SHADOWS

BRENDA DAVIS

BALBOA.
PRESS
A DIVISION OF HAY HOUSE

Library of Congress Control Number: 2012911809

Balboa Press books may be ordered through booksellers or by contacting:

Balboa Press
A Division of Hay House
1663 Liberty Drive
Bloomington, IN 47403
www.balboapress.com
1-(877) 407-4847

Because of the dynamic nature of the Internet, any web addresses or links contained in this book may have changed since publication and may no longer be valid. The views expressed in this work are solely those of the author and do not necessarily reflect the views of the publisher, and the publisher hereby disclaims any responsibility for them.

The author of this book does not dispense medical advice or prescribe the use of any technique as a form of treatment for physical, emotional, or medical problems without the advice of a physician, either directly or indirectly. The intent of the author is only to offer information of a general nature to help you in your quest for emotional and spiritual well-being. In the event you use any of the information in this book for yourself, which is your constitutional right, the author and the publisher assume no responsibility for your actions.

Any people depicted in stock imagery provided by Thinkstock are models, and such images are being used for illustrative purposes only.
Certain stock imagery © Thinkstock.

ISBN: 978-1-4525-5502-7 (sc)
ISBN: 978-1-4525-5504-1 (hc)
ISBN: 978-1-4525-5503-4 (e)

Printed in the United States of America

Balboa Press rev. date: 08/03/2012

To my husband, Hugh,
who is always there for me in everything that I do.
I will love him forever and ever.

CONTENTS

INTRODUCTION

The sun was creeping over the eastern horizon and without a cloud in the sky it was going to be another beautiful day. The night shadows began scurrying away as the sun rose, leaving no trace of the previous night. The shadows would return when the sun slipped down the western horizon and the darkness would cover everything again. Lily's life was like the approaching night, there were shadows in her past that sometimes were exposed by certain events. As much as Lily's consciousness could push the dark memories away, these thoughts would only to be exposed again later. Lily felt like she was an above average person; she certainly was very smart and well educated. She thought her best bet for a normal life was to fend for herself and make her own way, at least until she could figure things out. Lily had a past full of shadows that hid secrets, scandal, betrayal and murder. The only way she could manage her life now was to start over. She was totally alone and knew she could not out-run the past but by starting over maybe she could deal more successfully with her demons.

As Lily attempts to start her new life in a new location, she reflects on her past through memories and flashbacks. She has hidden many of these memories because with these recollections also brings pain. Lily hopes she can unravel her past by understanding the problems of her mother and grandmother so she can assure herself that she will not follow in their footsteps. Through heredity, Lily fears she will have the mental problems and an addictive personality from her mother and grandmother. She is constantly vigilant to avoid these problems.

Lily has to look deeply into the shadows which hide many things such as, mental illness, child abuse, spousal abuse, substances addiction and sin, in order for her to understand what she survived as a child and young adult. Lily has learned that a person's mind has the ability to hide things that they do not want to remember. Her insight into these many issues prompts her to dedicate her life and skills to the plight of women and children trapped in a life of pain and fear.

PART ONE

CHAPTER 1

LILY AND JANE

L ily Rose Baxter stepped down off the Grey hound bus in the middle of a small south central US town. She was not sure why she got off the bus here but just went with the fact that it felt right. She also felt the name of the town was a sign. The town was called Eden. She thought that Eden was where she needed to start a new and fulfilling life.

Lily left the bus station, walked a few blocks and was in the middle of the town. There were quaint streets with old, well-kept stores built in the old fashion of towns constructed many years ago. As Lily walked down the main street of town, she passed an aged drugstore on the corner of the intersection. As she peered into the glass windows she noted that there was a bar with a soda dispenser behind it and there were stools along the front of the bar with round, red, plastic seats that, of course, turned all the way around. She passed a five and dime store that she saw had the doors open with various items displayed on the street. There was no one around but she was sure none of the items would be stolen just from the feel of the town.

On the end of the block was a newsstand in the corner store. She saw every kind of the reading material through the open doors. Inside the store there was the musty smell of old and new printed material all mixed together. There was a train depot at the end of Main Street that had been refurbished as a traveler information center. Lily walked into the station and saw it had been decorated with the original décor of the days when train stations were the center of activity with passenger trains coming in and people traveling in great numbers.

Today there was one lady sitting behind a desk in the train station. The lady immediately greeted Lily and asked if she could help her. When the lady walked around the desk, Lily saw that she was about five feet two, slim with short gray hair. She had a lovely face and must have been very attractive when she was young. She appeared to be in good shape for her sixty something years as she stood very straight and walked quickly toward Lily.

Lily said, "Hello, I just got off the bus and I like what I see of the town. I think I would like to stay here a while. I will need a place to rent to see if I would like to make this my home."

The lady responded with, "I know you will love this town. I have lived here my entire life and have loved every minute of it. I am sure you can find a place to rent either an efficiency room or an apartment."

Lily answered, "Good. I don't need much but it needs to be furnished."

The lady looked at the one suitcase that Lily was carrying and said, "I will give you some names and addresses of some nice places to rent. Have a look around while I get that information for you."

Lily looked around the depot and noted that everything was restored and the room felt very cozy and inviting. She could almost feel the hustle and bustle of passengers switching places, either coming or going. She wondered if a passenger train even stopped here anymore. That would be something that Lily would like to research because she wanted to know everything about this possible new home.

Lily took the information that the lady handed her which had several names and addresses written in a careful, strict handwriting. Lily thanked her and then asked, "Which is the closest and how do I get there?"

Lily was led to the front porch of the depot then told, "Just go down this street a few blocks, turn left and cross the railroad tracks. Continue a few blocks and you will find the street names on this list. Nearly all the ones I wrote down are in the same area as I noted you were walking. Good luck and come by to see me again."

Lily thanked her and also promised to let her know what she found. There was not much traffic as she crossed the street and headed in the direction that the woman had directed.

This town, in the days when the train was a popular mode of transportation, was a very busy town. The town also had a major highway that ran right through the center of it. These travel modes were a great source of revenue for many businesses. However an interstate had been built a few years back. The interstate went around the town crossing both ends of it and making an arc around the middle of town. There were two exits off the interstate into town, one on each end. Therefore, most of the restaurants and gas stations had migrated to each end of town. The other factor that killed the middle of town was a Wal Mart superstore built at one of the exits of the interstate. Over time, lots of businesses flocked around that area to soak up the business that Wal Mark generated.

What saved the town from drying up was the poultry business. There was a poultry processing plant that provided numerous jobs and the farmers in the area started raising chickens for the industry. This greatly increased the income for the farmers. In fact, it probably saved many small farms that did not have enough land to support enough cattle to survive. Small farms could do well raising chickens since it did not take as much land to raise chickens. So farmers built chicken houses, used the chicken litter to fertilize their land and could then raise more cattle on less land thanks to the lush grass that grew when fertilizer was applied. Farmers bring in a lot of business because of the need for farm equipment and feed stores. So even though the middle of town was somewhat of a relic, it had survived because many long-time residents of small towns do what they can to support the old, established businesses.

Walking down the side walk, Lily noted the large oak trees that were in each yard and shaded the walkway. The houses had to be at least fifty to sixty years old but most had been well maintained. A few of the large homes had the sad, shabby appearance of being empty. Some of the shingles were missing, some of the paint was peeling, some windows were broken and the porches were sagging. Lily felt it was a shame that majestic homes, which represented a time long gone, were in such disrepair. Lily felt as though she were walking down a fairy tale street, as if she had stepped back in time. She wished she had lived in that period of time and that her life was normal or close to what she thought normal should be. Nice homes, with father, mother and children all happy, doing normal things would be on her wish list and she knew that she would never know that life except for seeing it in the movies. She felt her past had caused her to be damaged.

Lily almost missed the house she was looking for because she was day dreaming, so she had to back pedal a little to find it. There was a black metal fence around the house with a small gate at the front. She opened the gate and slowly walked up the walk, marveling at the beautiful, old house. It was three stories high with a wide porch across the front. There were large, round columns supporting the porch and there were rocking chairs all across the porch with a porch swing on one end. Lily could imagine everyone sitting on the porch after supper just discussing the weather. Lily knocked on the huge front door and waited patiently.

A petite, pretty lady in her mid-forties, answered the door, and said, "Hello, may I help you?"

Lily said, "I was told by the lady at the depot that you might have a room to rent."

The lady responded, "Yes, we do have rooms or they are actually efficiency apartments. Come in and we can discuss this."

Lily followed the lady into the house and noted a big entry way with a two story foyer with a beautiful chandelier hanging in the center of the hall. She saw a staircase was on her left and an opening on the right leading to a room that was used as an office. In the prime of life for this home, this room had probably been the front parlor. The office was furnished with heavy old furniture with a huge oak desk placed in the middle of the room. The lady went behind the desk and motioned for Lily to sit. "My name is Elizabeth Bristow, I am the manager here. We have five different units in this house. Each room has its own bathroom, kitchenette, queen size bed, TV and some living room furniture. We serve the evening meal in the dining room every night but Sunday night. This is included in the monthly rent. I assume you want to be here for at least a month?"

Lily responded, "Yes, I plan to find a job and stay here for a while until I get on my feet and become more familiar with the area."

"Good," Elizabeth said, "We do have a vacancy. I'm not being nosy, but what do you do for a living or what would you like to do?"

Lily smiled, "I went to college in California. I just finished law school and passed the bar exam. I will be looking for something in law."

Elizabeth was a little startled at this information but said, "We don't have any women lawyers in our town at this time. I'm sure a change won't hurt us at all. It may even shake up the "good ole boys" that have been around forever." She laughed and continued, "I, for one, am thrilled to have someone so young and educated move to our town."

Lily smiled and Elizabeth got back to business, "We do ask that you do not have guest overnight; but other than that you can do as you wish.

We don't wash your personal laundry but we pick up your linens weekly and wash them for you. I require a month's rent and one extra for a deposit which you will get back when you leave if nothing is damaged."

"That sounds very good. Is there a used car lot near here?" Lily asked.

"Yes, just a few blocks away, stop by here when you are ready to go and I will give you the name and some directions. We do have a cab company in town if you need transportation until you get a car. I hope you enjoy your stay with us and if you have any questions, please, let me know." Elizabeth pulled out an application and gave it to Lily to fill out. Lily filled out the application and Elizabeth gave her a key. "Your room is the first one on the left at the top of the stairs."

Lily got the money out of her purse and gave it and the application to Elizabeth. She took the key and said, "Thank you so much. I'll stop by when I get ready to look for a car."

Lily went out of the office and up the stairs. At the top of the stairs, she noted the room and unlocked the door. Entering the room she was pleasantly surprised to find a very nice, clean room. There were two overstuffed chairs to the left of the door that faced a portable television set. A small kitchenette was along the far wall. There were a few cabinets, a sink, a small refrigerator, a microwave and a small table with two chairs. On the far side of the kitchenette, was a queen size bed made up with a beautiful comforter set. There was a small chest of drawers, a night stand and a closet. There was a door beside the bed that led to a clean, small bathroom. Lily thought she could live here very well, and the thought passed through her mind that this was far better than anything she had lived in during her life. In college, she usually had a room in a house where several women and a few men lived. She had to share everything, wait in line for the bathroom, usually ended up cleaning more than anyone and there was never any silence. She always had to study in the library to be able to concentrate. She felt a sense of peace in this apartment and felt safe for the first time in a long time.

Lily set her suitcase down, put her purse on the floor and sat in the nearest chair. She was exhausted. There was a window unit air conditioner in the living area and the room was very cool. Lily laid her head back on the back of the chair and sighed deeply. She closed her eyes and began to drift. Out of the deep shadows of her mind, Lily went back as far as she could remember which was around five years old but these memories were sketchy. When she was six she started to school. She did have happy memories of school and she loved to learn especially when she excelled and she was given special recognition by her teachers. At least in school she felt noticed.

As she recalled her home life, Lily remembered a shabby, two bedroom house. The front screen door and the front steps were broken. She remembered this as she had fallen on the broken steps and her mom had forbidden her from going out the front door again. Thinking of her mother made Lily sad. She knew she should love her mother, as everyone loves their mother, right? And she did love her, but this love was so smothered with a sad history that she could not even say out loud that she loved her. She also knew she needed forgiveness for the things she would like to forget that she had done in her life.

At five years old, Lily thought her mother, Jane, was the most beautiful woman she had ever seen. Jane was an attractive woman; slim with a good figure, with shoulder length black hair and she had the most unusual, startling emerald green eyes. Lily favored her mother as she was a beautiful child with black hair and she had inherited the same amazing eyes. Lily remembered asking if anyone else in the family had their eye color. Jane got a sad look on her face and to Lily's surprise spoke quietly to her saying, "Lily, your grandmother, Bess, has these eyes. However, that's all I got from her as she is a wonderful lady and I sure as hell am not any of those things." Lily tried many times to get more information about her grandparents, especially since her grandmother was still alive. However, Jane would not talk about it anymore and told Lily to go to her room.

Jane was not a good housekeeper even though she was home all day. What Jane liked to do was drink liquor and smoke cigarettes. Lily had seen her mother sitting at the kitchen table for hours, with smoke circling her head and a drink on the table. Jane had a trust fund that she could draw from that was set up by her father. This money allowed her to stay at home and not work, but there were strings attached to the money from this fund. For some reason, even though she was able to stay at home to care for Lily, she appeared to not really be interested in Lily and always had a far-away look in her eyes. Many times when they were in the room together, Lily would have to call her mother several times before she would respond. Jane never hugged Lily but just went through the motions of a caretaker. Lily was very lonely and wondered what was wrong with her for her mother to not love her. The fact that Jane never told Lily she loved her, made her feel detached and alone.

Jane never said much about Lily's dad, so Lily did not know anything about him. She would tell Lily her dad had been in the army and was killed overseas. This was one of the lies that Lily told as the truth to anyone who ask, because she didn't know any better.

Jane enjoyed the night life which caused her to have to arrange some alternative care for Lily. Most of time, she would leave Lily with the neighbor whom Lily adored. Lily called the neighbor Granny and would have loved to have her as her real grandmother. Granny played with her, held her and read her books. When Lily was at Granny's house, she felt safe and for a brief time, felt like a normal child. After school Lily would run to Granny's house to relay all the days' events and snack on what Granny had made that day especially for her. Granny never said anything negative about Jane nor asked where she was going. She was afraid that if she made Jane angry, Jane would stop letting Lily come over. Lily was the light of Granny's life and made the days a lot less lonely for both of them.

Granny could tell that Jane had problems. She felt that addiction to alcohol was one of the major issues. Granny also had a feeling Jane had some mental problems. She had witnessed Jane being chatty and up beat then other times she was so depressed she could hardly talk. Granny just told Lily that anytime she needed company, she could come over to her house, whether it was day or night. She knew she could not solve Jane's problems, but at least she could make a safe haven for Lily.

Jane had several men that she dated but none of them lasted very long, especially when they learned Jane had a child. Men, or the kind of men Jane met, were not crazy about a ready-made family. Jane dressed in very sexy clothes and attracted men easily, but there was something odd about her personality. You really couldn't put your finger on it but she seemed to be false, it appeared she was playing a part in a movie. So even though she attracted men, they soon moved on. This was fine with Lily because she liked it to be her and Jane. Lily thought if she was really good and continued to work hard, Jane would come to love her soon. Of course maybe Jane did love her but just didn't know how to show her love for her daughter. There was always a chance that Jane would learn how to be a loving mother over time.

Everything was going along normally, as far as Lily was concerned, when Jake Henson came into their life. That's when everything changed. Life as Lily knew it was about to change and the events would have a long lasting effect on her and Jane.

Lily woke up from her nap, she pushed the unhappy memories that had invaded her dreams, back into the shadows of her mind and got up to start unpacking. She had plans to make and the unpleasant memories were not going to interfere with her new life. Tomorrow would be a new day and she thought she could escape her past.

A few hours later, Lily drifted back to her childhood memories again. When Lily was a teenager, she often wondered if she might evolve into a personality like Jane, whom she suspected was unstable. Children have no idea what normal is; they only know what is normal for them. Even when she was young, Lily knew Jane was different by observing how the rest of the world appeared to function. Jane never came to school or talked to any other women except for Granny next door. As Lily got older, she wondered about the possibility of Jane having some type of mental illness. All she knew about mental illness was what she learned in school which was that it had a hereditary tendency. She felt her mother definitely had episodes of unusual behavior. This was a nice way to say, her mother went off the deep end on many occasions. Lily was afraid that addiction to substances or an addictive personality could also be hereditary. Jane was addicted to alcohol and men. The men Jane wanted were not good men. Lily was not sure that there were any good men because she hadn't met any so far.

Lily wished she knew more about her grandparents and how Jane grew up. Maybe that could be a clue for her as to why Jane was different. If she had known Jane's history, maybe this would have helped Lily understand her own life or maybe her fate was sealed by genetics.

CHAPTER 2

JANE AND BESS

L ily would never know the entire history of her mother or grandparents. Jane could not tell her because she did not remember the events the way they actually occurred. In Jane's mind, she had a normal life and was a normal teenager. This could not be further from the truth.

To see the events that caused a family to fall apart, we have to start before Jane was born. Winding up with certain traits from parents is like rolling the dice. The emerald green eyes that were strikingly beautiful were first noted in Lily's grandmother. Then Jane had this trait which she passed to Lily. But what other traits were passed to Jane and Lily would not be known from many years. With the mixing of genes, half of them come from each parent. You may end up with the best traits of both parents or the worst traits of one or both. Some genetic results will be invisible to the eye but very visible in actions. A combination of the worst traits were carried by Lily's grandmother and passed to Jane in connection with their mental stability. Only time would tell if Lily was to have these dangerous traits. The only sure thing was all three had the emerald green eyes and jet black hair.

In the period of time when Lily's grandparents lived, mental illness in the family was a well-kept secret. You did not talk about being depressed or going to a psychiatrist because these things marked you as being crazy. If you had someone in your family that was odd or different, you kept them at home, away from the public. Therefore, mental illness could have been in the many families and no one outside the family would have known. It is sad that many mentally challenged individuals who could have been helped by our knowledge of mental illness today, never got the help they needed and they just existed; hidden away.

If a family had a member that had mental problems, their only alternative, other than keeping them at home, would be to put them in a mental institution. If the family did not have much money, they had to put the mentally ill member of their family in a state institution. In the early part of the 1900s, the state institutions were a catch-all for mental patients. There would be a range of patients from being clinically mentally disturbed all the way to being criminally insane. These institutions were overcrowded and the mixture of all levels of mentally ill patients housed together was a potentially dangerous situation. Many patients were injured or killed by other patients.

The overwhelmed institutions mostly kept patients sedated so they would not cause problems. Electrical shock treatments were popular. Even though electrical shock is a treatment that is still used today, there have been a lot of improvements made with the usage.

There were also experiments with brain surgery. Many of these surgeries left patients brain damaged beyond repair. There were some good institutions that were suitable for the mentally ill but only the rich people could afford this kind of solution for their mentally ill family member.

Lily's mother, Jane, was an only child born to parents late in their life. Her parents were thrilled to have a child and doted on her. She was given everything she wanted and as a result she felt entitled to a good life provided for her. Her father worked as a general manager for a hardware store in town and had been a loyal employee for twenty years. He was very meticulous and honest. He was always the first one to arrive at the store and the last to leave. He knew every item they carried, the ID number of the items, where the items were in the store and where to order them. He could add up a long list of numbers in his head faster than a calculator. This was before computers but the store was run just as well without a computer because of Henry Baxter, Jane's dad.

Jane loved her dad; he was her world. Henry took Jane to work with him many times and she stopped at the store on her way home from school. He taught her all the hardware items and how to help customers find things. Henry's boss, who owned several stores in the state, came in each month for a review of the business. He was a little older than Henry.

Mr. Miller was tall, handsome and always wore a suit. He came in with an air of a big business man which always impressed Jane.

Mr. Miller lived in another town with his wife of many years. He always drove a bright, shiny new sports car. Henry didn't even own a car; he walked to work, to the market and home so he couldn't see a reason for a car. There was a bus if they wanted to go on a trip to another town; which was not very often as Henry was always working. Jane's world was small so someone as flashy as Mr. Miller certainly caught her eye.

At thirteen years old and attending middle school, Jane was not attracted to boys her age but liked the older boys in high school. She could not wait to get into high school so she could be closer to the older boys. Jane did not particularly like girls her age, but ran around with older girls when they would allow her. Jane felt like an adult trapped in a young girl's body. Henry tried to keep a close eye on Jane and discouraged any older boys from coming around. He tried to get Jane involved with girls her own age, as he felt Jane needed to have some interaction with kids her own age. Her mother, Bess, was no help, as she thought Jane was better than all the kids her age and dressed her in the most expensive clothes that were a bit old for her. Expensive things were all Jane and Bess had in common when Jane was a young girl.

There was a deep, dark secret that the Baxter family kept. This secret was the reason Jane never had girls come over to her house and why the family did not go anywhere. Bess had what Henry referred to as "spells". Most of the time, Bess was very out-going, happy and had the normal dreams of a wife and mother. When she was in a good mood, she would buy many, expensive things for Jane. Henry had to be very stern with her to keep her in check concerning spending money and he did not allow her to handle any finances. Then there were times when Bess would go into her room, shut the door, turn off the light and go to bed. These spells could last a few days or as long as a month. Jane was not allowed to go into Bess's bedroom during this time. Only Henry went in the bedroom but only to take food to Bess and change the linens on the bed.

During Bess's spells, Henry slept in the guest room. Sometimes, Jane could hear her mother crying, sometimes moaning and every once in a while Bess would scream. It was out of the question to take Bess to a doctor; this was a mental thing that would label the family as having a crazy member of the family. Isolation and secrecy were the only solutions to Bess's problem and Henry coached Jane as to what to tell others. There were stories that they used when Bess was having a spell; she was either under the weather, or at her mother's house out of town, or busy with a project. They, themselves, did not understand what was happening, but were just trying to protect Bess from being labeled as crazy and praying she would get better.

The amount of time that Bess was in her room became longer and longer. One particular spell went on longer than a month. Jane missed her mother and one day she ventured into Bess's room. When she entered the room she had to take a moment to adjust to the darkness. Then she saw her mother lying on her bed on her side, with her eyes open. Jane moved closer and whispered, "Mother?" She got no response. She reached slowly, with a trembling hand and touched Bess's shoulder. She repeated, "Mother." A long moment passed and her mother rose up on her elbow and looked Jane in the eye. In a raspy, low voice that Jane did not even recognize as her mother, Bess said, "Don't ever come into my room again. I do not know you. Go away, go away, go away!" Each time she said 'go away' she grew louder and louder until she was screaming.

Jane jerked back her hand and backed up at first, then ran from the room as Bess's screaming trailed off. Jane ran to her room, slammed the door and fell on her bed crying and shaking. She knew that when she looked into her mother's eyes she was looking at madness. She would forever be afraid of her mother, even when she came out of her spell. Jane believed there was another person, an evil person, in her mother's mind and body and Bess never knew when that evil person would take over.

It was during one of Bess's worse spells when Henry asked Jane to sit so he could talk with her. Jane was twelve years old at this time. "We need to discuss your mother's condition and our future," he began to talk to Jane. "Do you understand that she has a mental condition that cannot be cured and will only get worse?"

Jane nodded and said, "I do know that when she is sick she can be very mean. She told me to get out and to not come back when I went to see her. I was scared because she was so different, even her face was different. How long do you think this spell will last?"

"I'm not sure but today when I was talking with her, she begged me to make arrangements for her to go into a mental institution for people with her condition. She told me that when she is sick that an evil spirit comes out of the dark shadows of her mind and whispers to her." He told Jane.

"What do the spirits say to her?" Ask Jane.

"She said she cannot tell what the spirit is whispering but she is afraid that when she hears what it is saying, it will be telling her to do something that she does not want to do. So I promised her if she got worse that I would take her to the institution. I wanted you to know so if you came home and we were gone, that's where we will be going. I know this is very hard for you because you love your mother and she loves you. It is her love for us that she has made this request. She knows when she is in the mist of this terrible condition she is not responsible for what she does. She does not want to hurt us or herself. At the institution they are equipped to keep her from hurting someone." Henry bowed his head; he was trying not to cry.

Jane had never seen her father cry and she began to sob. She laid her head in her dad's lap and he stroked her hair. He said, "We will get through this together. I love you and want the best for you. I also love Bess, but I am helpless with her condition."

CHAPTER 3

JANE

Jane was very sad after the conversation with her dad concerning her mother's future but she was more concerned for her dad than for her mother. Since her mother scared her so badly and could be so different, she did not feel the same about her. She felt like her mother had already gone, not physically but mentally. She still loved her mother but not the one laying in her bed. She missed the mother that laughed with her and held her tight.

Jane felt hollow inside and abandoned by her mother. She was also angry that this should happen to her. Jane was self-centered and looked at everything only as it affected her. This was not any different than how most teenage girls felt or how they acted. Teenage girls are usually self-centered because they were going through an array of hormonal and social changes. At this time in Jane's life it was all about herself and sadly Jane did not have a mother to help her make the transition from childhood into an adult.

Jane was different from other teenage girls as she lacked empathy therefore she took advantage of the fact that when her mother was sick that she had a lot of unsupervised time. At this time in her life that was not a good thing as she was not afraid of doing anything she wanted to do and it didn't really matter to her who she hurt or affected. These feelings and actions were definitely different from other teens.

Jane did wonder sometimes if her reckless feelings were connected to her mother's mental illness or if these feelings were normal. When her father told her about her mother hearing whispering, Jane thought she had heard whispering in her ear when she was contemplating something she knew to be wrong or she had unsettling evil thoughts. Again she wondered if this was a normal thing, but didn't think it was.

Since Jane did not have any close friends, her mother was unavailable and her dad was very busy working or caring for her mother, she had no one to talk to. She knew right from wrong as she went to church with her dad, but she did not care when she did something wrong. She did care about getting caught, so she did deter from some things if she thought there was a risk of getting caught. Jane was smart and a good talker so she got out of a lot of mischief by talking her way out. Between twelve and fourteen years old, Jane stayed under the radar and didn't do anything very alarming but she was heading in a bad direction and several other people were in her path of destruction.

CHAPTER 4

HENRY AND BESS

When Jane was fourteen, her mother was in bed sick and Henry started what he thought would be a normal day. Henry woke up early as usually. He was in the guest room where he stayed when Bess was sick. He took a shower, shaved and got dressed for work. When he went by Jane's bedroom door, he knocked and called for Jane to get up. He always cooked breakfast for all of them. He and Jane would eat first then he would take a plate up for Bess. Henry had hired a nurse to care for Bess during the day as Bess seemed worse in the last few months and he was afraid to leave her alone.

The nurse arrived at 7 AM, as Jane and Henry finished breakfast. Jane kissed her dad and left for school. She would catch the school bus at the corner of the block with several other kids from her neighborhood. Henry greeted the nurse as she came in, "Good morning, I fixed you some breakfast if you would like some and the coffee is ready. I am going to take Bess's breakfast to her."

As Henry started for the stairs with the tray, the nurse thanked him for the breakfast and coffee. "I will be up in a few minutes so you and Mrs. Baxter can have some time together. She was very quiet yesterday and would not respond at all when I spoke with her."

"Yes," Henry said, "She would not talk to me last night. I also heard her walking around during the night talking to herself. I did not interrupt her but I did lock her bedroom door so she would not wonder out while I was asleep."

When Henry got upstairs, he set the breakfast tray on a table in the hall and unlocked the door. He pushed the door open then turned to get the tray. As he walked in the room, he said, "Good morning, Bess."

18

However, that is all he had time to say before he felt a hard hit to the back of his head. He dropped the tray, breaking everything on it and he fell to the floor. He was not knocked out but he was stunned. The next thing he knew, Bess was on his back. She laid on him and put her mouth next to his ear. Henry heard her say, in a very low, gravelly voice, "I heard what the evil spirit has been trying to say to me. He is saying: *Kill him, kill him, kill him!* I am going to do as I'm told!"

The nurse heard the loud crash of the breakfast tray and ran upstairs. When she entered the bedroom, she saw Bess sitting on Henry's back with her hands holding a vase above her head. She heard Bess say, "He said to kill you!" The nurse grabbed the vase and pulled it out of Bess's hands. Bess screamed, "Leave me alone, go away, I hate you!"

The nurse discarded the vase and grabbed Bess's arms and pulled her off of Henry. Henry was able to get up although he was shaky. However, he recovered enough to help the nurse drag Bess to the bed. They laid her on the bed and Henry laid on her to keep her still. Bess was screaming and fighting. Henry said to the nurse, "Go get a shot, I can hold her for now." The nurse dashed down to the kitchen where her bag was with a shot in it to sedate Bess. She promptly returned and gave Bess a shot in her arm. In minutes Bess stopped fighting and screaming. She slowly went to sleep.

Henry looked at the nurse and said, "Please go call an ambulance to come get Bess. Also call the mental institution and tell them that we are coming. I will stay with her until the ambulance gets here."

After the nurse left to go down stairs to do the calling, Henry began to cry as he looked out the window at the sky. He lay down beside Bess and put his arms around her. He knew this was the last time they would lay together in the bed that they had spent their entire married life. He knew that for the Bess that he had known to be the sweetest, kindest person in the world to try to kill him, that she was completely mentally gone. The shadows in her mind that she so often had talked about had completely overcome her. The evil that she had told him was trying to whisper instruction to her had finally gotten loud enough for her to hear. The fact that she obeyed these instructions was evidence that the battle was over and Bess was gone.

Jane got in from school and immediately knew that something was wrong. The house appeared empty. She ran upstairs and saw the open door to her parent's room. She saw that the room was a mess with food and broken dishes all over the room. She remembered the talk her father had with her about a day when her mother having to go would be reality. She thought that it was easier to know her mother was where she could be taken care of properly but Jane was sad that this day had arrived. Jane then thought of the freedom she would have. She felt that life had dealt her a bad hand and she noted an anger that she had not felt before. That anger had been underlying for several years and now was mixed with adolescence hormones; this was a formula for trouble. This trouble would dwell just under the skin until Jane became a senior in high school then it would boil over, burning everyone near her.

CHAPTER 5

HENRY

In a small town like the Baxters lived in things did not go unnoticed. Henry knew sooner or later he would have to explain why Bess was not with them anymore. He thought about this a lot and then he thought about Mabel.

Mabel Winegardner was an icon in this small town. She was the only daughter of one of the richest men in town. Her father was the town mayor and the president of the bank. Mabel had two brothers that were both lawyers. Both brothers chose to work and live far away from their family roots, especially their father and Mabel.

Mabel was not very good in school so college was not an option for her. She thought she had to do something to be notable as she was the daughter of a powerful man and had two professional brothers. Mabel surveyed her options in this small town and the First Baptist Church came to her attention as needing some leadership. She started working her way into the upper leadership at the church which was made easier by the large contributions her father made to the church.

She took over the leadership of the choir which was in need of help. To be a member of the choir was a very important civic duty that all members took very seriously, especially Mabel. After Mabel took over the leadership of the choir, if anyone were to miss choir practice, which was on Wednesday night, they could expect a visit on Thursday from Mabel. She would have some kind of casserole or other food item as a token of sympathy, because if they missed choir practice they had to be sick or have a sick family member. Mabel ran the choir like her father had raised his three children. There was no excuse for failure.

Mabel was also the treasurer of the church. She kept very close tabs on who was meeting their tithing and who was not. Mabel had ways of encouraging folks to meet their obligations. She would start with some overt comments like "is your business having hard times?" or "I'm so sorry you are having financial problems." Then she would have a discrete meeting for a heart to heart talk about tithing obligations. Her methods were very affective as most folks wanted to stay off of Mabel's radar. Mabel also had very strong ideas of how the preacher should conduct his sermons. Mabel thought that a preacher's job was to scare folks into following their Biblical teachings. She liked hell fire and damnation sermons, loud and long, so the folks would remember it all week. Since she handled the church money she had control over how well the preacher was compensated over and above his salary. The smart preachers learned that the louder and longer the sermon, more money seemed to trickle to him in the form of extra expenses approved by Mabel.

Another thing Mabel thought was her duty was to spread all the news and uncover family secrets. She felt it her Christian duty to know who in the congregation was in trouble and might need extra support or guidance. Mabel soon got a clue that there was something amiss at the Baxter house. Mabel determined she had business at the hardware store and Henry was expecting her. Mabel entered the hardware store and was wondering around like she was looking for something. "Henry, can you help me?" She called out.

"Yes, Miss Winegardner, I will be with you in a minute." He answered. Henry finished what he was doing, then went to find Mabel. "How are you today, Miss Winegardner?"

"I am very well, thank you. However, I cannot find a washer for my water hose as the water is spraying out at the connection," She answered.

Henry led her over two rows and showed her several sizes of washers for her to pick from. "Will any of these do the job?" He inquired.

"Yes," she said, "I'll take six of them so I can have some spares."

Henry and Mabel walked up to the front of the store and Henry began to make a ticket for the items. Mable ventured to ask, "How are Bess and Jane doing? I haven't seen Bess lately."

Henry put down his pencil, looked down at the counter and was very quiet. Mabel looked at him and said, "Oh, Mr. Baxter, I hope I didn't say something out of line, is something wrong?"

Henry began to cry, at first he was faking a crying sound, then all the grief of losing his wife came over him. He began to sob for real and he sat down on the chair with his hands over his face. "Mr. Baxter, please, what is the matter?" Mabel cried. She walked around the counter and was patting Henry on the shoulder.

Slowly, Henry was able to talk, "Please don't tell anyone about my break down. I'm sorry to be so silly in front of you."

Mabel said, "Don't you fret, I would not tell anyone, please what is the problem?"

Henry was shaking his head but then he said in a very small voice, "Bess, my sweet Bess, has left me and Jane, for another man!"

Mabel gasped; she thought there was a story here but did not think it would be one this sensational. She knew that Bess was a mysterious person. No one really knew her and she did not go out very much. She seldom attended church even though Henry brought Jane regularly. Who would have ever guessed this!? For once in her life, Mabel did not know what to say.

Henry continued, "Oh, I should not have told you but I can't hold it in any more. Jane is doing pretty well but she is also sad. You are such a saint to listen to this, so please, don't tell anyone".

"Mr. Baxter, I would not say anything but you know this will get out somehow. But please, know we will all stand beside you and Jane and help you get through this grief." Mabel said, she could not help but ask "Who did she leave with?" She could not think of any man absent from town.

"You wouldn't know him. Bess knew him many years ago, before we were married. He called her one day because his wife had passed away and they began to talk. Things just got out of control. The important thing is, she is gone and not coming back." He began to cry again. His sorrow was coming from a different place, he knew Bess would not be coming back physically and mentally and she was forever lost in an unknown place where something was slowly taking over her mind.

The shadows that had haunted Bess her entire life had finally turned her mind dark. Henry would rather have everyone think she had left him than for anyone to know she was mentally ill. If that fact were known by the town's people it would put a stigma on him and Jane. Jane especially, would bare the weight of that information as folks would assume that Jane had the same insane genes and would eventually lose her mind. Henry would have to admit to himself, he often wondered if Jane did indeed inherit some form of mental instability. He hoped maybe the environment that she grew up in with a mentally ill person had somehow affected her in a negative way. He hoped with Bess gone, Jane would have a normal life. Many people thought that mental illness was contagious and isolation of the mentally ill was best for everyone.

CHAPTER 6

BESS AND HENRY

After Mabel left the store, Henry closed and locked the door. He put up the closed sign even though it was just 3 PM. This very seldom happened but Henry was in no shape to work after this ordeal. He went back and sat in the chair behind the counter. He thought of Bess; up until she went to the bottom of mental illness, all the memories were good and very sweet.

Bess, short for Elizabeth, had been the youngest of four daughters of a prominent farming family. Bess's dad, Robert Hampton, was a kind man who loved his wife and daughters. He was well respected in the community as he owned a great deal of land and ran a large farming business. His oldest three daughters were very ambitious. All three went to college and carved out productive careers and had nice families. Bess, however, did not like school. She loved the farm and being at home. She loved cooking; she did caning and took care of cleaning the house. Her mother was pleased to have at least one daughter appreciate the importance of being a homemaker. So Bess happily moved through her twenties doing the things she loved in her parent's home. Her father became concerned, as the years passed by, that Bess was not making any effort to develop her own home and family. He did not want a daughter that would become an old maid and never leave home. He loved Bess, but he did not want to enable her to stay hidden in the family nest.

Robert was a frequent customer at the hardware store where Henry was a young man who appeared to be working his way up in management. He liked Henry because he was knowledgeable about his work, he was very polite and he was low key. Robert had never heard anything negative about Henry and he knew he had lived in this town his entire life. He noted that Henry was a short man but was slim and stout. He wore his hair very short and wore heavy, black rimmed glasses with very thick lens. Henry was a couple of years older than Bess but was not dating anyone. So, Robert made a plan.

On the next trip to town, Robert, insisted that Bess go with him. He told her she needed to get out of the house and she could learn some of the town business that had to be attended to each month. Robert had on his agenda that Bess accompany him to the hardware store. Bess was a slim, petite woman, with black hair and she kept it cut in a short hair style. She was very shy but when she looked at someone they were immediately taken with her emerald green eyes. So when Henry asked if he could help them, he was unable to look away from her eyes and was unable to keep his mind on his business.

After the first time Henry saw Bess, he looked for her around town and at church. Fortunately for him, Bess attended the same church as he did. He could not imagine why he had not met her before. He learned he had not seen her in the church service because she took care of the nursery during church, therefore, was never at the service. After a few months, Henry ventured to ask Robert if he might ask Bess out on a date. Robert was delighted and gave his consent. After the first date, Henry was immediately head over heels in love. Bess was the sweetest person he had ever known. When he was not with her, he could not think of anything but her. Bess was equally in love with Henry. However, she had a secret that she could not keep from Henry, if he were to ask her to marry him. Henry did ask Bess to marry him, after they dated for a year. He knew he did not have much, but he had a good, steady job and promised to do everything in his power to make her happy.

When Henry popped the question of marriage, Bess took a deep breath and said, "Henry, I love you with all my heart. I know you would be the best husband ever. But I don't know if I would be a good wife. I know I can make a good home for you and hopefully I could be a good mother to our children. But, I have a problem. I should not have gone this long without telling you, but I fell in love with you so quickly, I just couldn't handle something coming between us. I can't marry you until I tell you this and I will not hold you to your proposal if you decide this is more than you can handle." Tears came to her eyes as she spoke.

Henry was very concerned, "Bess, what is the matter? Nothing is too much for us to work out. We are meant to be together." He said.

"No this is something very personal and could affect us in the eyes of the town, if they knew. I have times when I get very depressed. I get so depressed that I have to be alone for a while. I become unable to function and all I can do is sleep. I don't know if this condition is genetic or not. You want children, but I would be afraid this might pass on to our child. I'm so sorry," Bess started to cry.

"Bess, no one is without problems, I'm very near sighted and have to wear thick, ugly glasses. Poor eyesight could be passed on to our children. We can't live on fear of what might happen we have to live with hope and love and let God take care of the rest. When you have one of your episodes, we will deal with it. It will be our business and no one else's. We may never have another chance at love; let's not throw it away because of something that may not happen." He took her in his arms and kissed her.

She looked at him and smiled, "Yes" she said, "I will marry you. I promise I will be the best wife I can be and I will love you forever".

So, it was settled, they were married in the church with all her family there. Henry did not have any family. He was an only child of parents that were in their forties when he was born. His parents had passed away while he was in college. His parents were very devoted to each other and had married in their teens. After so many years of marriage, when his mother died, his father followed quickly, dying of a broken heart.

Henry and Bess did want a child, but they did not particularly try. They felt if they left it up to God, things would be fine. After several years, they had given up hope of a child and were content with each other and their life together.

Bess was 42 and Henry 44, when Bess began to feel ill in the mornings. Since the thought of a child was not in their mind, Bess went to the doctor in fear of having something awful wrong with her. After many tests, her doctor called with a congratulations message.

The doctor announced, "Bess, you are pregnant!" He then went on to talk about this being a high risk pregnancy due to her age. He told her that since she was in good health and he would watch her closely, things should go well. "The main thing, Bess, is not to worry and enjoy your pregnancy," he concluded.

Bess really didn't hear anything past the "you are pregnant" part of the doctor's message. She could not wait to tell Henry the good news.

She had not had one of her spells in over two years, so she was hopeful that her life was going to be stable.

When she told Henry about the baby, he was quiet. "What's the matter, Henry, are you not happy about the baby?" She asked.

"Yes, I am happy. But you are the most important thing to me and I worry about your health and the strain on you carrying a baby," He said.

"Do you remember what you said many years ago, when you ask me to marry you? You said we can't live on "what ifs", but must live our lives and have faith in God. I have faith, do you?" Bess ask.

"You are right, this is the best news ever and we will cherish this time and will love our baby completely." Henry said. He hugged her tight to him and whispered a prayer in his mind that Bess would be safe as he did not know how he would live without her.

The pregnancy went well. Bess had never felt better in her life. When the baby girl finally arrived, Henry and Bess were very happy. The baby girl was a perfect, healthy baby and they named her Elizabeth Jane; they were going to call her Jane. Jane was a beautiful baby, but she was a cranky baby. She cried all day and would not sleep at night. Henry and Bess were both exhausted the first year with the baby due to constantly having to hold her or rock her. The doctor told them Jane was a colicky baby and she would grow out of this stage soon.

The second year was easier. When she outgrew the colic, Jane was a happy, easy child. When she began to walk, again Henry and Bess were exhausted. However, this was a happy exhaustion. They loved to run after Jane as she toddled around the house experiencing all the new discoveries that every toddler finds.

Then things changed again and not for the good. By the time Jane started to school, she was becoming a difficult child again. After she was in school a few years, Henry and Bess knew she was a smart child because she made good grades. However, every parent/teacher conference was the same.

The teacher would tell them, "Jane is smart and does all her work in record time, but", and the "buts" would run on and on describing Jane's disruptive behavior that caused the other children in the class to be upset and rowdy. Jane was a leader but not in a good way because she encouraged the other kids to go against the rules. Bess and Henry always left the meetings with a heavy heart and no idea what to do with their daughter.

CHAPTER 7

JANE AND HENRY

As Jane entered her teenage years her life began to spiral downward. Jane liked to do or say things that were shocking. She liked to wear clothes that were different and she insisted on clothes of odd colors, odd styles and mostly tight fitting. Jane liked to embarrass the adults by saying inappropriate things or asking startling questions. Most folks said she was doing this for attention or acting out. Henry and Bess knew that Jane was a strong willed child and she never felt any remorse for what she did or who she hurt.

Sadly, Henry admitted to himself that he knew Jane would lie for no good reason, even when the truth was evident. This Henry knew by the time Jane was thirteen years old, but he was not prepared for the years ahead as she grew older. When Jane turned thirteen, Henry was also a single parent as Bess was in the mental institution. The only thing he felt he could do was love Jane, accept her for who she was and have faith that things would work out. He knew in the deepest part of his soul, that Jane was headed for a complicated and destructive life. He just hoped she would not leave any poor souls in her wake.

Jane was a physically beautiful child and grew into a beautiful teenager. She was five feet, two inches tall and well put together. She had a tiny waist with early developing, ample breast and small hips. Her hair was jet black and hung past her shoulders, very straight and shiny. She parted her hair on one side and allowed one side to slightly hid one eye. Her skin was very smooth and she did not have a blemish. The most striking feature adding to her beauty was her emerald green eyes. Her eyes were what she inherited from her mother. Jane was accustomed to people taking a second look when they saw her startling eyes. She became very adept at using every physical asset she had to her advantage and other folks had to beware.

During middle school and the first part of high school, Jane was mostly just being disruptive and doing minor irritating things. She was in the principal's office often and Henry was a familiar sight at school having been called many times for conferences concerning Jane's behavior.

When Jane got to her senior year in high school, Henry was worn out with lectures and grounding. Jane did not appear to care what punishment she got, she just did the time for grounding then went right back to her old ways.

In Jane's senior year in high school, she was a very busy girl. However, she found she was not as smart as she thought she was, she discovered she was pregnant during her senior year. Two months before graduation Jane had a problem, she needed money. Money for an abortion was her priority, but she had greater aspirations than just getting out of this mess. She wanted money to get out of this town and on her own. Then another thought occurred to her. Maybe she could get out of town and fix her financial problem another way.

CHAPTER 8

JANE

J ane played basketball throughout high school. During her generation, girls played half court basketball. There were six girls on the court for each team. Three played on each end of the court with the center line being their limit. Three girls were forwards and did the scoring; the three other girls played guard and defended the goal. Jane liked playing guard because she could take out her aggressions by playing rough. She also loved wearing the basketball suits because the suit consisted of shorts and a tank top. She loved being in front of all the people and being the center of attention. She played to the crowd and enjoyed their clapping and calling her name.

However, this all took second place to her attraction to the coach. Her coach was just out of college and coaching his first team when Jane was just starting high school. His name was Luke Mason and he was married with one child and one on the way. He was very nice, dedicated to his job and he loved his wife. Jane was patient but persistent.

Jane began her quest the first year she played basketball. She used the innocent approach to be with Coach Mason. For example, Jane would fake a hurt ankle that needed special attention such as soaking and wrapping. These things usually had to be done before the team began to arrive to get ready for the game. Luke was very professional and remained unfazed by Jane's flirting for the first couple of years. By the time Jane was a senior, however, she was ready to get results, so she increased the intensity of her advances.

Luke was having a bad season and if his team did not starting winning he was going to be out of a job. He and his wife, Mary, were not doing well due to the stress of the job and having their second child. Mary had quit her job to take care of the two children. He liked having Mary at home but the money was tight. Mary wanted to be home with their child, but some women that have a good career that they love also want to be at work. Mary's conflict in being a good mother, at home with her children, versus being in the supervision job that she had worked so hard to get, was taking a toll on her. Mary and Luke began to quarrel more. Luke was gone a lot to games. Mary felt overwhelmed being isolated with two young children all day and she began to resent Luke's absence. The formula for trouble was in place. Tight money plus Luke's shaky job plus a wife that is conflicted, equaled trouble in the marriage.

This was the opportunity that Jane was looking for. She could sense that Coach Mason was having problems at home. Jane decided to put on her best act one night after a game. She was the last one in the locker room when Coach Mason came in thinking everyone was gone. Jane was just getting out of the shower and had just a towel around her. Coach Mason didn't have a clue or a chance. Jane flashed him her best smile and batted her eyelids over her brilliant emerald green eyes. Jane also had a beautiful body so the deck was stacked against Coach Mason. When she dropped her towel, Luke's defenses fell and they had sex for the first, but not the last time.

Coach Mason was mortified when he realized what had happened. He begged Jane not to say a word as his job and marriage were at stake. Jane had no intention of telling, she was just happy that she succeeded after two years of pursuing the coach.

When Luke was pleading for her not to tell, Jane laughed and said, "I have no intention of telling anything as long as you and I continue to see each other."

Coach Mason answered. "Please, don't ask me to do this again. I love my wife. You are a beautiful girl, but I have children to think about."

Jane asked, "Did you have fun?"

Coach replied, "You were great, but I need to stay with my wife." He did not want to make Jane angry but he realized his mistake and was very remorse. He realized he had just put a noose around his neck and Jane had control over how tight it got.

"Don't worry, no one will ever know." Jane said, "See you around." And she was out the door, leaving Coach Mason to worry and regret what he had done. Jane was right though, it was not the only time they had sex. Each time he crossed the line, Coach Mason was devastated but he could not keep from being lured in by Jane and he was afraid she would tell his wife about their affair if he did not comply with her wishes. He did avoid her as much as he could and as long as he could, but ultimately he would give in to lust and fear.

Coach Mason was not the only man that Jane had in her sights. The First Methodist Church had just welcomed a new, young preacher assigned by the Methodist Counsel. Reverend Robert Leslie was very excited about his first assignment. He was very devout and felt called to God's service when he was in high school. He had gone straight into the seminary after he had obtained his bachelor's degree. Reverend Leslie liked people and he was very good with all ages. He was a good speaker so his sermons were well received. He took real interest in all his flock and was very sensitive to their problems.

Reverend Leslie wasn't married and had never had a serious girlfriend. He was a very attractive, clean cut man with a slim build and he dressed very preppy. Robert was not aware of his physical attractiveness as he was very involved with his vocation. Therefore, he was no match for Jane Baxter; he learned his faith was not a match for the devil.

Jane knew exactly how to work the reverend. She would go to him with stories of being motherless and not having anyone to care for her. She had lots of stories complaining she was not accepted by her peers due to being so beautiful and being a threat to steal their boyfriends. Jane cried and prayed with Reverend Leslie. She was so sincere she seduced Robert before he knew he was even tempted. He fell hard for Jane even though he was aware of being six years older than her. He would day dream about Jane being his wife, sitting on the front row of church during his sermons and encouraging him with her beautiful emerald green eyes.

Jane didn't want anyone to know about her affair with Reverend Leslie, so she was careful about when and where they met. She told Robert that her dad would not understand and convinced him that she wanted to wait until she was out of high school before she said anything to him. Robert would have been proud to openly date Jane but due to Jane's request they continued their secret tryst. However, Robert was feeling more and more guilt about this adulterous affair but his guilt was not enough to compel him to stop seeing Jane. He was in love for the first time in his life and was planning for Jane to be his wife. It was very hard for Robert when he and Jane were in public or at church to not talk to her and they also had to avoid being seen physically close to each other.

"We will be fine," Jane would tell him after they had sex late in the night in the church office and he was feeling especially remorse. She continued, "After graduation I will be able to talk to my dad and he will feel like I am an adult. I know everything will be fine." Then Jane would go on her way, leaving Reverend Leslie to pray for forgiveness. He had never had a passion for a woman like he had for Jane and he did not know how to handle it. However, he knew he and Jane were sinning and that was very disturbing to him. He had no idea how much worse his sins would become before Jane was through with him.

Jane was not satisfied with her two young men. It surprised her that she did not have any feelings of remorse about jeopardizing the life and careers of two men. In fact she felt satisfaction and powerful by seducing two men. Jane felt in control and that is what her life lacked. She was angry that her mother was gone and her dad was grieving for her loss. Jane felt like she was drifting and abandoned without a family to anchor her. If Jane had not of had some mental issues, she could have handled her home situation better, but she needed to have all the attention, all the time.

Jane was still restless and unsatisfied. She worked after school in the hardware store with her dad and she was very impressed by her dad's boss, Mr. Miller. Mr. Miller drove a flashy car and dressed expensively. Of course, he was a lot older than her but that was exciting to Jane. He had an air of superiority when dealing with any of the people that worked for him in his many businesses. He and his wife had been married many years but were only together to make a good show of stability for social reasons.

Mr. Miller had several affairs while being married and had no remorse for any of them. It was easy for him to have affairs because he was always traveling and met lots of people. He had not taken notice of Henry's young daughter when she started coming to work with Henry. Jane did surprise him when he did take notice of her when she turned sixteen. He saw that she had grown into a very nice looking young woman. He could not get over those eyes but she also had a great body. He was an easy mark for Jane, because he thought it was his idea and he felt every empowered when he accomplished his pursuit of young Jane. He was a little surprised that Jane was very mature and appeared experienced.

But he didn't care, she amazed him and he was happy about this affair. He did not care that Jane's father worked for him nor did he care what happened to Jane.

Jane's senior year was a year of juggling her schedule and the men while still making good grades. The grades were a snap as she was smart. She was having a great time with her three conquests. All of them were so different. Coach Mason was strong and athletic; he made love to her mechanically with no real passion but he was great. Reverend Leslie was timid and slow going. He was really in love with Jane, so he put all his passion into their sex. Mr. Miller was very aggressive and took charge of everything, commanding their sex to be as he required.

It was not the sex that Jane enjoyed; in fact she was not even engaged mentally during sex. She would put her mind on something else and just go through the motions. She sometimes would sing a song in her head that she liked or day dream about being somewhere else. She really found sex boring and felt it was just something to entertain and control men. What she really enjoyed was the power she had over men. She liked to pull the strings while letting them think they were the leader. She was surprised how easy it was to take them in. She felt like an actress in a movie and made up scenes in her head to keep things exciting for the men.

Jane had them all eating out of her hand, she thought. But, she was mistaken about Mr. Miller. She thought she had the power, and he did like her a lot, but he was always in control of the situation. Jane had some day dreams about marrying Mr. Miller, and being the wife of a rich, powerful man. Of course in her dreams, Jane was in control and he was helplessly under her spell. But Jane was in for a surprise, she was not as worldly as she thought and she had never met anyone like Mr. Miller, or maybe he was just so much like her that he fooled her.

As Jane looked at the big plus on the pregnancy test stick, she was angry at first as this was not what she had planned, but she recovered quickly. She felt she could either make it an advantage for her or she could get an abortion. Of course, she did not know who the father was, as she had three men she was seeing. However, she felt sure this might be her chance to get Mr. Miller to make a move to divorce his wife and marry her. She knew he and his wife were only married in name and did not love each other. She knew Coach Miller and Reverend Leslie would not say a word because of what they had to lose, and she did not have a desire to be a poor wife living on the small salary of a teacher or a preacher. Jane decided to go for Mr. Miller for her first target.

Late that night, Jane went to the office of Mr. Miller because he was in town that week. He was glad to see her saying, "What a surprise, I didn't expect you tonight but I am glad you have come by. I have missed you very much." He walked around his desk and put his arms around her and kissed her. "You seem tense, are you okay?" He asked.

"I'm fine just a little upset by something that happened today." She said.

"What is it? Is it your dad? You can tell me" He continued. He actually sounded concerned.

"Well," She said quietly, "I'm pregnant."

Mr. Miller immediately dropped his arms, his concern immediately evaporated. "Oh, my God! You said you were on the pill! Did you lie to me?" He exclaimed.

"I am on the pill, but it is not 100%. So I guess it failed, it is not my fault." She sounded distressed. She continued in a softer voice, "This might be a good thing as I graduate soon and we could be married before the baby comes."

Mr. Miller laughed bitterly, "I am not going to marry you. I thought you knew that! Have you lost your mind, why would I marry someone so young? I'd be ruined in the business world. I'm not going to be accused of robbing the cradle. I will give you the money for an abortion, and things can go on just as they are now. That's best for both of us." And he went around his desk to his chair and pulled out a lock box that had the petty cash in it for the store.

Jane was shocked; she couldn't breathe much less say anything. She wanted to kill him. How did he think they would go on like before and her be just a mistress for him to play with? He was crazy if he thought he could pay her off and they would continue their relationship. She would see that he would pay, but not just with money. Jane was not used to being taken so lightly and being insignificant. She was furious that he laughed at her, but she contained herself. She would need the money, if she expected to get out of this mess.

Mr. Miller came back around the desk and gave her five hundred dollars. "There, this should take care of it. I will give you some names and numbers of people that can take care of this. You will be fine." He told her. Jane could not believe he was acting like this was a business transaction and just business as usual.

Jane looked at the money. She wanted to spit in his face and walk out. But she didn't; instead she said, "Ok, get me those names. I think I'll go as I have had a very disturbing day and I am very tired." And with that she took the money and turned to walk out.

Before she got out of the office, Mr. Miller said, "Jane, we wouldn't want anyone to know about this. It could have a very bad effect on your father's job and future. I don't see how I could have anyone work for me with a bad situation between us. You understand, don't you?" The last part of what he said had a sinister tone to it.

Yes, she knew what he was telling her and she also understood that she had been a fool. She realized now she was dealing with a cruel, ruthless man who mistook her for a young, naïve girl. He did not know who he was dealing with. Well, maybe he had just made the biggest mistake of his life.

CHAPTER 9

COACH MASON

J ane met Coach Mason in his school office. When she knocked on the door and went in, he was very nervous. He said, "What are you doing coming here during school? We have to be careful. Please, don't do anything that may cause me to loose my job. Think of your future, you might be expelled and not allowed to graduate if we were discovered."

Jane sat down across the desk from the Coach. She said, "It is my future I am looking thinking about. I'm pregnant."

Coach Mason was shocked beyond words. He dropped his head into his hands and moaned. It never occurred to him that he might not be the father because he thought he was the only one Jane was with. "What are you going to do?" He inquired. He was very fearful as he could see his entire life, job and marriage, drain away.

Jane said, "Don't worry; I don't want to marry you or have this baby. But I need money for an abortion and I need it now. I think with what I have, five hundred dollars will be enough."

He looked at her and for the first time he saw a cold, damaged girl. Why did he not see that before? How stupid could he be? "I don't have that kind of money!!" he exclaimed.

Jane looked him in the eye and said, "Get it, or else, I tell all! I need it in two days." She got up and walked out of his office. He dropped his head on his desk and cried.

That night after supper, Luke took his daughter up stairs for her bath and to get her ready for bed. He read her a story and kissed her goodnight. He stood a long time in her room watching her sleep. She was so beautiful and sweet. She and her brother were the most important things in the world to him and yet he had risk it all for a sleazy affair. He could even go to jail as Jane was his student.

Luke thought of his wife. She was smart, sweet and very devoted to her husband and her marriage. There was no comparison between his wife and Jane. What did he ever see in Jane? She was so artificial and evil.

Luke walked to the kitchen where his wife, Kate, was cleaning up the dinner dishes. He sat at the table and motioned for her to come and sit down. She poured them a glass of wine and sat down with a big smile, "Where have you been my whole life?" She laughed as that was a joke between them. When they had been apart, even for a few minutes, one of them would say that to the other. When Kate saw that Luke was not laughing, or even smiling, she continued, "Why so gloomy? Are you okay?"

Luke was silent for a good while, then in a very low voice he said, "This is the hardest thing I will ever have to tell you. I love you and our children so much. I have done something so bad that I'm not sure you and I will get through it."

Kate said, "Please, your scaring me, what is it? Are you sick, did you get fired?"

"No, I almost wish that those things were the problem but they're not. Kate, I had an affair, with a student and she is pregnant. I don't know how it happened? I know it's a cop out to say she is pure evil in a beautiful body and I was weak. That's no excuse, I have screwed up. She says she'll get an abortion and not say anything as she wants to go on with her life. She knows I don't love her. She has to have five hundred dollars to put with money that she has for an abortion."

Kate sat stone still. Her face drained of all color. Her mind went blank. All she could think was their fairy tale life was over. She was silent so long that Jake finally looked at her and asked, "What are you thinking? I know you want to kill me and believe me I would not resist as I deserve it."

Kate looked him in the eye; she got up and went to the kitchen cabinet. She pulled out a tin container that used to have a fruit cake in it. She opened it and took all the money out of it. She counted the money; there was five hundred dollars with ten dollars left over. She pushed the five hundred dollars over to Luke.

Kate said in a very determined, stern voice. "Luke, you have done the unforgivable to me and our children. I don't know if I will get over it or not. I don't know how to process it but I know I am angry and hurt. You take this money and get yourself out of trouble with this girl. You can't lose your job because you have children to support. After you give this girl the money, you come back here and deal with making this up to us. It may not be possible, but you are going to have to work your ass off trying to put this marriage back together. You will have to work as hard as you can, odd jobs or what ever, but you will replace this money. This money was for our children. I've decided I am going back to work. I can't handle this if I have to think about it all day long here in this house. I love our daughter and son but I am geared to work with adults, to be challenged and productive. The time I spend with our children will be better if I can have my life back. Now get out of my face until I can calm myself enough to be in the same room with you."

Luke looked at her and was filled with relief and fear at the same time. He did not know if he could ever make it up to her but at least she was giving him the opportunity. He knew he would give it a good try as his life depended on it. He slowly nodded and said, "I will do everything in my power to fix this. Thank you so much for your faith in me and taking a chance on me and our marriage." Kate gave him a stern look and went upstairs to their room. He heard her shut and lock the door. This was going to take time and energy, but he deserved to have to work hard. He knew he would never cheat again.

The next day, Jane went to the coach Luke's office. He handed her the money and said, "I'm sorry you are going to have to go through this. We can never be together again. I told my wife everything and she has given me a second chance so I am working on my marriage. I know you didn't get pregnant by yourself or on purpose, so good luck."

Jane shrugged, "Don't worry about me, I'm fine." She turned and walked out of the office. She thought this was going rather well, she had a thousand bucks and one more prospect. The next one would be hard as she did have sympathy for the pastor because he would be the most wounded by his actions. She actually had feelings for Robert, which surprised her that she cared about him. Robert was so sweet and sincere and she could tell he really did love her. At this time in Jane's life, she was not mature enough to realize that this was a special thing for a man to be that much in love with her.

CHAPTER 10

REVEREND LESLIE

Reverend Leslie was in his office at the church working on his sermon, when Jane knocked. He called out for her to come in but he was very surprised that it was Jane. "What are you doing here, Jane? Are you okay?" he asked.

Jane sat down and with the best innocent, quiet voice she said, "Robert, we are in trouble. I'm pregnant."

The reverend was so shocked he could not speak and his face went ghost white. Before he could recover, Jane continued, "Don't pass out, I don't expect for you to marry me. I have bigger plans with my life which does not include marriage and children. So all I need from you is money for an abortion."

If Robert was shocked with the news of the pregnancy, he was even more shocked with the thought of an abortion. He found his voice and said, "You cannot get an abortion, it is a sin!"

Jane countered with a flip attitude, "Well, we have already committed one sin, numerous times, so one more won't even be noticed."

Robert laid his head on the desk and started to cry. What had he done? Not only did he commit adultery but now he was going to be a party to an abortion. He said, "Why get an abortion? Many couples want a baby so badly they will give anything to adopt one."

Jane said, "I don't want to invest that much of my life and body just to give the baby up for adoption. If you don't contribute some money for this abortion, I will be forced to talk to your superior. I would have to say that you raped me and that I was innocent. You could go to jail as I am under age."

Robert was cornered and he knew it. No one would believe him if Jane put on a good act and he knew she could do it. He said, "I don't have that much money. I don't make much money as this is my first job and they supply me with an apartment as part of my salary."

"You need to figure it out and fast" Jane got up and walked out leaving Robert in shock and with a dilemma.

Robert thought what am I going to do? First he had to deal with the fact that he had gotten into this mess. Why had he fallen for the oldest trick in the book? What kind of a preacher was he if he couldn't even stand up to a teenager's advances? Granted Jane was very persuasive and knew what she was doing, but that was not a good reason for him to go against everything he believed in. But the fact remained that he would be more than ruined if Jane went through with her threat, he might even lose his freedom. The only thing he could think of to come up with the money was the church collection money. The collection from the last Sunday was still in the safe to be deposited on Monday. To take the money from the church would be stealing, and technically he would be stealing the money intended for God's work. Robert went into the church sanctuary, knelt at the foot of the cross and prayed. He stayed in this position for a long time trying to express in prayer how sorry he was and how broken he was. Would he ever get through this? At last he felt he had gathered his thoughts and had come to a conclusion.

Robert went into the church office, opened the safe and pulled out five hundred dollars. He sat down at the desk and started to write a letter. In the letter, he addressed all the church members. He said he had decided the ministry was not for him. He asked for forgiveness for leaving without more notice but he couldn't continue at this position. He said he had borrowed five hundred dollars from the church. Part of it would cover his last salary check and he would pay back the rest as soon as he got a job. He wrote that he loved his congregation and his position but he felt he needed to get out into the real world for a while.

It wasn't just taking the money that was wrong, it was his soul that was tarnished and his faith that was broken. The best he could hope for at this point was that he could get a job, pay back the church and heal his soul, if that was possible.

Robert put the money in an envelope and addressed it to Jane at her home. He had to leave the envelope with the money in Jane's mailbox because he could not stand to see her again. He knew behind those beautiful, emerald green eyes there was evil brewing, and he had failed to resist the oldest temptation known to man. If Robert was more educated in psychology, he would have realized that Jane was dealing with mental illness and he may have helped her at that time. Chances are at this time in Jane's life, she would not have listened to anyone that may have tried to help her. It would take many years and many hard times before Jane would reach the realization that she needed help. For Robert, this incident changed his life but right now he had no other options so he got into his beat up old car and drove out of town, his destination unknown.

CHAPTER 11

HENRY

Henry was having a normal day. Everyone that came into the store was very nice and easy to please. He had been really busy as he also had to unpack the freight and inventory the stock. He got home tired and ready for some rest. He picked up the mail as Jane had not come home yet. She was always doing extra things at school, either playing basketball, or practicing for a play. What he didn't know was Jane also had other things that she did after school which had gotten her in a lot of trouble. In the mailbox, there was one piece of mail that looked strange. It was addressed to Jane, but there was no stamp and no return address on it. It was also thick which appeared different. He put the envelope in his pocket; he would ask Jane what this strange envelope contained.

Jane had gone by the church when she got out of school thinking that Reverend Leslie would have her money. When she got there she noticed several cars in the parking lot which was strange this time of the week. There weren't any regular meetings or choir practice on this night so there must be an emergency meeting. Jane went into the church and saw a group of church members sitting together in the first two rows of church pews. She noted most of the members were the upper level committee leaders. Jane moved to the side of the sanctuary and quietly moved down the wall. Everyone was so intent on the meeting that they did not see her. As she got closer she heard one of the elders speaking. He spoke very loudly as if he was agitated.

He said, "I can't believe Robert left without even saying good bye. He seemed fine the last time I saw him and in fact he gave a really nice sermon last Sunday. I would not have ever believed he would take money from the church. It's outrageous. We must report this to the council and the police."

Another member spoke up saying, "He did leave a letter saying he would pay the money back. He could have taken all the money rather than just five hundred dollars. I believe we need to show some forgiveness here."

One of the ladies on the council said, "I don't think that we should report this unless he doesn't return the money. If he had asked us, we would have loaned him the money. Also some of the money would have been his salary at the end of the month."

The final thing that Jane heard before she slipped out was, "We need to call in a council leader and discuss this with him before we do anything. We will just have some of the elders put together a church service this next Sunday, until we get another preacher."

Jane left for home. She knew that Robert had at least gotten the money but how did he plan to get it to her. She hoped he did not plan on going by her house as this would alert her father that something was going on. When she got home, her dad was already there. He was in the kitchen preparing dinner for them, which was normal. Jane causally went into the kitchen. "Hi, Dad, how are you?" She asked.

"I'm fine" He answered. "Are you doing okay? Is there anything going on at school?"

"No, everything is fine, just normal things going on at school. I'll go get ready for dinner." She said as she started to walk away.

"Oh, by the way," her dad, wiped his hands on a dish towel, and pulled the envelope out of his pocket. "This came in the mail addressed to you. It's strange as it does not have a return address or a stamp. Someone must have placed it in our box. It's pretty thick. You want to open it?"

Jane froze; she immediately knew what the envelope was. It had to be the five hundred dollars that Robert took from the church that she heard the church members talking about. She tried to remain calm and causal as she said, "Oh, well I'll take it with me." And she reached for the envelope.

Henry said, "Well, I'm curious, open it here. I can't imagine what it could be."

Jane was trapped; she did not have an escape. She took the envelope and slowly tore it open and looked inside. Sure enough, it was money, without counting, she knew how much it was. She removed the money and stood looking at it. Henry was astonished, "Who would send you that much money, is there a note?" He asked.

Jane knew she would have to tell her dad the truth or a lie if she could think of a good one. She looked at her dad and said, "Dad, I'm in trouble and this money is to help me get out of that trouble."

Henry looked at her, he was stunned. "What kind of trouble are you in that would take this money to help you out? And who sent the money?"

Jane looked down at the floor and said, "I'm pregnant. This money is for me to get an abortion."

Henry almost fell to the floor. He was more shocked over this admission than anything in his life. "How can you be pregnant? How could you do this to us? Who is the father? Who sent the money?" He demanded.

"Dad, I can never tell you who the father is." This was certainly the truth, as she didn't even know who the father was. "And I cannot tell you who sent the money. I have to get an abortion as marriage is out of the question and I do not want to ruin my life having a baby to take care of."

"No," Henry shouted, "Abortion is a mortal sin; your soul will be condemned to hell if you kill this baby. You know I would help you raise a baby; you would not have to work. Maybe when the child is older, you could go to college. Please, do not do this."

"What if something happened to you? I would not even be able to keep this house with no income. And I know it cost lots of money to keep mother in that hospital, her care would take all your savings. I'd have nothing, no education and no job. I don't have any other choice." She said.

"Yes, you do. If something happens to me, I have a trust fund set up for you that would give you an annuity every month. It would help you provide a home for you and your child for the rest of your life. I also have one for your mother. You'd be fine without me." He begged.

"Dad, I do not want a child. You know that insanity is hereditary. What if my child ended up like my mother? What if I end up like my mother? Who would take care of the baby then?" After saying this, Jane ran out of the room, up the stairs and into her bedroom, slamming the door.

Henry sat down at the table and put his head in his hands. This could not be happening. What had he done wrong in his life to deserve this? He could not let his only daughter commit this sin by getting an abortion. Jane was still a child and Henry knew she would regret this action the rest of her life. He had to come up with a solution.

Henry suddenly felt faint and the room began to spin. To much stress he thought as he got up to get a drink of water. As he started over to the sink, he had a pain in his neck and left shoulder that caused him to grip the edge of the kitchen counter. After a minute or two, the pain eased off and the room stopped spinning. Henry had been feeling more tired lately and was not sleeping very well, but he was sixty years old. He felt this was what getting older was all about. Slowing down and new aches and pains were to be expected at this age.

Henry turned off the stove and left the kitchen as it was. He slowly went up the stairs. At the top of the stairs, he looked at the closed door to Jane's room. What was he going to do with her? He needed Bess, he felt very inadequate as a single parent. If Bess was here, and was not sick, he thought she would be able to talk to Jane as a mother would to her daughter. Tomorrow he would do something; he just did not know what.

The next day Henry visited his lawyer and had some new provisions put into his will. He was afraid that Jane had made a terrible mistake but he wanted to prevent her from making a bigger mistake. He did the only thing he thought he could do. Now he just had to tell Jane.

That night Jane came home late and was surprised to see her dad still up. She did not want to talk to him or see him. She had made up her mind and he was not going to change it for her. She walked in, slammed the front door and started up the stairs. Henry called from the kitchen, "Jane, come into the kitchen, we have some things to discuss."

Jane called back, "I'm tired and don't want to talk right now."

Henry called her again and it sounded very much out of his nature as it was a demand, "Jane come to the kitchen immediately, you have to face this tonight."

Jane swore under her breath and stomped into the kitchen with a scowl on her face. Henry ignored her attitude and began the discussion. "As you know, I am very disappointed that you have become pregnant. It was a very bad choice that you made. But I know you didn't get into this mess by yourself. Therefore, you need to tell me who the father is."

Jane laughed, "I will never tell you who the father is. I am going to take care of this myself!"

Henry was getting more upset, "You will tell me; the father must take responsibility for this child, if only with money."

Jane retorted, "I told you I am not having this baby!"

Henry calmed a little and said, "Very well. If you insist in not telling me who the father is, how will you support your self with a baby and no job or education?"

Jane was getting louder, "I am not having a baby! I am going to college and make my own life!"

Henry sighed and was quiet for a minute then said, "If you have an abortion, I will no longer help you financially in any way which would include not giving you college tuition or money to live on. However, if you have the baby, I will support you until the baby is born and then you can stay home with your child. You could go to college at night as I will take care of the baby at night for you. We can do this together; it is the right thing to do! We need to stay together as a family. If something happens to me, you will get financial support on a monthly basis, as long as you have this child and take care of it properly. My lawyer will be in charge of monitoring that you are with your child and making a home for the child. If you don't keep this child, no money now or ever will come, from me, to help you. I am doing this for your own good, so you won't make the biggest mistake of your life."

Jane jumped up from the chair and pounded the table, "How dare you try to control my life! You are the worst father in the world! You are as crazy as mother! You need to get a bed beside her and you can both just be crazy together! If I were to tell you who the father is, your life would be ruined also. Your job would be gone!"

As this information slowly soaked in, Henry became aware of the implication of her words. His face turned red and he began to shake. He said, "Are you telling me that my boss, Mr. Miller, is the father? He is older than me!"

Jane screamed a lie that would cause a terrible twist of fate, "Everything would be fine if you weren't intent on ruining my life! Mr. Miller gave me money for the abortion and said if I told anyone he was the father, he would fire you. He raped me! I did not want you to lose your job. You have worked there all your life, you can't do anything else! You must let me take care of this and everything will be fine." After she delivered her bomb, she ran upstairs to her room, slammed the door and fell on her bed. She pounded the pillow and screamed to no one, "How can he ruin my life. It is my life and I will live it like I want to." After a while she grew quiet and fell asleep.

CHAPTER 12

HENRY AND JANE

Outside the night sky was filling with heavy, low, angry clouds. Thunder was rolling in with the clouds and lightning was streaking across the sky. This storm was not the only thing brewing. Henry sat in a kitchen chair not knowing how to process the things that Jane had told him. He did not have any personal relationship with Mr. Miller even after working for him for so many years. He had not had any conversations with him except what was necessary for business. Mr. Miller had a reputation of being a hard business man. When he came to town, it was strictly for work, or so Henry thought. But now Henry knew some of the long nights that Mr. Miller was in his office working he was doing other things.

In his rage, Henry did not take into account that for Mr. Miller to have sex with Jane, she would have gone to his office. She had no business in his office especially at night. However, Henry could only think about his daughter being pregnant and that she said Mr. Miller raped her. At this point, Henry also forgot that Jane was a good liar. Henry was still in physical pain from the weak spell he had the night before but now his emotional pain was overwhelming. To think Jane was a willing participant in having sex with Mr. Miller was more than Henry could bear; so he chose to believe that Mr. Miller raped Jane. Henry became aware that a storm was coming but he remembered Mr. Miller was working tonight at the store. Mild mannered Henry was beside himself with rage and felt so helpless in this situation.

Henry thought there comes a time in every man's life when he has to act to protect his family. He thought he could talk to Mr. Miller and get to the truth and just in case he already suspected the truth which was that Jane lied about the rape, he still had to convince Mr. Miller that he had to support his and Jane's child.

Henry went upstairs; he knocked on Jane's door and got no response. He went to his room and went to the closet. He moved several boxes to find the one he wanted. He put the box on the bed and opened it. Inside was a Western Marshall Colt .45 pistol. This was his prize possession. This beautiful gun looked like the pistol that the cowboys carried in the old west. It had a long, sleek barrel and a cylinder that held the bullets. The handle was made of beautiful wood buffed to a shine. He had not shot this gun in a long time. The last time the gun was shot was when Henry taught Jane how to shoot it. He felt she needed to know how to handle a gun in case she needed it for protection. He filled the chamber with bullets and went down the stairs. He did not have in mind to shoot Mr. Miller; he just wanted to scare him into doing what was right. He wanted him to say he would talk Jane into keeping the baby and that he would help support the child. Henry though this was the right thing to do for all of them.

Henry went out the front door and was surprised that the wind was so strong that it jerked the screen door out of his hands and slammed it against the house. The thunder was very loud and the lightning was so constant that the night was illuminated by the flashes. Walking against the wind was a chore and made the walk to the store much longer than normal.

In her room, Jane jerked awake when she heard the slam of the screen door against the house. She became aware of the thunder, lightning and wind. She got up and went into the hall. She saw the door to her father's room open and wondered what he was thinking going out at night in this storm. She looked into the room and saw the box, open on the bed. She immediately knew this was the gun box and the gun was gone. It struck her that her father was going to the store to confront Mr. Miller and he had his gun. This was very serious, she thought as she ran down stairs.

When she ran out of the house she was confronted by the same strong wind that Henry battled just a few minutes ahead of her. She bent into the wind and pushed toward the store. Normally she would have been afraid of the lightning but now she was just glad that the light from it was helping her find her way to the store.

When she finally reached the store, the front door was open which surprised her. She went in and adjusted to being out of the wind. It took a minute for her to get the sound of the wind out of her ears then she heard voices from Mr. Miller's office. Even though the store was dark, she knew it well and was able to go straight to the office. The office door was open and Henry was standing in the middle of the office with Mr. Miller standing behind his desk.

Jane noted her dad did not look right. He was bent over slightly, he was sweating profusely and his face was ashen white. Jane thought this was the results of him being so upset. Mr. Miller appeared relaxed and had a smirk on his face. He knew Henry was a mild man and he did not feel the gun was a threat of violence from Henry. Henry had always complied with his demands without any resistance.

Mr. Miller was saying, "Henry, you are mistaken. I never raped anyone and especially not Jane. I know you are her father and it will be hard for you to realize this but your daughter is a whore, a slut and a liar. I gave her money for an abortion which is what she wanted after I assured her I was not going to divorce my wife and marry her. She had this ridiculous idea that I would marry a little nobody like her."

The cruel words hurt Henry beyond his endurance. At the same time he was beginning realize what he suspected was true, that Jane was not telling him the truth. Henry was not feeling well and he was having that pain again in his neck and shoulders. His head was hurting and it was hard for him to focus. Mr. Miller kept going in out of focus for him and he was seeing dark spots in front of him.

Jane saw her father fall to the floor. She screamed and ran to him. She knelt by him and rolled him onto his side. His face was a bluish color and his eyes were staring but not seeing anything. Even Jane could tell he was dead. A wave of desolation swept over her. Everything in the room faded out and all she saw was her father's face and the gun beside his hand. For a second her mind turned black, and she heard a whisper in her ears that grew louder and louder until she heard loud and clear, "Kill him, Kill him. Kill him"

Even though it seemed an eternity, it only took seconds for Jane to pick up the gun and stand up. Mr. Miller said, "look what you have done you stupid bitch. You have killed your father. You have told a lie that has destroyed your family."

Jane held the gun in her right hand. With her left hand she took the palm of her hand and pulled the hammer of the gun back. She moved her left hand onto the handle with the right hand and stretched out her arms straight in front of her. The first shot hit Mr. Miller in the abdomen. His face turned to complete surprise and he grabbed his abdomen with both hands and sat down in the chair with a thud. He whispered, "You shot me, you little bitch. I will see that you burn for this."

As Mr. Miller was talking, Jane repeated her motions and the second shot hit him directly in the heart and he died immediately. His head fell back and his arms fell by his side. Blood was seeping into his expensive suit and dripping onto the floor.

Jane was surprising calm inside. She took the tail of her shirt and wiped the gun clean to remove her finger prints. She placed the gun in her father's right hand and pressed his fingers around the handle and on the trigger. She held his hand on the gun and put her finger over his on the trigger and shot a third time toward the dead man. This shot missed the body and went into the wall just above Mr. Miller's head. Jane knew that there would need to be gun powder residue on her father's hands to implicate him as the shooter.

Jane was not sure what put this thought process in her head as she felt like she was moving like a puppet with someone else pulling the strings. Jane looked at her dead father and felt sorrow but also felt detached. She turned and walked back through the store and out into the storm. The thought occurred to her that she just walked out of a disaster and into a storm. The rain had finally started to fall with a vengeance. Jane did not hurry but walked normally through the rain. The lightning was still steady so she was able to see how to get home with no problems. When she entered the house, the electricity went off. She felt her way up the stairs and into her room. She pulled off all her wet cloths and fell onto the bed and went into a deep sleep that even the storm in its prime did not wake her. As she slept, the storm raged through the town leaving a trail of destruction. Lying in the darkest shadows of mental illness, Jane had left a trail of destruction even more devastating than what Mother Nature had just yielded on this town.

CHAPTER 13

JANE

As the morning broke, the massive clouds from the storm were gone. Everyone in town started assessing the damage from the storm. It would be later that morning before anyone noticed the hardware store was not open for business. Jane woke up and at first was not clear what had happened. Then like a flood, the memories from the night before came back.

Jane felt no remorse for shooting Mr. Miller to death. She had told herself he would pay for treating her like common white trash; she just didn't know she was going to make him pay with his life. She did feel sad for the loose of her father. He had been a good man, working hard for his family. When Bess had to be committed to the institute, he lost the love of his life. Jane knew when he heard the truth about her from Mr. Miller, the rest of his reason for living was gone. In Jane's mind, she decided her father wanted to die and had given up on life. This is how she shifted the blame back to her father for his own death. Once again she had absolved herself of blame for the tragedies left in her wake. Jane's thoughts now were "what to do from here."

First she had a lot of acting to do to get through what was to come in order for there to be no suspicion on her. She took her wet cloths to the dryer. She was lucky the electricity was back on so she could clean up her trail. While the cloths dried, she cleaned up the kitchen and fixed some breakfast. When her cloths were dry she took them to her room and hung them in the closet. She got ready for school and before going down stairs, she closed the door to her dad's bedroom. She walked to the corner and got on the bus, just as usual. The only thing that was on her mind was to make a plan for her life. Since she was trapped into having this baby, she knew she could not stay in this town. Someone would make the connection of her being pregnant and her dad's attack on Mr. Miller and to Mr. Miller's death. Also she would be a complete outcast due to having a baby and not being married. During Jane's generation having a baby and not being married was a major mistake. Not only would the mother but the child and the mother's family would be shunned by everyone even the church attending Christians turned their head the other way. The saddest part of this was the children labeled a bastard and treated as an outcast when they were the innocent victim of a scandal.

It was late in the morning; Jane was in her third class of the day, when the principal of the school knocked on the door. The teacher went into the hall for a few minutes. When she returned she went to Jane's desk and in a serious voice, told Jane they needed her in the hall.

When the policeman told her that her father had passed away at the store, Jane fainted. As she started to fall, the principal caught her and helped her slid to the floor. A policeman carried her to the nurse's station where the nurse had some smelling sauce. When Jane revived, the policeman offered to drive her home.

When they arrived home, the police finished the story of what they found, "Jane it appears that your dad had a heart attack. But it also appears that he shot Mr. Miller before he died. Do you know of any problems between the two of them?"

Jane gasped and began to cry. As she began to calm down she said, "Dad worked for Mr. Miller for years. Dad never discussed anything with me directly. As you know, I work at the store sometimes and once when I was there, I heard dad and Mr. Miller auguring. Later I ask dad about it but all he would say was that Mr. Miller was so tight and he never gave him a raise or any other benefits. That's all I ever knew. You know my dad was a good man and would never do anything like that unless he was seriously provoked. This is terrible, what am I to do?" She began to cry again.

The officers looked all through the house. The only thing out of order was the gun case open on the bed. The officer brought the box down and asked Jane if she knew what had been in the box.

She said, "That box is what dad kept his Colt .45 pistol in. He loved that gun. He told me someday he would teach me to use it but we never got around to it. He thought he would always be here for me." As Jane told this lie, she did remember her dad patiently teaching her how to use the colt. Like everything that Jane did not want to deal with, she put this memory in the shadows of her mind so she did not have to feel any emotion that might cause her to weaken.

The police left and the church folks began to come. They brought food and patted Jane on the shoulder saying things would be fine. The next two weeks were a blur. The funeral was agonizing and Jane became tired of all the "good" folks. She just wanted to be by herself to think.

Graduation was the next week; after graduation she didn't know what to do. First she needed to see the lawyer. Jane had the one thousand five hundred dollars from the three possible fathers of her baby, but that would not last long. She could sell the house, but that would take a while and that money was probably slated for her mother's care since it belonged to her now. Jane wondered how everything had gotten in such a mess. Of course, she did not carry any of the blame. She thought if everyone else had not been so stupid, things would have worked out differently.

Jane thought she was smart enough to figure out how to make some sense out of her life and what had happened. She thought things could not get much worse but she had no idea what else awaited her in the shadows of her mind and in her life.

CHAPTER 14

ROBERT

B efore the terrible storm ravaged the town, Pastor Robert Leslie was escaping town in his old car. He was not running from the forecasted storm but the turbulence that would occur if Jane shouted rape to the world. Robert was a broken man in so many ways. He had broken his vows to the ministry, but he had betrayed himself and everything that he thought he stood for.

As he analyzed what happened, he blamed two things for his down fall. His thought process was not necessarily rational because he was trying to use reasonable explanations for his unreasonable actions.

First he blamed his parents. His parents were very average, normal people that were very satisfied with their life. His father, Jim, was a CPA with a good income. His mother, Mary, worked in the school system administration building. Jim and Mary were respected in the community. They had three children with Robert being the youngest with an older boy and girl. Robert was that one in a million kid that was born gifted with above normal intelligence. He was so smart that his parents felt in awe of him. They could never find anything that he did as anything but awesome. He sailed through high school and won a full scholarship to college. Robert never heard anything but praise from everyone, especially his parents. Robert had never failed at anything. After he finished college, he decided to enter the seminary. His parents again were elated. When Robert was assigned to his first church as an assistant, he felt above reproach. He felt entitled. Jane fed into his ego and he did not feel that he could do any wrong. He reasoned now that if his parents had kept him more grounded and had introduced him to reproach, he might have recognized the possibility that he was screwing up. Of course this thinking was only a mechanism for him to cope with his failure.

The second thing he decided contributed to his downfall was lust. He wondered why God would create man with such a flaw as lust. He was completely out of his comfort zone with sex because he spent all his time on his studies and had no sexual experience at all. What he did not take into consideration was that God made man capable of making choices. He had made the wrong choice but he was not capable at this time to accept his part in this disaster. Robert had asked God to forgive him but he was not asking for the right reasons. Therefore, he did not get any comfort or understanding for his choices. It would take a while and some growing up for Robert to reach a place of inner peace.

Robert drifted through the country. He stopped at the first "help wanted" sign that he saw which was in a café washing dishes. He slept on a cot in the back of the café and washed dishes there until he paid all the money back to the church. He felt a little better about himself with this one sin rectified, but he was still restless. He continued across the country until his car gave up running and was not repairable. He was now back packing and hitch-hiking. Robert's life was deep in the shadows as he wondered across the country. Until Robert was able to take responsibility for the choices he made, he would have to hide his transgressions in the shadows of his mind so he did not have to deal with having flaws.

CHAPTER 15

SARG

One night Robert was at a shelter when he heard some young men talking about available work. Horse racing season was beginning and that opened jobs at the race track caring for the horses. If you worked at the race track, you were allowed to sleep in the barn and eat at the track, so you did not have these expenses. Horse racing was exciting; the money was pretty good and if you got a good tip, you might make some money by betting. Robert got his back pack and headed out.

It was getting dark and the wind was starting to blow rain around as Robert was walking. He had given up on getting a ride, when to his surprise, a long horse trailer pulled by a diesel truck pulled to the side of the road. Robert took off running to catch up to the truck and climbed in the cab. He looked at the driver and saw a thin, rugged man in his late-fifties. The driver was clean shaven except for a mustache and he wore a beat-up cowboy straw hat that was sweat stained all around the brim. One thing Robert noted was the man had the biggest hands he had ever seen. The cowboy said, "Welcome aboard. My name is Sarg."

Robert said, "Thanks so much for stopping. It was getting very nasty out there. My name is Robert Leslie."

Sarg was surprised at this young man. He had picked up lots of young men looking for work but Robert was different. He was well groomed and sounded educated. "What are you doing out here tonight?" Sarg asked.

Robert said, "I'm just drifting. I always wanted to see the country. I've been pretty sheltered my whole life so I'm working my way around the country. Are you going to the race track?"

Sarg answered, "Yes, I've been going there for the last ten years. I have six horses that I'm training and racing for my boss. If you want a job, I have one. It's cleaning and grooming but you'll have a place to sleep. Ever been around horses, son?"

Robert said, "No sir, but I can learn and I really need a job, so thank you very much."

Sarg began to explain, "Horses are sensitive. They can smell fear in a person a mile away. So if you are afraid of them they will take advantage of that and they can be very dangerous. Horses are fright and flight animals. They react to danger by running and if they have to hurt you to get away, they will. But, I take care of the horses; you will just be cleaning stalls, feeding, grooming etc. Where are you from?"

Robert had not told his family that he was on the road so he was not going to reveal where he was from so he said, "Up north. My folks are just hard working, normal, good people. I'm kind of a disappointment to them right now, so I need some space for a while."

Sarg said, "You better get some sleep, we will get to the track later tonight and unload the horses at sun up."

Robert slumped in the seat and went to sleep as Sarg drove through the night. At sun up, Sarg woke Robert up to get started to work. All the stalls had to be cleaned and fresh straw put in before the horses were unloaded. Sarg was surprised how fast Robert worked and how well he did what he was instructed to do. Soon the horses were in their stalls eating their meal.

Robert was working hard but having a good time as he had never been around this kind of environment and had never worked this hard. Robert found Sarg to be a man of few words. Sarg talked to the horses more than to anyone else. Sarg spent all his time with the horses, getting them ready to race. One night after all the work was completed, Sarg was sitting on a bale of hay outside the stalls working on repairing a bridle. Robert flopped down near him. Sarg said, "I guess you're tired?"

Robert answered, "Lord, yes. Didn't know I had all these muscles until they all started hurting." Then he ventured a question, "Sarg, how did you get into the horse training business?"

Sarg was quiet so long that Robert thought he was not going to answer at all but he started out slowly. "I was one of ten kids in a family so poor that just getting enough to eat was the main goal. When I turned fifteen, I took off. I hopped a train west and rode it until I got into ranching country. I knew the only thing I could do was hard work so I hired on as a ranch hand. It was hard work, day light to dark building or mending fences or just doing ranch work. The rancher brought in a herd of horses each year that needed breaking. I was immediately hooked on horses. I seemed to have a way with them. I think they sensed that I was not going to hurt them. The boss put me in charge of breaking. I did not do the rough breaking which was just throwing a saddle on them and riding them until you or the horse gave up. I hated to see the fear in their eyes as they had no idea what was going on and they only knew to fight. I spend time with them and get their confidence.

'I watch each horse and determine their temperament. Then if you assess their movements, they will give you a sign when they are ready to trust you. First, they come to me then they just want to please me. When the boss got into thoroughbreds, I worked myself into training for the track. I watched a lot of good trainers and paid my dues on the track, mucking stalls and grooming just like you have worked. It gets in your blood and it becomes your life. It's a hard life and lonely, but I never learned any social skills, so me and the horses get along fine." Sarg got up and went into tack room where he slept. This was more conversation than he had engaged in a long time and it surprised him that he had said so much. However, he liked Robert. There was something about Robert that invited people to open up. Robert listened to people so it was easy to open up to him.

A few days later, as Robert and Sarg finished another day of working with the horses, they were sitting by the stalls resting when Robert asked, "Sarg, do you mind me asking, how you got that name?"

Sarg thought for a while then began a story that he didn't think he would ever tell anyone but decided it was time for him to let it go. "When I turned eighteen, it was the mid '60s. The Vietnam war was just getting started and the draft was in effect, but I went ahead and joined the army. I hated to leave my horses, but it was the thing to do. I loaded onto a bus with lots of other kids and we went to base for training. When we got off the bus, it was like stepping into hell. We were yelled at continuously, belittled, harassed and you name it. At times, we were even hit by the drill sergeants. They weren't playing around and they meant for us to grown up and do it fast. We were taught to do what we were told and not think about it. In combat you had to work as a team and protect each other.

'We trained non-stop and were immediately sent to Viet Nam without even a break to go home. Of course, I didn't have a home to go to so it didn't bother me, but some of the other guys were very depressed over not getting leave. But when we got to Vietnam we didn't think about anything but staying alive. That place was such a nightmare. It was such a strange land to all of us. None of us had ever been exposed to these elements. It was a jungle, with rain and cold every day. The jungle was so tough to navigate through and there was danger everywhere. There were a lot of men wounded and killed every day. We were on constant alert for attack.

'After I had been in Vietnam about six months, my unit was assigned to scout out a new area where they thought the Viet Cong had set up a base. There were eight men in my unit. I had been picked as second to the Sargent and I was in charge of the radio. It was dark and we were moving slowly. We were directed to walk through the jungle and see that it was clear of any enemy. On the other side of this area we would be picked up by helicopter to take us back to base.

'After about an hour, the unit stopped for a rest. Everyone sat down while the Sargent and I reviewed our map. Suddenly we were under attack. The first shot hit our Sargent. I held him as he died and he told me, 'you are the Sarg now' before he died." Sarg had to stop talking for a few minutes. Robert waited patiently as he knew this was hard for Sarg to tell.

Sarg began talking again, "Just the week before this the Sargent and I were walking down a road just outside a village. As we were walking we saw a bicycle coming toward us. When the bike got closer I saw it was a native boy around eight or nine years old. From out of the blue, the Sargent grabbed me and we both crashed in the ditch. Immediately when we hit the dirt, an explosion occurred right where we were walking. As the smoke cleared, I looked up and saw the bike turned upside down with the front wheel spinning. There was blood everywhere along with body parts. I was in shock until the Sargent shook me and made me get up so we could get out of the area. I ask the Sargent how he knew there was a bomb on the bike. He said as soon as he saw the kid riding the bike he knew it was rigged because kids never got to ride a bike, only the adults had that privilege. Robert, sometimes when I see a bike, if my defenses are down, I will relive seeing that bike wheel spinning with all the blood. I think about that poor young child whose life had no value to his own people. I break out into a sweat, start shaking and get sick to my stomach." Most of the time, Sarg could keep his bad memories in the shadows of his mind but if he was not on guard, these horrible memories would slip out and haunt him again. Many suicides are the results of war memories that cannot be repressed and becomes unbearable.

Sarg started his story again, "After I knew the Sargent was dead, I didn't have time to grieve or even process that our leader was gone and I was in charge. Everyone was stunned but I had to act now as we were under a lot of fire and not much time left to get to the pick-up spot. If we were not at the pick-up spot on time, the helicopter had no choice but to leave us because if they waited, they became a target. All I knew was to get the men up and moving. We would have to send a recovery team in to get the Sargent's remains. That is if any of us survived to tell where he was.

'We started to move through the trees, going from one hiding place to the next. The entire time, we were dodging bullets. We had two others wounded by now, and had to help the wounded move forward. We finally reached the bottom of a hill that we had to go over to get to the pick-up place. At the top of that hill was a machine gun nest and the Viet Cong were continually firing. It was placed where the gun could spray a 180 degree area. We were stalled and if we did not get to the pick-up place we were done for. The men looked to me for a plan." Sarg paused and lowered his head.

After a few minutes Sarg started again, "I had nothing! No plan or idea what to do. Then from somewhere I got an idea. I had my men spread out on the perimeter. I had them start firing at the nest from different places, when the machine gun was spraying an area on one side of the hill, it left the area I was in free of fire for a few minutes. I took off up the hill with my grenade in hand. When I got to the top of the hill, I pulled the pin and threw the grenade in the nest. I fell to the ground and started rolling down the hill as the grenade went off. As soon as the smoke cleared it was evident that the nest had been disabled. The men of my unit raced up the hill. They grabbed me and we took off for the field. The chopper was hovering as we began to jump on board. We helped the wounded up and I was the last one pulled on. As we were going up, a big group of Viet Cong ran out of the woods shooting at us. I got shot in the leg but we got away. When we were in the air, the men looked at me and said you're our Sarg from now on.

'I don't know why I stormed that nest; I'm not aggressive or heroic. War does something to you and all the training you have snaps in and you just react. That bullet in my leg is still there, but it got me home. They did recover the remains of the Sargent and sent him home. He was a good man, but a lot of good men died. I've thought and thought and I can't find an answer to who dies and who lives. I guess there is no answer." Sarg looked at the ground and was near tears.

Sarg looked Robert in the eye and said, "When we came home from the war, we were not welcomed with parades or slaps on the back for a good job. No, people would not even look us in the eye. Or if they did it was with scorn and some returning warriors were even spit on. There was a wave of apathy causing Americans to lose their pride in their country and to forget that freedom is not free. Someone had to fight and die for that freedom. It was a very sad time in America. I still grieve for the men that came home and were lost forever in a silent hell for what they went through in the war. I still wonder if God can forgive me when he said 'thou shall not kill' but I killed anyway."

Robert was so moved that he had tears running down his face. He had never heard any war stories before. He had no idea how bad it was by hearing a story where someone was in dire danger as well as being responsible for other men. Robert waited until Sarg looked him in the eyes and he said, "Sarg, you are a hero. I want you to know I think you are the bravest man I have ever known. I want to thank you for your service to our country." Robert got up, walked over to Sarg and grabbed him in a heart-felt hug.

Sarg was very surprised, he said, "That means a lot to me, Robert. You're a good man too." There were a lot of other things that Sarg had seen and done during the war that he could not talk about. These things that a man is trained and ordered to do to other men, is something that has to be hidden in the shadows of their mind in order for them to be able to live with the memories. When these memories emerge during times in a person's life, it can have devastating effects to them and others around them. This is called post-traumatic stress disorder and has moved out of the shadows in more recent times. PTSD has become a highly recognized and treatable aftermath of war. There are countless numbers of lives that have been lost to PTSD before awareness of the problem shed light into this mysterious syndrome.

CHAPTER 16

ROBERT

O ver the next few weeks, Sarg learned more about Robert. He found Robert to be a lost soul. After the night Sarg had told him the war story, Robert had felt close to him. Robert began to open up little by little and began to confide in Sarg. Sarg learned that Robert was very smart and well educated. He was the first college educated person that Sarg had any interaction with.

The other thing that really intrigued Sarg was that Robert was a preacher trained at the seminary. What was this talented, caring, educated man doing cleaning stalls? Every night Robert and Sarg would sit on a bale of hay and talk. Robert finally told Sarg what he had done and how he had failed God and himself. He had failed his vows to God and committed adultery. Sarg listened to his story and felt Robert had set unreasonable standards for himself. Robert had forgotten he was human and he would have to pick himself up and try again. Sarg was working on a way to tell Robert some things that would hit home with him and get him back in the human race. Sarg was also getting some information and comfort out of his conversations with Robert.

One night Sarg had burning questions, "Robert, You know so much about the Bible as you have studied it, so I have some questions. I have been in the war and I have seen men, good men, die at my feet while I go on. Why did I survive and others did not? All of those men that came home in coffins had families somewhere praying for them. I also know many of them were very devout and faithful. So *Why me?* I am a poor example of being what I should be. I grew up in a rough environment and I did some bad things as a kid."

Robert thought for a while before he spoke, "Sarg, I don't have the answers you are looking for. I don't know if there is one answer. If you take the Bible as it is written, and if you believe, trust and love God, your sins are forgiven, if you ask. Jesus gave his life for our sins to be forgiven.

'I can only speak from a Christian point of view. The ultimate goal of a Christian is to be with God and Jesus in heaven. Heaven is described in the Bible as the place where we will live free of pain, with no worries and resolved of guilt. The point would be; to die is not necessarily the tragedy but to survive the death of a loved one is the hard part. However, we have that element of fear of the unknown. No one has come back from death to tell us what it is like on the other side. There are many near-death experiences that are described by people that have been revived. They all have a common recall; they feel a sense of peace, a white light calling them and the sight of deceased loved ones waiting are described vividly. So if we believe that our loved ones are going to be in a better place, we should not grieve for them as they are going to heaven, but we are grieving for ourselves because we are the ones who have to continue to live without those we love. All we really know is the ones that feel the pain are the ones left behind to carry on without their loved one. A child without a parent, a wife left without her soul mate or a mother to lose a child is a pain that you cannot describe.

'Of course, we know suicide is considered a sin. When someone takes their own life, there are some serious mental issues going on that many times, goes unnoticed. To lose someone to suicide is the ultimate pain and betrayal. We feel we could have helped in some way to prevent this senseless act.

'We are all born with an internal instinct to live. We all fight to live in order to stay with those we love and we fear the unknown. I, personally believe, that those that go before us, are ready and those of us that are left behind still have things we need to do for ourselves or for others. We need to understand, it is up to each of us to develop our interpretation of what is written. People must determine what their faith is and how true they are to themselves.

'In theory, the door is open to so many different dominations of Christian religion but we have one Bible. People have a choice as to what to believe. To make their choice, they need to explore what feels right for them. I know that sounds like a circle, but there is no single answer. Everyone needs to explore the word of the Bible, research the different religions to see what they wish to stand for and, above all, pray for guidance."

Sarg shook his head, "It's too big for me to comprehend, but you have given me a lot to think about. I have never had anyone explain things to me in this way. Thank you, Robert. These talks over the last few weeks will stay with me forever."

A strange friendship had developed between a rugged, war torn, world wise cowboy and a young, privileged, exceptionally smart, fallen preacher. Somewhere in the night, their paths crossed and forever changed the course of their life and maybe even changed the course of their eternal life.

Sarg was so enlightened by his conversations with Robert and he felt close to Robert. He hated to see Robert in so much pain about his past and so uncertain about his future. He felt he had to do something to help Robert, like Robert had helped him.

Sarg had five horses in his racing string but he stabled six horses. Robert ask him one day about this extra horse. Sarg said, "That is my horse. He used to be the best one I've ever seen. He won me a lot of money that I was able to put back for my retirement. So, I take extra good care of him. He goes with me every racing season, then home again, even though he no longer races. We are going to both retire in a few years."

Robert asked. "How did you get a great horse like that?"

Sarg answered, "I got a lucky break. He was owned by a big stable that could buy the best horses around. This horse was up and coming, winning well. I was watching him and for some reason, I liked this horse.

'One day, I was watching this horse race. When he got on the back stretch, he was challenged by another horse. The other horse was on the outside, with him on the rail. The other horse swerved over on him pushing him over and causing him to hit the rail. He flipped over the rail throwing the rider. He wasn't hurt, just bruised up. But after that, any time a horse pulled up beside him and they were nose to nose, he would slack off. No matter how much the jockey pushed him, he just faded. The owner was done with him. I ask if I could buy him and we made a deal. I took him off the track for the rest of the year and let him rest.

'I thought about this horse's problem and by watching old racing films of him after his accident, I noted when a horse pulled up beside him and he made eye contact, that's when he would give up. I decided he doubted his ability to beat the horse next to him because he was afraid he would get hurt again. I call it having a "Shadow of Doubt" that caused him to give up.

The next year, I put blinkers on him. That's a device attached to the bridle that shades the side view of the horse. With blinkers on, he had to just look forward and he could focus on the track ahead of him and not the horse at his side. After that, he ran and won time after time. We made a good team. He took care of me financially, so I will take care of him till he dies."

Robert thought this was a good story, but Sarg had a bigger point to make with Robert, "Robert, I think that there's something you need to think about from this story for your life."

Robert was puzzled but listened. Sarg continued, "You, like my horse, got a good bump that threw you off track. You gave in to lust and you committed a sin against God's word. Now you think you are flawed, but you are not flawed. You have for the first time in your life experienced doubt. Doubt in yourself to reach the impossibly perfect standards that you have set for yourself. It's this shadow of doubt that has paralyzed you. It has taken you out of life. You are hiding here, doing manual work so you won't have to face cleaning up your life. People sin, get over yours, ask for forgiveness and get back to work. Don't let the shadow of doubt rule the rest of your life. You have too many more races to run." With that he turned back to grooming his horse. Robert just turned and walked away.

The next day, Robert said to Sarg, "When the racing season is over here, I'm going home to tell my parents what I have done. Then I will get back to my life. I don't feel I will ever be a preacher again, but I think I will get back to school and pursue a PhD in psychology. I think I have a lot to give. You are right, I am afraid; I have doubt that I can recover from my sins, or be worthy again. I need to believe the things that I have been preaching and have faith. Thank you, you didn't have to apply blinkers to me, but you did have to open my eyes."

When the horses were all loaded and ready for the ride home, Robert had his back pack ready. He shook hands with Sarg and hugged him, "I won't forget you and I will be visiting race tracks in the future to see you again."

Sarg smiled, "Robert, you have a lot of important work to do. I better not see you hanging around race tracks again. Good Bye." He climbed in the cab of the truck and never looked back. Robert started walking toward the bus station to buy a ticket home.

CHAPTER 17

JANE

When Henry passed away of a heart attack, he left financial support for Jane. He also wanted his grandchild to have a good life. Henry's lawyer, Mr. Mason, had documented what Henry wanted and it was all legal. Jane hated what her dad had arranged and she felt trapped. She had neither money nor any other support unless she kept her child.

Jane had to get out of town after the scandal of the decade centered on Henry Baxter. If she stayed in town she would create an even bigger scandal being pregnant without naming a father. She decided she would leave after she graduated from high school, which was in a month.

Mr. Mason took control of the estate and had the family home sold and the money was put in a trust so Bess would be assured of the best care she could get for the rest of her life. He also discussed with Jane the conditions in Henry's will about her support. Since Henry had lived very frugally and had made some good investments, he had left enough money that Jane could live on and care for her child if she lived modestly. He had also set up a trust for higher education for his grandchild when the time came.

Jane had stipulations on her money. She had to report to the lawyer to show proof that the child was living with her and was being well kept. This was all that Henry could do from the grave. He felt he was keeping Jane from committing a moral sin and making a life for his grandchild. Jane, on the other hand, felt her father was manipulating and controlling her life, even after death. Jane's mind set was not going to assure a nurturing environment for her child. She knew she had to have the baby, but that didn't mean she would love this child. As a spoiled child often does, Jane was determined to spite her father even if it deprived her of having a loving relationship with her child.

Once again, Jane's behavior was going to make the life of another human being miserable. Jane conveniently stored all the things she did not want to deal with in dark shadows of her mind. All the destructive things Jane did were all signs of mental illness. However, Jane did not have anyone around her to point this out to her. She thought she was normal. That is one of the tricks of mental illness; the person that is affected is the last one to see the problems and sometimes never believes there are any problems. These people continue their destructive patterns, causing other people untold misery, unless they are forced to face their illness and get help.

When everything was settled after the funeral and Jane was not implicated in the murder of Mr. Miller, Jane decided to leave town. She was going to the institution where her mother was living as she felt she needed to tell Bess about Henry passing away. She did not know if Bess would comprehend what she told her but Henry had visited Bess each week. Therefore, Bess would need to know why he would never be back to see her.

Jane rode the bus to the town nearest the institution. This town was larger than her home town and Jane liked the look of it. She felt she could blend into the town without being the fodder for gossip. She also felt that she needed to be close to her mother. It surprised her that she had that feeling of needing contact with one parent when the other was gone. She loved her mother, as much as Jane could love someone, and knew that inside Bess's damaged mind there was a women that loved her above all else. Jane needed that love now even if Bess could only express it on her good days.

Jane found a car lot with used cars and picked out a very modest four door sedan with the essential options. She drove out to the institution to talk to the staff about her mother. She visited with her mother's doctor and learned that Bess was violent at times but still had days of complete clarity. The doctor thought for Jane to live close and visit often would make a big difference in Bess's life. Bess was on a lot of medications but the doctor said he kept her on the lowest dosages possible to increase her opportunities for normal days. This way Bess was not just being maintained in a comatose condition.

Jane entered Bess's room and saw that the lights were low. The room was bare except for the bed and one chair. There was a TV extended from the ceiling in one corner. There were several pieces of equipment around the bed that was for monitoring vital signs and dispensing medication. Jane slowly approached the bed. Bess had her eyes closed and looked calm. She had not changed in her physical features since Jane had last been there. Jane had to admit she had not been a frequent visitor and it had been a while since she had seen her mother. She had been too involved in her own life as a teenager to make the long trip often.

Bess stirred and opened her eyes and ask, "Who is there?"

Her voice sounded calm and normal so Jane approached the bed and answered. "Mother, it is me, Jane. You look wonderful, how are you feeling?"

Bess pushed a button on her bed that raised her head up and then she focused on Jane. "Oh, Jane, how good to see you. Is your father with you?"

Jane did not speak right away but reached out to touch her mother's face. Then she said. "Mom, I am very sad and I know you will be also. Father had a heart attack and he was gone very quickly. He did not suffer any."

Bess's face looked puzzled as she struggled to understand what Jane was saying. Then she began to cry. "What will I do without my Henry? He loved me no matter what and he was the love of my life. What will we do?"

Jane sat on the side of the bed and held her mother's hand. "Mother, we will miss him. You will be taken care of and so will I. You know dad took care of everything."

Bess cried for a few minutes then was able to talk better. "What will you do? What about the house?"

"The house has been sold and I am moving to a town, which is close to you so I can be here for you. I am going to buy a small house in town and come see you a lot. Maybe sometime you can go outside and we can walk around the yard."

Bess sighed and said, "I'm very tired now, I need to sleep. Please, come back soon. I hope someday I can travel to visit where Henry is buried."

Jane replied, "That would be nice and I will talk to your doctor about that." Jane did not want to tell her mother yet that she was pregnant as she felt Bess had dealt with enough for one day.

Jane found a small house near town that was suitable for her and the baby. There was a small back yard that was fenced and shady. It was a safe neighborhood and close to schools so Jane felt comfortable. She was comfortable but not happy. This was not the life she had envisioned for herself after she graduated. She had been through a lot and should have learned that certain actions and choices could have a tremendous impact on others. But, Jane still had her wild streak. She had resolved herself to the fact that she would have to take a break from what she wanted to do until this baby was born. She was not going to drink, would stop smoking and wait. She was determined to have her life back but knew she had to keep the money coming in so she did not have to get a job. She had no skills so the job market for her would be slim.

In Jane's short sighted view of the future, she thought when the baby was born she would be free to live her life again. Jane was only eighteen, so she was not mature enough to project the future in terms of reality but only in terms of what she wanted. Except for having real feelings for her mother, Jane did not have any empathy for anyone else. Sadly, this included the baby. In her mind, she felt when the baby was born, she could put the child in the back ground and then she would be free.

Jane decided to meet the neighbors so she could build a support system by taking advantage of good neighbors. This would help her with someone to take her to the hospital when the baby came and by watching the child so she could go out. She wanted a very solid foundation and would keep her night life separate from her family life. So she did what she was best at which was convincing people she was something she was not.

She met her neighbors slowly and causally, weaving into their lives slowly. Her next door neighbor was a widow about her mother's age. She was just what Jane needed. A Grandmotherly, sweet, lonely lady that wanted to be called Granny, was the first neighbor that Jane met. The story that Jane told people about the father of her baby was that he was killed in the army. This story was accepted and real sympathy came from all that Jane confided in.

This new start might have been the perfect way for Jane to turn over a new leaf and change her life. She could have realized that she caused grief to a lot of people. To some extent Jane did do better while she was pregnant. In some women who have mental instability, when they are pregnant, they are more stable, even happy. The hormonal changes have a lot to do with these changes. Jane was a jumble of mental problems. If she were diagnosed by a professional today the list of possibilities would include: bipolar disorder, border line mood disorder, narcissism and the list goes on. Without medication, counseling and monitoring, Jane would never have a normal life.

Many times people that are on medication for various mental conditions will stop taking their medicine as they think they are cured. Actually, these people usually don't think there is anything wrong with them. It's usually close friends or family that gets them to go to a doctor. In Jane's case she had two things against her. One, she had no support system to tell her she had problems and two, in this period of time, these conditions were all lumped into one category which was labeled crazy. Medication was not widely used for mental conditions except when the person was in an institution.

Jane spent her days getting her house settled, getting the baby's room ready and checking out the town. While she was pregnant, Jane had feelings for the baby she was carrying. But that would change when the baby was born and her hormones went back to normal and her life was back to abnormal.

One day in early fall, Jane had a visitor. She was expecting this person or not so much a particular person, but a person with the social services. She greeted the woman that introduced herself as Mary Adams of the Family Services. She said she was commissioned by Mr. Mason for Jane's deceased father to keep a continuous vigilance on Jane and her child, when he or she was born. Jane was happy to show her the small two bedroom house. She showed her the room that was for the baby. It had a baby bed, baby changing table, bassinet and a rocker. Mary noted baby toys and some baby cloths. Everything looked in order and ready for the special event. Jane encouraged Mary to talk to some of the neighbors for information about her. Jane was all smiles. She knew that her money was dependant on the report that the lawyer received.

Jane visited her mother each week. Some visits were good, some were not. The ones that were not good could go from; Bess just not speaking then escalating into screaming that a strange person was trying to kill her. Sometimes she had to be in restraints and did not even know what was going on. Bess's doctor told Jane that he was giving Bess some morphine, due to the tremendous headaches she complained of, in an attempt to relieve her pain. The roller coaster that Bess was on with her mental health did make Jane sad and nervous each time she visited. The surprise was that Jane really cared about her mother and wished that she could get better. Bess was the only relative that Jane had in the world.

In the fall of the year, Bess was doing a lot better. Her mental condition was definitely related in some ways with the time of the year. Winter was her worst time with spring and fall the best time. Years later there would be a lot of research on seasonal depression that would result in medical intervention helping in these seasons. Mental illness in the decades that followed Bess's life time would become a major research item. Some of the debilitating illnesses would move out of the shadows and into the light of diagnosis, medication, counseling and management. However, this revolution would not come soon enough to help Bess.

CHAPTER 18

BESS AND JANE

One day during the spring, with the approval of her doctor Bess was allowed to go on a road trip with Jane. Bess wanted to see the resting place of her husband. She could not get closure until she saw his name on a tombstone. Jane picked Bess up and they headed out on their road trip. As they drove, Bess was quiet at first. She was enjoying the landscape that she had not seen in several years. Suddenly Bess ask, "What happened when your father died? I'm not a child; I should know the whole story."

Jane knew she would have to lie about part of the story but was sure Bess would hear from someone from their town what the gossip was. "Well, dad and Mr. Miller had an argument. Dad snapped one night and took his colt .45 to the hardware store and shot Mr. Miller. Then dad suffered a heart attack. He died instantly is what the doctor said. Dad had not been feeling well and I tried to get him to go to the doctor. But you know how stubborn dad was; he would just say he would go later. I'm sorry mom, I hate to tell you these things but someone else might tell you and I want it to come from me." Jane looked at her mother and found that she was staring straight ahead. "Mother, are you alright?" Jane asked.

"Yes, I can handle this." This is all Bess would say for the rest of the trip to the cemetery.

Jane and Bess arrived at the cemetery and walked out among the graves. "Over here" Jane said, "dad bought two plots in a very pretty and private part of the cemetery."

They walked up to the head stone that had Henry's name on one side with the dates of his birth and death. On the other side was Bess's name and birthday. Under Henry's name, was written, "Wonderful Husband

and Father, may he rest in peace." Bess knelt down and touched the grave. She took her finger and traced the writing on the stone. Jane brought a nice bunch of flowers that she put into the vase that was attached to the base of the tombstone. Bess told Jane, "I want to stay here a moment alone please."

"Sure Mom, I'll wait in the car. Call if you need me." Jane said as she turned to go to the car.

Bess sat on the ground at the tombstone; she wept and talked to Henry. She also appeared to be listening at times, but to what, no one would know. Eventually Bess got up and made her way to the car. She got in and nodded that she was ready. After driving a while, Bess ask Jane to pull over at a rest stop for a few minutes. Jane pulled into the next rest stop and parked the car. She asked her mother, "Do you need to use the restroom?"

Bess reached over and took Jane's hand. She looked Jane in her eyes and said, "Jane, I knew your father better than anyone on this earth. Your dad was not capable of killing Mr. Miller. What part did you play in the death of your father and Mr. Miller? Do not lie to me as I know when you lie."

Jane was astonished, she could not speak for several minutes and then she took a stab at what happened. "Mother, what I told you happened is the truth. I don't know why dad was fighting with Mr. Miller. It must have been something big for dad to be so upset."

Bess sat very still, her eyes did not waiver from Jane's eyes. "Jane, before I was taken to the institution, I tried to kill your father. I hit him with a vase and would have killed him, if the nurse had not stopped me. You know how much I loved your father, but I would have killed him that day. I have a very evil part to me that takes control sometimes and I have no way to fight against it. I do what the voice tells me and the evil voice was telling me to kill him. I believe I passed this evil gene to you so now you need to tell me what you did?"

Jane put her head in her hands, "Yes mother you are right. I do have that evil in me. Dad did take the gun to the store because I had told him Mr. Miller had raped me and I was pregnant. Dad flipped out. He went to get his gun and went to the store. I followed him and tired to stop him. Mr. Miller was telling him terrible things about me and dad fell dead. When I saw dad lying on the floor and knew he was dead, something came over me and I picked up the gun and killed Mr. Miller. And yes someone was whispering in my ear to kill him. I heard *kill him, kill him.* I had no will of my own." Jane started to sob, "I am the one that caused my dad to die, as I told a terrible lie. I was not raped. Mr. Miller was one of three possibilities of being the father of my child. I do things and I don't know why I do them. I know right from wrong, but at times I don't even care."

Bess released Jane's hand and whispered, "The two people in the world that Henry loved and who loved him, are the ones that killed him. We both caused your father's death. Even though I did not directly kill him, I passed evil genes to you that caused you to do very bad things. I am the most responsible because I was not there to guide you and give you the help you needed to deal with your problems. In combination we did cause his death." That was all Bess said for the rest of the way back to the institution. When they arrived at the hospital, Bess went straight to her room and to her bed. Jane followed her and tried to hug her. "Mother, please forgive me, please." Jane pleaded. Bess turned her head away and fell into a deep sleep. Jane continued to visit her mother each week. They never talked about Henry or what happened again.

CHAPTER 19

LILY ROSE

In the early spring Jane's baby was born. A girl she named Lily Rose Baxter. When the nurse bought Lily to Jane the first time, Jane looked at the baby and felt nothing. She felt disconnected from this baby. Lily could have been anyone's baby. Jane refused to nurse Lily so the nurse worked to get her on the bottle. Jane also refused to put a name of the father on the birth certificate. Actually, she didn't know who the father was. She thought she might see some resemblance to one of the men she had sex with, but all she saw was a baby that looked like every other baby she had seen. There was one exception; Lily had the most beautiful emerald green eyes which were not like any baby Jane had ever seen. Jane could not deny that she passed on her distinctive green eyes to her baby girl. Everyone in the hospital was fascinated by Lily's eyes and made special trips to the nursery to see her. However, it was not so odd for Lily to have those eyes, just look at her mother. Lily got those eyes from her mother. The big question in Jane's mind was what else Lily inherited from her and Bess?

Jane took Lily home. The neighbors were there to welcome them home. They had a pot luck meal with balloons and a banner saying "Welcome home Mom and Lily Rose."

Everyone was excited, except for Jane. She just wanted them to all go away. But she smiled and chatted with everyone. Then she said she was tired and so was Lily, so everyone went home. Now it was just the two of them. Jane put Lily in the baby bed and she went to bed. She got up to feed her and change her. She did all the normal things to care for a baby except love her. Jane had no love in her heart for Lily. Lily had a rough future ahead of her.

Lily's memories until she was about five were that she had everything she needed. She was well cared for by her mother. However, Jane never touched her unless it was necessary and she seldom spoke to Lily. Lily's only look at how life should be is when she got to go to Granny's house next door. Granny loved Lily. She held her, read to her, gave her treats but most of all talked to her. Granny was an angel for Lily because without Granny, Lily would not have had any bonding or people skills which are so important for a child. Jane did not let Lily go out much to play as she was afraid Lily would have an accident and that social services would investigate. The only thing Jane wanted was for Lily to grow up and for the money to continue to come in.

Jane and Mr. Mason were the only ones that knew about Bess and where she was now. Years later Jane would relate some of this information to her daughter, Lily. Lily learned some of this history when her mother would get drunk and then would want to talk about her past. Jane would say after she told her the story, "So you see, Lily, we have a crazy gene in us, and we never know when it will come out and cause us to do things that are evil. You better be a good girl and do as I say or the crazy gene may come out in me and I could kill you!" Then she would laugh; a fake, mean laugh. Lily believed her. After all Lily only had her mother, so she had to believe her. Therefore Lily tried to be good all the time and did as her mother said.

Jane did tell Lily the part about her grandmother, Bess, going crazy and going to the institute many times, but she did not tell her anything about her life after Bess went away and before Henry died. She also never told Lily the circumstances of Henry's death.

Even if Jane had told Lily about her teen age years, she would not have told her the truth, mainly because she did not recognize what she did as being wrong. She preferred to believe she had a normal childhood because if she acknowledged the truth, she would have to recognize the lives she had destroyed. It was easier for Jane to push her history to the dark places in her mind, the places where the shadows hid the ugly things so she could continue to live her life the best she could. However, what she could not hide from herself came out in a viscous way and was pointed at Lily. Lily remembered Jane slapping her on many occasions and then she would cry and beg Lily not to tell anyone. The physical pain for Lily was not nearly as devastating as the mental abuse dished out by

Jane. There were many days Jane would not speak to Lily or if she did it was just to make her go to her room.

Jane would say, "Get out of my sight. I can't stand you. If it weren't for you I would be free. Free to do what I want to. I could find a man that would marry me, instead of them running when they see you." Jane never thought that her unpredictable mood and strange personality was what sent men out the door. Jane chose to forget that if not for her father's money, she would have had a different and difficult life.

When Lily turned six, Granny made her a birthday cake and got her a small present. Jane ignored the day. However, Jane did recognize that Lily would be starting to school. Jane took the school supply list and got all that was required for the students. She did get a pink back pack with Snow White on it. Lily was so excited to have these things that signified that she was starting to school and that her mother got these things for her. She had no idea what to expect in school but she was ready to start something new and exciting. Granny had told her about what went on in school but Granny hadn't been to school in years. Lily was sure things had changed drastically since Granny went to school.

Lily could not sleep the night before school was to start. Jane took her the first day and walked down the school hall with Lily tagging along behind. Jane met Lily's teacher, told Lily to have a good day and was gone. Lily was very surprised to see other first graders clinging to their mothers, crying and saying they did not want to go to school. Lily was even more surprised to see the mothers crying when they left their kids on this first day. Lily thought "Gee, they will see them this afternoon. It's not like they will never see them again." Lily could not think of any reason her mother would cry over her.

Lily entered her class room. All of the desks had name tags so each child would know where to sit. Lily found her desk on the second row and second seat on that row. She sat down at her desk and looked at the room in amazement. She had never seen a more beautiful room. Everywhere there were bright colors with different things on every wall. The letters of the ABCs were in big print all around the top of the wall. A bulletin board that took up one wall was covered with pictures of kids going back to school. The best thing was one whole wall was covered with book shelves full of books. Lily could not wait to learn to read. She knew her ABCs, how to print her name and knew some words. Granny had spent hours working with her to get her ready for school.

Lily was not, however, ready for interacting with the other kids. She was shy and had no idea how to introduce herself to others. Lily looked to one side of her at a girl whose name tag said Mary Beth. Mary Beth was very pretty with dark red hair that was in a thousand curls and she had a thousand freckles on her face. She had bright blue eyes and seemed to smile a lot. When Mary Beth looked a Lily, Lily quickly turned away. But Mary Beth said "Hello, I am Mary Beth how are you?" Lily said hello but didn't know what else to say. This was not a problem as Mary Beth could talk enough for both of them and from that day forward, Mary Beth and Lilly were best friends throughout their school years.

Lily's teacher came into the class room and asked for everyone to settle down. Sarah James had only been teaching for a few years, but she loved her job and the kids. She spoke to the class, "Good morning class. My name is Sarah James. You all can call me Miss Sarah and I am your teacher for the year. You will see that your name is on the desk that you will sit in until I learn everyone's name, then I will allow you to pick where you want to sit. So, let's get to know each other. Each one of you, please give us your name and tell us something about yourself. Let's start on the first row"

As the kids started giving their name and telling something about themselves, Lily became very nervous. She did not know what to say other than her name. When it became her time to stand and talk, she could not move. She was griping the desk so tightly that her knuckles were white. Miss Sarah became aware that Lily was terrified. She walked to Lily's desk and knelt down by Lily. She said, "Lily, just take a deep breath, no one here will say or do anything to hurt you." She took Lily's hand and pulled her to her feet. She turned to the class and said, "This is Lily. Lily is shy and I hope everyone will talk to her today." Miss Sarah then asked Lily, "Can you tell us something about yourself."

Lily looked around and said, "I live with my mother. I have a neighbor that I call Granny. She's not my real Granny, but I stay with her a lot." Lily looked at Miss Sarah Miss Sarah said, "Thank you, Lily we are going to have a great year." Lily was so relieved and she was so grateful to Miss Sarah that she had tears well up in her eyes as she sat down. Sarah thought that this child is missing something very important in her life. She hoped she could in some way help her find her way. She also thought that she intended to follow Lily throughout her school life and see that she made it through.

Lily learned very quickly that if she did everything she was supposed to and did it well, she was praised by Miss Sarah. Lily was always the first to get her work done. She always made the best grade in class. She took books home to read every night. Lily had lots of friends at school but never had any over to her house and was not allowed to go to their house. Jane did not want Lily to see that other families lived differently than they did. Lily thought how they lived was normal. Granny was always home after school for Lily to come over and tell her about school and show her the papers she completed that day. Jane barely looked at the papers but was quick to show the social worker Lily's grades from school which were always A's.

Lily had a different life compared to other kids. She was physically and mentally abused and she got used to not having any connection to her mother. Jane went out several nights a week, most of the time after Lily was in bed or when she sent her to Granny's house. She never brought men home with her or introduced any of her boyfriends to Lily. When Lily was in the third grade, she was surprised when her mother came in with a man. Jane introduced him to Lily as Jake Henson.

Jake was a good looking man. He was over six feet tall; slim with substantial muscles in his arms and upper body. He had lots of wavy black hair and was very tan. He smiled a lot showing straight, white teeth. However, his smile had a very false look about it.

Lily had never seen her Mother as happy as she was when Jake was there. Jake lavished attention on Jane. He spent more and more time at their home until after about a month, he had moved in. Jake appeared to not notice Jane's different personalities, but mostly because he was more interesting in himself to notice much of anything else. As charming as Jake was with Jane, he never even looked at Lily. Lily was invisible to him. More and more Jane pushed Lily out of the room when Jake was there to keep Jake happy. Lily suspected Jake told Jane he didn't like having her around. Lily would stay in her room or most of the time stood in the shadows of the hall just out side of the living room. From there she could hear what Jane and Jake said and what they were doing. They would dance to the radio or sing along. Jake also liked to drink beer and whiskey and he wanted Jane to drink with him, which she did. Most nights, they ended up sleeping on the living room couch as they were to drunk to get to bed.

Jake did not have a steady job but was gone some of the time for several days. Lily never heard what he did and she thought her mother didn't know either. However, Jane was not concerned with what Jake did as a job as long as they could party at night and sleep in the day. Lily noticed that Jane was drinking more and more. Even when Jake was gone, Jane drank all day, sitting at the kitchen table with a cigarette, waiting for Jake to come home. Since Jane was in a much better mood when Jake was there and Jake never bothered her, Lily was fine with her life for a while.

After a year with Jake in residence, Lily noticed that she and her mother had less money to spend. Lily asked her mother if there was a problem with the money. Jane was not happy with the question and said, "That's none of your concern. Keep your nose out of my business. You have food to eat and cloths for school so keep your mouth shut and you'll be fine."

However, after a while, Lily noticed that they did not have much food and she was not getting any new cloths. This was a problem as Lily was growing taller and beginning to fill out and her old clothes were getting tight and short. Lily thought her mother must be giving Jake money as it was going somewhere. But Lily did not say a word as she got the message from her mother the first time she ask and that was "don't' ask."

Even though Miss Sarah was not Lily's teacher now, she still kept up with her. She made it a point to see her daily and talk with her. She kept up with her grades and always praised her on her accomplishments. Miss Sarah also noted the clothing problem and thought she had a solution. Miss Sarah had a younger sister that was about the size of Lily and her clothes were really nice and stylish. The problem was how to get them to Lily. One day Miss Sarah was carrying a bag and she saw Lily, "Hi, Lily," she greeted Lily, "please come by my class room after school, I have something for you." After school Lily went to Miss Sarah's class room. Miss Sarah handed her the bag and said, "My sister has tons of cloths that she has outgrown. I think you could wear them and she really wanted to give them to you. Do you think that would be alright with your mother if you accepted them?"

Lily thought a minute, she really wanted the clothes and needed them so she said, "I think I can get her to see that I need these and we are tight on money right now. Thank you so much." She took the bag and could not wait to see what was in there.

When she got home, she knew she had to be careful and that her mother's mood would be important. Fortunately, Jane was in a happy mood because Jake had just returned from a trip so she hardly listened to Lily about the clothes. She just said "Okay, that's fine. Thank her for me." Lily eased away and did not mention it again. Jane never noticed that Lily had new clothes every now and then. Lily was thrilled with the clothes and was especially happy that someone was thinking about her and cared that she had nice clothes.

Physical abuse as a child is a terrible thing and leaves lasting scars. However, emotional abuse can be just a detrimental to a child's life. Withholding love and communication from a child can leave extensive mental problems later in life. Lily did get a lot of support from Granny and Miss Sarah, but they were not her mother. Jane did not do this to Lily on purpose, even though this is not an excuse, but Jane did not have the ability to have loving feeling for Lily. Jane was blocking out her behavior that caused Lily to be conceived therefore, she had to block feelings for Lily. Jane knew that if it was not for the money from her father, she would have aborted Lily. She felt that she cared so little for her as a fetus, she could not care for her now.

There are many situations where the mother will be compelled to take the life of her children. When you put Jane's behavior in that context, Lily was fortunate to be alive. There is a natural instinct for a mother to protect and cherish her babies, but due to some malfunction with the brain or hormone imbalance, this instinct can be over ruled. It was a life saver for Lily to have Miss Sarah and Granny to support her and love her. This gave Lily a chance at a normal life when she grew up. There are angels among us and Granny and Miss Sarah were certainly those angels.

CHAPTER 20

JANE AND BESS AND LILY

ane was keeping a diligent watch on her mother. She went once a week to visit with her. She talked to the doctor and the nurses to keep up with her progress. When Lily was out of school she went with her mother to see her grandmother. When Lily went along, if Bess was not having a good day, Jane did not let Lily see her. However, when Bess was having a good day Lily loved to visit with her grandmother. All three of them would stroll around the beautiful grounds at the institute. Bess and Lily shared a sweet disposition that Jane did not have. Jane would join in with conversations but did not put a lot of feeling into the topics. Frankly, these meetings bored Jane, but Bess had such a good time being with them that Jane was usually pleasant.

What Jane had not shared with Bess was what she found out as some crucial information at the lawyers office concerning the things her dad had set up concerning the estate. Jane learned that she and Bess both had life insurance policies that the estate kept current. The amount of the benefit was one hundred thousand dollars on each of them. In addition to this if something happened to Bess the remainder of her trust would go to Jane. There was a slight stipulation on these two sizeable amounts of money, which was that Jane visited her mother regularly and made sure her care was the best available. Jane also had to see that Bess saw Lily as often as possible so she could get to know her grandchild. Jane always met these requirements because the lawyer kept a close eye on what she did. Anyone who saw what Jane was doing for her mother would think she loved her mother and wanted her to know Lily. But as usual for Jane, she had other motivations besides family love and loyalties.

Lily really loved her grandmother. Jane had told Lily many scary stories about Bess, but Lily had only experienced good times with her grandmother. She did feel a connection with Bess that she did not feel with her mother. Lily and Bess had many good conversations that Lily would remember for her entire life. She wished many times that Jane was as sweet as Bess and that Jane would have the feelings for her that Bess appeared to have.

When Lily was around fifteen years old, Bess became progressively worse. She had long spells of being catatonic. Then she would have severe head aches that took very strong medication to control. At times she would be in such pain that she was uncontrollable. It was during these episodes that restraints had to be used. Jane was spending more time at the institute to monitor the treatments. She knew all the medication and how they were administered. Jane was fulfilling her obligations of seeing that Bess had the best care available.

CHAPTER 21

JAKE

During this time Jane was under a lot of pressure from caring for her mother as Bess was descending into a deeper state of mental illness. As usual Jake was more interested in his own best interest and he came up with a big idea and Jane was his only source of money to finance that idea. He knew there was money held in trust for Jane and Lily, but he just didn't know how to get his hands on it. One night he decided to spring his idea on Jane.

Jake said to Jane, "I have a friend that told me about a great opportunity for us. There is a club in a town about 20 miles from here that is for sale. It has a bar and a place for music and dancing. The liquor has the largest income possibilities, so we would need a liquor license. This could be a gold mind for us. I have waited all my life to get a chance to be my own boss in my own business. What do you think?"

Jane asked, "Why is the guy selling the place?"

"He is tired of working and wants to retire to Florida." Jake answered. "There are a lot of possibilities for the club that could turn it into a money maker. We'd be on easy street."

"What other possibilities are you talking about?" Jane asked.

"A gentleman's club with dancers would draw in a lot of money." Jake said.

"You mean a strip club with strippers and pole dancers?" Jane said skeptically.

"Well, yes, what would be wrong with that? Men pay big money for a place to relax, have a drink and watch some girls dance." Jake told her.

"Well, I'm not crazy about your being around strippers all the time." Jane said.

"Oh, baby you are the only one for me, I don't care about those kind of girls. If I did like those girls, I could have them all the time but I have stayed with you." He said as he hugged her and kissed her. Jake knew how to sway Jane because he had been doing it for years now.

Jake was happy with the relationship he had with Jane. Jane gave him money, a place to stay and he came and went as he pleased. What could be better? Right now he needed money so he could get into business. This is something he had always wanted to do but he was always held back by a lack of money. This was his best shot; he just had to work it right. He knew Jane was sitting on a lot of money even though she did not have control over it, yet.

Jake turned his attention back to Jane and changed the subject, "How is your mother? I know you said she was getting worse."

"Yes, she is very bad. She is in pain all the time and doesn't know me half the time." Jane said. She was surprised that Jake inquired about Bess because he had never been interested before.

"I know you wish you could help her more" Jake said and then he dropped the subject for now.

The next few weeks Jake stayed close to home. He was more attentive to Jane and even talked to Lily. When Jake wanted to be charming, he was the best. Jane was elated, she even slacked off on her drinking because with Jake there, she didn't have to just sit and wait on him and drink. Jake encouraged Jane not to drink as he thought a sober Jane would be more equipped to come up with a way to get some of that money from the lawyer.

Jake needed more than money from Jane. He had not told her that he had a felony record from years ago. He had driven a car as a get away for a robbery. Because he was so young and did not have a prior arrest, he got off with probation. However, the felony was still on his record and he would not be able to obtain a liquor license with a record. A night club without a liquor license would never make it, so Jane would have to come up with money for the business and apply for the liquor license.

Jake's first idea to get the money was for Jane just to ask her lawyer for a loan from the trust that her father had put back for her and Lily. They could pay it back over a period of years. Jake had been talking non-stop about the business and Jane was getting pulled into the idea. When Jake mentioned the loan, Jane thought this was a good idea so she visited Mr. Mason.

Mr. Mason had personally known Henry for years before Henry died. He and Henry had many conversations concerning his wishes and the circumstances at home. Henry was a good planner and he was fugal. He had saved a great deal of money. He also invested wisely and had good income from these investments. Mr. Mason could still hear Henry saying, 'I trust you to see that this money takes care of Bess, Jane and my grandchild for the rest of their lives. The only way to do that would be to not let any of them be in control of the money. Bess is not mentally capable of the responsibility. She would spend it all in a short time. Jane is not able to take care of herself much less money.'

Then Henry was gone, Mr. Mason felt bound to his responsibility to be sure these two women and a child was taken care of. So when Jane approached him with the idea of a loan, he very patiently told her, "Jane, your dad was very specific about what I was to do with his money. He wrote it all down for me. He wanted me to control and administer his money so that it would last long enough to take care of Bess, you and now Lily, for the rest of your lives. I can not possibly loan that money out for any reason."

Jane became very upset, "Dad would want me to have a chance to start a business. I would pay back the principal and interest like any regular loan."

Mr. Mason said, "Jane, you do not have any education in business. Also you have never worked outside the home. It takes a lot of training and experience to run a business. You would not be able to qualify for a loan from any lending institution."

Jane said, "I have a business partner that is going to run everything. He will make it work."

Mr. Mason looked at Jane over the top of his glasses and asked, "Who is this business partner? How much money is he putting into the business?"

Jane truly did not see what the lawyer was getting at. She said, "Don't you trust me to make this decision?"

"Jane you can't be serious, you have no experience working with businessmen. The bottom line is I can't make a loan from your dad's estate for you or anyone. It is very clear the money will go to you when your mother passes away. You would get the insurance money but the trust would still stay in place for you and Lily's future."

Jane was furious and Mr. Mason saw for the first time, what it was like to be on the bad side of Jane. She got up and pushed most of the stuff off Mr. Mason's desk. Then she screamed, "You can't tell me what I can do! You are not going to keep me from doing what I want with my money. Who do you think you are? You pompous, over-blown, sorry bastard, you go to Hell."

Mr. Mason stayed calm and said, "Yes, I do control the money Henry put in my care. And yes, I can tell you what you can do with the money. Now please leave my office or I will call security."

Jane stormed out. The secretary had already called security when she heard the raised voices. Jane ran right into a huge security guard who took her arm and escorted her out to the street.

Jane was so furious she could hardly drive home. When she got home, she got a drink of liquor straight from the bottle and started to think. She did not want to disappoint Jake. She thought he might leave her. She could not stand the thought of that. She did not know how she would live without him. It is common for a mentally ill person to be obsessively attached to another person. Sometimes it is a relative such as a mother unable to break her attachment with a child, usually a boy. Most times it is one of the people in a romantic relationship. This obsession can turn into a deadly event when the relationship breaks down. Obsessive jealousy is a common sign of a relationship that is headed for trouble. The obsessive person reasons in their sick mind that they want the one they love to be dead rather than letting them go.

One thing kept coming back to Jane's mind that Mr. Mason said. 'If your mother dies, you would get the insurance money.' As she continued to drink, she started thinking. What use was her mother anyway? She was just laying up there in the institution, costing money. She didn't even know what was going on most of the time. Then she asked herself, "What are you thinking? That's your mother. How could you want her to die?" What surprised her was she didn't really, deep down care if her mother was not around. This thought scared her as she wanted to have feelings of love and caring but the few times that she had these feelings for her mother, were gone now.

When Jake got home he asked Jane, "Did you talk to the lawyer?"

Jane responded, "Yes but the news is not good. I can't get any of the money now. The trust can not be tapped at all." Jane hesitated, she was not sure she should tell Jake anything else but then she decided she had to. If he found out she was withholding information from him, he would not trust her any more. So she continued, "There is a life insurance policy that I am the beneficiary, and I would get the money as it is not in the trust. It is a life insurance policy on my mother."

Jake was not happy but he simply said, "Well, the idea of a business is out. I guess I will have to leave this town to find a job as I need more money than you have. Guess that's the way things go for me." Then he went to the bedroom and went to bed.

Jane couldn't sleep. She was desperate to keep Jake from leaving. She didn't have anyone else that cared about her or so she thought. She brooded for several hours and consumed a fifth of whisky.

The next day she was forming a plan. Jane had watched the nurses that regulated the medication for her mother's IV set up. Bess was on morphine now as she was having very severe headaches that other medications could not control. Morphine was given in her IV continuously and was controlled by a machine that put a specific amount of morphine into the IV fluids. The nurses set up the IV with a new bottle of morphine at 5 PM which would run until 10 PM before it was empty. The machine controls were contained in a locked unit to keep anyone from tampering with it because morphine at excess levels would be lethal. With high levels of morphine, the patient would stop breathing and die. Jane only had to figure out how to get into that machine and alter the settings. Getting a key was not an option as the nurse kept the key on her key ring attached to her belt so she never laid the key down. Maybe Jake would have a solution, Jane thought.

The next day, Jane described the plan to Jake. He said he could teach her to pick the lock with a particular tool that he could obtain. A couple of days passed and Jake came home with the lock tool. He began to teach Jane how to use it. It was not an easy job to pick a lock. Also to figure in the factor that she would be nervous doing this as a nurse could pop into the room anytime to check on her patient. Jane worked on learning to pick a lock and continued to fine tune her plan.

Jane normally visited her Mother every Wednesday afternoon. Everyone knew her and her schedule. Jane took note of the routine that the nurses kept in their duties. They fed Bess diner at 4 PM then came in again at 5 PM to change the morphine drip and take vital signs. The nurses seldom revisited the room until later in the night, sometimes not until 10 PM to change the morphine bottle. Jane visited with the nurses and learned who was on the schedule for the rest of the week. She also became familiar with the rest of the hospital.

The hospital had two wings that were connected in the middle by the central nursing stations. The building was four stories tall with the same configuration on each floor. There were a lot of people coming and going all the time. Visitors for the patients, doctors, lab workers, nurses, cleaning people and maintenance men were always in the corridors. Jane took notice of everything to make sure her plan was flawless.

Jane made her usual visit on Wednesday. She spent some extra time with her mother so she could be sure the routine was the same. Of course, she thought she should see if she could communicate with her mother for the last time. She sat on the edge of the bed and leaned close to her mother's ear and said, "Mother, its Jane. How are you tonight?" At first there was no response and then Bess roused up a little. She said, "Hi, Jane, how is Lily?"

Jane was surprised that her mother was awake, but she responded, "Hi, Mom, Lily is great. She is so busy with school she could not come today."

Bess was silent a long time then she whispered something. Jane leaned closer and asked "What did you say? Mom, tell me again."

Bess whispered again, "Jane, you should kill me. I am in terrible pain. You are capable of doing this. I don't want to live. Help me go to your father. You have the evil in you like I have in me; use it for doing a good thing."

Bess then fell into a deep sleep. Jane could not believe her ears. She had to sit down and take a deep breath. The nurse came in at that moment and Jane told her, "Mother just talked to me. She whispered in my ear."

The nurse said, "Honey, your mother has not spoken in several weeks. The medication she is on is very strong. You may have thought she said something but she is not able to talk." The nurse then left.

Jane was in shock. Did her mother just give her permission to kill her? Or did she just imagine Bess said those things to make it easier on herself? Bess had known that Jane had killed Mr. Miller over her father's dead body. Did she and her mother have some kind of genetic link that somehow was connected through an evil being? Jane went home but did not sleep all night. Her mind kept running around and around on what had happened and what did it mean. Jane had no illusions about herself. She knew she was evil. She had caused so much pain for so many people she felt she was doomed. So whether or not her mother knew what Jane was capable of, Jane was going to follow through with her plan.

CHAPTER 22

JANE

It was a Thursday, Jane had visited her mother the day before but she was preparing to go again. However, she dressed in baggy pants with a hoodie jacket and a scarf on her head. When she got to the hospital she did not park in her usual place but went to the end of the hospital parking lot. She got out and brought a large vase with a big bunch of flowers in it. She entered the hospital at a side door that was in the wing opposite the wing that her mother was in. She walked near the wall with the flowers hiding her face. She passed a few nurses but they did not take notice of her. She went to the elevators that were in the area between the wings. There were four floors in the hospital. Bess was on the second floor. Jane got in the elevator and rode to the forth floor. A few people were in the elevator but none noticed her as it was common for family members to bring flowers to the patients. When she got to the fourth floor, she changed elevators and went back to the second floor. As Jane went down the hall, she noted a door to one of the rooms open with the patient asleep. She slipped in and left the flowers on the tray by the bed. Someone would be surprised that they had flowers the next day.

Jane slipped into her mother's room. All the lights were off except the one over the bed. Jane went to the bed and looked at her mother. For a second she felt weak and almost turned around to leave. Then she saw the IV machine that was pumping the morphine into her mother at a rate that just kept her out of pain and unconscious. She took a small tool out of her pocket and began to pick the lock the way Jake had taught her. She had practiced a lot but she was nervous and dropped the tool twice before getting the lock open. The door popped open and she saw a knob that was turned to 1 unit. Jane turned the knob until it was at the highest reading. The IV changed from a slow drip to a steady stream. Jane closed the unit door but did not let it lock. She moved to the far side of the room and stood behind the drapes and watched the IV. Her heart was pounding. It was not sorrow for her mother that she was anxious about, but fear that a nurse would come in and catch the change in the IV drip.

After approximately an hour the IV of morphine stopped. Jane went back over to the bed. Her mother's breathing was very slow. In fact, Jane thought at first she had stopped breathing. Jane opened the monitor, turned the knob back to 1 unit and locked the door. She noted that her mother's face was beginning to turn a bluish color and her breathing was even slower. Jane put her hand on her mother's face. "Good bye Mother, I am sorry for this. I hope God will understand and forgive me." Then she turned and slipped out of the room. Jane retraced her footsteps going back to her car. No one paid any attention to her. She drove home and awaited the phone call telling her that Bess had died.

At the 10 PM room check, when it was time to change the morphine for Bess, the nurse found it empty as usual but she did not see Bess breathing. She rang the code alarm. Within seconds the room was full of nurses, with a crash cart. The doctor on call arrived. At 10:30 PM the doctor directed that the patient Bess Baxter was dead.

Jane received the call at 10:45 PM saying her mother had died in her sleep. There would be an autopsy then she would be sent to the funeral home. Jane was a little nervous about the autopsy but the amount of morphine in her body should be normal for the time it took for the nurse to find her but there was a chance of a problem.

The autopsy report was normal and Jane made arrangements to bury Bess next to Henry. Jane and Lily rode in a limo behind the hearse that was carrying her mother to her final resting place. Jane surprised Lily by talking about her mother while they traveled.

Jane said, "My mother was a beautiful person both inside and out. When I was little, she and I had so much fun. She would dress me up and we would go to town. We would put on music and dance around the room. Mother laughed and sang. I have to remember the good times because as her mind went bad, there were fewer and fewer good times. Bess had a very evil spirit that would talk to her and cause her to do evil things. The person she loved the most, which was Henry, she tried to kill. I am so sad to have lost her so many years ago. Only her body has been here for the last few years. I will always miss her" then she cried and it was a sincere emotion. That, however, was only one side of Jane. Jane secretly was terrified that she too would come to the condition that her mother was in. She recognized that she had experienced the evil spirit coming out when she killed Mr. Miller. She also knew it took a dark person to kill their mother, for money.

CHAPTER 23

JAMES

Lily was entering high school. She was fifteen and starting the tenth grade. Lily was a beautiful girl. She was five feet ten, which was taller than most of the girls her age. She had beautiful jet black hair that hung straight down about three inches below her shoulder. She had a great figure and walked with confidence. Her face was smooth without a blemish and was highlighted by beautiful emerald green eyes.

Lily was very popular because she was so nice. She had lots of friends both boys and girls. She had a way of being a good listener and taking an interest in each individual. She, however, did not have a boy friend.

Due to Lily's life at home, she was not allowed to hang out after school or go to the after school activities. This made it difficult to have a boyfriend since her socialization was limited to school. Lily was not upset over this. She was very involved in making good grades and reading. Also she was used to this life style as this is the way it had always been. There were no negotiations with her mother; she simply did not think to go against Jane. High school was a new venue; there was a different vibration among the kids. There was more electricity between the sexes that changed friendships into romances. Lily was not prepared for this change; she did not have anyone to help her navigate through serious relationships. Jane hardly talked to her and her only personal example was the roller coaster relationship Jane had with Jake.

As Lily was getting used to her high school schedule, she did not have a clue that someone had taken special notice of her. James Wilson was a junior. Everything that Lily did not have, James had. James had a large loving family, lots of old money and a social position in the community. James was the carrier of the family name. His dad had big hopes for his only son. James was also determined to make his dad proud of him. Then James met Lily. He had no idea how their relationship would test the very core of his family loyalty.

James was not flashy with his position or money. He had friends of all kinds, from all parts of town. James was taller than Lily by a few inches. He was blond with a tanned face and beautiful sky blue eyes. James was very handsome and life was easy for him. He thought that Lily was classy and he was going to go slow so as to not scare her off. He was aware that Lily had not dated anyone and even though she had lots of friends, there were no romances.

James had some of his friends introduce him to Lily then he took it from there. He would try to be where Lily was during the day at school, but he was puzzled that he never saw her anywhere around town. He soon learned that Lily had a very strict single mother. That's all he was able to find out as Jane and Lily did not appear to have family ties in town and stayed to themselves.

James decided he would have to win the mother over first so he went to Lily's house one evening. Lily was very surprised and was uncomfortable as she did not know what her mother would say. However, James was a very nice looking young man and Jane had an eye for men. James' manners and natural way with people quickly won Jane over. James sat in the living room with Jane and Lily talking and watching TV on several occasions before he even approached Jane with the question of Lily going out with him. He started with asking if they could go to an early movie, get some dinner then he would bring Lily home. Jane thought that was fair so agreed Lily could go.

James and Lily made a beautiful couple and they fell in love. On their first date, James was able to tell Lily some of the things he felt for her. The first thing he told her was "You have the most beautiful emerald green eyes I have ever seen."

Lily was equally taken with James. Her first observation was "You have the most beautiful sky blue eyes I have ever seen." They laughed at what they both immediately liked about the other.

James could not wait to see Lily every morning at school. He was so in love with her. He loved her sweetness, how smart she was and how beautiful she was. He could not wait to have her meet his parents. He invited Lily to have supper with his family. Lily was so nervous; she just did not want to embarrass James.

When James pulled up at the front of his house with Lily, Lily was shocked. She had never been in a house so big. It was three stories with big columns in the front. James led Lily to the door and took her in. They were met by the entire family. Of course, Lily knew both of James' sisters so she was happy to see familiar faces. Both of the girls were very nice, one was Lily's age and one younger than her. James' dad was a very handsome man and was definitely the master of the house. He gave Lily a hug and welcomed her. James' mother was an average height with a pretty face and short hair that was perfectly fixed. Her life revolved around her home and family. She just wanted everyone to be happy.

As they began to eat, Mr. Wilson ask Lily a question, "Who is your father?"

Lily responded with what her mother had told her so often, "My father was killed overseas while he was in the service which was before I was born. My mother raised me as a single parent."

"Oh, I am sorry about your dad." Mr. Wilson continued, "Does your mother work?"

"No, her father, my grandfather, provided her with a trust to take care of us. He passed away when my mother was still in high school. He had a heart attack."

"Again, I am sorry that you never knew your grandfather. What brought your mother to this town? I assume your grandfather did not live here as I didn't know him."

"Well, I'm not sure why we moved here as it was before I was born. I assume it is because my grandmother is in the hospital a few miles out of town. She's been there my entire life."

As Lily was innocently telling this history, Mr. Wilson's face took on a look of surprise. He said, "You mean the Crawford County Mental Institute?

"Yes, that's the name of it." Lily was unaware that this information would not be welcome in the conversation. She had never associated her grandmother with being mentally ill because when she visited her she was always doing well. Lily also did not realize her grandmother's condition was considered a flaw in your family history.

Everyone finished their meal with some chit-chat concerning school and the end of the school year. James was the president of his class and in the national honor society. James' dad was very proud of James and commented in the conversation, "James has a very bright future in front of him. I believe he will be accepted at Harvard or Yale. If he keeps his mind on school and continues to make good grades." When he said this he looked at Lily and smiled. However, the smile was not a happy smile but a forced attempt at a smile. Lily felt there was a hidden meaning in his comment even thought James did not appear to notice.

After supper they all went into the family room and watched TV, talked and laughed. This was a treat for Lily as she did not have a family life like this at home. There was no joy in her house and it was even hostile when Jake and Jane were drinking. Since Lily knew that Mr. Wilson would naturally be protective of James, she decided maybe she was making too much of the comment he had made about James' future. It was natural for a father to want his only son to do well. Lily just didn't know how far Mr. Wilson would go to see that James reached the top of his potential with out any distractions. She loved James and would not ever want to hold him back in his pursuit of a good career. She also honored their family ties enough that she would not knowingly cause a problem for the family.

James drove Lily home. When they were in the front of her house, he pulled her toward him and kissed her. "They loved you, I knew they would." He said.

Lily said, "Well, I don't think your dad is excited about me being in your life."

James shrugged, "He will come around. He is just anxious for my future." He kissed her again and said, "I am in love with you. We have so much to look forward to and I want us to be together."

Lily said, "I want that also. I love you too." Deep down inside, Lily felt a small twinge of dread. Anytime she had ever felt happy, she knew that around the corner there would be something to complicate the situation.

This period of time was before the sexual revolution. Of course, there were girls in high school that everyone knew to be "loose" or "easy", but having sexual intercourse was not the normal event for the majority of the students. James and Lily were very close. They would kiss and cuddle but the thought of intercourse before marriage was not there.

After James returned home that night, he was surprised when he saw his dad still in the living room when everyone else had gone to bed. "Hi, Dad," James said. "Did you like Lily? Isn't she the most beautiful girl you've ever seen? Besides mother, of course."

"Yes, James, Lily is a lovely girl. I do want to talk to you about her family. Her grandmother has been in the mental institute for years. I assume that there is insanity in her family. You know that is hereditary? I have to advise you not to get serious with this girl."

James was so shocked he couldn't speak for a minute, he said, "Dad, you must be kidding. All of that is just rumor. Lily's mother is normal and has raised Lily well. Lily is at the top of her class and is very active in many school activities. I love her and plan to do everything I can to keep her with me."

Mr. Wilson's face grew red and he raised his voice, "You will not jeopardize your future with this girl. I demand that you break this off now before it gets any more serious!"

James had never gone against his dad but he also had never been in love, he raised his voice for the first time ever to his father, "You cannot tell me what to do with my life. I will be with Lily unless she calls it off." Then he stormed out running to his room and slamming the door. Mr. Wilson was shocked and was dismayed that James was so involved with this girl that he thought he was in love. It occurred to him that breaking James and Lily up would be a hard task, because James might be seriously in love.

Lily started her junior year in high school very excited about the possibilities and she was in love. She and James were together at every opportunity. It was still fashionable to not have sex before marriage. They came really close but were both disciplined and kept it at kissing and caressing. They were devoted to their studies and did not allow their grades to drop. With James graduating this year, he would be in college a year before Lily but they felt they could survive a year of a long distance relationship. Mr. Wilson was hoping for the opposite. He wanted James to be free of Lily. Lily had a strong chance of having a streak of insanity in her family. Mr. Wilson felt there were other secrets in Lily's family and her family certainly did not have money. He did not want to be a snob, he just wanted the best for his son and he did not think Lily was anywhere near the best.

CHAPTER 24

JANE AND JAKE

Jane and Jake had their money for their business venture. The insurance money for Bess came through a few weeks after the funeral. Jane had not seen the property that Jake was so sure was a gold mine. The day they were to sign the contract for the purchase, Jake took Jane down to the club. She was shocked to see that this was not a club but a dive. The building was in a bad part of town and it was run down also everything on the inside was just sad looking. The bar was small with a few tables and about ten bar stools. There were two pool tables in the room with the bar but both of them needed complete recovering to be functional. Then behind the bar was a room with a stage in the middle surrounded by tables. The stage had three dance poles built in with a ramp that lead out into the room. Behind the bar and dance room there were a small office and a small dressing room. There were two nasty restrooms where all of the fixtures were broken and leaking. Jake assured Jane he was going to give it a face lift but Jane thought it needed an overhaul rather than a face lift. Jane was committed to the venture so she left it to Jake. The name of the business was the Swing-in Bar and Grill and since there was a marque with that name on it, they kept the same name. Of course, all the lights were burnt out in the marque but it was there.

Jake did spend some money getting the place cleaned and some painting. He added some lighting and a sound system. He hired a bar tender and one waitress for the front and two girls to do the dancing. He did not intend for them to strip but get as close to having nothing on as they could. He intended to be the business man and the bouncer. The patrons could come in the bar for no cover charge if they ordered drinks. However, to get into the dance bar there was a five dollar cover charge. Jake got a percentage of the girl's tips. He felt he paid them an above average wage and deserved some of the tips.

Jake started out with an opening special of half price for drinks. He had a good first couple of weeks, but then things slacked off some. It didn't get bad until one of the dancers took off to get married. The dancing girls were a big draw and only having one would not keep the show moving.

It was illegal to have a strip show, but Jake was right on the edge with his girl's pole dancing with skimpy clothing. Just one girl dancing got boring for the customers quickly, so Jake's business was in trouble. He was barely covering the overhead and the financial situation caused Jake a lot of stress.

Jake did not realize how hard it would be to manage the money with the money being so assessable to leaking away. The things that were an easy money leak were; cash for drinks making it easy for employees to slip money out, being sure drinks did not exceed the limit causing the overhead to increase, employees drinking without paying for their drinks and a lot of the customers were slick about stealing money. With a narrow margin of profit, every penny counted so these sources for money evaporating could cause the business to go under.

As Jake racked his brain for a solution to his money squeeze, he got the idea that Lily should contribute to the business. He would not have to pay her as she was benefiting from the business and she was young and beautiful. Jake needed Jane to help out to stop the money leakage by monitoring all the business transactions she could.

Jake told Jane, "Lily is living the good life. She does not have to do anything but go to school. She could do some dancing, there's nothing wrong with it. It's no worse than her being a cheerleader jumping around in front of a crowd of people in a short skirt. And you could come down and help me watch the money and do some waiting on tables. It's tight on money right now and we need to all pull together to get this business off the ground." At first Jane was adamant that she contributed the money so he could run the business. However, times got desperate and they were close to losing the business. Jake's attitude became pretty nasty. Jane began to think he could be violent as he became more aggressive and forceful toward her.

Jane called Lily in to the kitchen for a talk, "Lily, Jake is in a bind at the business. He needs us to help out. We can go down and wait tables or handle the money. Since you are a cheerleader at school you could do some of your routines on the stage and drum up some money. You are out of school for the summer so you won't have a problem being up late at night."

Lily was astonished, "Mom, you want me to work in a strip bar! Isn't that illegal with me being under age and liquor being served?"

Jane responded, "It is not a strip bar, it is a dance bar. You have had a free ride so far; it won't hurt for you to help out. No one around here will know. It is dark in the dance room and the bar is in another town. Jake says the police hardly ever come around and won't notice you being under aged."

Lily had always done what her mother told her to without an argument. She also knew Jane was capable of harsh punishment if she was upset. But Lily told her, "I won't do it" and she went to her room.

When Jane told Jake this, he became enraged. "Who does she think she is? I will teach her a lesson. You have been too easy on her."

Jake started toward her room but Jane stood in his way. "Get out of the way!" He demanded. Then for the first time, he hit Jane in the face and knocked her down. He grabbed her by the neck and started to choke her. Hearing the commotion, Lily came in the room. Lily screamed, "Stop Jake, leave her alone."

Jake looked at Lily and said, "If you don't come dance, I swear, I will kill her!"

Lily said, "I'll do it, just let her go." Lily was shaking; she had never been as scared of someone as she was of Jake.

Jake let Jane go and walked out of the front door. Before he left he said, "I will see both of you at the club tonight, or else."

After he was gone, Lily helped her mother up and said, "What has he done? You have to call the police. He can't treat you this way. He has no authority over us."

Jane looked at Lily and said, "Yes he does. He knows something about me that could put me in prison for a long time. Please, we have to do what he says."

Lily ask, "What did you do, mother?"

Jane just turned away and said, "I can't tell you but it is real." Jane went to the kitchen to get some ice for her face.

Lily and Jane did show up at the bar in the evening. James was gone for the summer working at a page job in Washington, DC. This was good for Lily because she did not want him to know what she was doing.

At first the job started off alright. Lily did not mind the work in the bar of waiting on tables. The bar was not busy early but as the night wore on, business picked up. Many of the patrons were asking when the show was starting. Lily did not know what they were talking about. She ask Jake and he just brushed her off without an answer. Around eleven, Jane came to Lily, "Lily, the dancer has not showed up so Jake needs you to do some dancing on stage. He advertized that there would be a dancer. Many guys have already paid their money for the show."

Lily was unhappy, "Mom, I do not know anything about this type of dancing and I will not strip. How can you ask me to do that?"

Jane responded, "Just get out there and do a cheerleading routine. It's dark; no one will know who you are. It's no different than performing in front of all those people at a ball game."

Jake walked up at that time and added, "People come to the ball game to see you girls in short skirts. They come to see yours legs, ass and tits. This is no different, so get out there now. There are costumes in the dressing room." He walked off.

Lily stormed off to the dressing room. She was more scared than angry. She found a couple of outfits in the dressing room. They were essentially a bikini bathing suit. When she put on the bathing suit, she felt naked and did not know if she could go out on the stage or not. She started putting on some make up when her mother came in. Lily told her mother, "I'm scared; I have no idea what to do out there. I can't believe you are making me do this."

Jane said, "I'm sorry. I never wanted this to happen but things have gotten out of control. Just do your best and I promise you will be okay."

Lily finished getting ready and went to the stage entrance. She put a sheer robe on over her outfit and did not intend to take it off. There was a big crowd of men in the room. It was dark so she could not see anyone's face. On the stage there were three silver poles. She had heard about pole dancing but had never done this. The music started and Jake got on the stage with a microphone. "Thanks for coming, gentlemen, I hope you enjoy the show. Our dancer tonight is Lily, so be nice. No touching, but if you want to contribute some money to her, just put it on the stage. Okay, Lily come on out!"

Lily was shaking but she walked out. The cheers began as the music got louder. Lily put herself into a mind-set that she was at a game. So she began one of the cheerleading routines. It looked athletic and not very sexy. Jake got on the stage and took Lily to the side to talk to her, "You got to be sexier. Take off that rob, you know how to dance. Give them a show! Just remember, I will hurt you and Jane if you don't do like I tell you."

Lily felt trapped but she decided she could give them a show. She started improvising and moving more provocatively. The crowd began to get loud and happy. Money started hitting the stage. Lily began to use the poles with some simple moves. After about an hour, Jake got on the stage and said it was intermission time, but Lily would be back in thirty minutes. He then turned to Lily and said, "Take a break then we will give them about thirty more minutes."

Lily began dancing several nights a week, when the other dancer did not show up. The patrons began to demand Lily dance more and more. Lily had gotten more comfortable dancing but she was still not happy about any of this. She told Jane that she would not be able to dance when school started. She said, "I have to have good grades if I'm going to get a scholarship so I have to study at night. Please, talk to Jake and make sure he knows this."

Jane said, "I'm sure he won't expect you to dance during school." But she was not sure at all about this as Jake was adamant that the business do well and Lily was a big draw. No one expected what was to come.

One night during Lily's first dance, a commotion suddenly started in the bar. Almost immediately the doors of the room burst open and the police SWAT team swarmed into the room. One of the team jumped on the stage and grabbed Lily by the arm and pulled her off the stage. Lily screamed for Jane as they took her out the door. She vaguely remembered flash bulbs going off as she was put into the back of a police van. As she found out at the police station, she was under arrest for being an under-age person in a place where liquor was being served. The owner of an establishment is not even allowed to have anyone under age waiting tables and an under-age dancer was certainly illegal. Jake was booked as the owner and had to be bailed out of jail along with Lily. Lily and Jane were glad this happened for the reason that it freed Lily from working in the club, but the raid would have some far reaching consequences for Lily's life.

CHAPTER 25

JAMES

James returned home from his job in Washington DC in late summer so he could get ready to enter Harvard. His dad was very happy that James was accepted into Harvard. However, he was not happy that James was still insistent that Lily was the one for him.

James came downstairs for breakfast the first day he was home. His dad stood at the breakfast table with a stern look on his face. When James sat down, Mr. Wilson pushed a newspaper over to him. James looked at it in shock. On the front page was a picture of Lily. Only she did not look as he had remembered her. The picture showed her in a skimpy outfit with a lot of make up on, being led by police to a police van. The head line above the picture of Lily was **Under-age stripper arrested in Swing-in Bar and Grill.**

Mr. Wilson said, "Isn't that your girlfriend, Lily? She was arrested for dancing in a strip bar in a bad part of town! Can you see what this will do to our family's reputation? This could hurt you with your career. I told you this girl was bad news. Not only is she from a family with an insane grandmother, she is an under-aged stripper in a sleazy bar! Now do you see what I was telling you is for your own good? Please, don't jeopardize your future. You must break off with Lily now before you leave for college."

James did not have anything to say. He got up and left and headed for Lily's house. When he got there, Lily opened the door and gave him a hug and a kiss. He immediately pushed her back and said, "How could you dance in a sleazy bar? Are you crazy? This will cause my family a lot of embarrassment. What were you thinking? Why did you not tell me?"

Lily was stunned, "How did you know?"

James answered, "It's all over the newspaper. My dad hit me with it first thing this morning."

Lily said, "I can explain. Jake needed me because his business was going under. I had to do it for my mother. I didn't want to do it but I had no choice. I'm sorry this has upset you and your dad, but I'm still the same person I was, I just had to do something I didn't really want to do."

James was not convinced, he said, "I don't know what to say."

Lily saw the look on his face, she knew this was the end. She said, "You don't have to say anything. I'm sorry I embarrassed you or anyone. Don't worry; I will not cause you or your family any more problems. Good bye." And she shut the door. James stood on the porch a while, then left. Lily thought he would knock on the door and tell her it was fine, he loved her anyway. But that did not happen. Lily was crushed and cried all day. When Jane asked what was wrong and Lily told her, Jane's response was, "You are better off without him. You can make your life on your own merit." Lily did not get any sympathy or hugs from Jane, but she should know by now how what to expect from Jane.

Lily went to Granny's house with her sad story. Granny was really sorry for her. Granny was the one that gave Lily a hug while she cried. She said, "I know right now this is very devastating and I understand, but someday you will see this experience will help you. The people that really care about you will be there through thick and thin. James should have known the real you and known that you had no control over the situation. He should have given you the benefit of the doubt and helped you get through this. I think his father is a big part of why James reacted as he did but that's his family and if he picks them over you, you are truly better off."

This was good and comforting advice, but Lily was still heart broken. She stayed in her room for a week before she began to feel a little better. School was starting soon so she thought getting back to school and being busy would help her move on.

As a cheerleader, Lily was prepared to start practice a few weeks before school started. When Lily went to the gym for the first practice, the cheerleading coach asked Lily to come to her office.

When Lily got there the coach said, "Lily, as you know to be on the cheerleading squad, each member must be an example for the rest of the students. I am concerned about some publicity that you received during the summer. This certainly is not what we advocate for our students. Therefore, I have to tell you that you are released from the squad. I'm sorry, as you are one of our best girls, but the school board was adamant that you be dismissed."

Lily was surprised and disappointed, "Please, could I have some other kind of punishment but be allowed to stay on the squad?"

The coach shook her head, "I'm afraid that I can not let you stay."

Lily left, she was again devastated. She did not know what else could be worse. She did not know if she could even show her face at school this year. Like most scandals, it would blow over when something else came along. However, at this time it seemed to Lily that everyone was talking about her. She was disgraced and embarrassed. At school she kept to herself and kept her head down. For the first time in her life, Lily knew people were talking behind her back and some kids avoiding her. However, some of her good friends stayed loyal. Lily's good friends were what kept Lily strong and by the second semester things were better and Lily was looking forward again.

Lily thought about James less and less as time went by. She'd never forget her first love, but she would also never forget her disappointment that he did not stand by her in her time of trouble. The pain ran deeper when Lily was also dropped from the debate team. Being on the debate team was important when it came to college applications. Lily became afraid she would not be accepted at any of the colleges. She went to see her long-time friend, Sarah Watson. After she told her the problem, Sarah told her, "I will write you a letter of reference as I have known you from the first grade on through school. I will also ask some other teachers to send letters of recommendations for you. You will get into college, I promise. I am very disappointed in your mother. It appears she does not care about your future. Please be strong and it will be okay."

Lily was very thankful for Sarah's advice and help. She felt things had to get better, but she had no idea how much worse things were going before the light would shine in some of the shadows of her life.

CHAPTER 26

JAKE

At home, Jake's business was struggling after the raid and the loss of Lily as a dancer caused the attendance in the bar to go down. This resulted in the liquor consumption going down. Things were getting near the breaking point for Jake. He became more and more hostile to Jane and Lily as time wore on. Lily noted that Jane had more and more bruised eyes, arms and face. Lily heard them arguing more each day. The tension at home was very thick.

A couple of months after the raid, Jake and Jane were arguing when Lily came home. She tried to pass through the kitchen and go to her room without them noticing her. But, Jake turned on her and said, "You are going to dance again. Everyone is asking for you and my business is really hurting."

Lily looked at him and said, "No, I am not dancing. If I get caught again, I will go to juvenile court and reform school. I can't believe you'd even ask me. Dancing in that bar and getting arrested has ruined my life. I lost my boyfriend, many of my friends are avoiding me, I was thrown off the cheerleading squad and dropped from the debate team. You have no idea how this could hurt my chances to get into college."

Jake was hostile, "How sad, little Lily's love life is ruined and she can't squeal with the other squealers. I'm losing my business, so forgive me if I don't cry for you. *You will dance!*"

Lily screamed, "I will not dance!" Lily ran to her room with Jake right behind her. He grabbed her by the arm and jerked her around and hit her in the face. The blow knocked her down on the bed. He jumped on her and started slapping her face. Lily was screaming and kicking. Jake was much bigger than her so she didn't have a chance against him.

From the door way of Lily's room, there was a deep, gravely voice that came from Jane, **"Jake, leaveee her aloneeee!"** Lily knew her mother was home when she came in and she was glad she was not alone. Lily was truly afraid for her life.

Jake stopped his assault on Lily and slowly turned around to look at Jane. He said, "Who the hell do you think you are telling me what to do? I will kill you both."

Then he stopped and looked in surprise at Jane. Her face was dark; she didn't even look like herself and did not sound human. When Jane saw Jake run after Lily, she knew he was out of control and intended to harm her. Her mind went dark and her focus became one thing, stop him. She went to her room and retrieved a box from the closet. She removed the Colt that had belonged to her father. It had three bullets left in the chamber since the incident when her father died. When Jake saw the gun in Jane's hand, he laughed, "What do you think you are going to do with that gun? You don't even know how to use a gun?"

Jake got the answer to his question when Jane pulled the trigger. The bullet hit him square in the chest. The smirk on his face froze then melted away as the life drained out of his body. A bullet from a Colt .45 at this range will leave a hole you can put your fist in, so it was the end of Jake's life. He was dead when he hit the floor. Lily was in shock; she got up and ran to Jane. She threw her arms around Jane and said, "Mother, what have you done!?"

Jane was very calm, she held Lily for a moment then pulled away from her, "Lily, it was self-defense. I thought he was going to kill you and then me. I got us into this by bringing Jake into our lives. I had to save you. We have to call 911 and explain to the police what happened. I do love you and I am sorry this has ended this way." This was the first time Jane had told Lily she loved her.

When the police arrived, they found Jane and Lily huddled on the couch holding hands. The paramedics attended to Jake and pronounced him dead. The police officer told Jane, she and Lily would need to go with him to the police station to make a statement.

When they got to the police station, Jane and Lily were put in separate rooms. A different detective went into each room to question them. The detectives were Jim Roman and Tom Cramer. Detective Roman was a veteran of many years but Detective Cramer had only been at this job a couple of years. After the detectives completed their interviews, they sat down to compare notes.

Lily and Jane both told similar stories. The basic facts that the detectives agreed on were: Jake Henson had become enraged that Lily was no longer going to work at the club due to the incident the month before. Even though he knew Lily was under age, he insisted the business was in trouble of closing and he needed her to dance. Jake had chased Lily into her room and was beating her severely. Jane could not get him to stop hurting Lily so she got her dad's gun that she kept for protection and shot him. Jane was adamant that she thought Jake was going to kill Lily, then turn on her. They both stated that Jake did not have a weapon but that he was very strong and out of control with rage.

The detectives decided to talk to the women again to be sure they had everything. They ask Jane and Lily if there were any other conflicts between them and Jake. They both said no, the only conflict was that Lily would not dance. Then Detective Roman asked Jane who owned the club known as the Swing-in Bar and Grill. Jane said she put up the money and held the liquor license, but Jake was the manager.

Detective Cramer told Jane that since she had shot and killed a man, she would have to be booked and held in jail or bailed out of jail until there would be a hearing the next morning. Lily was free to go for now.

Later that evening the two detectives were discussing their information that they had gotten from the Baxter women. Detective Roman said, "Ms. Baxter seems to be a pretty hard case. For a woman that just lost her significant other, she was not very emotional about it. She apparently was into the guy as she gave him the money for the club and made him boss. I think Henson was also knocking Jane around, I saw some bruises on her arms and on her face. I don't know why a great looking woman like that would need a guy that beats her up. Isn't it something how mother and daughter both have the same emerald green eyes and are beautiful to boot. Jane could have been looking for an excuse to get rid of Jake. I think I'll go down to the club and nose around. I'll talk to the bar tender and some of the other girls that work there. What did you find out talking to Lily?"

Detective Cramer replied as he flipped through his note book, "Lily appears to be just a kid that is caught in a nasty situation. She's a good student and plans to go to college. She seems a little afraid and cautious about her mother. I don't think they are very close. I don't think the girl had anything to do with shooting of the guy. She was pretty beat up. I'll go with you and see what the club looks like."

When Roman and Cramer entered the Swing-in Bar and Grill there were only two men at the bar. They noted that the place was pretty much a dump and in a bad part of town. Detective Roman asked the bar tender, "Do you work for Jake Henson and Jane Baxter?"

He nodded and said, "So what's going on? They didn't come in tonight. I had to handle this by myself except for the two girls that dance here did come in."

Detective Roman said, "Mr. Henson has had an accident and has been killed."

The bar tender was shocked, "Man, that's bad. What happened?"

"Apparently there was a problem between him and Lily Baxter and Jane Baxter shot him." Detective Roman continued.

The bar tender said, "Well, Jake could be a son-of-a-bitch at times. He was also heavy handed."

Detective Roman asked, "Did you see trouble between Jake and Jane?"

The bar tender answered, "I didn't see anything. They spent most of the time in the office or with the dancers. I mind my own business."

Detective Cramer asked, "Could you have the two girls that dance come out here for a minute?"

The answer came as the bar tender yelled for Kitty and Martha to come out for a minute.

Two women came in; both were dressed for dancing and had on heavy makeup. They were both pretty with Kitty being the cutest. Kitty was also a lot younger than Martha. "Hello girls, I'm Detective Cramer and this is Detective Roman. We have some bad news for you. Your boss, Jake, has been killed."

Kitty began to scream and then broke into sobs. Martha just looked mildly shocked. Kitty was crying, "No, not Jake. What will I do now?"

Detective Cramer tried to help Kitty calm down, "Kitty, you seem very upset. Did you have more than a professional relationship with Jake?"

Kitty began to pull herself together and said, "Well, we were fond of each other. He was going to help me get a big break in show business.

He had connections out west. Now I won't even have a job here, because if it is up to Jane she will fire me. Jane doesn't like me much."

Both detectives looked at each other and continued to take notes. This might turn out to be more than it appears on the surface. They would be talking to their boss soon.

CHAPTER 27

RAYMOND MCCOY

T he chief of police contacted the prosecuting attorney, Mike Anthony, to discuss the evidence in a homicide that had taken place the night before. He caught him up to date on Ms. Baxter and her daughter, Lily, in connection with the death of Jake Henson. He said to Mr. Anthony, "My detectives have gathered some interesting facts that shed a different light on what Ms. Baxter contends, which is the shooting of Mr. Henson was committed in self-defense. They have uncovered some other possible motives for the incident."

Mike Antony was in his early thirties. He had risen up the ranks quickly as a motivated, ambitious lawyer. He was handsome and dressed very well. He was charming when he needed to be but could cut right to the bone when the occasion arose. He replied to the chief, "I will be glad to look into it. Give me until tomorrow and I will go to Ms. Baxter's hearing. Thanks for the tip."

Mike spent the night in his office going over the evidence submitted by the detectives. By morning, he had drafted a motion for the judge to charge Ms. Baxter with second degree murder or manslaughter.

Jane and Mr. Mason, Henry's lawyer, were in court the next morning for what they thought would be a short hearing, then Jane could go home. However, when the case was called Prosecuting Attorney, Mike Anthony, stood and announced he was submitting documentation to request that the court charge Ms. Baxter with murder 2 or manslaughter.

When Jane heard this, she almost fainted and Mr. Mason was so shocked he could not speak for a moment. Then he said, "Your honor, my client acted in self defense to protect her daughter from being killed by Mr. Henson. We had no idea Mr. Anthony thought otherwise."

The Judge called a recess so he could look over the documentation that Mr. Anthony had submitted. When the court reconvened he said, "After reviewing this motion, I find that this case has enough evidence to go to court. Unless Ms. Baxter wants to plead guilty to the charges a court date will be set."

Mr. Mason spoke briefly with Jane and replied, "Your Honor, my client pleads not guilty to the charges of murder 2 or manslaughter. I will ask that I be removed as counsel for Ms. Baxter as I am not a trial lawyer. I will assist her in obtaining adequate counsel for the trial."

The Judge said, "I agree. Mr. Anthony will work with your new lawyer and I am setting bail at four thousand dollars. We are adjourned."

Jane was in shock and could not speak so the lawyer said, "Jane, I'll take care of the bail. You go home with Lily and wait for my call. I'll get you a good lawyer."

Jane's new lawyer was Raymond McCoy. All his friends called him Ray-Mc and he had a lot of friends. Ray-Mc was what could be called a colorful character. He had an easy way of connecting to people especially people on a jury. He came off as every person's best friend and appeared to be talking to each individual in the jury rather than a group.

Ray-Mc was in his early sixties and had spent his entire professional life trying cases. He loved the law and being the center of attention when trying a case. He also had a good sense of humor that made people relax and think of him as a "good ole boy". However, he was a smart, cunning individual that did not like to lose cases. This case was his favorite kind of case. This kind of case would be a high profile and would certainly make the media go crazy. They did not often have a murder case in this small town so the trial would be attended by a lot of the people from town.

Of course, when he met Jane, Ray-Mc was immediately smitten by her beauty and her classy attire. He noted that Lily resembled her mother and just as beautiful. He introduced himself to Jane and Lily using his best manners, "Hello, my name is Raymond McCoy but you can call me Ray-Mc, as most people do. I have reviewed this case and I believe you have a very good chance to get acquitted of these charges. However, you never know how a jury will look at the evidence and it will be important for you to be calm and collected during the trial. I think you should not testify as that just opens up the door for the prosecuting attorney to come at you and that could hurt us. I do see that Lily is on the defense's list of people to testify. I will coach you very closely, Lily, so don't worry too much about this. I need for you, Jane, to tell me everything leading up to this incident and what happened the night you shot Jake. I do mean everything, even the bad stuff. I do not want to be blind-sided by something that has been dug up by the prosecution. I would also like to know some of your life history because that gives me more sense of who I am defending. So take your time and let's get started."

Jane started from the beginning of her life. Lily was very surprised at the story as Jane had never told her any of these details. Ray-Mc quickly picked up on the information that Jane's mother had been in an institution for the mentally ill many years before her death. He wanted to know her exact diagnosis. Jane told him her mother was an extreme case with several disorders and a steady downward spiral. He asked her if she had ever been evaluated to which she said no. Ray-Mc said, "I will need to get you evaluated, if you have any of these tendencies, it might play a big role in your defense."

What Jane left out of her story was the part that could have put her in jail for a long time which was that she murdered a man a few years prior whose name was Mr. Miller. She also left out the part that she played in the death of her mother. These would be secrets she would forever keep in the shadows and take to her grave.

After several hours, Ray-Mc said he had enough information. He told Jane and Lily to go home and keep a low profile. "Do not talk to the media. They will take anything you say, no matter how innocent, and make it ugly just to create more drama. We don't want drama. We just want this to be a self defense case and the fact that you might have some mental issues from your mother may play a part in why you snapped." With that Ray-Mc let them go and began his work. This is the part he loved, when he was putting together a case, he was in his element. He was anxious to see the results of the mental evaluation that he would request for Jane.

Ray-Mc requested and was granted an extension on the trial in order to get the mental evaluation completed. He was given two months to prepare. Lily returned to school while Jane closed the club and put it up for sale. Jane began her evaluation with a doctor selected by Ray-Mc. This doctor had worked with Ray-Mc on several cases and was very good on the stand. So now, everyone just had to wait for the mental evaluation.

Jane was not happy about the mental evaluation. It is typical for people with mental problems to think they are fine and everyone else is screwed up. Therefore, at first Jane was defiant and guarded with the doctor. It did help that the doctor was a woman, Debbie Sampson. Jane was comfortable with Debbie so she soon began to open up. Dr. Sampson moved slowly with Jane but after two months of meeting with her three times a week she had made her determination of Jane's mental condition. Her evaluation was double edged. Some parts would help determine why she would kill Jake, but some things she had discovered would not be to Jane's advantage.

Since Mike Anthony knew and respected Doctor Sampson, he did not request his own expert to evaluate Jane. He had dealt with Dr. Sampson on several cases, some when she was on his side and some when she was on the other. She always reported the facts in a non bias way therefore she was very credible as a witness. So the trial started on time with the Judges' schedule.

CHAPTER 28

JANE

J udge John Martin had been a trial judge for thirty years. He was tough but fair so both sides felt they would get a fair trial. On Monday morning following the jury selection, Judge Martin entered the court room ready to get this trial on the road.

Prosecuting Attorney Mike Anthony was ready. He was always prepared and very meticulous about the facts of the case. Raymond McCoy, Jane's lawyer, was also ready. Mr. McCoy had 20 years of experience over Mr. Anthony and was very relaxed in the court. Ray-Mc knew many ways to get information out of people and them not even be aware of what he was doing. Ray-Mc had determined from his many conversations with Jane that she was a tough cookie. He felt her cold detached attitude was not going to be in their favor. He really didn't want to put Jane on the stand but would have to see how things were going.

Ray-Mc knew the fact that Jane was beautiful would be in her favor. He had found that attractive people always got the benefit of the doubt from others. He also felt that Lily would be a good influence on the jury as she too was a beauty and was innocent to boot. Ray-Mc was a little worried that Mike Anthony was a very good, aggressive lawyer and would not leave anything to chance. All things accountable, this was going to be an interesting case and Ray-Mc fully intended to win. Mr. Anthony was also confident he had a good case.

The people in the court were instructed to stand as the judge entered the room. With the crack of the gravel on the bench, the judge took charge and was ready to get to work. He first instructed any witnesses to wait outside the court as they were not to hear the other testimonies. That included Lily and Granny as they both had been notified they would be called by Mr. Anthony to testify. They sat together in the hall and waited nervously to be called.

The beginning of the trial was basically boring, but in two days the jury was selected from the pool of people summoned to the court for jury duty. The selected jury consisted of seven women and six men. Eleven of the women and men were married with children and two were single without children. They ranged in age from 25 to 65. They were all middle class citizens. Ray-Mc was pleased with the jury and was ready to rock and roll. He was always excited at the prospect of a new and exciting trial. He was a little concerned with some of the evidence that did not put Jane in a good light. He just hoped he could pull this off as he really liked Lily and felt she needed a break in life. He thought that Jane would be a different person if she had help with her mental problems. If she was found not guilty, he was going to try and assist her in getting help.

On Wednesday morning, the judge addressed the court. He went over the rules and instructed the jury on their responsibility for all of them to agree on a verdict. The Judge said, "Mr. Antony, please begin with your opening statements."

Mike stood, adjusted his expensive suit and walked to the podium, "Ladies and gentlemen of the jury, I thank you for your time and know you can come to a fair verdict. As you see sitting at the table, the defendant is Ms. Jane Baxter. She is a single parent of one daughter, Lily Rose, age sixteen years old.

'Ms. Baxter shot and killed Jake Henson. Mr. Henson was a young man in his mid-thirties. Mr. Henson and Ms. Baxter had lived together for several years and they were also business partners. They owned and operated a club called Swing-in Bar and Grill, located in the east part of the city of Rome, which was about 20 miles from their residence.

'Ms. Baxter contends that she shot Mr. Henson in self-defense in defending her daughter. However, I think after you hear all the evidence, you will see another side to this story. I intend to prove beyond a shadow of a doubt, that Ms. Baxter shot Mr. Henson in cold blood because of reasons of her own. I know it is difficult to look at Ms. Baxter and believe that such a lovely woman could do such a thing. Ms. Baxter does not look at all like a gun totting killer. But don't let her looks fool you. Look into Ms. Baxter's beautiful, emerald green eyes and try to see the real person sitting there and believe me, Elizabeth Jane Baxter is a cold blooded killer. Thank you." Mr. Anthony returned to his seat.

The Judge said, "Mr. McCoy please, present your opening statements."

Ray-Mc slowly got up. He was wearing an old suit that was out of style but was very neat. He did not walk to the podium but went right to the jury box. He put his elbow on the half wall in front of the jury. He leaned in toward the jurors like they were having a personal conversation. He started, "Good morning Ladies and gentlemen. It's a wonderful day, I want you all to relax and listen to all the evidence carefully. You are going to get to know the woman sitting at the defense table. She had a very tough childhood. She is a single mother, which can be a lonely life. She was taken in by a good looking gigolo named Jake Henson. Jake zeroed in on her isolation, took her out for the fun she didn't have as a teenager. But all along he was taking her money, living in her house for free and talked her into investing all her money in a run-down bar/strip joint in the worst part of town. He even talked her into having her under aged daughter, dance at the joint. You will also learn of some mental issues that affected Jane's mother. Jane grew up in the house with her mother who was mentally ill and in fact, when Jane was fifteen years old, her mother was institutionalized for being diagnosed as insane.

'Ms. Baxter found Lily being brutalized and possibly in danger of being killed, she stepped up and did all she knew to do which was stop Mr. Henson any way she could. She shot him, with her father's gun in defense of her child. Folks it is the right of every citizen in this great country to defend themselves and their family from immediate danger. Thank You." Ray-Mc walked back to the defendant table where he patted Jane on the shoulder as a show of support.

The Judge then instructed Mr. Anthony to call his first witness for the prosecution.

Mr. Anthony stood and called to the stand the 911 operator that took the call from Jane on the night of the incident. He questioned her and established that Jane had identified herself on the call, gave her address and requested an officer to come as there was a dead man in her house. He asked the operator, "How did you think Ms. Baxter sounded on phone?"

She answered, "Well, it was kind of like she was reading a script. She showed no emotion. She gave all the information in a clear manner. Usually when folks call in a 911 call they are so excited they can't even remember what day it is."

Mr. Anthony ask his next question, "Would you say, Ms. Baxter sounded rehearsed and not surprised that she had killed Mr. Henson.?"

The operator answered, "Well, I think she would have been more upset or excited than she appeared."

Mr. Anthony said he did not have any more questions for this witness so the judge indicated that Ray-Mc was next. Ray-Mc approached the witness box, gave the lady a big smile. He asked her "How long have you been an operatora?"

She answered, "About 4 years."

"How many calls in that time would you say you received that involved a dead or dying person?"

She looked puzzled then answered, "Well, it doesn't happen very often. In this small town we usually get calls about minor things like cats in a tree or someone trespassing. So I'd say this is my first one of this kind and severity."

Ray-Mc asked kindly, "So you are not really an expert on how someone should sound when they are calling in an incident of this magnitude."

"Well no, but I would think she should have been excited or scared and she didn't sound that way."

Ray-Mc asked, "Have you heard that when some people are traumatized they go into shock? Sometimes they can't even talk or they go into a trance and act on instinct."

The operator thought for a minute then said, "I've heard of that and I've seen it on TV so I guess you are right, I might not know how she should sound in any particular situation."

"Thank you for your honesty," With that Ray-Mc said he did not have any more questions for this witness. He was confident that he had established that the 911 call did not have any significance as to Jane being cold hearted concerning the death of Jake.

Mr. Anthony called his next witness which was the first officer on the scene of the crime. He requested that he give the details of his investigation. The officer pulled out his note book and began. "I arrived on the scene at 8 PM. I found Ms. Baxter and Lily sitting on the couch in the living room. I noted a gun on the coffee table which I bagged as evidence.

'Ms. Baxter said that Jake Henson was in the bedroom and that he was dead. I ask her to remain on the couch with her daughter while I went into the bedroom. Mr. Henson was lying face down on the floor. I checked for a pulse and when I did not find one, I determined he was dead. I returned to the living room and asked what had happened. Ms. Baxter said Mr. Henson chased Lily into her room and was beating her. She could hear Lily screaming. She said she got her gun out of her closet in her room and ran into Lily's room. What she saw was Jake on top of Lily on the bed. She stated Jake was beating her with his fist. She said she told him to leave Lily alone. He then turned and started toward her. At that time she shot him and he fell to the floor. She said she checked on Lily then called 911. By this time some more officers had arrived and I told both Jane and Lily they would have to come down town with me to make another statement. I turned them over to the detectives who were on the case."

Mr. Anthony asked, "Did you find any weapon near Jake or in the bedroom?"

The officer responded, "No sir, I did not find any kind of weapon around Jake. Like I said earlier, there was a gun on the coffee table in the living room which I bagged."

Mr. Anthony then said he had completed his questioning. Ray-Mc approached the officer on the witness stand. "Officer, at any time during your questioning did Jane tell you that Jake said anything to her when he turned around and started toward her?"

"Yes sir, she said when Jake turned around, and I quote 'I'll kill you both, bitch'."

"Officer, what size man was Jake Henson?" Ray-Mc raised his voice when he ask this question and looked at the jury. He wanted to be sure they knew how much bigger Jake was than Lily.

"He was about six feet, two inches tall and around two hundred forty five pounds."

Ray-Mc then asked, "Was Mr. Henson in good physical condition?"

"Yes, he had big upper arm muscles like he worked out a lot." The officer answered.

"Officer, if you saw a man of Mr. Henson's size and build, coming toward you, who also said, 'I will kill you both, bitch?' would you fear for your life?"

"Yes, I probably would be concerned that he could do harm to me." The officer stated.

"Thank you, no further questions." Ray-Mc returned to his seat. He smiled at Jane as he returned to the table hoping to boast her confidence.

Mr. Anthony slowly rose from his chair, this was not going well for him but he had just gotten started. "I'd like to call Mrs. Vivian Watson to the stand."

The guard opened the door to let Granny enter the court room. She was a tiny lady dressed nicely in a well fitted suit and low heels. She held her head high and walked quickly to the witness stand. After she had taken the oath, Mr. Anthony requested what her address was and established that she lived next door to Jane and Lily. He then asked, "When did you first become acquainted with Jane Baxter?"

In a clear voice, Granny said "When Jane moved in next door to me she was pregnant with Lily. She had moved there to be near her mother who was in a nursing home near town. Her father had just passed away of a heart attack. She did not have anyone to help her."

"What kind of person did you find Jane to be?"

"She was very serious. She did not make friends very well but we hit it off. I think I reminded her of her mother and she needed someone at the time."

Mr. Anthony asked, "How much time did you spend with Lily as she grew up?"

"Oh, I saw her every day and when she started to school, she came to my house every day after school. I was a like a grandparent to her. Lily is the sweetest, most wonderful girl in the world."

"Spoken like a proud grandparent, thank you. What kind of a mother do you think Jane was to Lily?"

Granny looked down at her hands and took a second before talking, "Well, Jane had some problems in her life that kept her from being the best parent. But she loves Lily very much and Lily loves her."

"Would it be true to say that Lily stayed with you more than she did with her Mother?"

"Lily did love to come to my house. I had a lot of time to spend with her. Jane visited her mother often so Lily stayed with me when Jane went to see her mother."

"Did Jane have a problem that you knew of that would contribute to Lily staying with you so much?"

"I'm not an expert on other people's problems and I don't meddle." Granny sat up straight and had an indignant look on her face.

"I'll be more specific, Ms. Watson, did Jane have a drinking problem?"

"Jane did drink a lot of the time. As to her having a problem with drinking you would have to ask the experts as to what is a drinking problem as opposed to just enjoying a drink."

Mr. Anthony decided to get straight to the point, "In your opinion, Ms. Watson, did Jane at times neglect Lily?"

"That is a question that I can't answer as I was not in her home that much. I do know Jane always made sure that Lily was taken care of if she was indisposed or away from home. She kept a clean house and always had food in the house. She saw that Lily was always in school."

"After Mr. Henson came to live with them, how did he interact with Lily?"

Granny said, "Lily never talked about Mr. Henson except she did say he never seemed to notice her and never really talked to her."

"During this last year, how did things change for you and Lily?"

"I didn't get to see her that much this last year. Jane and Mr. Henson had started a business in a town near here and Lily helped them out at night. She also had her school activities. Lily is very popular and active in school and a very good student. I understood that as she got older she would become less able to spend time with me, that's the way life is."

"Thank you, Ms. Watson. I think Lily was lucky to have someone like you to be a big part of her life. I don't have any more questions for now."

Ray-Mc approached the witness stand with a big smile for Granny. "You are a remarkable woman, Ms. Watson. I know Lily is very fond of you. Since Jane was a single parent and had no relatives, would it not be natural for her to be happy to have some extended family to help her raise her daughter?"

"I think it is natural and I was glad to be there for her and Lily."

Ray-Mc then asked, "Did Jane pay you for the time you spent caring for Lily and help you with groceries?"

"Well, yes she did. The money really helped me. I never worked and I live on my deceased husband's social security benefits. Money gets tight sometimes."

"So Jane did not take advantage of you but actually you probably kept Lily as much as a day care center would have kept her if Jane had to work? Would that be a fair assessment of equal time that other children spend with a sitter if their parents have to work?"

Granny was hurt, "I am more than a baby sitter to Lily. She is precious to me and I am thankful to Jane for sharing her with me."

Ray-Mc was contrite, "please don't take offense. I know you have a special relationship with Lily. I was just making the point that a lot of children spend a great deal of time with someone other than their parent but they still have good, caring parents. I do not have any more questions for Ms. Watson."

As Granny left the stand, the judge declared the court would adjourn for the day and reconvene the next day at 9 am.

The court was called to order at nine AM the next morning. Mike Anthony spent the morning calling several teachers to the stand who taught Lily in school over the years. He spent a lot of time with each one but the main point he made was that Jane had not been a participating parent in Lily's education. The teachers all noted that Jane did not come to school for events or parent/teacher meetings. One teacher also told the court that she had given Lily the clothes her sister had outgrown because Lily did not have nice clothes to wear. Ray-Mc did not cross examine any of these teachers as he felt he could not make anything positive for Jane out of their testimony.

After lunch, Mr. Anthony called Mr. Mason to the stand. Mr. Mason identified himself and told the court he had been the family attorney for the Baxter family for many years. He also stated he was the executor of the estate of the late Mr. Henry Baxter in charge of the trust Mr. Baxter left for his wife's care and the trust for Jane and Lily.

Mr. Anthony's first question was, "How did Mr. Baxter make the money he put in these trust funds?"

Mr. Mason answered, "Mr. Baxter worked his entire life for a man who owned several businesses. Mr. Baxter was very frugal and saved a large part of his salary. He did not even own a car for many years. Mr. Baxter made several successful investments over a period of years. Mr. and Mrs. Baxter rarely left the house due to Mrs. Baxter's illness."

Mr. Anthony asked, "What kind of illness did Mrs. Baxter have?"

Mr. Mason replied, "I never was informed of her diagnosis, but it had to do with a progressive mental disability. Mr. Baxter was forced to have her institutionalized when Jane was fourteen years old as she became uncontrollable and dangerous to her family."

Mr. Anthony asked, "Were you ever informed that this condition might be passed on to any children that Mrs. Baxter might have?"

Mr. Mason answered, "I was told this might be the case and that is one of the reasons I have been in control of the trust for Jane and Lily."

"Mr. Mason, was there another reason that Mr. Baxter did not feel secure in allowing his adult daughter handle her money?"

Mr. Mason looked at Jane for the first time; he was familiar with her temper and hoped she would remain calm as he revealed this information. "Jane was sixteen when she got pregnant. She would not reveal the father of the child to her father or to anyone. Jane was very rebellious at this time and she was determined to have an abortion. Mr. Baxter was a devout Catholic and strongly opposed an abortion. He offered for Jane to live with him and he would help her go to college and help take care of the baby. However, if she did get an abortion he said he would not support her in any way and she could not live in his home.

'Mr. Baxter had always given Jane anything she wanted and let her have her way, but on this subject, he stood firm. When Jane refused the offer, Mr. Baxter came to me to rewrite his will. He set in his will that if something happened to him, Jane could only have the trust money paid out monthly, if she had her baby and provided a proper home for the child until the child was grown.

'I was instructed to have periodic home checks if she kept the child and determine if she was to get the money. As it turned out, when Mr. Baxter told Jane what he had done they had a huge confrontation. Mr. Baxter at this time also had some problems with his boss. I think Mr. Miller had not given Mr. Baxter raises for several years and when Mr. Baxter confronted Mr. Miller there was a fight. The police determined Mr. Baxter shot and killed Mr. Miller then he had a heart attack and died immediately after. Jane was very traumatized by this tragedy and she came to the conclusion the best option for her was to have her child and raise her as per her father's wishes."

"So would it be fair to say the motivation for Jane to keep her child was money, because she was adamant about an abortion?"

Mr. Mason reluctantly nodded his head and said, "That could be assumed but only Jane knows her true feeling as to why she made the choice she made. I do know Jane loves Lily and cares about her welfare."

"Thank you, Mr. Mason. When Mrs. Baxter passed away last year did she have a life insurance policy?"

Mr. Mason answered, "Yes, in the event of her death she had a hundred thousand dollar pay out that would all go to Jane."

"Mr. Mason, how did you advise Jane to use this large amount of money?"

"I advised her to invest the money in some safe bonds for her future and Lily's education. However, Jane told me she was going to invest the money in a business that she and Mr. Henson wanted to buy."

"And did they buy a business?"

Mr. Mason replied, "Yes, they bought a business called the Swing-in Bar and Grill."

"Mr. Mason, did you give Jane any other advice concerning this venture?"

"Yes, I did. I advised that since she was putting up all the money that she should take out a life insurance policy on Mr. Henson so she would get her money back if something happened to him. The nature of the business and the location of the establishment made it a high risk that Mr. Henson could get killed. I was not sure Jane could run a business by herself if she did not have a partner. Jane has no education in business nor has she ever worked outside the home. I did not want her to lose everything if something happened to Mr. Henson."

"Mr. Mason, did Jane purchase this policy on Mr. Henson as you advised?"

Mr. Mason again looked at Jane and reluctantly replied, "Yes she did."

Mr. Anthony looked at Ray-Mc and said, "Your witness."

Ray-Mc rose and approached the witness stand, "Mr. Mason, as you know sixteen year old kids make rash decision and one minute later change their mind. Do you think it is possible that Jane changed her mind when she faced the reality that her father was gone and his last wish was for her to have her child and not get an abortion?"

Mr. Mason thought a moment and said, "That is possible as she never mentioned it again. She made the decision to sell the family home and move to a small town near her mother. She told me she was going to start a new life and raise her child."

Ray-Mc then asked, "Did you ever get a negative report on the living conditions that Lily was being raised in?"

"No, in fact, the report always noted that Lily was a happy child and doing well in school. She was well liked and appeared stable."

Ray-Mc was satisfied, "I do not have any more questions."

The judge dismissed Mr. Mason and instructed Mr. Anthony to continue his case.

It was after lunch and the court room was very warm so the jury had become a little bored with the last testimony and some of them were even nodding a little with sleepy eyes. However, the next witness woke everyone up. Mr. Anthony called Miss Kitty Conway to the stand.

Through the door a petite young woman emerged. She was wearing a very tight skirt with a sweater that was low cut at the neck and fit extra snug over her more that ample breast. She had her bleached blond hair pulled back in a bun with small strands of hair curling around her face. She had a lot of make up on and the reddest lips anyone had ever seen.

When she entered the small gate into the area in front of the jury box, she stopped just a split second to look the jurors in the eye and then she proceeded to the stand. She took the oath and was seated. Every person in the court room had their eyes on her watching her every move. Kitty was used to being watched and knew how to give everyone a show. She would tilt her head and give a little smile and presented her best profile for full effect.

Ray-Mc was not amused; he leaned over to Jane and whispered, "What is she got to say that I don't know?"

Jane replied, "We may need a recess for us to talk."

Ray-Mc jumped to his feet and addressed the court, "Your honor, I object to this witness as she was not on the discovery list that was provided by the prosecution."

Mr. Anthony answered, "Your honor, it was an oversight on my part that Miss Conway was not on the list. I will not object to a recess and I will supply the defense with all the information."

The judge said, "I agree, we will recess for two hours. That will give everyone at least an hour for discussion."

Ray-Mc followed by Jane left the court room. He called Lily to accompany them to a conference room to talk. When they were in the room and Jane and Lily were seated at the table, Ray-Mc leaned over the table and stared at them both, "What do I not know here, and I mean I want all of the information. From the looks of Miss Kitty, I'm sure I'm not going to like this!"

Jane looked at Lily and said, "Lily heard something that she told me. It might not sound very good for us. I didn't think they would find out. Lily tell him what you heard."

Lily began in a very small voice, "I had forgotten my purse in the club one night when mother and I were in the car ready to leave. I ran back into the club to get it. When I was near the office I heard Jake and Kitty talking. I didn't intend to listen but they were talking loudly. Jake was telling Kitty to be patient, that in a couple of weeks everything would be in place and they could take off. Kitty said to Jake, 'you promised that you had big connections in Las Vegas and you'd get me some great jobs.' I entered the room like I had just hurried in and I saw them kissing. They quickly separated and Kitty left the room. I just grabbed my purse and ran. I debated about telling mother but I did not want her to wake up one day and Jake and Kitty be gone and her left alone at the club. So I told her what I heard. I knew the club was in trouble and I was also afraid Jake would take all the money they had if he took off."

Ray-Mc was getting red in the face as the impact of this information sank in. "Jane, this is not going to look good for you as it gives you a motive to kill Jake other than self defense. Also the insurance information has not been in our favor. Tell me every bit of dirt you can on this Kitty gal so I can try to discredit her as a reliable witness."

After Jane and Lily had told them everything they knew about Kitty, Ray-Mc stood up and headed for the door. Before he left the room he turned to Jane and said, "Don't keep anything from me again. This may be what sinks our case." Then he was gone.

Lily and Jane sat in silence for several minutes. Jane got up to leave but Lily stopped her with a question, "Mother, did you kill Jake to protect me or because you were pissed off that he was fooling around with Kitty?"

Jane stood very still, then spoke without turning around to face Lily, "Lily the damage is done, I can't change things now. You need to prepare yourself that I may not get out of this but at least we are both rid of Jake Henson." She walked out of the room without another word. For the first time, Lily contemplated the reality that she may be all alone in the world. She had never felt so desolate in her life. She was almost paralyzed with fear. The door opened and Granny walked in. "I thought you would be in here when I saw Jane leave. What's the matter you look like a ghost?"

Lily looked at Granny and tears ran down her face, "Granny, things are not going well. Some things have come out that make mother look guilty of wanting Jake dead for other reasons. I am so afraid of being alone."

Granny went to her and put her arms around her, "Lily, you always have me. I know I'm not your mother, but I will be with you until you are ready to go on your own. Don't give up yet, there's still time for Ray-Mc to do his job. You will need all the courage you can come up with as you are the next witness on the list." They walked out of the room together ready for what ever came their way.

When court reconvened, Kitty Conway was reinstated on the stand and reminded of the oath she had taken. Mr. Anthony approached the witness box and smiled at Kitty. He wanted her to be relaxed and tell all. "Miss Conway, you are looking especially lovely today, thank you for your presence. Could you state your full name please?"

Kitty smiled at Mr. Anthony and was obliviously pleased to talk to such a handsome lawyer. "My name is Kitty Jo Conway." She was very strong on the southern accent and took her time in answering. She loved being the center of attention.

"Miss Conway, would tell the court what your profession is and where you are currently employed?"

"I'm am a exotic dancer employed at the Swing-In Bar and Grill owned by Jake Henson and Jane Baxter." When Kitty said Jake's name she paused and became teary eyed.

"How long have you been an exotic dancer at the Swing-in Bar and Grill?"

"Well, about six months, I think."

"Miss Conway, how well did you get along with the defendant, Ms. Baxter?"

"Jane was not really very friendly to me or anyone. She is all work and very serious all the time. She wasn't mean to me and didn't yell at me or anything like that but she was cold."

"How did you get along with Jake Henson?"

"Oh, Jake, he was so much fun. He was always joking around and having fun. He was really nice to me." Kitty made sure when she said the last part that she looked at the jury members in a way that implied she had more to tell on this subject.

Mr. Anthony continued, "Do you know Lily Baxter?"

"Oh, yes, Lily worked at the bar. She was a dancer some of the time. She was really sweet to me and everyone liked her."

"Miss Conway, did Jake Henson ever have a conversation with you concerning your future?"

"Yes, he told me I was a really good dancer and should have a great future in entertainment. He told me he had lots of contacts in Vagas and that he knew he could get me a great job in one of those big time shows."

"Did he tell you when he might call his contacts on your behalf?"

"A few days before he passed away, he told me if I would give him a couple weeks he would get me an interview but he needed me to work for him a little while longer. He also said they were short on cash and wanted me to work a while for my tips."

"What did you think about that request?"

"I really didn't mind as I made good tips and Jake let me have my meals and drinks free."

"Miss Conway, did you have a personal relationship with Jake?"

"If you mean were we fooling around together, no. Oh, Jake would flirt and kiss me every once in a while but it never went any further than that."

"Would you have liked to have a more intense relationship with Jake?"

"Well yes, Jake was a good looking man. He told me he and Jane had a long history and he didn't want to mess that up."

"Do you know if Lily ever overheard any of the conversations that you had with Jake about your career?"

"One night, Lily came in the office after we had closed and she may have heard something but she never said or acted like she knew or expected anything."

"Thank you, Miss Conway; I do not have any more questions for you."

The Judge declared, "Your witness Mr. McRoy."

Ray-Mc approached the witness stand, he was not smiling. He wanted Kitty to be a little intimidated as he was not going to be easy with her. "Miss Conway, how old were you when you left your childhood home and went on your own?"

"I left home when I was fifteen years old." Kitty answered.

"Was there a reason you took off at such a young age?"

"We were very poor; sometimes we didn't even have food. My mother had lots of different boyfriends and some of them couldn't keep their hands off me, so I split."

"Wasn't it tough on the streets by your self?"

Mr. Anthony stood up and said, "Objection, Miss Conway is not on trial here."

The Judge addressed Ray-Mc, "Do you have a purpose in this line of questioning?"

"Yes your honor, I am just establishing a history to assess Miss Conway's character and thus her perception of the situation."

"Over ruled, but please move along to the point."

"Yes, your Honor. Miss Conway do I need me to ask the question again?"

"No, thank you, "Kitty answered curtly. "I was lucky, as I was mature for my age and attractive and I landed a job quickly."

"And what was that job?"

"I was a escort."

"What exactly does an escort do?" Ray-Mc got as close to Kitty as he could so he could look her straight in the eye to let her think he knew the truth already.

"We accompany gentlemen to different functions." Kitty was getting a little nervous and was moving around in her seat as if to straighten her skirt.

"Does the escort also provide sexual favors?" This question certainly got the jury's attention; they were all looking at Kitty.

Kitty acted offended when she replied, "No sir, the escorting position was a very professional job."

Ray-Mc decided to get to the point, "Miss Conway, have you ever been arrested?"

Kitty hesitated but knew Ray-Mc would have documentation as proof so she said, "Yes, I have."

"How many times were you arrested and for what?"

Kitty was silent so long the Judge instructed, "Miss Conway, please answer the question."

Kitty said, "I believe it was three or four times."

"I believe it was four, and what was the charge?" Ray-Mc persisted.

"OK, so it was four times and it was for prostitution." Kitty said.

"I guess you were mistaken when you answered my question about sexual favors?"

"Yes sir, I was." Kitty was no longer looking at the jury box and was very contrite.

"Miss Conway, when you are performing as an exotic dancer, do you also strip?" When Ray-Mc asked this he looked at the jury with a smirk on his face.

"Well, I usually dress in layers, so I do remove some of my clothes."

"So you really are a stripper and a prostitute." Ray-Mc raised his voice so this point was heard by everyone.

"Objection," Mr. Anthony roared, "Mr. McRoy is trying to discredit this witness but her profession has nothing to do with her testimony in this trial."

The Judge stated, "overruled, the creditability of a witness has everything to do with this trail,"

Ray-Mc said, "I do not have any more questions for this witness."

Kitty left the stand quickly. She hurried out of the court room and did not make eye contact with anyone on her way out. Ray-Mc had made his point, Kitty was a liar. However, it was sad that a child, like Kitty, had to grow up in such a bad situation that she had to resort to the streets and do what she had to so she could survive. It was also sad that someone like Jake would take advantage of Kitty and build false hopes of a better life. Ray-Mc hated to crush someone on the stand when they were the product of a cruel world. However, his client's freedom was at stake here.

CHAPTER 29

LILY

Mr. Anthony announced he was calling his last witness, Miss Lily Baxter.

Lily was called into the court room and took the oath. Lily was dressed conservatively in an A-line skirt that was grey with a black turtle neck sweater. The jurors were surprised to see the strong resemblance between Lily and Jane. The most noted features were their jet black hair and their emerald green eyes.

Mr. Anthony said, "Please state your full name."

"Lily Rose Baxter."

"How are you related to the defendant?" Mr. Anthony asked even though it was obvious.

"Jane Baxter is my mother," Lily answered.

"Who is your father?"

Lily looked at her mother and answered, "My father was killed overseas in the military before I was born. He and my mother were not married."

Mr. Anthony asked, "Has it always been just you and your mother living together."

"We lived by ourselves until I was around six years old. Then Jake Henson began to live with us." Lily answered and decided to put everything on the line so there would be no doubt that she was telling the truth.

"How would you describe your relationship with your mother?"

"My mother always provided me all the essentials in life. She is not a very warm person and does not show her emotions. I do know she loves me."

"How did you and Mr. Henson get along?"

"Jake barely acknowledged that I was around. He chose to ignore my presence. So you could say we did not have a relationship at all."

"We have learned that you got your nurturing from Vivian Watson whom you call Granny. Is that a fair statement?"

"Yes, I spend a lot of time with Granny. I love her dearly and will always be grateful for her in my life." Lily looked at Granny in the court room and smiled her appreciation to her.

Mr. Anthony paused to review his notes; he presented his next question, "Lily, what were the circumstances that led to you working at the Swing-in Bar and Grill that Mr. Henson and your mother owned."

Lily knew this was coming and she tried to remain strong and calm, "The business was a little slow to start off so mother said I needed to pitch in to help since it was summer and I was out of school. So I started going in with them to help out." Lily looked at Jane while she talked.

"What exactly did you do at the bar?"

"I waited on tables, cleaned off tables and worked in the kitchen cooking and washing dishes."

Mr. Anthony waited to see if Lily was going to say more and when she didn't he continued. "Did you have anything to do with the entertainment in the bar?"

Lily looked Mr. Anthony in the eyes and said, "I did some exotic dancing along with Kitty."

Mr. Anthony looked at the jury and said, "We have already established what the exotic dancing consist of according to the other dancer, Miss Kitty Conway."

Ray-Mc objected to that on the grounds that Mr. Anthony was making speeches instead of asking questions. The Judge agreed but the damage was done as the jurors were replaying Kitty Conway's testimony in their head.

"Lily were you aware that you were under-aged and it was illegal for you to be working in the bar under any circumstances?"

"Yes, I was."

"And what happened along those lines?"

Lily reluctantly began her answer, "We were raided and Jake, mother and I were arrested."

"Were any of you charged?"

"No, as this was the first offense for me, I was put on probation. Jake and mother were given a fine and a warning."

"Lily, did this raid get in the media?"

Lily lowered her head and said, "Yes it made the front page of the paper."

Mr. Anthony held up a newspaper and slowly walked down the jury box so all the jurors could get a good look of a full body shot of Lily in her dancing attire. He then gave the judge the paper to look at.

Mr. Anthony asked Lily, "How did this affect your school life?"

Lily said, "When I started my senior year, I was supposed to be on the cheerleading squad but was told I could not be on the squad as I had set a bad example for students. I was also ejected from the debate team."

Mr. Anthony went farther, "What happened with your boyfriend, I believe he had been accepted at Harvard."

"We broke up." Lily said quietly.

"I guess his family was not thrilled to have an exotic dancer/stripper in the family?"

Ray-Mc jumped to his feet, "Objection, Mr. Anthony can't presume what the boyfriend's family thought."

"Sustained," The judge said, "Mr. Anthony, you need to watch yourself. I think you know the rules."

"Yes your honor, I am sorry," Mr. Anthony said but, again he had gotten his point across.

Mr. Anthony said, "Lily how did that make you feel toward your mother and Jake when they had literally ruined your senior year in high school and implemented the break up with your boyfriend?"

Lily remained calm and said, "I was really sad about my senior year."

"Come on, Lily, were you not mad as hell that your mom and Mr. Henson had completely changed your life?"

"Yes, I was very upset." Lily admitted.

"Lily," Mr. Anthony got very close to the witness box and looked at Lily, "What did you hear Kitty Conway say to Mr. Henson the night they did not know you were there?"

"I heard Kitty ask Jake when he was going to use his contacts in Vagas and help her get a good job out there. Then Jake said to give him two more weeks and he would have everything worked out and he would take care of her. When I walked in, Kitty was saying he would not regret it and she kissed him."

"Did you think that Kitty and Mr. Henson were having an affair and planning to leave together?"

"I didn't know what to think."

Mr. Anthony said, "Did you think your mother would think that if she had the information?"

"I didn't know what mother would think."

"Did you tell your mother what you heard?" Mr. Anthony looked at Jane as he asked this question.

"Yes I did. I didn't want mother to be blindsided or left holding the bag?"

"By the bag do you mean the Swing-in Bar and Grill that was not doing so well financially?"

"Yes sir, that's what I meant," Lily responded.

"Lily, in your upset, angry state of mind, were you hoping to get a little revenge and maybe told your mother a story slanted toward Mr. Henson and Miss Kitty having an affair?"

Lily began to get tears in her eyes, "I did not intentionally want to cause trouble, I was just hurt and acted badly. "Lily looked at Jane and said, "Mother, I'm so sorry, I am so sorry." Lily began to cry.

Ray-Mc stood and requested a recess which was granted.

After the recess, Mr. Anthony began again, "Lily, I'm sorry to upset you, but I need to ask you a few more questions. When Mr. Henson came into your room that night, what did he say and do to you."

"Well, he was drunk and he was mad. He insisted that I dance at the bar. He said I was a spoiled brat and I was going to have to dance along with Kitty even if I did not want to. I told him that I could not dance because if I was arrested again, I would be put in jail. When I said that he slapped me and I fell on the bed. Then he jumped on me and started hitting me with his fist. I nearly blacked out but then I heard mother shout at him to let me go."

Lily began to cry again, "that's when Jake stopped hitting me. He stood up and turned around. The next thing I hear was the gun shot. Then he fell."

Mr. Anthony walked back to his table and said, "Lily, it is very important that you answer this question honestly and not just what you think your mother wants you to say. Do you think Jane shot Mr. Henson out of fear that he was going to hurt or kill you or do you think she was mad and jealous and wanted revenge?"

Lily took her time in answering even to the point that the judge requested that she answer the question. "I do not know what was on mother's mind or in her heart. I just know that I was in trouble and she came to my rescue. I truly think Jake would have severely hurt me or killed me if she had not intervened."

Mr. Anthony walked back to his table and reviewed his notes for a minute then he said, "Lily, I have one more question for you. Do you think your mother was having second thoughts about the business adventure she and Jake Henson were in and thought the insurance money would at least get her money back?"

Lily gave a surprised look at Mr. Anthony that turned to anger, "No, my mother never would have killed anyone for money. I don't think that thought crossed her mind."

Mr. Anthony sat down at his table and announced that he had no more questions for Miss Baxter. He felt good that he had gotten the money motive injected into the testimony. It had to help his case.

Ray-Mc stood and slowly walked to the witness box, "Lily I am not going to prolong your ordeal but I need to ask a few questions. Do you love your mother?'

"Yes sir, I do, very much." Lily said.

Ray-Mc continued, "Did Jake Henson take advantage of your mother during the time they lived together?"

"Yes, he took money from her, lived with us for nothing, came and went as he pleased and in the end was very abusive. He had started hitting mother on a daily basis."

"Do you think Jane was afraid of Mr. Henson?"

"Yes, especially in the end when he became so mad all the time and was violent."

"So after Mr. Henson and Jane bought the bar, would you say that's when Jake became aggressive?"

Lily answered very positively, "Yes, since he was at the bar most of the time, he drank a lot more than before. He was rubbing elbows with all kinds of tough guys and developed a very hard core approach to everyone. At the bar he treated mother like dirt and yelled at her all the time. I think he was showing off for the other men and did not like it that mother had put in all the money."

"So, with this change in Mr. Henson, do you think it is reasonable, for your mother to believe that he was capable and in fact would kill you and possibly her?"

"Absolutely, Jake was progressively getting worse and that night he was very drunk." Lily was very convincing.

Ray-Mc turned and went back to his table, "No more questions, your Honor."

The judge stated, "The witness is dismissed."

Lily felt drained and miserable. She knew what she said was strong and convincing but did not know if it had helped her mother's case. She looked at her mother as she walked from the stand. Jane's face was completely blank.

Jane could not honestly know in her heart what her motive was when she killed Jake. She could only remember a voice in her brain saying "Kill him, kill him". At the time, she did not harbor any bad will toward Jake, nor did she particularly feel she was protecting her child. She just did what she was being told by the voice that she had held in check for a long time. However, once again, from out of the shadows of her mind came the voice. She had no will to block it out and she just reacted. The events of the trial were looking as if Jane might pay a higher price this time for following the voice in her head and killing another human being.

Mr. Anthony stood and said, "Your honor the prosecution rest."

The Judge responded, "Mr. McCoy you will call your first witness for the defense first thing in the morning. Court is dismissed for today."

After court was convened the next day, Ray-Mc started the day by announcing that Jane Baxter would not be testifying in her defense. He then called a series of professional witnesses all working in the family relationship fields. Among them were a child physiologist's, a social service expert and some scientists that specialized in mind studies for instinctual responses in animals and humans. He worked to establish that there is a mother and child connection that causes an instinctual response to protect the child if they are in danger or in perceived danger. He reviewed scientific observation of animals and people when a mother would protect her off spring no matter what the danger was to her.

Ray-Mc's next witness was Debbie Sampson, MD. After she was sworn in, he asked his first question, "Dr. Sampson please tell the court your profession."

Debbie answered, "I am a clinical psychiatrist and have practiced for 20 years. I also have a doctorate in criminal justice."

"How many times have you been called for testimony to assess the mental condition of a defendant?"

"I have testified in over 100 trials over the years. Sometimes I have testified for the defendant and sometimes for the state."

Ray-Mc asked, "Did you complete a clinical analysis on Ms. Baxter?"

Debbie answered, "Yes. I completed 24 sessions with Ms. Baxter. I found her corporative and willing to work with me in this short time. I prefer a longer period of time to make a more complete analysis with someone as complex as Ms. Baxter. I believe it will take a life time of counseling to help Ms. Baxter dig deep enough within herself to find who she really is and the reasons why she does the things she does. However, I feel confident that I have a good handle on this diagnosis."

Ray-Mc asked, "And what did you determine as the diagnosis?"

"I found that Ms. Baxter has a history of mental illness in her family. Her mother was institutionalized for many years and died in a complete comatose state. Ms. Baxter was traumatized in childhood by her mother's condition. She also witnessed her father's death when she was 16 years old. As a single parent, Ms. Baxter was conflicted with feelings of inadequacies as a parent and doubted her feelings for her daughter. She suffered considerable abuse at the hands of Mr. Henson. I found her to have limited social skills with obsessive tendencies toward Mr. Henson. She has impulse control problems and unrealistic visions of the future. I diagnose her as being bi-polar with borderline destructive mood disorder."

Ray-Mc asked, "Dr. Sampson could you tell us how the diagnosis you made on Ms. Baxter could have caused her to shoot Mr. Henson?"

"Ms. Baxter definitely would have been protective of her daughter, Lily. However, as obsessive as she was about Mr. Henson, she would have been inconsolable if she thought he was being unfaithful or leaving her. Her lack of impulse control would have prevented her from making any other decision when she saw Mr. Henson attacking her daughter other than to kill him."

Ray-Mc then completed his questioning, "So, if I may summarize, are you saying that whether the reason Ms. Baxter shot Mr. Henson was to protect Lily or because she thought Mr. Henson was unfaithful, Ms. Baxter would have killed him either way?"

Debbie concluded, "I would have to agree with that. I would venture to add that Ms. Baxter probably does not know her reasoning for her pulling that trigger any more that we do."

Ray-Mc turned to Mr. Anthony and said, "No more questions."

Mr. Anthony stood and addressed the judge, "I have no questions for this witness, your honor."

The Judge said, "You may step down Dr. Sampson."

Ray-Mc's defense was very impressive but he was not sure if the jury was convinced. He knew that he had taken a big chance by having Dr. Sampson testify that Jane could have another motive for killing Jake. He was hoping that the reasonable doubt would register with the jury as to Jane's motive and they would opt that she was protecting Lily. Only time would tell and he was afraid that time was running out for Jane. At the end of the day, Ray-Mc stood and addressed the Judge, "Your honor, the defense rest."

The Judge stated, "Tomorrow morning both sides will present their closing statements. We are adjourned for today."

CHAPTER 30

JANE

The next morning after the Judge called order, Mr. Anthony slowly walked in front of the jury box. He made eye contact with each juror. He wanted to have a personal contact with each one of the jurors so they would be listening to every word he said. "Ladies and Gentlemen, this is a very tough case. We have a beautiful, single mother who has raised a lovely, sweet daughter. However, we have learned that Jane Baxter was not your normal, loving parent. Mrs. Watson, Jane's neighbor was responsible for the majority of the Lily's raising. Mrs. Watson was the force behind Lily being a good student and an obedient young girl.

'We have also discovered that Jane is deep into alcohol addiction. She spent a lot of the time drinking or passed out drunk. As per the testimony by Dr. Sampson, Jane has extensive mental problems. Then along comes Jake Henson. He basically was a parasite to Jane. He soaked up her money and lived with her for nothing. He then talked her into investing all her insurance money from her mother's death, into a sleazy business, the Swing-in Bar and Grill. He began beating Jane on a regular basis as times got tough at the bar. As if that was not enough, he demanded Jane bring in her sixteen year old daughter to work and dance.

'We did establish that the dancing was actually stripping. The bar was raided and Lily was arrested and plastered all over the news papers. Lily's reputation was ruined. She is off the cheerleading squad and off the debate team. On top of all this her boyfriend dumps her. Lily certainly did not have good feelings toward Mr. Henson. Even if she did not intend to, she made an incident she had seen between Mr. Henson and Kitty Conway sound like an affair when she informed her mother of what she

saw. She also hinted that Mr. Henson and Kitty were going to run off together,

'Jane was the one that gunned him down by shooting him straight through the heart. I agree that the fact that he was beating Lily could have been a self defense move by her mother. However, there could have been other ways to protect Lily besides shooting Mr. Henson. We have other facts that show another motive to get rid of Mr. Henson. The business was declining and there was a chance they would go under and all the invested money would be gone. Remember all the money was invested by Jane. Jane had a life insurance policy on Mr. Henson for one hundred thousand dollars. That insurance money on Mr. Henson would at least return Jane her investment.

'Mr. McCoy will argue that Jane was protecting her daughter. He spent a lot of time educating us on the inborn instinct of a mother to protect her young. However, there are a lot of cases where animals actually eat their young and many cases where human mothers kill their own children. There is no way to know if Jane was defending her child by instinct. Where was Lily's mother when she was growing up and why did she not protect her against illegally working in a bar and being a stripper? Jane's history does not scream that she is protective or even concerned with Lily or her welfare. We even learned that when Jane was a pregnant sixteen year old she wanted to get an abortion but her father attached his support on the condition she have her baby. Therefore, Jane is forced to have the baby who turned out to be a beautiful, sweet daughter, Lily.

'Mr. Henson was unarmed, why did Jane not just wound him? Why not just grab Lily and run? How convenient to all of a sudden, for Jane to become the protective mother of her daughter who is being beaten. Jane certainly had more to gain from Mr. Henson being dead because of the money from the insurance police and also he was possibly cheating on her. A scorned woman has no limits. I hope you all will search your soul and I think you will see, with all the evidence, that Jane Baxter took the opportunity to get rid of her problem, which was Mr. Henson. She murdered him in cold blood and deserves to pay the price for her actions. Thank you." Mr. Anthony again looked at each juror before he returned to his table.

The judge then stated that Mr. McRoy would present his final statements.

Ray-Mc was determined to do all he could to win this case. He presented himself with confidence and marched up to the juror's box. He stated in a strong voice, "Ladies and gentlemen, through-out time when the first woman had a child, there was a bond between that woman and her child. This is an instinct that is in a mother's genes. As you have heard from many experts on this subject, a mother will react from instinct to save her child. This reaction does not hinge on past history or outside circumstances. This reaction to save their child cannot be denied. Jane Baxter heard Lily screaming. She walked into the bedroom and saw Jake Henson beating Lily. Mr. Henson is a big man. He had huge arms and muscles. He could easily kill Lily with his bare hands. Jane knows she would not be a match for Mr. Henson, who was also drunk and in a rage. Jane knew that in the recent past, Mr. Henson had become more and more aggressive. He had been hitting her on a daily basis. She does the only thing that she can think of that would stop Jake. She grabs her gun and reacts. She shoots him. This is self-defense, protecting her child and herself was the only thing on her mind. Please, send this woman home to be with her daughter. Lily is a beautiful, innocent teenager who needs her mother. Thank you."

After Ray-Mc returned to his desk, the Judge began a long and boring speech to the jury. He laid down all the laws and rules that they must abide by in order to come to a fair and supportable verdict. After thirty minutes the speech finally ended and the jury was sent out to start their deliberation. Ray-Mc had a heavy heart as he felt he did not see mercy in the eyes of the jurors. He felt he noted several jurors turn cold, hard eyes on Jane. Even though he believed Jane was protecting Lily, he did feel coldness from Jane that made him doubt that Jane did not have other motives in her mind when she pulled the trigger. But it was out of his hands. He felt he had done the best he could. It was up to the jury now.

CHAPTER 31

GRANNY AND LILY

That night, Jane and Lily sat across from each other at the small kitchen table in their house. Neither one of them had touched their meal nor had they talked to each other.

Finally, Jane spoke, "Lily, I want you to know that things did not go well in the court room. The prosecutor has a strong case. If the jury finds me guilty of manslaughter, it will mean I will go to prison. I want you to know you will have enough money to live on and go to school, from the trust. I talked to Granny, and she wants you to live with her until you graduate. So you will have a home.

'I know I have not been a great mother to you. I have allowed my self to fall into addiction when I should have resisted. I brought Jake into our lives and he was trouble. I will accept any verdict and sentence because I have done bad things in my life. I have hurt many people that didn't deserve it. I know I have evil in me like my mother had. When I saw Jake hurting you, the voice in my head was shouting "Kill him, Kill him". My mother told me that the voices in her head said the same thing when she tried to kill my father. She adored my father, but the voice was so controlling, that she attempted to kill him.

'Even if they find me not guilty, I know I need help. I am so sorry for what I have done but if I don't get help, I may do something worse than I already have. Please, go on with your life. Make something of yourself and be strong and independent. If I go to jail, I do not want you to visit me. We can write but I don't want you to waste your time visiting me." Jane stopped talking and had tears in her eyes.

Lily was crying softly. Jane slowly reached for Lily's hand and held on to it like her life depended on it. At that moment, Lily felt sure, that

Jane did love her and killed Jake to protect her. It was the first time she had ever felt a bond between the two of them. They sat that way a long time before they both went to bed. In the middle of the night, Jane slid into Lily's bed and hugged Lily to her the rest of the night. They both thought they were ready for the verdict.

The next day the jury was ready with a verdict. Everyone assembled in the court room. Lily and Granny sat together behind Jane. The Judge stated that the defendant and her lawyer were to stand and he asked the jury foreman to read the verdict. The foreman stood and began, "We the jury find the defendant, Elizabeth Jane Baxter, guilty of murder in the second degree in the death of Mr. Jake Henson."

The Judge said, "The verdict is guilty. I will set a sentence tomorrow morning. Court is dismissed." The judge banged the gavel on the bench and rose to leave.

Two guards moved behind Jane and put handcuffs on her and led her out of the court room. Lily bent over as if she had been punched in the stomach. She was sobbing. Granny held Lily's head in her lap and rubbed her back until she became calmer.

Lily said, "Granny, this hurts so much! I have no mother now. I am an orphan."

Granny continued to rub Lily's back and said, "I know it hurts and the hurt never really goes away. However, it will eventually become more bearable.

'I want to tell you a story. When I was your age, I met a young man that stole my heart. We were so in love we ran off and got married. The next year I became pregnant. We were so excited about having a baby.

'I had a very hard pregnancy and almost died giving birth. But when I saw our baby girl, all the pain disappeared. She was the most beautiful baby in the world. I held her in my arms for two hours, then she just slipped away and God took her to be with him. I thought I would die when we buried our sweet angle. Why would God give me this precious gift and then take her away so quickly. Of course, I didn't die like I wanted and the world kept turning and time moved on.

'We tried to have another child but I never became pregnant again. Ten years later, my husband passed away from cancer. The only good thing was, he didn't suffer a lot and he was gone quickly. I know he is with our daughter but I thought I would surely die this time as I was all alone. Again I didn't die. The hurt is still there and I know it will not go away.

You will get better with time. For now, you have to get up and we will go home." They left the empty court room together. Lily was thankful to have Granny. Even though she loved her mother, Granny was and always would be her lifeline.

The next day they all, for the last time, assembled in the court room. The Judge requested the defendant to stand. He then said, "Elizabeth Jane Baxter, you have been found guilty of manslaughter by a jury of your peers. In reviewing this case, I am disappointed in your parenting skills. I feel you have neglected your duties as a mother to protect your child and by encouraging her to participate in illegal acts. So I am also outraged that you would attempt to hide behind your daughter in order to get rid of your lover and business partner. Therefore, I am giving you the maximum sentence which is no less than eight years and no more than ten years in prison. That means you cannot be paroled until you have spent at least eight years in the Women's Correctional Institution. I suggest as you are a young woman, that you utilize this time to get your life together and become a better citizen of this country. You also need to make amends to your daughter for not giving her the stability she deserved as a child. Guards please, remove the prisoner. Court dismissed."

Jane looked back at Lily, who was crying and she mouthed, "I love you." Then she was gone.

Lily was better prepared today than yesterday. She left the court room with Granny holding her hand as she cried quietly.

CHAPTER 32

JANE

J ane was scared for the first time in her life. She did not like the fact that she had no control over any part of her life for the next eight or more years. The next day she was loaded on a bus with several other inmates. She had cuffs on her hands and chains around her ankles. As the bus drove across the state, Jane watched the landscape and knew she would not see this again for a long, long time. She was afraid of having to go into detox cold turkey. It had been years since she had gone a day without a drink. She had never attempted to stop drinking.

The first week that Jane was in prison, she was in a cell alone. The warden had her in a solitary area with extra observation as she knew this was going to be tough on Jane. However, Jane would have to tough it out. The first day Jane became very nervous then she began to have the shakes. Next, she ran a fever and had a pounding head ach. By the end of the first day, she was sweating profusely and crying for help. Help was near, watching but not interfering. For three days Jane's body rebelled from not having alcohol. She had illusions and screamed in pain and fear. It was five days before she was able to sleep then she slept for twenty four hours.

When she awoke, the guard went into the cell and said, "It's been a rough few days, but I think you have made it. I'll take you for a shower and get you something to eat. Then you will go to your new home in a cell with another prisoner. Follow me."

The days after detox were still rough because Jane still wanted a drink but other than that, her days were much the same routine. She was assigned to several jobs, from working in the kitchen to doing laundry.

She was numb and went through the motions. She did not know how she would do this for eight years.

Every prisoner had to attend sessions with a counselor, so Jane began her therapy. In accordance with the diagnosis of Dr. Sampson, Jane was given several medications and after a few weeks she began to come out of the fog and she began to think more clearly. She felt calm and was better than she had ever been in her life. She realized life could have been so different if she had known she could be helped with medicine.

Jane began to see the damage she had caused and the people she had hurt. For the first time in her life, she felt empathy for all the people she had hurt in the past. Her biggest worry was how she had affected Lily. She was in awe that Lily was such a wonderful daughter in spite of her poor parenting skills. Jane hoped she would get a chance to show Lily how much she loved her and maybe even be a part of her life again. She had a long time to work out her problems and try to keep the lines of communication open with Lily. Hopefully she would have the rest of her life, when she got out of prison, to make up for the time she had wasted when Lily was a child.

Jane would never be cured of her addiction and she would have to work at getting better all the time. She and Lily were exchanging letters regularly and Lily was very happy to see the changes in her mother. They were able to write all their feelings in these letters so for the first time in their life; they began to know each other.

One day the guard came and delivered a letter to Jane. Jane knew she was not due a letter from Lily so who could it be from? She opened the letter and read it:

Dear Jane,

I am a friend from your past. I have kept up with you throughout your life without your knowledge. I felt you might need a friend just now and felt compelled to write to you. I have learned that you are on medication to control the mental imbalances that you have. I am very happy you are doing so well. I just want to encourage you to take advantage of your incarceration to prepare yourself for a productive life when you get out. I would suggest that you look into the educational opportunities that you have in the institution. I happen to know the prison where you are is very proactive in educational opportunities for prisoners. You are smart and I know you could do well. I will write again sometime but for now just know you have a

Sincere Friend

Jane had no idea who could have written this letter, but it did give her some things to think about. The letter prompted her to look into taking college courses. She tried not to dwell on who her "sincere friend" was but take it as an omen. One month later another letter came, this one included an address for her to write in return, but still no name. Jane wrote back and the correspondence became a big part of her life. She had the odd feeling that she could tell this friend anything and she would not be judged. Jane actually found being in prison a good environment for her to be diagnosed and treated for her mental illness. Jane functioned well having a strict structure to her life. She knew when she would eat, work, study and write her letters. She did what she was told and followed the rules. The routine made it easier to deal with her past and start healing a little at a time. In the dark cells of prison, the light was beginning to clear away shadows that had covered Jane's mind and actions all her life.

PART TWO

CHAPTER 1

LILY

G ranny stood at the bus station waving good bye as Lily's bus pulled away. Granny was very sad to see her go but was excited that she had been accepted at a good university in California. After the trial, Lily had lived with Granny the rest of her senior year in high school. It was the best year in Granny's life, but she knew it would come to an end. She would never hold Lily back from pursuing her career. She also wanted Lily to get away from this town where the gossip about Jane and Lily was still a hot item. Granny wanted Lily to start a new life and she thanked God for her time with Lily.

Lily arrived in California on the bus after a long ride. She was exhausted but excited to start a new life. She had made contact with another student that was looking for a room mate so she had an apartment waiting on her. The only way she could leave all the past behind her was to move on. She did not want to forget her past; she just did not want it to define how she would live the rest of her life.

Lily was a stable person emotionally even though she had a very difficult childhood. The main void that Lily felt was that she did not have a relationship with her mother. That could have been devastating to Lily in developing other relationships, if it were not for Granny. Granny showed Lily what it was like to have someone who was totally interested in her well being and development. That left Lily with a deep appreciation for Granny and she hoped to be an important influence in someone else's life.

Of course if she had a child, she would definitely develop the connection with her child that her mother did not pursue with her. But if she had an opportunity, maybe she could be am important part of someone's life who was not related to her the way Granny had been in her life. Lily also had a deep desire to help women be independent and not to look for a man to make their decisions and put limits on their life. Lily felt that if Jane were able to stand up for her self she would not have let Jake take over her life. Those kinds of relationships nearly always end in disaster. In her case, that disaster included Lily as an innocent child in the middle, a man dead and her mother in prison. Lily thought that if she could get her education in law she could defend women that had been caught up in a harmful relationship.

Lily also wanted to be an advocate for children caught in a situation that they had no control over. In some ways the life that Lily led had inspired her to help people that were held deep in the shadows of child abuse, addiction, spousal abuse and mental illness. She knew she had to get all the education she could in order to be effective in her endeavor. It seemed like a long road because school would be at least six years or longer. At nineteen, Lily had a hard time seeing the big picture but she knew she had to get started.

Lily was very intelligent and she read many different types of books in her life therefore, she was very well rounded. The first four years of college were very enjoyable. Lily made lots of friends consisting of both women and men friends. She did not date but went out with groups. Long term romantic relationships were not what she was looking for because she had other goals. She was accepted to law school due to having excellent grades and being active in student affairs. Lily was very surprised that the first four years of undergraduate study went by so fast.

The summer before Lily was to start law school, she received the call that she knew would come sometime. Granny had a stroke and was in the hospital. The prognosis was grave. Lily immediately took a flight home to be with Granny. When Lily got to the hospital and she entered Granny's room, she was asleep. Lily sat down by the bed and took Granny's hand into her hand.

Without opening her eyes, Granny said, "Lily, I know that's you."

Lily answered, "Yes, Granny. I'm here. How did you know it was me?"

Granny opened her eyes, "I could feel you in my heart. I knew you would come but I'm sorry it's under these circumstances."

Granny was very weak. Lily sat with her day and night. She slept in a chair in the room so she would be close if something happened. On the second night, Granny called out for Lily; she said, "Lily, I saw my dear husband and he was holding our sweet baby. He wanted me to come and be with them. I'm really tired and I think it is time for me to go. I hate to leave you, but you are strong and you will make a good life for yourself." She drifted off to sleep and after an hour, Granny slipped away to be with her family. Lily was devastated and did not have any idea what to do next. However, Granny had made all the arrangements for the funeral. She even had the dress picked out that she wanted to be buried in.

On the day of the funeral, Lily was very surprised at the number of people that attended the service. She didn't realize how many people knew and loved Granny. The church service was beautiful and the day bright and sunny at the cemetery. Later that afternoon, Lily returned to the cemetery alone to have a quiet time with Granny.

Granny was buried between her husband and the tiny grave of her baby girl. Lily read the headstone that Granny shared with her husband. Written on Granny's side was Vivian Rose Watson. Lily did not know Granny's middle name was Rose. Then under the name it said "loving wife and Mother of two Roses". Lily was puzzled at that until she read what was written on the stone on the tiny grave next to Granny which said "God took her to heaven to be with him, but she was our Rose Marie". Lily had not known the name of Granny's baby either. Lily was in a lot of pain and once again felt alone in the world. She remembered something Granny told her that she knew she must remember to make her feel better. Granny had told her that deep emotional pain never went away but it got easier with time. Lily would just have to see if that was true for her and her pain.

Lily found law school to be a different story from undergraduate studies as far as school goes. The increased intensity of studying was staggering. The main difference was the amount of self motivation necessary to keep up. The attitude of the professors was different. They did not have the personal interest in a student making the grade. You either did well enough to pass or you were out. Because of this shift of attitude of the facility, students became more dependent on each other. Some students wished to stay independent but most sought out students of similar work ethics and interest and bonded together.

Study groups of about four to six students formed. Since law consists of a massive amount of material which is subjective, it is essential that the ideas of individuals in the group are shared, analyzed and a solution agreed upon. These groups met several times a week at different places. Group study members would naturally get close to each other because of the time they spent together however they tried to keep their feelings for each other strictly professional. This helped keep conflict at a minimum and the environment calm and conducive for learning.

Lily found a group that she felt she clicked with. There were two women and two men in her group. The other woman in the group was also Lily's roommate. Her name was Anna Fisher. She was very petite with long brown hair. She was easy going, very smart and she and Lily bonded. The two men in the group were very different from each other. Gary was very intense. Even thought he was very smart, he lacked some common sense and did not have good people skills. Gary was married and his wife was a student in undergrad studies.

Then there was John Jackson. He was not married and came from an extremely rich family. His dad was a lawyer who also owned a very large law practice. John's father, Mr. Jack Jackson, was a self-made man and he expected John to make his way on his own. He did not indulge John in the extra things that you would think the son of a rich family would have.

John was smart and did not have to study very hard. He loved to have fun and he had a good since of humor. The fact that he was also very handsome made him very popular with the girls. At first, Lily did not think John was a good fit for their group. She felt he might not be as dedicated or serious about the material they were going to be covering. But he did add some fun to the group and kept the mood lively. He appeared to hold up his end of the study material so she decided to give him the benefit of the doubt.

The way the group worked was they divided the reading material load. Each member took part of the material, read it, made notes to share and made an analysis on the material for the group to discuss. At the meetings each person would present their material with a copy of the notes. Then they discussed each case and came to a conclusion. Due to the amount of material that each instructor gave for the students to cover, it was almost impossible for one person to cover it all. Being in a functional group was an important part of being able to do well in law school. These groups worked very well if everyone in the group did their part. Trust in each other was essential for the group to work together well.

During the second year of law school, John started to become interested in Lily. One night after a meeting, John asked to walk Lily and Anna home. They thought this was fine and it became a routine. Lily actually thought John was interested in Anna. So she tried to give them some private time together by making excuses that she had other things to do or go to bed early when John came in for a drink.

After the third year started, John asked Lily if he could talk to her so they walked home together. Lily thought John wanted to talk about Anna with her.

John said, "Lily, I know you think I am interested in Anna. But the truth is I would like to spend some time with you. If you're okay with that, we will talk to the group to see if they have any issue about it. After two years having a successful relationship with the group, I don't think they would have a problem with it. What do you think?"

Lily stopped walking and looked at John, "John, I thought you and Anna made a good couple. So I have not thought of you in any other way but in the group and in being a couple with Anna. I think you are a great guy, but I have a lot of baggage with me. I have not had a nice, rosy life like you have had. There are some members of my family that have mental problems. You have no idea what you are asking to get involved with."

John smiled and took her hand, "believe me, being from a rich family does not mean it was rosy. We have as much drama in our lives as anyone else. I have spent enough time with you to know you are an intelligent, beautiful and kind person. I don't care about your past. I care for you and want to get to know you better. Could we try to get to know each other better and go on a real date?"

Lily thought for a minute then said, "Okay, let's give it a try."

When presented to the group that they wanted to date, Lily and John were told that it was alright with them as long as the integrity of the goal for the group was in tact. John and Lily began to see each other every day. They quickly went a step further and had sexual relations. John was very sweet and thoughtful with Lily. He did not rush her and wanted her to be happy. Their love life seemed fulfilling for both of them. Lily began to believe John might be the one for her. John knew Lily was the only woman in the world for him. Lily and John spent a great deal of time together but were still intent on doing well in school

John was very easy going and was the life of the party but he did not have any close friends. He enjoyed Lily because they could talk about law or anything they wanted to. The only subject that John would not go into details was about his family. He was an only child and had what he considered a normal but privileged childhood. This was the end of his description of his family. He did not discuss that his famous father was a bully and a tyrant. He did not tell her that he hated his father. He did tell Lily that his mother was the most wonderful, beautiful, caring and loving woman alive. He adored his mother and attributed all that he was to her.

Lily gave a scant description of her childhood. She left out that her grandfather was accused of killing his boss and died of a heart attack at the time. She did not discuss that her mother was in prison for murder. Nor did she disclose that her grandmother was committed to the insane institution until she died. She left out about being a dancer in a strip club and being arrested once. She did talk about Granny in great detail as Granny was the center of her life and the best part of her life. The bottom line was both these young lovers had big secrets so there was a gap in their knowledge of each other from the start. These secrets were sure to damage their relationship.

CHAPTER 2

JOHN AND JACK

After being together for over a year and with just a few months until graduation, John wanted Lily to meet his parents, his mother in particular. Lily was very nervous about this but if they were to continue to see each other it was inevitable. They planned a trip to John's home during spring break. The weather was getting very spring-like and Lily was looking forward to the trip but not very excited about meeting the parents.

John picked Lily up in his snazzy sports car. The car had been a present from his mother. John's dad was adamantly against him getting the car. However, this was one time that John's mother had persisted and went against John's father. As John packed the car, he barely had room for the luggage and in fact, Lily had to abandon one piece of her luggage. Lily didn't mind as this was an adventure. The day was beautiful and John had the top down on the car. As they sailed along the interstate, Lily was in heaven. She felt like all her problems were blowing away. John was very happy at the beginning of the trip but he got more and more quiet as they got near his home.

John looked at Lily and said, "You look so beautiful. I know my mother will absolutely love you. I know you two will get along very well. She has the same sunny attitude as you do."

Lily commented, "I hope she likes me. I know she is a great lady. What about your dad?"

John looked very stern when he said, "He is very proper and stern. You just have to take him as he is. He won't be around much anyway. I don't even know what kind of a mood he will be in as he is in a very high stress job. Sometimes he brings home the stress." What John did not tell

Lily was that his dad was a controlling person and expected everyone to jump when he was around. John and his dad did not get along at all. John started talking again, "We will have a great time. We can ride horses. We have a beautiful stable. We can walk in the woods, play some tennis and swim. Thank you for coming with me. I do love your company."

Lily was impressed and said, "Thank you for asking me. I love being with you. This will be such a welcome break from school."

John said, "Not far now." Lily noted he had a very serious look on his face. He hardly ever appeared stressed or tense but now he was both. Lily thought something was wrong, but she let that thought fade away. This was too much fun for it to be spoiled by her assumptions.

Suddenly John turned off the main road onto a small paved road that passed through two huge brick columns with lion statues on the top of them. John slowed down and said, "This is it, the beginning of our estate." He then approached an iron gate. On the drivers side of the car was a post with a control panel on it. John punched in a six digit number and the gates opened. Lily was looking for a house, "Where is the house?" she asked, "I only see a road and forest."

John floored the accelerator and squealed the tires which surprised Lily and he said, "You'll see soon enough."

They drove about a mile and the scenery was absolutely breath taking, but no house yet. Then they went around a big curve and the forest stopped. The land which was perfectly mown opened up on both sides of the road and up ahead was a startling view. A circular drive went around a huge water fountain that was shooting water high into the air then the water fell over several structures creating a water fall that ended in a large pool. Behind the fountain was a mansion like Lily had never seen before. It had huge columns in front of a three story gothic structure. Then on each side of the main structure a two story wing ran in opposite directions. There were so many beautiful things to see that Lily was stunned.

John jumped out of the car and ran around to Lily's side and opened her door. He bowed deeply and said, "Madam, may I present my modest residence." Lily laughed and stepped out of the car. John hugged her before they walked up to the front door.

John threw the door open and ran in yelling, "Mother, I'm home! Where are you? Come see who I have brought for you to meet."

John's mother appeared at the top of the magnificent staircase that went straight up the middle of a huge entry hall. At the top there was a platform then a stair case ran up on each side of the platform. John's mother was dressed in a sun dress that was a beautiful aqua color and flowed around her legs. Her hair was a deep brown falling below her shoulders. She was a stunning woman. She had a big smile as she descended the stairs in such a fluid way as to look like she was floating down. She grabbed John who then lifted her and turned in circles spinning her like a child. She was laughing and gave John a big kiss. She then turned to look at Lily. She walked over to Lily, took both of Lily's hands and said, "Oh, you are so beautiful, just like John described you. I'm so glad to meet you. Anyone that John likes as much as he likes you must be very special. Please, call me Maggie."

Lily blushed for some reason and felt very shy but said, "Thank you, Mrs. Jackson, I mean Maggie. You do have the most wonderful son in the world."

Maggie beamed with pride and said, "Well, come with me, I have a snack set up on the patio for us to relax and visit." She continued to hold one of Lily's hands and lead her through several huge, lavishly decorated rooms to a veranda at the back of the house. They passed through some French patio doors on to a large patio that overlooked a beautiful garden that ran for what looked like miles. Every flower Lily had ever seen was in that garden. Lily was thinking that this was like a fairy tale or something out of a magazine.

Maggie began to talk as she poured some lemon aide, "Lily, I hope you enjoy your stay. Anything you want just asks anyone for it. Now tell me about school, John, how are you doing?"

John had a big smile on his face as he said, "Thanks to Lily for helping me study and keeping me focused, I have all A's. Can you believe it?"

Maggie was so happy she clapped her hands and said, "Oh, I am so happy. And your father will also be happy."

John's smile faded, "Oh, I bet, he is always so interested in what I do," He said very sarcastically.

Maggie touched John's arm and said, "Now, John, give him a chance. He will be here for dinner tonight."

For about an hour, Lily and Maggie chatted about many things then the question Lily dreaded to hear came up. She knew she would have to lie. Maggie asked, "what about your parents?"

Lily took a deep breath and said, "Well, my father passed away before I was born."

Maggie said, "Oh I'm so sorry."

Lily continued, "My mother still lives near our home town. She does not work as my grandfather left her money when he passed away of a heart attack when she was seventeen years old. As I said, my father was killed overseas while in the service before I was born. So I don't know much about him except he was a home town boy that was a star football player that volunteered for the service right out of high school. My grandmother on my mother's side of the family, passed away about a year ago of a terminal illness. And that's it. Nothing very fancy just down to earth every day people. My grandfather was the manager of a hardware store in their home town for thirty years."

Maggie said, "Lily I think you have done very well for yourself in getting such an extensive education. I know they would all be proud of you. Let's all go get some rest and get ready for dinner which will be at seven. John, please, show Lily her room."

John led Lily up the stairs, down a hall and into a huge, beautifully decorated guest room. John said, "Here is your room, your majesty." He closed the door and grabbed Lily and they fell on the bed, laughing. Lily said, "I am so happy." John added, "Me too." Then they made love.

Lily felt something different with John during their love making. He seemed rougher and more urgent. He did not do any of the usual sweet things that he did that made her feel special. Lily decided it was being back home that made fooling around in your childhood home seem forbidden and strange. She was wrong, John was feeling like his dad, this was his property and she was his property. Just being back where John spent his childhood, bullied and intimidated by his father, he could not help having some rebellious feelings. He wanted to have the power now and Lily, unfortunately, was the only one he had any influence over.

At 7 PM, the dining room table was set for four. It looked like the queen of England was coming to dinner. Maggie sat on one end of the table, Jack was to sit at the head of the table, Lily sat to the left of Jack and John sat across from Lily on the right of Jack. Jack had not arrived so everyone sat in their place waiting. The maid did serve the wine during the waiting. At ten minutes after 7, Mr. Jack Jackson walked into the room. He was a very tall man, with broad shoulder. He had his hair cut very short and was dressed in an expensive looking suit. When he walked in Maggie stood up and said, "Hello Jack, we have a guest and our son with us tonight. Isn't this nice"

Jack stood in the door a minute then said, "Yes, how nice. Hello John and I'm guessing this is Lily. Welcome to our home." He sounded like he really was glad they were there.

John stood up and went around the table and shook hands with Jack. Lily got up and shook his hand also and said. "It's nice to meet you Mr. Jackson. Thank you for allowing me in your beautiful home."

Jack looked hard at Lily, he said, "Jack, you have a beautiful girl friend. I don't think I've ever seen anything like your emerald green eyes"

Lily said, "Thank you very much. My mother and grandmother have the same eyes so I guess it is hereditary."

Jack then sat at his place at the table. The parade of maids began bringing all kinds of food. Soup was first, followed by salad, then the main course. It was all delicious; the cook must have come from a five star restaurant. As they started the main course, Jack looked at John and said, "How is school? Don't you graduate soon?"

John said, "Yes sir, Lily and I graduate together. We have been in a study group together for 3 years. She has really helped me stay focused and I have really good grades."

Jack said, "Good, I'm proud of you for that. I hope that you will consider joining my firm when you graduate."

John dropped his head and said, "I have not made a decision about what I want to do. But thank you for the offer."

Jack looked at Lily, "I'm not a fan of women being in law, but I guess it is a sign that things are changing. What are your plans after graduation?"

Jack's remark stung Lily and she flinched a little but kept her composure. She looked him in the eye and said, "I have definite plans and do not intend to waste my knowledge of the law or my opportunity to practice law. I'm interested in working with mentally and physically abused women. Not just protecting their legal rights but having an interest in them to help them rebuild their life without an abusive partner."

Jack had stopped eating and was intently looking at Lily. He responded, "Don't you think you should practice real law work and not dabble in unprofitable, charity work? Most of those situations occur involving the poorest people."

Lily was fuming, she put down her fork and continued to look Jack in the eye, "Mr. Jackson, domestic abuse is not just a poor people problem. Abuse, both physical and mental, occurs at every economic level. In America today, the family unit which is the very basis of American life, is in danger of dissolving. The next generation of Americans is struggling to grow up in dysfunctional or broken families. I think everyone deserves to be represented no matter what their economic status. I don't believe working to try and preserve families or getting women and children out of an abusive situation would be considered 'dabbling'."

Jack looked at John and said in a flippant manner, "Well, you have certainly found a feisty, head strong woman. I would think she might want to wear the pants in her family. You need to think about your future and who you need for a partner. A proper wife is only concerned about her husband's career and supports him."

John responded, "Dad, I don't need a wife to support me. If Lily and I are good together then I support her doing what she wants. She is very smart and will make an extremely good lawyer."

Lily had to fight hard not to explode with words, but she said, "Mr. Jackson, I see we do not agree on this issue. I'm sorry you have an antiquated view of women today. Someday you may even have a women lawyer as a partner in your firm."

Jack slapped the table with his hand, "Never! It will never happen as long as I am in control. I resent being told I'm antiquated by someone who has no idea what she is talking about. Being a lawyer requires being tough and women just don't have the fortitude for this kind of work. Now if you will excuse me. I have some calls to make in my office." He got up and stalked out of the room.

Lily could not believe what she was hearing. She had never known anyone that was so rude and narrow minded. Lily looked at Maggie. Maggie had a look on her face that Lily could only describe as fear. Lily said, "Maggie, I am sorry that this lovely dinner has been spoiled. Forgive me for my part in this and ruining the mood for dinner."

Lily looked at John. He was staring at his plate and looked like he had been slapped by his dad.

Lily said, "John, are you alright? You are a grown man with a very bright future. You have the right to lead the life you want to in order to fill like you have made a difference. We have a right to our own opinion and life."

John looked up and his face was very dark, his eyes were cold and hard, "I will have hell to pay for going against him. You have no idea how vengeful Jack can be. You could have placated him and avoided this scene."

Lily was surprised at not only what John said but how he looked. She said, "I think you know me better than that. You should have warned me if you wanted me to play a part." Lily was also surprised at how irritated she was at Mr. Jackson and at John's attitude.

John quickly recovered and had a transformation, his face changed to a smile and his eyes lit up; he said "Of course, I would not want you to be any different than you are. That's why I love you so much. But tomorrow is another day. Let's take a walk and then get some sleep. Tomorrow we will ride horses." He got up from the table and walked around to Lily, took her hand and said, "Mother, would you like to accompany us?"

Maggie had recovered some and said, "No thank you, I'll stay here in case your father needs me." John and Lily left the house and walked down the lane in the twilight. The moon was full so it was almost light as day. It was such a lovely walk, Lily relaxed some. She could not get rid of the feeling that she had seen something in John that he kept hidden in the shadows of his mind and sometimes it slipped out and was out of his control. It crossed her mind that John had two personalities, one that Lily knew and loved. The other John had repressed resentment and anger at a father that had mentally abused him for his entire life.

Lily was concerned that John was so affected by his dad that he actually appeared to revert back to the child that was starved for affection from his father. Even as a man, he was in constant fear of his dad's wrath. She knew there might be a scary element within John that could reach a point where he could be dangerous. She hoped it did not manifest itself in her presence.

As they walked, John said, "I'm sorry, Lily, about the way my dad acted. He is very controlling. I am guilty of avoiding confrontation with him and I really hate to upset my mother, so I just dance around him. I know that's not right but it works. Please, don't let him ruin our trip. This is such a lovely place and you have to admit, I have the best mother in the world!"

Lily was smiling now, "yes, your mother is wonderful. I hope to have some time to visit with her while we are here."

John stopped and hugged Lily to him, "You are a lot like my mother. But not so much that I will forget that you are the sexiest woman I have ever known. I can't wait to get you alone!" With that he kissed her.

The next day John was back to his old, happy-go-lucky self. He came down stairs in a run. Lily was already at the breakfast table with Maggie. Maggie was enjoying Lily as she rarely had any one visiting her. Most of the visitors were Jack's friends and she had to be a good hostess and politely stay quiet. Now she and Lily were talking like old friends. Lily liked Maggie but felt sorry for her. Lily saw a picture of a very attractive and intelligent woman who traded her independence and creativity for a huge mansion with all the amenities. What she did not consider in this life decision was how lonely she would be. Then Lily considered the fact that Maggie really loved Jack and was ready to assume any life that he wanted for her. Life choices are never easy and an individual's confidence and self-esteem are vital in these choices. These two qualities are developed in childhood. The ideal situation for a child to develop into a confident adult is being a part of a strong family with both a father and mother who work together to develop an adult that is a strong, valuable addition to society. Lily had learned one thing growing up, you should never judge a person's actions until you know their life story.

After breakfast, John and Lily headed for the stables riding in a golf cart as the stables were about a mile from the house. The stables were beautiful and the fields around the barn had several horses grazing. Some had foals that were romping around with each other. Lily was amazed at the sight. It was like a scene out of a movie. The stable manager walked out of the barn leading a black and white spotted horse.

John said, "Lily this is Joe, our stable manager, and this beautiful lady is Molly. I grew up riding Molly. She took care of me like a baby sitter. She has the sweetest nature and loves first time riders to take care of."

Joe nodded a hello and returned to the barn. Molly was saddled and ready to go. John helped Lily mount her horse and was giving her some instructions when Joe returned with another horse. This was a very different type of horse. He was a very tall, solid back magnificent animal. He was bobbing his head up and down and snorting. He was also prancing and kicking his back legs. Joe said John, "He's very stirred up today. Did Mr. Jackson give you permission to ride him? You know how he is about this horse."

John ignored Joe's questions and looked at Lily, "Lily this is Thunder. He's a hand full but I can handle him." John then looked at Joe and said, "You just need a strong hand and take control when you are riding a head strong horse. Thanks for getting the horses ready to ride." He dropped his voice and leaned close to Joe and said, "And thanks for your concern."

John took Thunder's reins and gave them a sudden, sharp jerk. Thunder and Lily were both surprised. Thunder threw his head up and attempted to rear up to which John responded to with another stronger yank on the reins. Thunder started to back up with his head up. Fear came in his eyes and his nostrils were flared so big Lily could see the pink inside of his nose. Lily said, "John, don't be so rough."

John responded with, "Lily you don't know anything about horses. Just pay attention to Molly. I'll take care of Thunder."

Lily said, "I may not know much about horses but I do know nothing good comes out of violence or from inflecting pain." She turned Molly around and urged her to start up the trail. She could hear more commotion and John yelling at Thunder but she did not look back. Before Lily had gone very far, John caught up with her. "I'm sorry Lily. I did not mean to be short with you. Thunder just needs a strong hand; see he is doing fine now."

Sure enough, Thunder was matching his gait with Molly's stride. Lily relaxed and started enjoying the scenery. Spring was just around the corner. The bare trees were budding and the grass was starting to turn green. They were riding down a trail that had a white wood fence on each side. Soon the fences stopped and the trail started up a mountain. As they rode the scenery became more and more beautiful. At the top of the mountain they stopped to enjoy the view. In the far distance they could see the Jackson mansion. Lily had a sudden thought and she realized that maybe Maggie had not necessarily made a bad choice to live in this fairy tale. But what had she given up and was it worth the loneliness?

John reached out and took her hand. He said, "Lily, I love you. You have been the reason I have become serious about life. This can give you an idea of what life could hold for us."

Lily smiled at him but she was so conflicted between being herself or taking a back seat, as a supporter, for a rich and powerful man. Either choice had good points and bad points. The difference would be the individual person. Lily would have to do some soul searching to make this kind of a decision. However, she was sure she was not going to be controlled by anyone and she could not love someone that just wanted to control her. She was not going to reside in the shadows of a powerful man

They turned around to head back to the stable because it was several miles and it was getting late. John said, "Thunder needs to run. Just give Molly her head; she will go back to the stables." With that he kicked Thunder and made him take off with a big jump. As she watched, John had Thunder in a full run but he was still hitting him on the rump with a quirk. This behavior concerned her as many times you could evaluate a person's enter feelings by how they treated animals.

When Lily reached the stables, Joe was slowly walking Thunder. Thunder was soaked in sweat with white foam dripping off of him. His head was down and he was breathing hard. Even Lily could tell the horse was in distress. She dismounted and led Molly over to Joe. "Joe, what happened, is Thunder okay?"

Joe looked very angry, he said, "It's not my business but John rode this horse into the ground. He may be winded."

Lily was surprised and asked, "What is winded?"

Joe said, "When a horse has to run far pass his ability he gets fluid built up in his lungs. This then causes him to bleed into his lungs and may leave him with permanent lung problems. After a horse is winded, they cannot run any more without wheezing and essentially the animal is not good for much activity."

John walked up at that moment, "Joe, Thunder is not winded. Just keep walking him around. He will be fine by tomorrow."

Joe gave John a look of distain, "That's easy for you to say but I'm the horse trainer and I say you pushed him too far and may have ruined him for life. Just because you hate your dad does not mean you can take it out on this poor animal."

John grabbed Joe by the shirt front, his face was red, "It's none of your damn business how I feel about my dad. This horse is our property and I can treat him any way I please."

Joe roughly pushed John away from him, "John you don't want to try and push me around; I will mop this yard up with you if you don't back off."

John changed immediately and said, "Joe, hey I didn't mean any thing by that. You know anything about my dad causes me to flare up. Just take care of the horse." He turned to Lily and said, "Let's go, we need to get ready for dinner as dad will be home tonight." Lily reluctantly gave Joe Molly's reins and said, "Thanks Joe for taking care of Molly. I really enjoyed riding her." She really did not know what else to say so she got into the golf cart.

John chatted as they drove along but Lily did not have anything to say. She was getting to see more and more of a side to John that scared her and that she did not like.

Dinner started much the same as the night before. Jack was ten minutes late, so again they waited. When he arrived he said hello to all and they started to eat. Suddenly Jack looked at John and said, "You rode Thunder today, didn't you?"

John froze and it took a minute for him to respond. He said, "Yes, I did. Lily and I went up to the top of the mountain. Lily road Molly and I rode Thunder."

Jack was putting butter on his roll; he pointed his butter knife at John in a threatening way and said, "Do not ever get on Thunder again. Don't even go near him or touch him. If that horse is permanently injured, you will have to answer to me."

John looked at his plate and murmured, "Yes sir."

Jack then continued to talk, "I have also made a decision today. I am putting some conditions on my offer for you to join my firm when you pass the bar."

Jack had everyone's attention; no one was eating now. Maggie looked like she was ready to faint and John's face was hard and unreadable. Jack continued, "You will not be offered a job in my firm if you and Lily marry. I do not think she has the attitude that a lawyer's wife should have in order to further his career. I have to take every precaution to see that my firm is successful which means everyone is on board with my policies." Jack was talking about Lily as if she was not in the room.

John looked at his dad and for once he was stern when he said, "So now you are going to tell me who I can marry. Will you stop at nothing to ruin my life?"

Jack put down his fork and looked at John, "Well, someone has to see that you don't screw up your entire life and squander our estate." He leaned back in his chair and looked pleased with himself as he dropped the next information on them. "I did a little research today. Were you aware that Lily's mother is in prison for manslaughter? Did you know;

Lily's grandmother resided many years in a mental hospital and died completely insane? Did you know; Lily worked as a stripper in a sleazy bar when she was sixteen years old? Also in all my searching, I could not find any information about Lily's father. There is no soldier or boyfriend known to be associated with Jane Baxter. From the look on your face, I guess you didn't know any of this scandalous information about your girlfriend."

Maggie gasped and put her hand over her mouth. John looked at Lily. Lily said, "John, I can explain these things. I was going to tell you when the time was right."

Jack laughed wickedly and looked at Lily, "I guess the time would be right after you had snared my son as a good catch so you would be set up for the rest of your life?"

Lily was shocked beyond words. How could a father be so controlling as to dictate who their adult son should marry and how that wife should act? How dare Jack talk about her like she was a piece of property and invade her privacy. She looked at John and after a long silence, she said, "John, tell him what you want to do with your life. You are a grown man and should not be told what you can and can't do. It is our business what is in my past and not any of your dad's concern. You know me well enough to know I would not trick you into anything and I would have told you everything if we got more serious." She looked at Jack and continued, "How dare you snoop in my past. Who the hell do you think you are?"

Jack narrowed his eyes and glared at Lily, "I am the one smart enough to catch you in your goody-two-shoes act. I am not blinded by your beautiful eyes and body like John is. I did the research to protect my son from the likes of you."

John did not say anything he just looked a Lily. After a few minutes, Lily said, "Well, I guess I have your answer." She stood up and looked at Jack, "Jack, you are the most controlling freak that I have ever seen. You have ruined a very good man by putting him through years of mental abuse. You are worse than the meanest child and wife beater that ever lived. The only difference is you don't leave visible scars. You will not have to worry about John marrying me because I would not marry a man who did not stand up for himself and the girl he professes to love." Lily turned to Maggie and said, "Maggie, thank you for opening your home to me. I would have loved to have more time to spend with you but I think you know that this is good bye." Lily walked over to Maggie and bent down to give her a kiss on the cheek. Maggie was crying softly but she gave Lily a hug and whispered in her ear, "I wish you the best."

Lily left the table and went to her room, shut and locked the door. She immediately packed her bag. She used the phone in her room to call a cab. She told them to send the cab to the estate address and wait by the front gates. She slipped out her door leaving it locked and went down the back stairs to the kitchen. She went out the back door and started the long walk to the front gate. She was thankful that the full moon was still as bright as it was last night. However, this was not a happy stroll with her boyfriend and she was carrying her luggage. She was grateful that John's car was too small for the luggage she had packed; the two she was carrying were heavy enough. This was an escape from what she realized was the worse case scenario of a dysfunctional family that had completely destroyed two lives. She knew she could not stay no matter how she felt about John. She was not going to be a casualty of Jack Jackson.

Lily realized that once again her past had come out of the shadows and sabotaged her life. She had to ask herself would her life ever be normal. One thing for sure, she resolved she was going to be alone in this world and would have to depend on herself for her future.

It struck Lily that she and John were born and raised in complete opposite ends of the economical spectrum. But both families were riddled with abuse. Lily felt she had survived her childhood but she was not sure if John would.

Lily finally reached the front gate. She had not thought about the fact that she may not be able to get out without the code for the gate. However, on one side, next to one of the big columns, was a small gate that allowed her to exit, but not to enter, the property. She got in the cab and asked him to take her to the nearest bus station. When she reached the bus station she paid the cab driver and went to the front desk. She requested a ticket on the first bus to the university. She found out it would not be leaving for the university until 6 AM in the morning. She was not deterred by having to sleep in the bus station. She found a long bench and settled in for the night.

The next morning the ticket seller woke her up and offered her a cup of coffee before the bus left. She could not wait to get home.

Back at the estate, while Lily was drinking coffee at the bus stop, John was knocking on her bedroom door. When she did not answer he knocked harder and called louder. He panicked when she did not answer; he stood back and kicked the door as hard as he could. It took three kicks before the door flew open. He could tell immediately that Lily was gone. His fear that she had left him turned to rage. He was not going to let her walk away from him. He might have to consider some of the information that his dad told him but if anyone ended this relationship it would be him, not her. He ran down stairs where his mother and father were eating breakfast. He stormed into the dining room. "Lily has left! Jack you have run off the woman that I love and that has been the best thing for me in my life. I hope you are happy."

Jack said, "Well, yes I am happy. I did what you would not have had the nerve to do. I have done you a favor."

John just turned and ran out the front door to his car and sped down the drive.

Maggie looked at Jack and said, "You have made a big mistake. You have just alienated our son from us. You have also run off an intelligent, caring and sweet girl. For once, I can not support you on this decision. You need to fix this!" Then she went to her room.

Jack had never seen Maggie so angry. For a moment he felt some fear that she might leave him. Then he recovered, he didn't need any of them, let them go if they wanted to. They'd be back; they couldn't live without his money.

CHAPTER 3

LILY

When Lily got home, she was exhausted. She went into her bedroom and dropped her suitcase and purse and fell on the bed. She was still in a deep sleep when she heard knocking on her door. She got up and went into the living room. She looked through the peek hole and she was surprised to see John. She thought John looked transformed; he was wild eyed and scary looking. She felt sorry for him, but she was just as determined not to let him back in her life. She backed away from the door and said. "John, go away. I don't think we need to see each other any more."

John said, "Lily open up the door. I just want to talk to you."

Lily said, "Maybe tomorrow we'll talk. But for now, go home and get some rest."

John said, "If you don't open this door, I will kick it down."

Lily moved back away from the door, "No John, go away. I will call the police and have you arrested."

For the second time today, John kicked a door. By the second kick the door crashed open with splinters flying.

Lily screamed, "John what are you doing. I've never seen you like this. You must get out of here." She turned to escape to her bedroom.

John grabbed her arm and turned her around to face him. Before she knew it John had smashed his fist in her face. She fell to the floor and was stunned. John jumped on her and started hitting her in the face. Lily started fighting with all her might. She took her fist and hit John in the face hard enough that she was able to roll him off of her. Just as she was trying to get up, John grabbed her again and was turning her back around to face him. Lily knew she would have to fight for her life as John was out of control and was intent on hurting her or doing worse. Lily swung her foot as hard as she could and buried her foot into John's testicles. He slumped over and grabbed his groin and let go of Lily then she was able to get up. She grabbed the nearest lamp and smashed it on the back of John's head. He crashed to the floor. Lily ran for her bedroom where she immediately went to her bedside table. In the drawer she found the Colt .45 that her mother had given her. She whirled around and found John getting off the floor. He said, "I'm going to kill you. You don't lead me on and have secrets in your life. You thought you would marry me and get my dad's money. Well, that's not going to happen. You made me love you. You reeled me in like a big fish. You're just like Thunder, needing a strong hand to control you. No one fools with me and gets away with it." He started for her with murder in his eyes.

Lily tried to remain calm even though she was shaking she held the colt as steady as she could. She said, "John, this is a Colt .45. It has two bullets left in it. It holds six. The other four bullets killed two men. I hope I don't have to make you the third man to be killed with this gun."

John stopped in his tracks, "You won't shoot me Lily; you don't have the guts."

Lily looked him straight in the eyes, she wasn't shaking now and her voice was solid steal, "Oh, yes I do. You have no idea what I am capable of. I have had a hard damn life and I do know how to use this gun. I have seen the damage that a bullet from this gun can do to a man and it's not pretty. One bullet will blow your heart out of your body. I am tired of being run over and intimidated, so don't make me shoot."

John lay back down on the floor; he believed what Lily was saying and the way she was holding the gun that she was serious. Lily picked up the phone and dialed 911. She gave the dispatcher the address and asked for the police to come. Then she looked at John and said, "John, you are very lucky I choose not to shoot you. When I first got the gun, I heard a whisper in my ear that said 'Kill him, Kill him'. That's what my mother told me she heard when she was faced with a monster. The difference is; I chose not to listen to the voice like my mother did. She is paying the price for not using some self-control and she's in jail right now for man slaughter. I don't intend to go to prison for killing you, but I will if I have to. I don't want to ever see you again, next time I might not be strong enough not to shoot."

The police came through the door with guns drawn. The lead policeman told Lily to put down her gun and kick it to him. The paramedic recommended taking both of them to the hospital. John had a concussion and had to stay in the hospital overnight then he was taken to jail.

Lily had a broken cheek bone that required surgery. Her face was swollen and her eyes were black. She was hospitalized for a week. When she got out of the hospital she took out a restraining order on John.

Lily got back to her studies as it was only two months till graduation and the bar exams. She decided not to press charges against John because she did not want to prevent him from graduating. Even though she was afraid of him, she could not help but feel his dad had driven him to have these rages. However, his rages may have been a genetic trait that his dad had passed on to him. Lily knew about this from her own family. Either way, she did not intent to deal with him or anyone else with this problem.

CHAPTER 4

JOHN

John did not return to school. No one seemed to know where he was. Lily got a lot of questions about what happened to her face. She explained to everyone that she was in a car accident. A month later, graduation came and John still had not shown up. Lily was proud to walk across the stage and receive her degree. She was sad that she did not have anyone there to clap for her or give her a big hug of congratulations. She walked through the crowd of graduates and happy parents taking pictures but no one took a picture of her.

Lily missed Granny. Granny had been at her high school graduation but she was gone now, so Lily could only keep her in her memory. Lily had written to her mother about graduation and Jane wrote back to tell her she was proud of her. Jane was a different person after she was able to control her alcohol addiction. Jane had also been reading a lot trying to determine why she did the things she did. She had hopes of making up for lost time when she got out by getting to know her daughter. That was if Lily would have her around.

Lily had one more hurdle to get over and that was the bar exam. She planned to stay where she was and study hard and in three months she could take the exam. She had not been out on a date since she and John broke up. She could not handle another relationship now or maybe ever. Even though she had healed from her physical injuries, she felt beat up on the inside and it was going to take a while before she trusted another man. It seemed every man in her life, so far, had only caused her pain. The next man would have a tough time getting past the barriers that she put up for protection.

A month after graduation, Lily decided to take a break from studying and take a walk down town. The day was very nice with a slight breeze and the flowers all over town were blooming. Lily saw lots of people were milling around, enjoying the town. She decided to stop at the local coffee house. The university kids loved this place as it was furnished with couches and comfortable chairs so they could relax and visit. There was always popular music playing in the surround sound system. Lily ordered a latte and found a table to sit at. She set her coffee on the table and noticed the newspaper was spread out over the table next to her. She picked up the sports section and scanned through it. Then she reached across the table for the front page section. A large picture caught her eye as it looked familiar. There were big head lines above the picture that said, "**Local Prominent Citizen Loses Only Son**". Lily took a long look at the picture. It was a picture of a young man in a suit. The picture appeared to be a high school graduation picture. Lily gasp when she recognized it was John. She started reading the article.

Prominent Lawyer, Jack Jackson and Maggie Jackson, his wife, lost their only son in an accident. John Justice Jackson, 26 years old, was riding one of the horses in the Jackson stable when he was apparently thrown. The fall did not kill him but the horse, a big back stallion, stomped him to death. There was no explanation why the horse reacted violently as he had been ridden for several years by Mr. Jackson, John's father.

Lily was so shocked she could barely comprehend what the article was saying. John being dead was beyond belief for Lily. Lily remembered how John had been so violent with the horse when they rode just a few months ago. He had forced the horse to run beyond his ability and almost ruined him for the rest of his life. No wonder the horse reacted violently with John. She also sadly saw in the article that the horse was euthanized by a veterinarian. She finished the article which spent more time describing how wonderful and successful Jack was than talking about John. They did have in the article that John was close to graduating from law school. She noted the time and place for the funeral which was scheduled for that afternoon. Lily got up and ran home. She quickly got dressed as appropriately as she could for a funeral and jumped into her car. She could just make it if she pushed the speed limit.

Lily arrived at the church where the service was being held and was glad she was late. This way she could slip in the back without being noticed. The church was full and the casket was in the front draped in flowers. The brochure said the casket would be closed due to the extent of the injuries to John's face.

As Lily sat there in the peaceful, quiet place, the reality of John being gone hit her. She began to cry. Even thought their romance had ended badly, she remembered the John that she first met. He had been the sweetest, funniest man she had ever known. He was such a gentleman and treated her like a queen. It was when they had gone to meet his mother and dad that things changed. Jack had been so mean to John and his mother that she could see that John's childhood had not been good. His mother was the light of John's life and she was surely the only reason he went home at all.

The service ended and everyone formed a long line of cars going to the cemetery. It was beginning to rain as the preacher gave a short talk and prayer over the casket at the grave site. Since it was raining Lily could hide under her umbrella. She certainly did not want Jack to see her and make a scene. Lily watched Maggie standing very straight but she could not see her face which was also hidden by the umbrella. As everyone began to disperse, Lily waited next to a tree near the parking lot. She was hoping to get to speak to Maggie as she couldn't go to her home. Maggie turned from a small group and started walking alone toward the cars. When she got near where Lily stood, Lily stepped out to meet her.

Lily said, "Hello, Maggie."

Maggie looked up and was surprised. "Lily, oh, I am so glad to see you!" She took Lily's hand, "I don't know if I will ever get over losing John." She began to cry again.

Lily stepped closer to Maggie and said, "I am so, so sorry. You know I loved John. But I could not make up for what Jack has done to him."

Maggie stopped crying, wiped her nose and spoke in an angry tone, "I should have stopped Jack years ago. I will never forgive myself for standing by while he belittled John continually. I want you to know, I am divorcing Jack. I have to get away from him. I see now that I traded my life and soul for the material things that Jack could give me. I did love Jack so much at first, but as he got older he became more abusive. He never wanted children but I insisted; now I'm sorry for bringing a child into the cruel world that Jack made for us. I know it is too late for John, but maybe it won't be too late for me. I have to try and find myself and find out what my purpose in life is."

Lily said all she could honestly say, "I think this is the best decision you have ever made. I want you to call me and give me your new address. I hope we will meet again under happier times." She kissed Maggie on the cheek and hugged her.

Maggie turned and walked away. She was a sad figure of a woman who had lost everything. Not everything in a material sense but everything that she thought would make her a whole person. A marriage flawed by having the wrong partner, a child that was damaged by his father and a life that was solely in the shadow of her husband. One day maybe she would be able to see that peace of mind and being her true self would come through new avenues. Maggie got into the back seat of one of the long black cars and was driven away. When everyone was gone, Lily walked to John's grave. The rain falling on the newly turned dirt made a pleasant smell. There were flowers every where. She looked at the new grave and the stone that said John's name with a script underneath saying; "He was a wonderful son".

Lily said, "John, maybe now you will find the peace your soul needed. Your mother and I love you very much. We saw in you the wonderful person that was overwhelmed by the fact that your father did not love you. I will think of you often." She returned to her car for the long drive home.

CHAPTER 5

MAGGIE

Who was Maggie Jackson? Everyone knew she was the wife of the successful and powerful Jack Jackson. She lived in a huge, beautiful estate. She hosted big important parties and numerous charities. But did anyone know her?

Maggie was born the second daughter of three children, with the third child being a boy. As if being the middle child was not hard enough, she felt she was the second child that was a mistake because she was not a boy so they tried again and "Wow!" they got just what they wanted, a boy.

The oldest daughter to Ralph and Ginger Young was named Raina Lynn. Maggie thought that was the most beautiful, rare name she had ever heard. However, her name was just plain Maggie Ann. Maggie was not short for any other fancy name, just Maggie. Maggie's brother was Ralph Regan Young Jr. They called him Regan but everyone knew he was a junior so he could carry on the Young name.

When Ralph introduced his children it was, "this is my oldest daughter Raina."

Everyone would say, "Raina, what a different name and she looks just like her beautiful mother."

Then he would say, "This is Maggie, my second daughter." No one had anything to say about the name Maggie and she was not as pretty as Raina, so they said nothing. Her dad would continue, "This is my son Ralph Regan Jr."

Then the conversation went; "Oh your son, what a chip off the old block." Maggie wondered if Regan was a chip off the old block, did that make her a splinter off the old block or maybe a knot hole in the old block?

Raina was outgoing and smart. She was a cheerleader in high school and the lead in the class play. She made good grades and the boys were after her all the time. When Maggie got to high school, everyone asked, "are you going out for cheerleader? Your sister, Raina, was a great cheerleader. Are you going out for the play cast, Raina was the lead." Her answer was always a shy shake of the head "no". One good thing that Maggie did hear by the time she got to high school was "you are just as pretty as your sister." These comments helped but still made it seem like she had a role to fill in for her sister instead of being herself.

If children could put things in perspective they would realize that life is never as bad as it seems. When Maggie was just entering her teen years, Raina was just becoming comfortable in her own skin as a teenager. Raina was becoming a butterfly while Maggie was still in the pupa stage. But Maggie only saw that she fell short on all accounts in comparison with her sister.

Years later, Maggie would also realize her parents were doing their best to treat each of their children equally. Parents are human and they can't help but connect with one child more than the other. Maggie's parents felt every bump in the road for all three of their children. They read all the books on raising children especially concerning the middle child syndrome. Most parents realize that the roll of being a parent is the hardest thing they will have to do in life and no matter how smart or educated they are, it is never easy. Watching a child, that you love more than anything go through the pain of growing up, is heart breaking. However, at the same time the most rewarding feeling is to see your child look at you as their hero.

Maggie loved to read and went through countless numbers of books. She loved peace and quiet. Her idea of a good Saturday night was a movie at home with her parents. Boys were attracted to Maggie, but her shyness was a barrier for conversation thus no invitations for a date. It didn't bother her not to have a date because she did not have a clue what she would say or do on a date.

Maggie did have a best friend, Linda. Linda lived next door to the Youngs' so she and Maggie became best friends. Linda was a little kooky. She wore wild clothes, funky shoes and her hair was naturally curly and always all over the place. Maggie was very neat and proper and kept her auburn hair the same way all the time which was always shiny and neat. Linda was skinny with knobby knees and long arms.

Linda and Maggie were total opposites and if they did not live next door to each other, they would probably never have gotten together. Regardless of the differences, they had fun together just like all girlfriends. They had sleepovers, went everywhere together and talked for hours on the phone. Together they plowed into high school and together they made their own space and were very happy.

When Maggie and Linda started their senior year in high school, they were already talking about going to college together. Since they both had good grades and they really wanted to go to a small school, the chances were good they would both get accepted at the same college. They were already planning how to decorate their dorm room the first year and then get an apartment the next year.

At the end of September, Linda was sick and stayed at home for a few days. Maggie went over to Linda's house after school every day and recounted everything that happened during the day. Linda appeared tired and sometimes would fall asleep while they were doing their homework. Linda's mother told Maggie that they were taking Linda to a really good doctor and would find out why she was not getting better. Maggie had noticed that on Linda's leg there was a big bruise. When she ask Linda's mother what caused it, she didn't know but said that was one of their concerns.

The day Linda went to the doctor, Maggie could hardly wait to get out of school to see what the doctor said. When she got home, she dashed into the house saying, "I'm going to see Linda; she should be back from the doctor's"

Ginger said, "Whoa, wait I need to talk to you. Please sit down for a minute."

Maggie was reluctant but did sit down. Her mother continued, "Linda did not get to come home. She had to stay in the hospital to start some treatments."

Maggie looked puzzled, "what kind of treatments?"

Ginger looked down at the table. This was one of those times that a loving parent wished they could take the pain away from their child. She said, "Maggie, Linda is very sick. She has leukemia. This disease is very aggressive and she will have to have a lot of treatment."

Maggie began to get a bad feeling in her stomach, "Leukemia! But Mother, people die with Leukemia! Is Linda going to die?"

Ginger could not lie, "Maggie, that is possible."

Maggie crumbled, she began to sob, "I can't lose the only friend I have. I love Linda like a sister!"

Ginger went around the table and held Maggie to her, she also began to cry. Her heart was breaking for her child but also for the pain that Linda's parents would be going through. Maggie said between sobs, "This is not fair. Why Linda? She never hurt anyone or did anything bad."

Ginger tried to explain, "This has nothing to do with getting sick because she was bad or good. This is just something that can happen. You need to have faith that God will help us get through everything that happens. This is why we go to church, so you can learn that God loves us but things don't always seem fair. You are going to have to do the hardest thing in the world and that is to be up-beat for Linda. You are going to have to show courage for her and treat her like your friend. You can't treat her like she is sick but fill your time together with fun. And we don't know that she won't get well, so many kids get well now with the new medications. In a year, you and Linda could be in your room at college and this will be a distant memory."

Maggie was not consoled, she jumped up and screamed, "I can't do this, I can't act like nothing is wrong. I can't look at her now without being sad." She ran to her room and fell on her bed sobbing.

Ginger composed herself and followed Maggie up the stairs. She sat on the bed by her precious daughter and began rubbing her back. "Maggie, you have to do this for Linda. She would do the same for you. It's okay that you are mad at what has happened. It's okay that you cry. It's not okay for you to abandon your friend when she needs you most. I know that you are a strong and caring person. You will do the right thing. I am always here if you need me or your father and I love you very much." With that being said, she left Maggie so she could process her grief.

Maggie did stand by Linda through out her painful treatments. When Linda's hair fell out, Maggie cut her hair very short for the first time in her life. She and Linda wore matching head scarves so people wouldn't know who the cancer patient was. They laughed a lot and they cried. Maggie did most of her crying at night in her room, alone. Or she thought she was alone but her parents listened helplessly while their child suffered heart break.

The holidays went well; at times Linda felt as good as she ever did. Everyone's hopes rose. In January things went very wrong. Linda got very sick again. Maggie slept at Linda's house on the floor in a sleeping bag so she could be near her. Linda's parents put a hospital bed down stairs in the den when Linda could not go up the stairs. They did everything they could to make things better, but for Linda, getting better was not going to happen.

Very late one night, as Maggie held one hand and Linda's parents held the other, Linda stopped breathing. She slipped away so quietly that Maggie didn't even realize it until Linda's mother began to sob. Maggie did not know what to do; she felt Linda's parents needed their time alone so she went home. She went into her mom and dad's room and sat on the bed. She felt really calm when she woke them up to tell them Linda was gone. But as the realization slowly came that her dearest friend in the world was gone, a pain began in Maggie's stomach that was so bad that it doubled her over. That pain was there for a long time and even years later Maggie would feel a twinge when she thought of Linda.

Maggie did not remember the details of the funeral. She drifted through it all. She even continued to drift through her senior year in high school. She continued to make good grades but could not remember the last part of high school after she graduated. Maggie did get into a good college which was bigger than she wanted to attend, but she got a good scholarship which would help her parents a lot. She did not have a specific career in mind but since she was good at math, she stayed on the business, economic and social studies side of the curriculum. She did date some but usually didn't get past the second or third date before she became bored and broke it off. Maggie felt like all her emotions had been spent over the loss of her best friend and now she was empty. She really didn't care about anything now.

One beautiful fall day at college, Maggie was sitting on a bench on campus just watching the leaves slowly fall off the massive trees. A stranger sat down on the bench, whom Maggie did no even notice until he spoke to her, "Beautiful day isn't it?"

Maggie looked to see if he was talking to her, then responded, "Oh, yes, it is." Then she took a real look at the person next to her. He was very handsome. He had dark eyes and dark hair with an olive complexion. She felt she had seen him before but could not remember where.

The stranger then introduced himself, "My name is Jack Jackson. What is your name?" Maggie had no idea that Jack Jackson had been watching her a while and was very taken with her striking beauty. He also liked her quiet manner, her auburn, long hair, blue eyes and just about everything else about her. He was surprised that he never saw her with a man and didn't see her at any of the parties or ball games. Maggie answered him with, "My name is Maggie Young." That was all she said. It looked like if he was going to make any head way with her he would have to make all the moves. So he said, "Are you a senior here?"

Maggie said, "Yes."

It crossed his mind that this might take more energy than he wanted to put into getting a date. He had scores of girls that would have been all over him by now. But Maggie had not even smiled at him. At this time in Maggie's life she was very depressed and was still recovering from losing her best friend. She was vulnerable; which caused her to be more likely to allow herself to be taken in by a controlling personality which is what Jack had.

Jack watched Maggie every day and made a point of being where she was and making it look natural. Soon he did ask her out. Maggie began to take notice of Jack and what she saw she liked. He was very considerate and attentive. Maybe he was a little to close all the time but she felt that was just because they had fun together. Gradually they became an item. It was always Jack and Maggie together.

Sometimes when things happen gradually they can get out of hand before it becomes apparent what is coming. Needing total control over another person is an addiction just as strong as a substance addiction. Jack was one of those people who had to have control over everything. Maggie was a prime target because she was naïve and needed someone to make the first move before she could connect. Jack recognized Maggie's weakness and knew how to take advantage of her.

Jack began to comment on the cloths Maggie wore and making suggestions on what he thought would be appropriate. He had to know where she was at all times. He convinced her it was for her safety that he was concerned. The biggest mistake that a woman can make is to think that a man has to know where she is and what she is doing at all times and is sure this means they are madly in love with them. In reality, this is a part of the control addiction.

At Christmas Maggie ask Jack to go home with her to meet her parents. Ginger and Ralph were so glad to see Maggie and see that she appeared happy. Jack was at his best and charmed them completely. Well, almost completely, Ginger was seeing some red flags that caused her to be concerned. When she finally had Maggie to herself, she ventured some advice. Ginger said, "Maggie, Jack seems very nice and does appear to really love you."

Maggie beamed, "yes, he is wonderful."

Ginger continued, "I have some small concerns that I would like you to be aware of. When Jack comments on what you are wearing and suggest something else, don't you think you should decide what you want to wear?"

Maggie shrugged, "Jack has a good eye for fashion and he just wants me to look my best. He has been to so many places that he has a lot of experience in what is in style. I don't mind that."

Ginger decided to go one more step, "Maggie, it appears that Jack decides everything that you are to do and is a little obsessive about where you are all the time. Don't you think that is pretty controlling and should he not trust you more?"

Maggie ended the conversation, "Mother, Jack has a strong personality. I like him just the way he is." Then she left the room.

Ginger sighed, she could only pray for Maggie now as Jack had complete control over her. It made her sad to think Maggie had lost her will and creativity.

The last semester of college, Maggie did not come home any. This was very out of character for her but she always had an excuse. Jack has something for us to do; or Jack thinks we need to study. It was always what Jack wanted for them, that they did.

When Ginger and Ralph went to the college for Maggie's graduation, they got a surprise. Jack had decided he and Maggie would get married in September. Maggie had a huge diamond ring. Her parents were happy but also sad as the red flags of doubt about Jack kept popping up. The last blow came when Jack told them about his job which was on the west coast. All the way across the US; so far away from everyone Maggie knew and loved. Ginger made one last plea to Maggie, "Maggie you need to think really hard about this as you are isolating yourself from all of us. Please don't do this if you don't really want to."

Maggie did have second thoughts but she did not know how to get away from Jack. She thought after they were married she could decide what she wanted to do with her education and career. But pride kept her from voicing her doubts so instead she said, "Mother, I love Jack, he loves me, everything will be fine."

This is typical when the shadow of control addiction of a person creeps in and takes total control over another person. Maggie had convinced herself that this is what she wanted when in reality; Jack had instilled his will into her. Maggie soon found that it was easier to live in the shadow of being controlled by another person to hide the fact that she had made a big mistake by marrying Jack. She had traded her independence and her will for the security of money and to be the wife of a powerful man.

CHAPTER 6

MAGGIE AND JACK

A couple of months after their marriage, Maggie and Jack were settled in California. Jack was working a lot of hours to get his business going. When Maggie brought up the idea that she also wanted to work, Jack was adamant that he was the bread winner. She needed to make their home and help him entertain his clients. Maggie had no idea what Jack's work was but she knew his clients were high rollers with lots of money.

In the second year of their marriage, Jack came home to tell Maggie he had bought them a large house on some acreage, thirty miles from the city. Maggie was shocked that he did this without consulting her and that the property was so far from the city. Jack responded to Maggie's concerns with, "I got this for you as a surprise. It cost a lot of money. Any wife would be happy to be treated like a queen but not you; you complain. We are moving and you will do your part!"

This was the first time Jack had spoken to her in this manner. But it would not be the last. Jack became more and more detached from her. If she did cross him or have an opinion, he was gruff and then would leave the house, slamming the door as hard as he could. Many times he would stay in the city at an apartment he rented, instead of coming home. They did entertain a lot at the mansion so Maggie was relatively busy. Now she also had staff to manage as it took several people to maintain this huge place.

As time went by, Maggie wanted a baby. She was in her early thirties when the hormones began to flow and the instinct for her to desire a baby kicked in. She ventured the subject to Jack, "Jack, wouldn't it be nice to have a baby?"

Jack's reaction was quick, "No, a baby would just take a lot of your time. You can't entertain with a big belly or a screaming kid running around. It's out of the question."

For the first time in their relationship, Maggie made a decision on her own as to her future. She stopped taking her birth control pills and after one month she was pregnant. Now that she was pregnant, she thought Jack would fall into place with the idea. But that was not what happened. Jack was not going to share Maggie with anyone, not even their child. Jack demanded she have an abortion.

Maggie was going to stand her ground on this one. Maggie actually said, "No, there will be no abortion. You will just have to deal with it." Jack ranted, but Maggie did not budge, nothing could change the way a she felt about her child.

Maggie had a baby boy whom they named John Justice Jackson. Maggie would one day regret bringing a baby into the world to be treated as badly as Jack treated John.

Maggie loved John with all her heart and they did everything together. Everything was fine when Jack was gone but when he was home everyone was on alert. John was a sweet baby but at times he displayed a temper that was uncontrollable. Maggie was afraid John had gotten this bad temper from his father. She did everything she could to teach John how to control his emotions. She tried hard to create an environment that would nurture John and build his self-esteem but she was always blind sided by the verbal abuse Jack rained down on John. Maggie had no way of knowing the worst was yet to come. Later in her life she realized that things might have turned out differently if she had taken John, when he was a child, and left Jack.

Maggie was ready for a new life after her divorce from Jack. She would have to recover from the loss of her child and the loss of her marriage. Maggie would have a long and difficult road before she would recover her confidence and have a good life.

CHAPTER 7

LILY

After John's funeral, Lily felt she had to be in a different place. She wanted to start over. It seemed every time she was in a place for a while a tragedy would penetrate that place and to get away from sad memories, Lily would have to hit the road.

Lily now found herself in a town and state far away from where she grew up or went to school. For some reason she had gotten off the bus in this town named Eden, and now called it home. Her next task was getting a car; then a job. She still received enough money from her grandfather's trust to live moderately but she did not want to waste her education and felt in some way that she had something to contribute to society. She just didn't know what that would be.

Lily got up early, straightened her room and called for a cab to pick her up. She ask the cab driver to take her to a car lot that had used cars and that he felt the owner would be fair with her. She had never owned a car, but was taught how to drive by John. Of course, she was not going to buy a sports car like John; John's car had surely cost a fortune.

The driver pulled up to a small car lot that had about 30 cars of all kinds, age and make. Lily paid for the ride and thanked the cab driver. She began to wonder around the lot looking at all the different cars of all colors. Shortly a middle aged, rather short and dumpy man came toward her. Lily extended her hand and said, "Hello, I'm Lily Baxter. I'm new in town and need a car. I want it to be not old as I don't want a lot of mechanical problems. A good economic car would be fine, but I would like it to be a little flashy."

"Great, you have come to the right place. My name is Randy Low. I've owned this car lot many years and I will help you. I stand behind my cars. So what do you like?"

Lily pointed at a red, two door small car. Randy beamed, "That is a jewel of a car. It is a Mercury Cougar. It is low mileage, one owner and I don't think there is anything wrong with it. If something does go wrong in the first 90 days, I always fix it. You also have the option to get it checked out by a mechanic. I think this car would just fit you. Do you want to drive it?" Randy asked.

Lily asked him what he wanted for it and since she felt it was a price she could handle she said she would take it. Like everything else, she was just going with gut feeling about what she did. They went to the office and filled out the papers and exchanged the money. Randy explained what she would have to do to get it registered and licensed. He went over all the things in the car and since it was an automatic transmission, Lily caught on quickly. When she left the car lot, she drove around the town and out on the interstate enjoying her first car at the age of 27 years old.

Lily loved the free feeling of driving and also seeing the sights. She found the high school at the end of Main Street, the court house on the square, the two main banks, many eating places and some interesting flea markets she hoped to be able to visit later. As she toured, she found three offices that had signs on the door announcing law offices. Lily decided to visit them tomorrow to see if any of them needed a new, fresh-out of school lawyer.

When Lily got back to her apartment, she stopped to talk to Elizabeth to tell her about the car. She really liked Elizabeth and found her easy to talk to. Elizabeth had told her she was divorced for many years with two grown children. Both her girl and boy were married and she had 2 grandkids. Lily told Elizabeth some things from her pass but not much. She certainly did not include the part about her mother being in jail for manslaughter but kept the story rather short. She did include a lot about Granny as the most beloved person in her life.

The next day, Lily began her search for a job. She had a resume written out even thought it was very short with no working experience on it. She did not mention her time pole dancing and being a stripper in the club as previous employment. She thought that might not be a positive and did not want to demonstrate her skills in the area of dance.

The first office was a single lawyer office. Lily introduced herself to the receptionist. The lady was nice but made it clear that her boss was not looking for anyone but would give him her resume. The other offices had the same story. Lily learned that all the lawyers were in court most days. She decided she'd meet them soon enough.

The job search was disappointing and when Lily recounted the day to Elizabeth, Elizabeth said, "Why don't you just start your own office. All you need is an office and there are plenty of vacant offices in town that could be rented for a small fee. You would not need much room for your office. There are no women lawyers in town so I think you would attract some women who would feel better talking to a women rather than a man."

"That's an interesting idea. I will have to think about it," Lily said, "Where would I go to find out about an office?"

"We have one woman real estate agent in town that has her own business. I'd start with her. I'll give her a call and set up an appointment for you tomorrow, if you want?"

"Sure," said Lily; "Sounds great. Great, but scary at the same time."

"I will tell you it will be hard to break into the "good old boy" click in this town. The lawyers here have been scratching each others back for a long time. You'll have to be tough to get established. I can talk to some of my friends at the local newspaper. They could write a good introduction and it could be a 'welcome you to town' article. The Chamber of Commerce will do a ribbon cutting when you open, which will spread the news also.

'I can help you get a receptionist as I know some good women in town that know everyone and can help you learn the lay of the land and who to trust. So does that make you feel better?" Elizabeth was smiling as she talked. She loved something exciting going on and was happy to be a part of it. Since she was already in the mist of this new adventure she continued, "I know a lot of women in town that have not gotten a good shake in divorces or other disagreements and would love to get another opinion. A woman's opinion would really be a breath of fresh air. I know you like this town for the friendly atmosphere but there is still an element of unfairness in some areas. This is going to be so much fun!" She clapped her hands and gave a thumbs-up sign indicating that this was going to be a good thing.

Lily was not so sure this endeavor would be fun but she was getting excited about the idea. She said, "Well, I'm not afraid of a little action and I have dealt with the worst of mankind so I'm ready for a shot at it. Let's get it going tomorrow."

It took two months for Lily to find an office space and get it ready for opening. She found a small space in the middle of down-town. The office was sandwiched between a furniture store and a department store. She had a reception room and one office down the hall off the reception room. At the end of the hall were a small kitchen and a restroom. It was small but all Lily needed. She had book shelves built in her office and found some used office furniture. She also found some very comfortable sofas and chairs for the reception room and a desk rounded out the room. Lily put in a table with a huge coffee pot in the reception room as she wanted the town's people to feel good about coming in and having coffee in her office. She was so proud of her name on the front door which announced: **Lily Rose Baxter Attorney at Law.**

In a small town the people are very friendly and welcome new comers. However, to trust a new comer with their personnel business and trust their judgment on legal business was anther matter. Most people in a small town have a long line of family history and new comers could take years to become a part of the community. Just opening a new business did not mean there would be business coming in. The Chamber of Commerce gave an opening ceremony with punch and finger foods. There were a lot of town's folks that came to the opening, ate the food and welcomed Lily to town but this did not mean they would be clients.

Elizabeth had helped Lily find a receptionist that was perfect for the job. Her name was Pam Walters and she had lived in the town her entire life as well as having relatives as far back as great-great grandparents. Pam knew everything that was going on as well as everyone in town. Lots of town's folks would drop by daily and drink coffer and talk with Pam. Actually getting business was slow to start off. This was fine with Lily, she had time and she loved being able to brush up on legal issues that she had been away from for a while.

So the first couple of months Lily was open for business was very laid back. Lily spent lots of time visiting different organizations and getting acquainted with the town officials. She also learned lots of town history and gossip from Pam whom she got to be very good friends with. Business began to build up; then word-of-mouth brought more interest.

Lily's personality and knowledge of the law were the two factors that increased her business. She also began to meet the other lawyers but it would be a while before she was considered a part of the legal click. This didn't bother Lily; she was having a good time and loved her job.

CHAPTER 8

ANNIE HALL

In early spring on a day when the sun was the only thing in the sky and the air was so mild that it was a sign that winter was dying, Pam had the door of the office open and lots of people were walking the streets enjoying the weather. Lily was busy reviewing a contract for a friend to see if it was solid. Pam came into her office, with a solemn look on her face and said, "Lily, there is a woman in the front that I think you need to see right now even though she doesn't have an appointment."

Lily responded, "Okay, have her come in."

Pam said, "I think you will need to come up here as she doesn't want to come into your office."

Lily was puzzled but got up and followed Pam out to the reception room. There stood a very thin, small woman. She was dressed in a very shabby dress with clunky shoes which were too big for her. Her hair was streaked with grey and pulled tightly back in a knot at the back of her neck. Her face was very smooth with no wrinkles, which was in contrast with her hair and stature; this made it hard to determine her age. The lady kept looking around especially toward the door and would not make eye contact with Lily. Lily walked up to her and extended her hand and said, "Hello, I'm Lily Baxter. I'm the lawyer here. It's nice of you to come in. May I help you?"

The woman did not take Lily's hand but said, "I'm Annie Hall. I just wanta talk to you bout a legal matter. First off, I'll have to pay you in a small payments, as I aint got much money. I wanta know that you won't tell nothin I say. Ain't it some kind of law that says you won't tell what I say?" Annie was very crude in her language which indicated she had not advanced very far in school. She also kept looking at Pam as if Pam might be an enemy.

Lily responded, "You are right, there is a code of confidentiality between a lawyer and the client. You can be sure everything you say is safe with me, so please come into my office so we can talk. Please, don't worry about the money; we will work something out on that."

Annie appeared ready to run out of the office but then decided to go with Lily. They went into Lily's office and Lily said, "please sit down. Would you like some coffee or tea?"

Annie responded, "No, I ain't got much time. I'll just start now. My husband is Ray Hall. He was a good man when we got married. I was just 15 when we got married. Ray, he was 20 and worked hard haulin' pulp wood out of the woods and he brung his money home. But the work played out and he lost his job. He's a proud man and when we went on welfare he started drinking. He gets mean when he drinks. I gots two children, Jenny six and Joshua ten. Ray, he starts beating on me when he gets drunk and I need you to do something for me. Something legal, something written down so it can't be changed."

Annie stopped and Lily said, "Annie, I can get you a legal separation and start divorce preceding. It will all be legal."

Annie got a look of terror on her face and started to get up to leave. Lily got up and took her arm and asked her to please stay, so she sat down again. "You don't understand. I aint here for no separation or divorce. Ray would never let me go. Anyways, I don't have no wheres to go. I only come to town once a week for groceries. I only get grocery money so I aint got no money to go anywhere."

Lily said, "Annie, can't you go to some relatives or neighbors. You could get a legal restraining order to keep Ray away from you and the children."

Annie shook her head, "You don't know Ray. All the neighbors know how mean he is, they'd never help me. I aint got no relatives. We live so far out in the mountains no way I could get away. Ray would kill me and anyone who helped me, that's why he can't find out what I'm doing."

Lily was puzzled, "What do you want to do, Annie. I will help you any way I can. Do you want to go to the police?"

Annie shook her head again, "No, no, no. I can't go to no police. They can't protect me. All I wants is for you to write me a legal paper that says that if anything happens to me, the social services will take my kids and put'em in a safe home away from Ray. As long as I'm there, he beats on me and leaves the kids alone. 'Cept he does beat on Joshua lots, but if I'm gone, he will get worse on the kids. I gots to protect them if something happen to me."

Lily was shocked. A woman so resigned to a life of hell, with no way out and only thinking of the safety of her children. Lily said, "Of course, Annie, I will certainly draw up a document for what you want. You will need to come in and sign it then I can file it with the courts. But Annie, what about you, surely there is something you can do to help yourself?"

Annie looked at her lap and started to cry softly, "No, there's no way out for me. My kids, they ride the bus to school in town so the right folks could get'em and keep'em safe. I will have to do what I have to do. I'll pay you two dollars a week out of my grocery money, till I settle my debt."

Lily said, "That's fine Annie. Please call me if you need anything. I can come get you if you need a way out of your house."

Annie got up, "I gots to go. You can't save me. Ray he would kill you too. You just do what I ask and that will be enough." And then she hurried out of the office. On her way out she gave Pam two dollars on her account.

After Annie was gone, Lily sat very still. She could not believe what she had just been through. She felt so hopeless for this poor woman. This was the first time Lily had been introduced to the cruel world that many women are trapped in. She thought she had been through a lot of trauma in her life but nothing to compare with this. Surely this was an isolated case; there could not be more women in this dire situation without any way out. She would have to open her eyes and find out about what was out there in the world. Right now she had to get a document drawn up that might just save two children.

Lily started studying court documents and arrest records through the freedom of information act to see what she could fine and if there was a pattern of women abuse. She went to the Social Services department in town and became acquainted with some of the social workers. She went to the schools and visited with school counselors to get an idea of the number of children at risk with family problems. She got Pam to help her with some of the charity services to get information on the economics and family issues in the area. She was very busy and what she found was very disturbing to her.

The information was there if anyone looked. The ugly side of life was documented in police records, social service calls, court records on domestic abuse and records from school counselors concerning troubled children. Then when Lily began to dig into these dark shadows she found things that shocked her and made her feel even more helpless in making a difference. Lily also learned this was not a one area problem. Over the entire United States the information was the same. There are a lot of social problems widespread that need to be taken out of the shadows so they can be addressed.

Lily also found that economic status did not make a difference in the prevalence of these problems. She found that the higher income group of people could get a lot of things covered up by applying money in the right places. This was especially notable in the cases of minors being in trouble. The rich kids got out of trouble a lot more often than the poor kids. This was the case because the rich could hire the best lawyers. This gave Lily cause to reflect on the profession she had chosen for her life. She never gave it a thought that all people would not be afforded the same level of protection and representation regardless of economic status. Lily did not consider herself being raised in a sheltered environment, but she had not been exposed to some of the hard facts of life.

CHAPTER 9

SWEETIE

Time seemed to slip away as Lily became engrossed in her research to determine the extent and severity of the plight of women. Summer went by and fall was beginning. The days were not as hot and humid and the air was crisper. The leaves began to turn all colors and began to drift to the ground. Many days, Lily would walk to work to enjoy the weather and get some exercise.

This time of year always gave Lily a feeling of new beginnings. She had gone to college for so many years, that fall signified new classes, new books, new friends and renewed energy to achieve a goal. She always felt sad that those days were over yet this is what she had worked so long for. To have a career and a life independent of schedules that ruled your life for nine months out of the year.

On this particular day, Lily was strolling along enjoying the weather and the town that she now called home. She became aware of a dog following her down the side walk. This was unusual as the town had a leash law and there were few stray dogs around.

Lily stopped and the dog stopped and sat down. Lily would then walk and the dog would follow. Lily noted the dog was a small shepherd looking dog with long hair. The dog had distinct black spots with the other areas a bluish color. The ears were all black, and black encircled the eyes making it look like the dog had on a Zoro mask. One ear stood erect but the other ear bent over slightly which made the dog look comical. The most remarkable feature of this dog was that both of her eyes were an ice blue color. This gave the dog a bit of an eerie look when it stared at you with those eyes. Lily could relate to that as her emerald green eyes were always the first thing people commented on when they first met her.

Finally Lily said, "Hello, sweetie, you look like a nice dog. Can you come here?" At the invitation the dog slowly walked, with head down, toward Lily. When she got close enough, the dog lay down and rolled onto her back. Lily noted it was indeed a female, as she lay on her back. Lily began to pet her and rub her belly at which the dog wagged her short, nubby tail. Lily did not know what kind of dog this was but thought she looked like a well kept dog. There was no collar so there was no way to tell who she belonged to. Lily walked on toward her office and was followed by the dog. When Lily opened the door to the office, the dog walked right in like she was a client. Lily had to laugh and Pam was amused, "Found a friend I see," Pam said.

Lily responded, "Well I guess I have. Would you call the local veterinarian clinics to see if anyone has reported missing a dog? And call the dog shelter also. I don't want them to pick her up; she can stay here until we find her owner." Lily went back to the kitchen, found a bowl for water and a half of a chicken sandwich in the refrigerator. She returned to the front and offered the sandwich and water to the dog. The dog gladly and daintily accepted the sandwich and drank the water. She then followed Lily into her office and lay down right beside Lily's chair.

Lily told herself, "Don't get attached, she must belong to someone. She is so sweet and beautiful. I think I'll call her Sweetie just for now." She then addressed the dog, "Do you like the name Sweetie?" the dog gently licked Lily's hand. "Well, I'll take that as a "Yes". So Sweetie, welcome to my office." Lily reached down and ran her hand down Sweetie's side and was surprised to find a place on her fur where there was what appeared to be dried blood. She looked closer and saw some wounds under her fur. Lily got up and called to Sweetie to follow her. "Pam, call the Vet and see if I can bring in Sweetie, she appears to have some wounds that need attention."

Pam commented, "So, I guess you have named her Sweetie. Does that mean you have claimed her?"

Lily responded, "No, I just don't want to call her dog and I know she probably belongs to someone who will be glad to reclaim her. I do not want her to suffer with some trauma until I can find her owner."

Shortly Pam called to Lily, "Dr. Davis is a local veterinarian located just a few miles out of town. She says she can see Sweetie as soon as you get her there."

Lily went to her car with Sweetie at her heels and opened the door of her Cougar. Sweetie jumped into the back seat and lay down. So off to the vet clinic they went.

Lily and Sweetie met Dr. Davis in one of the exam rooms. Dr. Davis lifted Sweetie up on the exam table. Lily asked, "Doctor, do you know what kind of dog this is?"

Dr. Davis said, "Well, she favors a bred called Australian Shepard. She is the size and color of that breed and the ice blue eyes are common in them. I don't think I have ever seen her but she looks very well kept. Now let's look at that side." Dr. Davis pulled the hair back and noted several small round wounds in the skin. "Well, just guessing, I'd say she got peppered by a shot gun with scatter shot. It's common for folks to shoot stray dogs with light shot gun loads to move them on down the road without killing them. I'll clip the hair and flush the wounds out. Then antibiotics should take care of infection while these areas heal. You can leave her for a while and come back this afternoon for her. I assume you will keep her if no one claims her?"

Lily liked Dr. Davis immediately, mainly because she never stopped petting and comforting Sweetie while she was conducting the exam. Lily could tell that Sweetie was the main focus for Dr. Davis and in order for Lily to take proper care of Sweetie; she was going to educate Lily on being a responsible owner. Lily also liked the way Dr. Davis was so interested in her and she smiled a lot. Sweetie was not just another patient to Dr. Davis, but an important new acquaintance that would have a long time connection. Hopefully!

Lily considered the question, "I've never had a dog before. I have no idea how to take care of them. Do you think she would make a good pet?"

Dr. Davis smiled, "I think the way she is staying close to you that she has picked you, so the question is do I think you will be a good owner?"

Lily smiled, "Well what do you think?"

Dr. Davis laughed, "I think with some education you will pass. I have found that dogs know people better that people know themselves, so if she picked you, I think you must be "good folks". You will also find that what you give a dog usually comes back to you as having a devoted friend."

Lily left Sweetie with Dr. Davis and went back to work. She could not wait to get back to pick her up, she already missed her. She had a lot to learn about being a dog owner but she was ready for this responsibility in her life.

When Lily returned to the vet clinic to pick up Sweetie, Dr. Davis had a list of things for her to start this adventure as a pet owner. Dog bowls, dog bed, brush, collar and lease were on the list. Another list was also made to include all the shots that Sweetie needed and about heartworm prevention and tick and flea prevention.

Dr. Davis told Lily, "If you keep her, I will go over all this with you and make sure you have all the information about keeping her healthy. Many people do not realize that it takes a lot of care for a pet and working with your Veterinarian is the best way to see that you don't miss anything. Now don't be alarmed when you see Sweetie, as I had to shave her side and part of her hip to expose all the pellet wounds to the air. A dog like Sweetie has a double hair coat. One is a fine layer of hair that lies right against the skin; the other is longer and is what you see as her coat. If a wound is covered by the fine hair coat, moisture will stay around the wound and allow bacteria to grow and what is a small wound will become a major skin problem. Now with the hair shaved off, the wounds will heal in two weeks and the hair will grow back in about six weeks. She will be as good as new in no time.

'Be sure to get back to me for her shots as there is a city ordinance that all pets be vaccinated for rabies and have a rabies tag and city tag. If you have any problems please call me night or day, that's what I am here for. No question is too small when it comes to understanding your pets and their needs. By the way, Sweetie is a great dog, and very smart. I'm sure she will teach you what you need to know about dogs in due time." Lily liked Dr. Davis' sense of humor and felt comfortable with her.

Dr. Davis then brought Sweetie up for Lily. Sweetie was so glad to see her that tears came to Lily's eyes. She had not realized that an animal could bring such pleasure by just loving you. Lily took the medication and the list that Dr. Davis had prepared and went back to her office. There was a small task of discussing with Elizabeth about Sweetie coming into her room. Lily was already prepared to move if Sweetie could not stay with her. She was very surprised at her resolve. What had started out as a normal day, walking to work, had ended in a wonderful beginning of an adventure. Now Lily had a partner and an unconditional commitment of love.

It turned out that Elizabeth did not have a problem with Sweetie being a roommate to Lily. So Lily's days were now filled with not only work but with Sweetie. Having Sweetie now prompted Lily to think about a place of her own. A house with a yard for Sweetie to run and romp was part of her criteria for a house.

Lily contacted her real-estate agent, Judy, to check on some homes for her to consider. Lily gave her a list of the things she wanted, which was not very long because Lily was used to living very simply. Her most important item was a place for Sweetie to run and exercise.

After a few days of research, Judy contacted Lily about a few places to look at. However, she had one particular place she thought would be ideal for Lily and Sweetie.

Lily said, "That's great. What is it like?"

Judy said, "I want to surprise you, so you will have to wait until we get there."

At 5 o'clock that afternoon Judy picked Lily up and headed out of town. Judy said, "It is just about 10 minutes from your office but it is out of town."

On the outskirts of town, Judy turned on a small paved road. After about a mile she turned onto a driveway. She stopped at the beginning of the driveway and commented, "The property starts here. It consists of an acre with the house on the back part of the acre. This drive winds around in the woods to the house. You can not see the house from the road so the house is very secluded." She started driving slowly down the drive. Lily turned to Sweetie, who was in the back seat, and said, "Sweetie you would love all these woods to roam in." Sweetie stood up in the seat and began to whine in anticipation.

The drive was about half a mile then there was an opening in the woods where a house sat. The house was a two story structure, with a pouch across the front and one across the back. It was country blue with white shutters. Lily fell in love immediately. There was a detached garage that was on one side of the house. Behind the house was a traditional, small red barn with a hall down the middle and horse stalls on each side of the hall.

Judy stopped the car and they walked on the front pouch to the door. The inside of the house was as good as new. There was a big country kitchen with a bar and kitchen table. A large living room with a fire place was off the kitchen. There was a master bedroom with a bath on the first floor that also had an attached office area. Upstairs there were two bedrooms with a bathroom. Lily was beside herself. This was her dream house. She told Judy, "I want this house, please tell me I can afford it."

Judy was sure she could afford it. They went through all the work of buying a house and in two months the house belonged to Lily. Lily was sad to leave her first apartment and Elizabeth, but she was ready to be a home owner. She and Sweetie moved into her dream home. Lily had a great time buying furniture. She loved flea markets and bought all slightly used furniture with some antiques thrown in. Sweetie loved running free, chasing rabbits and exploring the woods. Life for Lily had come full circle. She felt she was, at last, in a home. She had her own business, her own home and Sweetie was her constant companion. She had no idea that life was going to turn up side down and both good and bad was on the horizon.

CHAPTER 10

LILY

Lily was in her office with Sweetie by her side on a usual day when she heard Annie's voice in the reception room. Annie had slipped in to pay her usual two dollars on her bill. Lily rushed out to talk to Annie. "Annie, it's nice to see you. How are you?"

Annie was very nervous and kept looking at the door of the office. Lily noticed one of her eyes was swollen and blue and there were bruises on her arms. Annie said, "I'm fine, I have to go."

Lily stepped in front of the exit door to keep Annie from bolting. "Annie, it is obvious that you are being abused. Please, let me help you."

Annie looked at Lily as if she were from a foreign country, "You can't help me. You'll only make it worst. I thank you for what you done by writing that there legal paper for my kids, but you got to stay out'a my business or you'll get me hurt real bad!" She pushed passed Lily and dashed out the door. Lily was shaken by the accusation that she was going to cause more harm to come to Annie by caring about her.

Lily told Pam, "please, hold my calls; I need some time by myself to think."

Pam said, "Lily, I've lived here my whole life. Things like this have always gone on with folks and there's nothing anyone can do. Don't think you are the only one that cares. My advice is don't get involved. Annie is right; you could cause her a lot of harm, even death. Women like Annie, are very proud and don't want charity."

Lily's eyes began to tear up, she felt so helpless and angry at the injustice of the situation. She went to her office and closed the door. Sweetie moved close to her legs in an attempt to comfort her as much as she could. Lily began to think back over her life. She began to see the situations she had lived in as a child to be just as desperate. She knew she had a mother that was just as dependent on a man as Annie. Jane let Jake take all her money, her dignity and abuse both her and her daughter. The only time she stood up to him was when he turned on Lily. Even thought her mother never showed the least interest in her or love for her except when Lily was endangered. She remembered the isolation she and her mother lived in. Granny was the only person they ever associated with. The teachers at school knew there were problems but they could not help, except for the one teacher that gave Lily clothes. Lily began to realize through her own childhood, that the worse things got, the more her mother receded into the darkest shadows of abuse, addiction and denial.

Lily then thought of Maggie, the mother of the man she had been engaged to. Maggie had everything; money, beauty, education and position in society but she let a man completely dominate her and verbally abuse her. It was only after she lost her son that Maggie realized her husband was the problem and left him.

Why would a woman allow herself to be physically and mentally abused but would kill her abuser if her child was endangered? Lily was searching her heart to find some answers to this question. Lily could also not equate economic factors to deter abuse. It was happening with the very rich to the very poor. Of all the evil in the world, both mental and physical, this cycle of abusing the one that you profess to love, is the biggest issue hidden in the shadows away from the public eye. Even close families would not know one of their members was being abused by a spouse until something tragic happened. Lily had found the court records filled with these issues. Social Services were over run with cases of spousal abuse and children removed from families because they were also abused. Surely something positive could be done. But what?

As Lily continued to ponder this issue, she remembered something that Annie said to her. Annie had said, "I aint got no where to go and no one to hep me. I ain't got no choice but to stay." Annie had no alternative. That was the key that Lily was looking for. What if Annie had an alternative for a safe place to live temporally until she could get a job, or an opportunity to train for a job?

A safe house came into her mind. She knew there had to be government grants for educating people for new jobs and job placement for people. She also knew that if this community was ask to help that they might team together for a good cause. The first person Lily thought of was Elizabeth. Elizabeth was active in all the city projects and knew the town well. That's who she needed to talk to first.

Lily was so excited by her idea that she left her office and went right to see Elizabeth. "Elizabeth, I have an exciting idea and I need you to help me get it together." Lily said as she entered Elizabeth's office.

Elizabeth was intrigued and asked her to go on. "Well, I have discovered through a lot of research and personal contacts, that there is a huge problem with women being abused both physically and mentally. Some stay in bad relationships for reasons of their own, but some have no alternative. I want to launch a safe house project. A place where women can go with their kids, and be safe for a while until they either get training or education for a job or get a job and go on their own. This place could be in an area where police can keep a watch on it to prevent husbands from getting to the women or their kids while they get on their feet. What do you think?"

Elizabeth was speechless at first and had a frown on her face, "Lily, you have no idea what you are getting into. This would be a huge venture not to mention, a huge risk. Also, where would the money come from? And who would you get to run the place?"

Lily thought these were good questions, she responded with, "There are government grants available if we just look for them. There are lots of huge, old houses in this town that are empty and run down. We could get the civic groups to take this on as a project in helping to renovate the house. I know some people that I think I can get that would just fit the bill for managing the project. Elizabeth, just tell me I'm not crazy and that you will help me!"

Elizabeth thought for a minute, "Well, you are crazy, no doubt about it. But I will help you get some information. Just promise me if this does not look good after I do some research you will drop it before you get in to deep?"

Lily nodded and smiled, "I knew you would help, and I will make that promise. But I know this will be the biggest and best thing to happen in a long time."

The next few months were very busy for Elizabeth and Lily. They persuaded the city counsel to sell one of the empty houses in town for the price of the back taxes. They filled out mountains of applications for federal grants to help with the house and the education programs to help the women get jobs. They also spent considerable time talking to civic groups that might support the cause.

After securing the house, getting the house in livable condition was going to take a lot of help. Lily went to the local groups such as the Lions club, Rotary club and Junior League and persuaded them to volunteer time and to donate some money for the renovation. With the many volunteers, things began to move along well.

The house was three stories. It sat on a lot with huge trees shading the yard. There were six bedrooms on the second floor with one bathroom. Two more bathrooms were added so every two bedrooms would have a bathroom. There were two bedrooms on the third floor, but due to the amount of money it would cost to put a bathroom up there, those on the third floor would have to use the second floor bathrooms. On the first floor there was a big room to the left of the entry hall. This was made into a lounge with lots of donated sofas and chairs. There were also card tables for playing cards or putting together puzzles. The room to the right of the entry hall was a library. There were a couple of computer desks with computers in the library for working on line with courses or looking for jobs. There was a big kitchen and dining room behind the front rooms. At the very back of the house were two small rooms. One was made into an office for a director of the house and the other was an office for a counselor. In order to get certain federal grants they were required to have a counselor to help the women work through their problems. This was another thing that Lily had to work on, finding a director and a counselor.

As she was trying to get everything going there were some other issues associated with the introduction of the safe house in town. There were a number of people who were not in favor of this endeavor. They thought that the safe house would bring danger into town by housing women with husbands that were a danger to them and others.

One morning Lily found that the front of her office had been "egged". Another incident happened when someone spray painted the safe house writing "Not welcome in this town." Lily also had some calls that were not pleasant but she knew anything new would have some opposition.

Pam was a little nervous at work and urged Lily to get a gun for her self protection. Pam was good with a gun and carried one all the time. Lily agreed and bought a small pistol that would fit into her purse. Lily practiced and obtained a concealed weapon permit. Lily remembered she still had her father's gun, but it was too large to carry in her purse so Lily put the colt in Pam's desk drawer.

Lily could not help but have memories flood back when she handled the colt that had been her grandfathers. Her mother had told her the story about her grandfather shooting his boss before he died of a heart attack. She also vividly remembered the night Jane shot Jake with this very gun. Lily had yielded this gun at John when he had attacked her in her apartment. She had come close to shooting John as she had a voice in her mind that was saying "kill him, kill him". She knew both her mother and grandmother had heard these voices and had both acted on these directions. She hoped her restraint in not following the voice was a sign that she had developed a strong ability to use good judgment over impulse. Lily knew she stood a good chance of inheriting mental instability that could lead to destructive behavior. She hoped with knowledge and resolve she could lead a normal life even with the genetic tendencies she got from her relatives.

Lily had an idea to fill the position for a director of the safe house. She made a phone call to an old friend, Maggie Jackson. When Maggie answered the phone, she was very surprised, "Lily, what a surprise. Where are you and what are you doing?"

Lily responded, "You would never guess where I am. I'm in South central US, in a small town named Eden. I have a law office here and I am in love with the south. But more important, how are you and what are you doing?"

Maggie sighed and said, "I'm still in this huge house, doing nothing. I'm trying to get myself together after the divorce and find a purpose to my life."

Lily thought this was a good opening and continued, "Well, how would you like to do like I did and take a chance on life? I got on a bus headed east then south and just got off the bus in this town and decided to stay. I have my own law practice and a home. I even have a dog as my best friend. Life here is easy going, with nice people to work with. My reason for calling you is; I have a project going and I think you would be perfect for my project."

Maggie was very cautious as she responded, "You know I do not have any skills in the work place and I really don't need to work."

Lily continued, "Well this job does not pay much but it is a great opportunity to help other women. I'm starting a safe house for abused women. I have a house and it is being renovated but I need a director. You would be great. You have run that big estate for years. That's what I need. Someone to hire, fire, assign work, coordinate women coming in and keeping records. You would be great! Want to give it a try?"

Maggie was not sure, "I don't know, I will have to think about it. I'm older than you and I'm not as adventurous as you."

Lily knew she needed to help persuade her, "Who do you have there to keep you from moving here? You would be closer to your family here. Your house will be fine and if you don't like it here, you can always go back. This could just be a long vacation with a work option."

Maggie was silent then said, "let me have a few days and I will call you back. Good to talk to you and even if I don't come, good luck."

Lily was disappointed that Maggie was not sure about coming. But she knew this was really outside Maggie's comfort zone, so she would wait and hope she would come.

After Maggie hung up the phone from talking to Lily, she was very happy that Lily thought to call her. She was also excited that Lily thought she could handle the director's job of the safe house. Maggie had been on a hard journey. Getting the divorce from Jack was brutal. Jack was not used to losing anything and even though he did not love Maggie, he felt she was his possession and he did not like to give up what was his. Maggie had a great lawyer so she came out pretty good. She got the house and land plus money to live on for the rest of her life. At first she was happy with the arrangement.

Then reality set in. After the divorce, all the friends that she thought she had, turned out to be Jack's friends. She was very lonely in the big house. She found that there were so many memories of John in the house that it was a sad place to live. Maggie fell into a deep depression after the divorce. She had no one to turn too. She finally went to a doctor. She was diagnosed with depression and was given anti-depression medicine. When Lily called about the job, Maggie had been on medication about three weeks. She was feeling better and she was beginning to have hope. She now had the opportunity to change her life. She had an opportunity to do something that had value to other people. She was the perfect person to help women pull themselves out of an abusive relationship. She had been there and felt the deepest pain a mother can have which is losing a child. She had never used her college education in the workplace, but she did have a degree in business management. After several days of thought, Maggie was ready to take Lily up on the offer of a job.

Maggie called Lily, "Lily, I have decided to join you in your adventure. Tell me where to come and what to do."

Lily was elated and answered, "let me know your flight schedule and I'll pick you up. I am so happy, I know this will work and you will be an important part of the team. I will arrange for you to move into the apartment I lived in when I first got here. You will love the apartment and the lady that runs it. Welcome aboard! I know you will never regret changing your life and working for a good cause."

CHAPTER 11

JANE

Lily's next thought went to her mother, Jane. Jane had been in prison for almost her full sentence. Lily had been corresponding with her by mail but had not been to see her as per Jane's request for her not to come. It had taken eight years for Jane to come out of the shadows of her addition and mental illness. She had a history that was filled with things that had affected many people in adverse ways. These things could not be changed. Jane was trying hard to make amends for her bad past. She could not help those that she had hurt but she wanted to help others make a better life. She had no idea what she would do when she got out of prison so when she got the letter from Lily about an opportunity, she was excited about the possibility of a new life. She just had one big surprise for Lily and she did not know how it would affect them.

On the day that Jane was to be released from prison, Lily drove the long distance to the prison. She arrived early and parked near the entrance of the prison. While she waited she had time to reflect on some things in her pass. She was very thankful that she did not appear to have a mental illness that could have been passed to her from her mother. However, she had felt the burden of being born as the results of her mother's mental illness and living in the shadow of Jane's addiction and illness. Lily thought she had come to terms with her long struggle to become who she was and was surviving her past. But she did not know how she would feel when she came face to face with her mother after eight years. A lot would depend on how Jane embraced the future and how they interacted in a mother/daughter relationship that was now two adults facing a past filled with many problems.

As Lily watched, the big gates to the prison opened. Her mother emerged out of the dark interior of the prison into the sunshine. Jane stopped just outside the gates. She looked up directly into the sunshine and tears began to stream from her eyes. She felt so blessed and so undeserving of the magnificent sunshine.

Lily got out of the car and went to Jane. She was so surprised at the flood of emotion and love she felt for her mother. She embraced Jane tightly. For a moment, Jane was shocked at the contact with Lily after so long. Then she too felt the over whelming emotion for her daughter. These emotions had been hidden so long and only now were released. She threw her arms around Lily and they both cried.

The miracle for Jane was in controlling a debilitating mental illness and freeing her maternal emotions for her daughter. For Lily the miracle was that she was able to overcome her feelings of rejection and abandonment and let her love for her mother emerge. The sunshine had removed more than the physical darkness of the prison for Jane but had also physically warmed these two people. It had been a long road for both of them, but they were trying to bridge the gap and make up for lost time.

Lily and Jane finally got into the car for the trip south. They were talking to each other as if they had been friends for years. Lily went into great detail about the safe house and how it was progressing. Jane began to get tears in her eyes, "Lily, you are the best person in the world. I know I did not have anything to do with it, but I am so proud of you. Thank you so much for being who you are."

As they drove south toward Eden, they drove into the northwest part of Arkansas and the south west part of Missouri. They were driving through part of the Ozark Mountains. As the road wound around and was at times a roller coaster ride, but they marveled at the beauty of the land. There were miles and miles of forest with hardwood trees, pine trees and spruce trees to name a few of the majestic foliage. Lily pulled into a parking spot that was designated as an overview spot. Jane and Lily got out of the car and stood by the safety rail and looked at the deep valley that was boarded on two sides by towering mountains.

Lily remarked, "I feel like I am closer to the sky right here than anywhere on the earth."

Jane was awed, "I have not felt this free in my entire life. Even before I went to prison, I was in a prison of my own making. I want to tell you some things that I have learned and what I hope for the future.

'First, I hope you know how very much I love you. I am deeply sorry for the circumstances of your childhood. I don't know how you turned out this well as I certainly did not contribute to your character. I can truly say that going to prison saved my life in more ways than one.

'You know, you and I are in a gene line from our ancestors, which have mental illness. I knew my mother went insane but I did not recognize that I was in a mental fog. In prison, I was diagnosed with mental problems but with counseling and medication I have become much better. When my mind cleared, I was able to see what I had caused in my past and it took a long time to forgive myself. I can only forgive myself as I believe my mental illness was the cause of my actions. Another thing that I realized was I am an alcoholic. After I went through detox, I began working toward staying sober. It is an everyday battle that I will always be aware of. This is another thing that can be passed on genetically."

Lily touched her mother's arm and said, "Mother, you do not have to explain yourself. I know what you have been through and I admire you for being able to recognize your problems."

Jane persisted, "But I need to explain everything to you, as it is your right to know. I want you to be aware of the dangers you face with the predisposition for mental illness and addiction. Everyone has shadows in their mind where they can store things that they don't want to face or that they don't want other people to know. My shadows happen to be big and are filled with very scary things. I have to keep my guard up all the time to keep the evil in me under control. Medicine helps a lot, but I have to stay strong and always be aware that I can fall down at any time. You must also be ever vigilant."

Jane hugged Lily tightly and then they got into the car to continue their journey.

Lily asked Jane, "Do you want to live with me?"

Jane was silent a moment then said, "I would just stay with you until I fine my own place. After eight years of not owning one single thing, I want to own my own home. We can deal with that later, but now I have some other things to tell you. As you know I earned my BS degree while in prison, in social services specifically concerning women and children in abusive situations. I feel so lucky to achieve what I have and I want to give back something to society. I would like to work with women that have problems. The women that have been abused and need to start over, are the ones that I think I can help the most as I have been in their situation. I want to give back by helping women in trouble. Some I may help, many I won't be able to help, but I may be able to refer them to someone who can help them. It's the only thing I can think of that would be something to help society that I can do. If I only help one person, the world will be a better place."

Lily was elated. She had envisioned her mother being close to her and them being able to enjoy holidays together. She said, "Mother, I am so happy you have made this decision. Our safe house has a great team in the making. Maggie is coming. I think you will like her. Elizabeth helps us a lot. I think we can make a difference, even if it is a small difference."

Jane said, "Well of course we can. I want you to continue the life you have made and make memories, good memories, of your life. I will stay with you a while but I want a place of my own. I only have one more thing to tell you. I hope you will be happy about what I have to say."

Jane and Lily continued to drive south but in silence for a while. Jane told Lily she wanted to wait to tell her the rest after they got to her house. When they arrived at Lily's home, Jane was in awe at Lily's home. Lily led her upstairs and said she could have one of the bedrooms.

Jane said, "You'll never know how much this means to me. So many inmates don't have anywhere to go but the streets. Here I have a room in your home. I love you, Lily. I don't feel I deserve your love or your generosity after the poor parenting that I did for you. The judge was right when he admonished me for my treatment of you."

Lily responded with "I love you to, mother. We are going to look to the future from here on out."

A little later, Jane came down stairs and she and Lily sat down in the living room. The fireplace was going. Lily started the conversation with, "What surprise do you have for me?"

Jane took a deep breath and began, "About 6 months after I was incarcerated, I got an anonymous letter that was signed your "Sincere Friend". The letter said he was a friend from my childhood. That he had heard I was in trouble and he wanted to help. The next month I got another letter. This time there was an address that I could return a letter to him if I wanted to. So I began to write. It seemed we could tell each other anything. We explored our dreams and realities. He encouraged me to take college courses. He was a highly educated individual and helped me a lot. This continued until two years ago when he wanted to visit and see how our relationship would continue.

'So one visitation day, he was there. When I saw him I was breathless. I knew him when I was a teenager and he was a preacher at my church. His name was Robert Leslie. When I met him, I was a teenager and he had just gotten out of college. This was his first preaching job. He was handsome, nice and naive.

'But, I was not nice. I was in a spiral downward with a mental illness no one recognized. I was infatuated with Reverend Leslie so I worked hard to get him to notice me. I finally seduced him and we had a short affair. As a sincere preacher, he was very conflicted and felt very guilty.

'Then I found out that I was pregnant. However, Reverend Leslie was not the only one I had been fooling around with. I had no idea who your father was, but I did know I wanted an abortion. So that's what I told him and I told him I needed money. He was devastated with the news of the pregnancy and especially upset that I wanted an abortion. I told him I would tell everyone he raped me. This would have sent him to prison. He took the money I needed from the church and sent it to me, then he left town. He also left the ministry and he bummed around the country a while. He paid the church back all the money and then he met a man at a race track. This man was a war veteran and had been through a lot of trauma during the war. This man and Robert bonded and learned a lot from each other. The veteran made Robert see that he was hiding from life by doing manual work when he was so well educated. Robert then decided to go back to school as he did not feel worthy to return to preaching. He is a professor at a college now. He is the best man I have ever known and he loves me. He said no matter what I did he knew if I got help he might have a chance to see me again."

Lily was in shock, "Mother, this man waited for you all those years not even knowing if you would ever be there for him?"

Jane said, "Yes and Lily you inherited all your good qualities from him. Robert Leslie is your father."

Lily gasped, "Mother, how can you be sure he's my father? Didn't you say there were others?"

Jane said, "We thought of that too. So we had a DNA test by getting your DNA off of an envelope that you licked of one of your letters. He is your father."

Lily put her hands on her face and cried. "I always dreamed that someday my father would come and sweep me away to a fairy tale world. But mother, that was a dream, this can't be happening. Now I have a father after all these years. Does he want to meet me?"

"Oh, Lily, yes. That's all he can talk about. You will see you are so much like him. I didn't need the DNA test to know he was your father."

For a long while, Lily and Jane just sat on the couch, both deep in their own world which for Lily was changing rapidly. Jane said, "He wants to move down here and for us to get married. We want to be as close to you as we can. We just want a normal life with our family"

Jane began to cry. Lily began to laugh, "Why are you crying! We just made a new family." Jane then began to laugh.

Robert Leslie came south to meet his daughter. It was a joyous, emotional day. Lily had to admit that her mother was right. She and Robert were very much alike. They were easy going, level headed, loving and kind. Lily and Robert were an instant match. When they met, Robert put his arms around Lily and said, "I've waited all my life to have a daughter. You are the most beautiful daughter anyone could have. I am very lucky to find Jane and then find you."

Lily was overwhelmed with emotion. She had dreamed of this day but could not have imagined how wonderful it would be.

Jane said, "We would like to get married and have you with us. We are a family now."

So Jane and Robert were married with Lily as witness. They all three went on a trip together to celebrate their family unit. Jane and Robert bought a small home in town. Robert got a job at the local junior college that had become a branch of a larger university. Jane went to work at the safe house. It had been a long road for all three of them to come to a happy life together. They each had worked hard to shine light on their shadows that kept their life from being good. Jane now had a support system. Robert and Lily both knew she had to be constantly vigilant to her mental status and work daily on controlling her addiction.

CHAPTER 12

JOSHUA AND JENNY

As Lily's family was coming together as a happy unit, another family was self-destructing. Annie Hall still came in to Lily's office once a week to make a payment. One day she had her children with her. They stood behind her and were very quiet. Lily came out of her office and wanted to meet the children. Annie had them come around her and she introduced them as Joshua and Jenny. They both said, "nice to meet you, mam." They shook her hand then returned to their safe spot behind their mother. Both children were small for their age. They were wearing old clothes that did not fit them very well. They were both cute kids and Lily was impressed with their manners. Lily had no idea what their life was like and even if anyone had told her how they lived, she would not have been able to believe it.

Joshua was eleven years old but he felt a lot older. He actually did not know how a child should feel. He just knew that his first memory of being hit by his father he was three. From that time on, it was routine that he would get hit on a daily basis usually more than once a day.

Joshua was the son of Ray and Annie Hall. Ray was the hitter. He would hit Joshua on the back, in the stomach or anywhere that would not show. He knew if the kids went to school with visible marks, the social services would come around. He would not have sent them to school except it was against the law not to send kids. Ray did not want to attract attention from the law, Ray made the law in his world and that's the way he liked.

Ray was a big man over six feet tall with big strong arms. He had worked in the woods as a logger all his life. However, he was not working most of the time now as the demand for wood had gone down and the hard wood supply had gotten low due to unmanaged log harvesting. So now he was home more and that gave him more opportunity to hit Joshua.

It was Joshua's job to do all the chores. He had to cut and split wood for his mother to cook with as she had a wood cook stove. He also had to draw all the water for their use as they did not have any indoor plumbing.

The Halls lived several miles out of town and about one mile off the gravel road where the school bus would pick the kids up for school. So Joshua and his sister, Jenny, walked a mile to catch the bus. Jenny was eight years old. She had been spared being hit by her father as Joshua always stood between Jenny and Ray. He protected Jenny in every way because he loved her very much. Jenny was a sweet, shy little girl.

Joshua also tried to protect his mother but he was not able to keep his dad from hitting her. Annie was a small, mousy woman who had resigned herself to a life of pain and misery. She loved her children but hated that she could not protect them. She had married Ray when she was fifteen years old. Ray had not always been mean but when life dealt him some hard times, he lashed out at his family because that's all he had.

When Joshua and Jenny were in school they saw kids doing all the things a kid should do. However, even in school they were mentally abused by the other kids. They had shabby clothes, holes in their shoes and were not always clean. The kids at school would not play with either Joshua or Jenny. They were called white trash, jeered at and even had things thrown at them. The teachers tried to keep these things from happening but could not always be present.

Joshua and Jenny got the free lunch at school which was also embarrassing but they were so hungry they did not care what anyone thought. They were lucky if they got a biscuit in the morning before they went to school and at night they might get a scrap of meat and bread. Hungry children cannot think about anything but food, so doing well in school was not possible. Jenny did better in school than Joshua as he always split his food with her so she got more.

Joshua was small for his age but strong in his arms and legs due to the hard work he had to do at home. The one emotion that Joshua was most familiar with was fear. He tried to be invisible when his father was around hoping he would not get hit. He never spoke directly to his father and tried to always stay out of his reach. If Ray could not reach Joshua with his fist, he would use any object in his hand to inflict pain on Joshua.

Even though there is no excuse for an adult to abuse a child, Ray also had a terrible childhood. He and his twin brother Rafe were raised by their father as their mother died having them. Ray had been the abused child while Rafe had been his father's favorite. The amount of abuse he endured was unbelievable. He did not know any other way to relate to his children other than how he had been treated. His father had literally beat all the feelings out of him.

The only time Ray felt any emotions was when he first saw Annie. Annie was the most beautiful thing he had ever seen and he was instantly in love. Somewhere between first loving Annie and the loose of his job, Ray turned against life and his family. He also became an alcoholic. Drinking only brought out the mean in him and it was worse than when he was sober. Annie had no escape and she was resigned to an early death which she believed would be at the hands of her husband. She just needed to see that her children were safe before she died. That's why she went to Lily Baxter. She had heard that Lily was someone that would care about her plight and help her.

Joshua's typical day began around 4 am, when he was awakened by his mother to go bring in wood for the stove so she could cook breakfast for Ray. Ray monitored how much was cooked and made Annie keep it at a minimum so it was seldom that there was any left over for the kids and Annie. Annie had learned how to hid food and sneak it to the kids as they left for school.

Joshua had to draw water from the well twice daily to keep enough water in the house for the bare necessities. On bath night, he had to draw a lot of water to be heated on the stove and put in a large tub that he had to drag into the kitchen. Annie helped Joshua anytime she could but she was very frail and had so much other work that she was exhausted most of the time.

During the school year, Joshua had some relief from his father while he was in school. He did like school but he could not concentrate on his studies as he was always day dreaming about food and a plan on how he could escape. He knew he could run away. But he could not leave Jenny and she would be a burden on him if he took her with him. He also would not leave his mother. He knew he was not any help in keeping Annie from Ray's beatings, but he felt if he and Jenny were there, Ray would not kill her. It also crossed his mind that Ray might kill them all.

Joshua thought the day would come when he would have to kill Ray. He had several different plans, but knew he would have to be older to be able to stand up to Ray. He was ready to go to jail for the rest of his life if it meant Jenny and his mother were safe and happy. He figured that jail would be better than his home. At least in jail he would have some food and would not be beat on all the time.

In the summer, Annie made a large garden in an attempt to get enough food canned to help them make it through the winter. With a large garden, Joshua and Jenny spent their summer working from daylight to dark in the garden. They also helped prepare the vegetables for canning.

The Halls did not have any close neighbors and only Ray's brother was still alive as a relative. Isolation is the first element to keep Ray's reign of terror on his family hidden in the shadows. Fear was the next tool. Everyone that knew Ray knew he was capable of inflicting harm and even death so no one ventured near the Hall's house. There were a few people who would talk about how bad things must be at the Hall house as they saw Annie bruised and battered anytime they happened to see her. They also knew Ray was brutal to Joshua. No one had any answers as to how to help the situation, so they chose to just talk about it and do nothing.

Joshua and Jenny were in the shadow of child abuse by a parent. It was a very dark place for them, filled with fear and pain. Their entire life was a nightmare. Joshua was afraid to sleep in fear that his father would harm Jenny. Ray had tried to do some inappropriate things with Jenny but Joshua was always there. Joshua would submit to being beat by his father but he would fight him when Ray tried to touch Jenny. Since Ray was drunk when he tried to touch Jenny, Joshua had an advantage and could fight him off. But Joshua could not protect his mother. When Ray was beating Annie, he was in a rage and was deadly, so Joshua would just try to keep Jenny away so she would not see how Ray hurt Annie. To say the Hall house was hell on earth was correct. There was despair, pain and fear hiding in that dark place. Before this shadow was gone and the terror within exposed, there would be grave consequences for some of the members of this family.

CHAPTER 13

JOSHUA

One day Joshua was horrified to realize that his mother was pregnant. He was astounded that she would want to bring another child into this family to suffer like they did. He could not help but confront her, "Maw, are you pregnant?" He ask Annie,

Annie said, "Yes, Joshua, I'm goin'a have a baby. I'm about six months along."

He looked at her with so much pain and anger on his face, "Why would you get pregnant? A child in this family is only a punching bag for paw. There's not enough food to go around now. Do you really want to watch another hungry child take the abuse that Paw dishes out?"

Annie began to cry, "Ray wants another boy to help with the work. I don't have nothin' to say in this. We just have to make the best of this. I'll do the best I can." She turned and went into her room and shut the door.

Joshua was angry but he was also afraid for his mother. She was frail and he did not know if she could go through childbirth. Annie would not be going to the hospital. She delivered Joshua and Jenny at home with a midwife and that's the way this baby would be brought into the world. Joshua could only imagine what would happen to him and Jenny if their mother was not there to care for them. He did not know that his mother had Lily set up a legal document that would take them away from their father if something happened to her.

Three months later, Annie began having labor pains in the early morning. She awoke and told Ray to get the midwife as the baby might come quickly, since this was her third child. Joshua and Jenny decided not to go to school that day. As soon as Joshua got out of bed he began to draw water and got the fire going in the stove. After Joshua had everything prepared, he went to sit with his mother. He held her hand and told her he loved her.

When Ray returned with the midwife, he sent Joshua and Jenny outside. Even outside, they could hear their mother screaming. It seemed like the labor would go on forever. Annie was getting weaker but by the time night was falling, they heard the cries of a new baby. The midwife eventually came out and told them it was a girl and their mother was fine but needed to rest as it was hard labor and delivery.

After a while Ray took the midwife home. When he returned he told Joshua and Jenny to go to bed and not to bother their mother and the baby. After Jenny was asleep, Joshua wanted to see his mother. He eased toward her room and noted the door was ajar. He peered in the opening in the doorway. He was surprised to see Ray bending over the baby's crib, so he went back to bed thinking he did not want to disturb Ray. This was the first day in a long time that Ray did not hit him and he didn't want to take the chance he would want to take a swing at him.

The next thing Joshua knew, he was being shaken by Ray in the very early morning hours on the day after the baby was born. He got up and followed Ray into the kitchen. He thought he was going to start his chores but Ray said, "You go get the shovel and head out back to the edge of the woods. You goin'a have to dig a hole. There was something wrong with the baby and it died."

Joshua was shocked, "You mean the baby died?"

Ray violently pushed Joshua toward the back door, "You heard me, do what I say and don't ask any questions." Then he went back into the bedroom.

Joshua got tears in his eyes. He didn't know what could have happened but he was sad that his mother would surely grieve for the loose. He recovered enough to do as his dad told him to. He picked a spot under a nice, big cedar tree because the fragrance from the cedar was so sweet and he knew his mother loved that tree. He began to dig. He had no idea how deep to dig the hole, so he just kept digging. After about an hour, Ray walked to where Joshua was digging. The hole was about 5 feet deep by now as Ray could barely see the top of Joshua's head. Ray placed a blanketed bundle on the ground near the grave. He said, "That's deep enough. Get out of there and put the baby in and cover it up." Then he turned and walked away.

Joshua could not believe a man could be so calloused that he would not even bury his own child. He felt pure hate for this man. An inner rage welled up inside of him that mixed with the sorrow that he felt for the loose of his sister. Joshua looked up at the sky and a savage, visceral cry came out of his mouth and soul. Tears ran down his cheeks as he cried for all the pain in his life as well as his mother's pain.

He climbed out of the grave and looked at the tiny bundle on the ground. A blanket was tightly wrapped around the body. He had not seen the baby before she died and he wondered what she looked like. He knelt down and pulled the blanket off the baby's face. Then he wished he had never looked. The baby's nose was black and there was a definite outline of a hand print around her mouth. It was immediately obvious to him that Ray had killed this baby by holding her nose closed with his fingers and the rest of his hand over her mouth. Joshua fell back on the ground and lay there for a while. He remembered that his mother had said Ray wanted a boy. Joshua knew at that moment that Ray's soul was damned to hell.

A dark shadow covered Joshua's mind and he hid this terrible event in this shadow. This is the only way he could possibly continue his life. He eventually got up from the ground and placed the bundle in the grave and covered it up. He felt he needed to say something but all he knew to say was the Lord's Prayer. In an isolated place, a very small, young boy bore the weight of a terrible event on his thin shoulders. Surely God had something in mind for this child that would be good as Joshua had been through enough pain to last him a life time.

Annie lay in her bed for the next month. She was in a state of deep depression as well as physically spent. She ate what the kids brought to her and slept. Then one day in the spring, Annie came out of her room and took up her life as if nothing had happened. She did ask Joshua where the baby was buried. Joshua said, "I dug a deep grave under the cedar tree behind the house. I put a stake in the ground where the grave is. I can take you there if you would like."

Annie was quiet for a while then said, "Yes, that would be nice." After a good while she suddenly said, "I named her Emma Marie. Marie was my mother's name and I just like the name Emma."

Joshua said, "that's a nice name. Maybe we can get a stone some day with her name on it."

Annie nodded her head, "Yes, that would be nice."

Two months later a knock was heard at the door. Since they never had company everyone was interested in who it was. Annie moved to the door of the kitchen and the kids eased up out of their room to peek into the living room. Ray got up and opened the door. Standing on the porch was the midwife that had been there for the birth of the baby. She opened the screen door and entered the living room and smiled at everyone. "Hello, Ray. Hi, Annie, nice to see you mended and are getting' around. Hi kids, how are you'll?" She did not wait for an answer she continued to talk, "just was around today, and thought I'd come see the baby. I always check up on the babies I deliver later down the line. How is that sweet baby girl? I didn't even get her name before I left."

Everyone froze. No one spoke until a very soft voice came from Annie, "Her name was Emma Marie." Then she dropped her head like she could not believe she had said that. But something inside her wanted someone to know her baby had a name.

The midwife said, "Oh, what a nice name. May I see her?"

Ray took a step toward her and said in a loud voice, "The baby died. Somethin' was wrong with her."

The midwife was shocked, "That can't be true, that baby was a fine, healthy baby when she was born. I know babies. I seen a lot of them die, I seen a lot of them come into this world but not intending to stay. But that baby was tough and ready for life." She looked at Ray's face and the ugly truth came to her in a rush, "Ray Hall, you done somethin' to that child! You took her out of this world afor her time come. You killed that baby!"

Ray stepped closer to the woman and took his big hand and wrapped it around her throat and squeezed. "I said, the baby was sick and she died. That's the end of it and you need to go mind your own business."

When he let go of her throat, her eyes were bulged and her face was a dark red. She staggered out the screen door and let it slam behind her. She looked back through the screen at Ray and holding her hand on her throat she said "God have mercy on that poor baby's soul. Ray Hall, may your soul burn in Hell!" And she walked away.

Ray slammed the door behind her and turned around. Annie was standing stone still in the door of the kitchen with tears streaming down her face. Ray looked at her and ordered, "Go get me a beer, now!"

Annie looked at him and said, "Get it yourself." She turned around and went into the bed room and slammed the door. This was the first time the kids had ever seen Annie defy Ray in any way. They eased back into their room, they did not know what Ray would do next but they did not want to be there if he reacted by having a rage.

Surprising everyone, Ray walked out of the house, got in his truck and drove off. He was gone for three days. No one said a word about him or what happened. They all just went about their chores as if nothing happened. At the end of the third day, they heard the truck returning. Everyone stopped what they were doing and waited to see what Ray might do. He came in the house and had a bag full of groceries which he set on the kitchen table. He turned around without looking at any of them and said, "I got a job in town driving a delivery truck. They paid me for my first two days so here's some food." Then he went in the living room and sat down. Annie began to unpack the groceries and things went back the way they always had been in the Hall house.

After Ray got the truck driving job he was easier to live with. He was still a bully and loud but he had stopped hitting them. However, everyone knew this would not last but no one knew it would end in such a disaster.

A few weeks later, Joshua and Jenny were in their room waiting for supper when they heard the front door open and slam. The next thing they heard was Ray as he went into the kitchen where Annie was cooking supper. Ray shouted, "What the hell are you trying to do? Why would you be a-goin in to see that there Bitch Lawyer in town? A guy I work with said his wife seen you a-goin in that office last week. Are you fixin to get a divorce?"

Annie backed up against the cabinet and said, "No Ray, I wouldn't do such a thing. I was just talking to her but it didn't have nothin to do with no divorce." She knew from the look on Ray's face that this was going to be bad.

Ray was very red in the face and his eyes were bulging. He got in Annie's face so close that when he talked he sent spit flying in her face. "You don't go behind my back and do stuff. You ain't telling me the truth. I will beat the truth out of you." As he said this he hit her in the face. Annie's head snapped when she was hit and one of her teeth flew out of her mouth. Ray was not done yet and he hit her again. Joshua ran to the kitchen just in time to see Annie get hit the second time. As Ray drew back for another attack, Joshua grabbed his arm. When Ray couldn't swing his arm, he was surprised but quickly saw it was Joshua. "You think you can fight me? You'll get the same thing as your Maw." He said to Joshua as he took his other hand and grabbed Joshua by the neck and threw him against the far wall. Joshua hit the wall and slid to the floor, unconscious.

Ray turned his attention back to Annie who was barely still standing. The last blow that Annie would ever get from anyone knocked her down and her head hit the edge of the cabinet. Blood began to stream from a large gash on her head. Ray stood over Annie's lifeless body and his face changed from rage to shock. The fact that he had just killed his wife began to sink in. He backed away from Annie and then looked at Joshua lying on the floor. He decided Joshua was just knocked out and not dead. As Ray tried to figure out what his next move would be, he rationalized that this would not have happened if that bitch lawyer had not interfered. His thought process was that he needed to take care of her, too. He turned and left the house his focus was that he would settle this with Lily Baxter and he had the guns to do it in his truck.

Jenny heard the screaming in the kitchen then the sudden stillness. She had begged Joshua not to go in the kitchen because Ray was out of control. But Joshua went anyway. When everything went silent, Jenny heard the front door slam and the truck fire up so she knew Ray was leaving. She was trembling as she slowly moved toward the kitchen. She could hardly comprehend what she saw as it was like a horror movie. Her mother was still and laying in a pool of blood. Even at her young age, Jenny knew her mother was gone. She ran to Joshua and knelt down by him. He was breathing. She called his name and patted his face. Joshua slowly began to wake up. He was weak but raised his head to look at his mother. He started to cry and Jenny hugged him and cried with him. Joshua said, "Jenny can you help me get to the bedroom? My head is really hurting and I'm dizzy."

Jenny helped Joshua slowly get to the bedroom and on the bed, "Jenny, you are going to have to be brave. I want you to get a blanket to cover maw."

Jenny answered, "I can't, I can't go in there again. It is too horrible."

Joshua insisted she could, "Maw did everything for us, at least we should not let anyone come in and see her like that. So you have to do this, you have to."

Jenny went to the other bedroom to get the blanket off her parent's bed. She then went to the kitchen. For a minute, Jenny stood frozen looking at the body of her mother on the floor. She could not process that this lifeless, bloody mess was her mother just a few minutes ago. She felt an emotion so overwhelming and sad that boiled up from her stomach and she had to run to the sink as she began to throw up. Then she slide to the floor and sobbed. Who would take care of them? Would Ray come back and kill them too? She heard Joshua calling her from the bedroom, "Jenny, you can do this. Be strong."

Jenny got up from the floor and placed the blanket over her mother. Her life would forever be changed but she did not know if it would be for the better or for worse. She went back to sit with Joshua. They sat on the bed beside each other just waiting for what life would throw at them next. Joshua was resigned to the possibility that at any minute Ray would roar back up the drive to finish them off. As the afternoon wore on, the sun began to go down and shadows began to form. The room grew dim as the two small figures sat on the bed. They were deeply submerged in their own mental shadows of sorrow, fear and hopelessness.

CHAPTER 14

LILY VS RAY

I t was a warm day in the middle of summer. It was not very humid and about ninety degrees which was average for this part of the country. Everyone walking outside on the town streets were taking their time and enjoying the summer. Lily was working on some documentation that was very mundane, so she was feeling bored. Pam came to the door of Lily's office and stated, "We don't have any appointments this afternoon so if it's okay with you, I would love to get off early. The kids have been out of school long enough that they are starting to get bored. When kids get bored it usually equals trouble as they will be thinking up things to do "just for fun". So I would like to take them swimming and have a picnic."

Lily paused in her work and smiled. She had a little stab of jealousy that Pam would be going home to a house full of fun and noise from her three kids. Lily would be going to a quite house with just Sweetie to talk to. She thought maybe her mother and dad would want to go out to eat somewhere. Lily answered Pam, "Go ahead, I'll be finished with this soon and may go home early myself."

After Pam was gone, the office was quiet. Sweetie was a little restless so Lily took her outside a couple of times to walk around. Sweetie loved the warm weather; she had shed a lot of her thick coat so she was not too hot. After returning to the office, Sweetie settled down in her normal spot, by Lily's feet.

Around quitting time, Lily was surprised she had worked so long. She began to close up her work when she heard the office door open. She thought Pam had probably forgotten something and returned to get it, so she called, "Pam, is that you?" When she did not get an answer of any kind, she got up and walked into the reception room. She was very surprised to see a large man in the office. He had a full beard with long hair that was below his shoulders and he looked dirty. He had on a dirty, oily ball cap and wore overall over a dirty tee-shirt. It didn't take long for Lily to zone in on the most important part of the intruder. He had a pistol in his hand.

Lily told herself to remain calm so she politely ask, "May I help you? I'm Lily Baxter the lawyer in this office."

The man said in a low gravely voice, "I know who you are? I'm Ray Hall. Annie's my wife."

Lily fought to control her fear and was able to say, "Well, yes I know Annie. Is she with you? How is she doing?"

Ray stared at Lily with an unblinking stare. He said, "Don't you fret about Annie. You don't need to be worrying about Annie ever again; she won't need your meddling help no more. In fact, no one will be able to get help from you as you are going where Annie is now."

Lily was shaking, "Ray what have you done? Is Annie okay? Please tell me you did not hurt her."

Ray growled, "I'm not telling you nothin'!" He raised his pistol and was ready to shoot. Before a shot could be fired, Ray was shocked to feel Sweetie sinking her teeth into his thigh. Ray screamed and looked down at the dog hanging on his leg. His hand with the pistol flew up and he pulled the trigger. The bullet went wild and buried in the wall behind Lily.

Lily was high on adrenalin and acted on sheer instinct for survival. She ripped open the top draw of the desk and pulled out her father's colt .45. She cocked it and fired. The bullet hit Ray and he went down to the floor on the opposite side of the desk from Lily.

Lily grabbed the phone and dialed 911. "I need the police and an ambulance. A man has come into my office and I shot him. I'm Lily Baxter and I'm at my office." While she was talking she was looking at Sweetie who had come back to stand by her side. What she did not see was Ray rising off the floor. He was wounded but able to get up. Before she knew Ray was still alive, she felt a sharp pain in her left shoulder that spun her around. She still had the colt in her right hand, she raised it and shot the last bullet that was in the gun. This time Lily's bullet hit Ray square in the chest. When he fell this time he was not going to get up again. Lily had dropped the phone but she could hear the operator begging her to answer. Lily picked up the phone and said "just have them come now." Then she sank to the floor, holding Sweetie close to her.

The first police officer that was on the scene was Detective Ronnie Harris. Ronnie had been on the force for ten years and had been in the area when the call first came in so he responded immediately. He was over six feet tall and in good physical condition. Some people would describe him as rugged looking. His face had strong features and he had brown eyes and brown hair. Ronnie had not met the new lawyer in town, but he was aware of the things that Ms. Baxter had been working on. He was impressed that she was so interested in raising the awareness of families that had problems.

When Ronnie arrived on the scene, the paramedic was putting Lily on the gurney. As he approached the gurney, he was surprised to see what a beautiful woman Ms. Baxter was. He was especially astonished with her emerald green eyes. So much so that it took him a minute to recover and understand what Lily was saying to him. Lily looked up at Ronnie and immediately requested, "Please, send someone to Ray's house. I think he may have hurt Annie. The kids may also be there and need help. Please go now."

Ronnie turned and requested if anyone knew where Ray Hall lived. One officer stepped up and said, "I was dispatched out there last year for a disturbance. I'll go." And he turned to leave.

Ronnie turned back to Lily and asked, "Ms. Baxter, what makes you think Ms. Hall may be hurt?"

Lily tried to sit up but her arm was hurting, "Ray told me he had taken care of Annie, for me not to worry about her anymore."

"Ms. Baxter did you know Ms. Hall?"

"Yes, she came to me and requested legal help. I think Ray thought I was going to help Annie leave him. I would have helped her but she was adamant she could never leave Ray. She was afraid if something happened to her, her children would be in danger from him." Lily lay down at this point. The paramedic told Ronnie he needed to get Lily to the hospital.

Ronnie told Lily, "I will see that we check on Annie and will let you know. I also need to get a statement from you. So I will see you soon." With that Ronnie patted Lily on the hand as the paramedic pushed the gurney toward the ambulance. Just as the ambulance with Lily in it pulled away, Pam burst into the office. She was scared and asked, "Hey, where is Lily? Oh, lord, is she okay? I should never have gone home early. Tell me, is she okay?" She shouted as she grabbed Ronnie's arm.

Ronnie said, "Hold on Pam. Settle down, Ms. Baxter is fine. She has a bullet wound to the shoulder; but she is fine."

Pam looked down at Ray on the floor in a pool of his blood and said, "Lord, what an ugly bastard that is. He must have really scared Lily, but she's very cool and he got what he deserved." She looked down and saw Sweetie leaning against Ronnie's leg. "Oh, Sweetie," she said, "I'm glad you are okay." Pam looked at Ronnie and said, "If anything happened to Lily's dog, she would be devastated. That dog is her pride and joy."

Ronnie looked down at Sweetie, "I'll take her with me to the hospital and ask Ms. Baxter what to do with her. Sweetie seems to like me." Sweetie was wagging her tail and looking at Ronnie like he was an old friend.

Lily didn't remember the ride to the hospital but after the emergency room doctor looked at her, he assured her the bullet had gone in and out. He had some X-rays taken and determined the bullet had entered her upper shoulder and exited under the shoulder blade. He was surprised that nothing was broken. He dressed the wound and told her she needed to stay overnight just to be monitored. Lily was in no shape to argue. Jane had arrived at the hospital just as Ronnie got there. She saw that he had Sweetie and was very relieved. Jane introduced herself to Ronnie and said she would take Sweetie home and take care of her for Lily.

Lily was awake in her hospital room. She was reflecting on the dangerous day she had just gone through. Ray could have easily have killed her instead of her killing him. She was very thankful that she was alive. Lily was surprised to hear a knock at her hospital door. She said for the visitor to come in.

Detective Ronnie Harris eased into the room. "How are you doing?" He asked.

Lily smiled and replied, "Well, my arm hurts but I was just reflecting on how lucky I am that Ray just hit my shoulder. They gave me some pain medicine so I will be out of pain soon. Were you able to check on Annie?"

Ronnie was quiet a moment, then he said, "I hate to tell you this, but Annie is deceased. It appeared she was beaten but a blow to her head from being pushed against the cabinet is what I think killed her. There was a lot of blood loss from the head wound. I'm sorry; I know you knew Ms. Hall."

Tears welled up in Lily's eyes, "I really didn't know her except for doing some legal work for her. I know she had two children. Were they okay?"

Ronnie was touched Lily cared so much for someone she barely knew, "The children are okay. They were hiding in one of the bedrooms. They were afraid Ray was coming back to kill them. The boy had apparently tried to defend his mother and was knocked around some. He has a bump on his head but I think he will be okay. We'll get him checked out tonight. They will be taken to the social services office in town if the doctor says he is good to go. Social services have a temporary place for them until they get a foster family or find some of their family to take them."

Lily said, "They don't have any family, that's why Annie did not have anywhere to go to get away from Ray. Annie was the inspiration for me introducing the safe house getting it up and running. I guess it's too late to help Annie now." Lily wiped the tears off her face.

Ronnie asked, "Do you need anything that I can do?"

Lily answered, "No, you did enough by bringing Sweetie to me. I love that dog so much; I hope she was not any trouble. My mother can take Sweetie home with her. Sweetie is not just my dog, she's my constant companion. She is the reason Ray didn't get a good shot at me the first time he shot. Sweetie bit his leg and distracted him long enough for me to get my gun out of the desk. After I shot Ray, he fell. Sweetie and I thought he was dead; but he wasn't. He got up when I was calling 911 and that was when he shot me in the shoulder, but I was able to shoot him again. Sweetie just came to me by accident but I am fortunate to have her because she saved my life."

Ronnie said, "I agree, she sounds awesome. I'll go for now, and let you rest. I'll get your statement tomorrow."

Lily said, "Thanks for coming by with the information about Annie. I know it's late and I'm sure your family is waiting for you."

CHAPTER 15

RONNIE

Ronnie smiled, "No you're not keeping me from anything. See you later." As he left he thought how wrong it was for Lily to think he had a family; there would be no family waiting on him. Thinking about family brought back a flood of memories for Ronnie. He had lived in this town his entire life. He had one brother who was a couple of years older than him. His brother, Jason, had gone to law school. Jason had been the brains and Ronnie had been the muscle. Ronnie had been the star quarter back on the football team and of course, he had been very popular with his team mates and the girls. The crowd he ran around with preferred to go as a group, the boys and the girls. They would party at each other's homes; swim in the river or just hang out together. However over time, some of the kids paired up and became an item, but they still all hung out as a group.

Ronnie was drawn to one of the cheerleaders, Katy Nelson. Katy was a cute, petite blond with a sweet disposition. She was quieter than the other girls and wasn't silly and flighty. Katy was drawn to Ronnie because he was sweet, quiet and great looking. They seemed to fit together well. They could talk for hours or just be together quietly. They looked very good together and everyone knew they were an item.

In the late 60s and early 70s, the sexual revolution had not reached deep enough into the South to affect a lot of the kids in Arkansas. South Arkansas was deeply religious with a church of some demonization on every corner in town. It was still popular for couples to wait until after marriage to start their sexual life. Katy and Ronnie had been as close to having sex as they could without going all the way. They were both satisfied that they were meant for each other. As they talked about their future, Ronnie was very sure of his direction. He told Katy, "I want to be in law enforcement. I can go to the police academy for two years and then be ready to go to work. Do you think you would like for us to get married?"

Katy smiled at him, "I do want us to get married."

Ronnie was surprised that Katy did not seem excited about the prospect of getting married and she did not seem to have any plans for her life after graduation. He just felt she was thinking about her options. So they were engaged with a target of two years till the wedding. Ronnie was accepted to the police academy and he gently encouraged Katy to go to the local college for a business degree or accounting degree. She agreed to give it a try.

Katy was the only child of Ruth and Doug Nelson. She was the center of their life; she was her father's pride and joy. The Nelsons gave Katy everything they could and yet she did not appear to be spoiled. She was polite and people loved her. Even though Katy fit in well with a crowd, she really did not have any close friends. Then after she and Ronnie started hanging out together she did not seek other friends. Katy would just as soon be alone than to have to interact with another individual.

After Ronnie left for the academy, Katy had a lot of free time on her hands. She was not very interested in college, in fact, after the first semester she quit. She did not tell her parents or Ronnie that she had quit school. She just couldn't make herself go to class or to even listen while in class. She decided to use her approaching wedding as an excuse because it was going to take a lot of work to get everything ready.

To keep from having to face her parents about dropping out of school completely, Katy said she had night classes. At night she would go out as if she was going to class, but she did not go to class. Katy had become fascinated with religion. She had grown up going to church every Sunday but now she found regular religion boring. She was attracted to tent revivals.

These revivals were put on by a traveling troupe made up of diverse people. A huge tent would be set up by a team of rough neck workers. These workers also set up the benches for seating and a stage at one end of the tent. There would be other people with the team that put up advertisements and made sure the public knew the revival was coming. Then there were the singers that made up a choir that was essential to set the mood for the star of the show, which was the preacher. The show or service would start out with some very rousing hymns and testimonies from people traveling with the troupe. There was always a plea for donations so they could continue to do the Lord's work. Many people gave money that they could not afford to give as they were caught up in the excitement from the preacher. The preacher would start with a message from the Bible but the goal was to reach a climax of fire and brimstone preaching. The energy in the room would go up. Many people would start praising God, with some getting so emotional they would sometimes faint. Katy found that the only time she ever really felt emotionally charged and involved was at the height of the sermon. She soaked in the sermon about the streets of heaven being paved in gold and life in heaven being free of sadness and pain.

Katy had a secret that she did not share with anyone. She felt pain and sadness on a daily basis and most of the time, she felt hopeless and alone. She knew these feelings were not justified with the advantages she had in her life. She had loving parents, a comfortable life and Ronnie loved her. Why was she not happy? She felt a huge void in herself that she could not understand or cope with. She had fooled everyone by acting like everyone else, but how long could she go on like this? Katy did not have anyone to confide in that she was depressed and anxious all the time. She certainly could not tell her parents, they did everything for her now, how could they do anything more. Ronnie loved her so much that she could not tell him of her feelings for fear he would blame himself. She sat and dwelled on the sermons she had heard about heaven being such a peaceful place. Katy's only hope to be normal and happy was that after she was married things would be better.

Time passed quickly and Ronnie was back from the academy and he was ready to get married. Ruth and Doug spared no expense on their only child's big day. They got the largest church, had the most flowers and were ready for everyone to attend. There were eight bridesmaids and eight groomsmen. The town was excited about two of their native kids getting married and settling in their home town.

On the day of the wedding, Ronnie was a nervous wreck. Katy did not feel anything. Everyone else was ready for the show; like a train leaving the train station, there was no stopping it now. When Katy appeared at the door of the church holding her father's arm, she was the most beautiful thing Ronnie had ever seen. He didn't know if he could breathe after he saw Katy walking down the aisle beside her proud father. He felt he was the happiest and luckiest man alive.

The wedding went perfectly. Then the party began and went into the early hours of the morning. Finally, the happy couple made a run for it in a rain of rice and a string of clanking cans tied to the car. They took off for a resort town that was only a couple of hours drive away where Ronnie had made reservations at a beautiful hotel.

When long last, Katy came out of the bathroom at the resort hotel with her sexy gown on, Ronnie was elated. Katy sat down on the bed with her back to Ronnie. He reached for her and was surprised that Katy stiffened at his touch. "What's wrong, Katy?" Ronnie asked.

Katy shook her head, "Nothing, I'm just exhausted. Could we just rest tonight? This wedding has been a real strain on me."

Ronnie was disappointed but he said, "Sure, we can just lie here together. We have the rest of our lives to make love. I love you!"

So they lay together that night, and the next two nights before Ronnie began to be impatient. He questioned Katy, "Is something wrong? Do you want to talk about this? Are you just scared?"

Finally, Katy said she was ready and she reached for Ronnie. He thought things would be fine now. However, he found that Katy was not participating in their love making but just being there physically. Since the first night was a little painful for Katy, Ronnie considered that was the reason that she was so unresponsive to him. Maybe things would be better after they got home.

They had rented a cute house in town and bought all new furniture. Surely they would fall into a normal married life when they got home. Sadly, their sex life did not get better with time. Katy did everything she could to avoid sex, then when the excuses ran out, she would consent but she never was emotionally present. She just went through the motions. Ronnie knew things were not right. He requested Katy go to the doctor for a physical exam. Everything checked out good for Katy physically. Katy told the doctor she could not sleep well and she was sad all the time. The doctor gave her some sleeping pills and told her to get more exercise, get more sunshine and eat more nutritional foods. All of this was good advice, but not nearly what Katy needed to help her with her deep emotional problems. Anti-depressants were beginning to be used more frequently at this time, however, they were new and many doctors did not believe in dispensing them. The thoughts about depression had not elevated much and many doctors still thought people could just get over what they termed the "blues". Today many different options are available and medications could have been administered. This young couple did not get the help they needed.

Because Ronnie loved Katy so much, he resolved himself to the fact that sex was not going to be a satisfying part of their marriage. He felt their life was good enough together that he could overlook this problem. He also thought things would get better as he and Katy matured.

Ronnie and Katy were getting close to their fourth wedding anniversary. Ronnie had felt Katy had been more withdrawn over the last few weeks. He was thinking about talking to her parents about helping him understand Katy's moods. However, he decided it would be very awkward discussing their sexual problems with Katy's parents. He was worried about more than their sex life. He found Katy to be uninterested in anything. She slept most of the day then wanted to go to tent revivals at night. He was concerned that Katy had been going to more and more of these tent revival meetings. He did not have a problem with her exploring religion but he thought this might be why she was getting more withdrawn. Ronnie had decided that after their anniversary, he was going to address the problems aggressively to see what they could do together to get help.

The day before their anniversary, Ronnie received a call at work. When he answered the phone, he was pleased and surprised that it was Katy. She hardly ever called him at work so he said, "Hi, honey, it's nice to hear from you. I love you."

Katy said, "Ronnie" then she paused, "Ronnie" again she called him.

Fear gripped Ronnie's heart; this was not like Katy, "Katy, honey, what is wrong?"

"Ronnie—I need—you—to come—home." Katy slurred her words then dropped the phone.

Ronnie called, "Katy, talk to me, Katy." He put down the phone and dashed out of the building. He jumped in his squad car and as he raced toward his house, he dialed 911 and requested an ambulance come to his house. He just had a bad feeling about the call from Katy.

When he reached his house, he raced in the door to find Katy lying on the couch, unconscious with a hand full of sleeping pills. He started doing chest compressions and calling her name. The ambulance rolled in, the paramedics rushed in and took over. There was a weak pulse as they loaded her into the ambulance. Ronnie rode in the back of the ambulance with Katy, holding her hand and praying. At the hospital, Ronnie was left in the hall as Katy was taken into the emergency room. He heard the doctor call "clear" and he knew they were shocking her heart to try and get it started. Then "clear" again; then silence. What seemed like forever was in reality just minutes before the doctor appeared.

When the doctor came out to face Ronnie; he didn't have to say anything, the look on his face said Katy was gone. Ronnie sank to the floor and cried. How did this happen? Why did this happen? Ronnie was devastated. His next thought was how would he tell Katy's parents? Ronnie had never had a time in his life when he was this devastated. He had no idea that emotional pain could be so bad that you thought you were going to die.

The doctor took Ronnie by the arm and helped him up, "Ronnie, you will need to come in to verify identity. You need to have to face this now, it won't get any easier."

Ronnie walked into the emergency room. Katy was lying on the stainless steel table with a sheet up to her neck. She looked like she was asleep and any moment she would wake up, say hi and they'd go home. But that didn't happen.

She was so beautiful. Her skin looked like fine china. Ronnie was suddenly struck with the realization that Katy's face was completely serene. As he got near her body, Ronnie felt an energy almost like a spirit, come over him. He felt Katy's spirit was there trying to lessen his pain because she was out of her pain. He touched her face with his hand; her skin was soft but cold. He leaned down and kissed her lips. He told her good bye.

CHAPTER 16

DOUG AND RUTH

Ronnie knocked on the familiar door at Ruth and Doug's house. Ruth answered the door, "Why Ronnie, how nice to see you. Come in." She called out, "Doug, Ronnie is here."

Doug called back as he came into the livingroom, "Is Katy with him?"

Ruth looked behind Ronnie, "No," she answered.

Ronnie sat down on the couch in the living room. Ruth and Doug sat across from him. Ruth said, "Ronnie is everything alright? You don't look very good. Are you sick? You are scaring me."

Ronnie said, "This is the hardest thing I have ever done, but I am here to tell you Katy is gone."

Ruth looked puzzled, "Gone, where?" She asked.

"Katy passed away today." He said.

They both looked at him like he had two heads and for a split second they were frozen. Then Ruth began to scream, "My baby can't be gone. Tell me it isn't true." She fell back against the chair.

Doug finally spoke through his despair, "Was there an accident?"

Ronnie wanted to lie and say yes, but he knew they would find out, "No, she overdosed on sleeping pills."

Doug said, "NO! NO! My baby did not take her own life. You are lying to me."

Ronnie had heard that in times of extremely devastating news people would age in front of your eyes. Ronnie saw Doug's face crumble and turn an ashen color. In fact, he looked ten years older in seconds. Doug said, "Why? Why? We gave her everything. We loved her beyond belief. Oh my God Why?"

After a while, Ronnie said, "Katy left a letter addressed to you and me. She wrote on the envelope not to read this until I'm with you both. So we will learn what she had to say together." Ronnie cleared his throat and wiped his eyes, which were overflowing with tears. He pulled out of his pocket, a white envelope, opened it and pulled out two sheets of white paper that was folded one time. He unfolded the paper and read:

Dear sweet Mother and Father and my dear Ronnie,

I know you all are sad right now and confused at what I have done. Please do not think you did anything to cause this. Ronnie, I can not tell you how sorry I am that I could not be the wife to you that I should have been. You are such a dear person and you deserve more than I could give you. None of you are to blame! It is me, I am flawed. I am missing some essential component in my heart and mind that allows me to feel happiness. I am always deeply depressed. I am a pretender and I do not feel the things other people feel, I just emulate how other people feel. I feel a part of my mind is dark, so dark, that the light of any feelings can not penetrate. I pray to God to forgive me for my sin of causing my own death and if he can forgive me, I will be walking on the streets of gold, where the sun always shines and I will sit beside God and I will not be sad any more. Pray for me and know I love you all. Katy

Ronnie folded the letter put it back in the envelope and put it in Ruth's hand.

Deep depression is one of the causes of suicide in teens and young adults. Suicide is occurring at an increasing rate in America today with a large percent of the deaths being teens and young adults. Even with advances in anti-depressants, counseling and therapy many parents and loved ones are left all because young people feel such desperation and isolation that they feel suicide is their only way out. By hiding in the shadows, suicide can take even the closest families by surprise when their child is gone. We have to look deep into these shadows to see what we do not wish to see. We must be alert to red flags of depression, if we want to save a loved one. Essential to dealing with depression is to get professional help as soon as possible.

Ronnie sat with Ruth and Doug while they cried. He did not have anything to say that would ease their pain. A knock was heard at the door. Ronnie answered it and found the pastor of Doug and Ruth's church there. Ronnie took him to Ruth and Doug, and then he slipped away. He felt the minister might have some answers for them, but he knew there were no answers for him at this time.

At the funeral there were hundreds of people in attendance. The church was overflowing and flowers filled the entire front of the altar. Ronnie sat with Doug and Ruth on one side and his parents and brother sat on the other. Everyone wanted to shake hands with Ronnie or hug him in order to express their condolences. Ronnie thought he saw on their faces questions: What did you do to her? Did you hit her? Did you cheat on her? They all wanted an answer and he had no answers. To the world Katy was a beautiful, sweet, talented, privileged person who had it all. For Katy, life was a void, she was an observer that only saw how life could be but she could not live it.

After the funeral, everyone went to Doug and Ruth's house where the church ladies had prepared a huge meal consisting of every dish you could imagine. Ronnie wondered; why do people think food will fix sorrow and emotional pain? The people that are hurting the worst could not eat anything anyway.

As Ronnie was standing in the house of his in-laws feeling like an alien, Ruth touched his arm and motioned for him to come with her. They went up the back stairs of the house and into Katy's room. The room was just like Katy had left it before she and Ronnie were married. There was the big canopy bed with pink curtains and bed spread. There was a bulletin board with pictures of her high school friends. Ruth sat on the side of the bed and patted next to her for Ronnie to sit down.

"Ronnie," she started and stopped, took a deep breath and started again, "Ronnie, you are the best thing that ever happened to Katy. I know you were good to her in every way. That's why I am going to tell you some things.

'When we moved here years ago, Katy was just weeks old. We had moved to get a new start away from everyone that knew us. We had adopted Katy. We arranged to adopt her from a woman who wanted to give her child up. The woman was an alcoholic and had no way to take care of a child. It was all legal but we never wanted Katy to have to see her biological mother or any of her relatives in that area. We wanted her to have a good life. We wanted to protect her from a past that she did not have any control over. When I first held Katy, I thought she was the most beautiful baby in the world. Doug was over the moon; this was his princess. She was the best baby and she never cried. She never smiled either. I did not think that was normal. All babies cry and smile. Doug just thought she was special. As a toddler, she did all the right things but never laughed or giggled like toddlers. I thought maybe she was autistic. We took her to several doctors all across the country. They all said she was normal in every way. Just stop worrying; they advised. We were told that we were over protective and over anxious new parents. I have since learned that there are things we do not know about that can happen to the fetus when the mother drinks alcohol during pregnancy. The baby's brain can be affected. I believe now that Katy was damaged by her mother before she was born. Of course, we did not know that and would not have believed a beautiful baby like Katy was damaged.

'As she grew up, I did all the normal things a mother does. I took her to dance lessons and Katy was a beautiful dancer. Her instructor thought she would be a professional dancer. However, for no reason, Katy just quit dancing. Then she took piano lessons. Again, Katy was so gifted. The teacher thought she had potential for fame. One day, Katy stopped playing and would not touch the piano again. The only thing she stuck with was cheerleading. She appeared to really enjoy cheerleading. I ask her one day why she liked being a cheerleader. She said, 'It's like everyone is pretending to be happy and I am an expert at pretending to be happy.' I did not know what that meant until you read the letter to us that she left. When Katy said she felt a void and she didn't feel anything like everyone else, so many things she did began to make more sense. She was so sad inside and only pretended to be happy. How painful that must have been for her. I know Katy was looking for something in life and that's why she went to the tent revivals. She wanted to believe that there was a better place; a place where everything was good and everyone happy. She gave up on this life and hoped the next life would be better. I pray that it is better for her and someday we will see her again." She bowed her head and sat for a few minutes as if she were trying to feel the pain that Katy felt.

Ruth put her hand on Ronnie's arm as she continued to talk, "You need to know you did not do anything to cause this. Doug and I want you to go on with your life. You are young and need to find someone to share your life with. We want you to have a family. Of course, we wish it was Katy as your partner and the mother of our grandchildren but that can not be. So please, make peace with yourself. We love you." She kissed Ronnie on the cheek and got up and led him out of the shrine left to Katy.

Ronnie could not live in the house he had occupied with Katy. He sold all the furniture and moved into a furnished apartment in town. He asked to be put on the grave-yard shift at the police department. By working at night, he was able to enroll in college during the day and pursue his degree in criminal justice. He kept his life simple with his police work and going to college. That did not leave much time to think about how much he missed Katy. Even though their sex life was not exactly satisfying, he still loved Katy with all his heart. It would take a long time for his broken heart to heal and there would always be a spot in his heart for Katy.

Today the shadows are very dark that hide women who are pregnant and consume alcohol and abuse substances. These women are condemning their babies to a dysfunctional life. The babies may look normal at birth but they will have far reaching mental and many times, physical disabilities. Many unsuspecting adoptive parents, who have waited for a long time for a child, adopt these children and their life is forever traumatized by the fate of their children. There is so much support and outrage concerning abortion rights today. Maybe all that energy should be focused on demanding accountability of women that use alcohol or drugs during pregnancy because they are knowingly harming their fetus by making choices that condemn their child to less than a normal life.

CHAPTER 17

LILY

Lily had a shoulder wound where the bullet passed all the way through her body. She was lucky as the bullet did not break any bones. A night in the hospital was just for precaution. The day after the shooting, Lily was sitting up in bed with her arm in a sling. Her mother was sitting in a chair beside the bed. Officer Harris came in to make his report. He was a little disappointed that Lily's mother was there and intended to stay through the interview. He would have liked to talk to Lily alone; he was more than a little interested in Lily. From the first time he saw her laying on the gurney, he was awe struck by her beautiful black hair and emerald green eyes. However, he felt she was way out of his league even though she appeared to be very down to earth and easy to talk to.

After all the questions were answered, Ronnie pulled out the colt .45 that belonged to Lily. He said, "Here is your gun. It's pretty old but apparently in good working order. Which was lucky for you as Ray was intent on taking your life. I just have one question; why did it just have two bullets in it?"

Lily and Jane looked at each other, Jane said, "that was my father's gun and many years ago he loaded it with six bullets. He died of a heart attack after he shot it three times. Then I shot it once leaving two bullets. We did not have the heart to reload it."

The detective looked puzzled, "So all three of you shot this gun?"

Jane responded, "between Dad, Lily and myself, we managed to empty the chamber. However, every bullet was for a good cause. I guess we can retire it now."

Lily looked at Jane and said, "Or we may need to reload it for the next chapter in our life." With that Lily and Jane laughed. Ronnie did not get the joke so he just shrugged and continued to document Lily's report of the events as they happened the day before.

When he finished, he said, "Thank you, I will file this report. There will be a hearing but as of now no charges will be issued. Hope you recover quickly and if you have any questions, please, call me." He smiled at Lily and for a minute was frozen in his spot staring at her. Jane smiled at the obvious smitten look on the detective's face. She made a mental note to mention to Lily that the detective would be a good catch. However, Lily did not seem interested in men since she had such an unsuccessful track record with them.

Lily was released from the hospital that afternoon. When she left the building she was inundated by the media. The local newspaper and TV media from near by towns were clamoring for attention. Lily gave a brief summery of what happened and ask to be allowed some time to heal. The story was flashed on many TV stations across the country. Lily made one final statement, "The loose of Annie Hall is the tragedy here. Her two children are orphans now. Her only concern was that her children get a good home if something happened to her. I hope all of us work to see that happens. Next week we, the entire town, are opening a safe house as a place of refuse for women and children that are in a bad situation. This safe house might have saved Annie's life if the house had been available for her. We have decided to name the safe house the Annie Hall Safe House in memory of Annie Hall." The media crowd became quiet and moved aside for Lily and Jane to walk through in route to their car.

Lily took Jane to her house then Lily decided to go to the office just to look around. However, the office was roped off with yellow tape and she felt she should not go across the tape in case the police were not finished with their investigation.

Lily thought about Annie's children. She drove to the social services shelter to check on the children. The building had once been a hospital so it was built with several wings radiating out from a central station for nurses. Lily entered the central area and asked the lady at the desk where Annie's children were. She was told the room and directed down a long hall with doors on each side.

When Lily got to the designated door, she softly knocked. A very small voice said to come in. Lily was not prepared for the sight of two small children huddled in the corner of the room with a blanket over them. They appeared very small for their age and had old, tattered clothes on and no shoes.

Lily slowly walked over to them and sat down on the floor. "My name is Lily. I knew your mother and I liked her very much. She loved you both so much that she had me write a legal letter saying that you both should be taken care of by anyone but your father. She was afraid that your father would do harm to both of you if she were not around. Your father was very sick and he lost hope which caused him to loose himself. All he knew was to take his pain out on his family. You both need to know, I am the one who shot and killed your father. I never, ever, wanted to hurt anyone but he was going to kill me. He was in a rage and would not listen to me. I am so sorry you have lost both your parents."

Joshua was surprised to hear Ray was dead because no one had told them. He bowed his head and said, "Paw hit my maw and she fell. She hit her head and didn't move anymore. He had hit maw lots of times but never this hard and he wouldn't stop hitting her. I couldn't do nothing to stop him. Me and Jenny loved her a lot and we gona miss her." Jenny began to cry.

Lily pulled Jenny into her lap and hugged her. "I want you both to know it was not your fault that any of this happened. It is very strange what the mind can do when it gets all mixed up with pain and sadness. I want to help you both." Lily's heart was breaking to see these two orphans so afraid and sad.

Without a thought for herself, Lily knew she could not leave these sweet children alone tonight when they had just witnessed the death of their mother and knew their dad was gone also. Even when children are abused by a parent, they still see their parent as their connection to life. Also even if they know they cannot be hurt anymore, they still believe they will be punished in some way. Lily reached out and touched Joshua. He did not say a word; he just looked at Lily with wide eyes. She pulled Joshua over and put an arm around him also. Lily said, "I am going to see if you two can come home with me. I have a dog named Sweetie. She will be so excited to have you two with us. Would that be alright with you?"

Joshua took Jenny's hand and said. "Jenny what do you want to do?"

Jenny looked at Lily and said, "I think we should go with Miss Lily."

Joshua said, "I'm glad paw didn't kill you. I know he hurt you, Paw he hurt a lot of folks."

Lily led the children down the hall to the desk. "I'm taking Joshua and Jenny with me tonight so they won't be alone. I have the power of attorney from their deceased mother. I'll get in touch with the case worker tomorrow."

The Lady said, "Please, sign them out and leave a phone number."

When Lily brought Joshua and Jenny into the house, Sweetie met them. She was so excited to see them and licked their face. For the first time, Lily saw a smile on their face. It is always amazing how children react to animals, for some reason there is a connection between them that helps children feel at ease. "Let's get you guys something to eat, a bath and a bed made for the night."

Lily had twin beds in her guest room and she got the children tucked in after they ate and had a bath. Lily had just gotten in her bed when she heard a noise at her door. The small face of Jenny peeked around the door. Lily said, "Jenny, are you okay? Where is Joshua?"

Jenny said in a small voice, "Lily, Joshua is asleep. I'm scared. I ain't never been away from home at night."

Lily patted the bed next to her, "come sleep with me, dear. There's nothing to be afraid of but I have a big bed and you are welcome to sleep here. Sweetie won't mind; she sleeps on the foot of the bed anyway. Jenny, I don't want you to ever be afraid again."

Jenny ran and hopped into the bed. "Thank you, Lily" and she slipped under the cover. She was quickly asleep. Lily looked at her sweet face and love filled her heart. What was she doing? She did not know how to take care of kids. Sometimes things happen the way they should, especially when people listen to their heart.

The next day, Lily got all the paper work in order to be the foster parent for the kids. Since Annie had signed her power of attorney, it was no problem. Lily wasn't sure how she would get the kids through the funeral. She had called Jane to come and be with them so she had help on the way.

CHAPTER 18

ANNIE

On the next Monday after the tragic death of Annie Hall at the hands of her husband and the death of Ray Hall at the hands of Lily, there were two funerals. The first funeral was held early in the morning. Ray was buried with only a hand full of people present. There was a preacher and some police officers there. Ray's grave was in an isolated part of the cemetery, alone.

That afternoon, at the service for Annie, the funeral home was filled with standing room only and some town folks standing outside. The preacher gave a moving and appropriate talk. Everyone was surprised when Lily approached the podium. Her arm was in a sling but otherwise she looked stunning in a tailored suit. Joshua and Jenny were nicely dressed in clothes that Lily had hurried around to buy. Both of them clung to Lily's hand and stared wide eyed at the coffin in the front of the church. Jane was with them for support. Since Lily was the only one that knew anything about Annie, she asked the preacher if she could make a short talk.

Lily talked very softly into the microphone. She said, "I met Annie Hall in my office when she came to me for help. She asked for some legal documentation to protect her children if something happened to her. I could tell from her condition and bruises that Annie was an abused wife. I pleaded with her to leave her husband with her children for their safety. She told me she had no place to go, no money and no one to help her. How sad is it when someone knows their future is domed and they are all alone?

'The efforts of this town to build a safe place for women and children like Annie and her children, has come too late for Annie. The Safe

House that so many citizens in this town, have worked so hard to open is ready to open. I plan to name the safe house: The Annie Hall House. I think it is appropriate to have a memorial to the woman that gave me the inspiration for a safe house. Annie had a short, very hard life. I know I will always remember her and I will always regret that I could not help her. I want to assure everyone that Annie's children, Jenny and Joshua, have a good, safe home just like Annie wanted. I hope that they will be able to stay with me. I took the life of Ray Hall, Annie's husband; he was going to kill me so I had no choice. But to take a life no matter what the reason, is a very sad thing. I am very, very sorry, Jenny and Joshua, that you have lost your parents especially your mother." With tears in her eyes, Lily then returned to the chapel pew and hugged both Jenny and Joshua to her.

Annie Hall was buried in the same cemetery as her husband Ray. However, she was placed far away from his grave. At least in death, she was away from her cruel husband. Many beautiful flowers were on Annie's grave and a fund was set up for donations to an education fund for her children.

One week later there was another crowd of town folks gathered at the house that was now a safe house for women and children. The Chamber of Commerce sponsored a ribbon cutting and tour of the facility. The ribbon was cut by Lily, Elizabeth, Jane, Jenny, Joshua and Maggie. They all cried as it was an emotional event that signified hard work from the entire community. Everyone was very proud of the Annie Hall House. Again, there was wide media coverage for the dedication of the home. The attention was welcome as it would get the word out about the new facility. However, the publicity came at the price of losing Annie. Lily hoped that Annie's death would not be in vain. Lily realized that women still have to make the decision to change their life if they find they are in an abusive situation. Her hope was if they have a safe place to go and support, they would take the opportunity to make their life better.

CHAPTER 19

LILY

Lily was going to return to work after the dedication of the safe house but she needed a few days to heal from her wound and to mentally heal from all the events. Pam gave her some directions to a place that she thought would be a peaceful place for reflection. Lily had gotten the kids back in school and they appeared to be settled. Lily needed some time to think. Her life had taken a sharp change and now she was responsible for two children which was a big order.

Lily, accompanied by Sweetie, followed the directions that were given by driving along the main highway for twenty miles to find the Little Missouri River. This was not a river the size of the Arkansas River or the Mississippi River, but what Lily would consider a large creek. At the bridge the river spanned about 50 yards across but was shallow in comparison to the larger rivers. Lily took a sharp left just before driving over the river bridge. The road was just a logging road with two ruts and grass in the middle. She slowly followed the twist and turns of the road along the river for about a half mile. The road grew into a clearing that was obviously where cars parked even though no one was parked there now. She stopped the car and got out. Sweetie followed close behind her.

The first thing she noticed was the complete stillness, except for a slight breeze in the very tops of the tall trees around the parking place. She followed a well worn path down a small bank to the edge of the river. Sweetie charged ahead of her but stopped at the edge of the river. This appeared to be a swimming hole. On the left she saw a rocky beach that went into a shallow area of water just prior to some rapids. Above the wading place was a large round area of what looked like deep water where

Lily assumed was the main swimming hole. On the bank was a large tree that was right next to the water and leaned out over the swimming hole. A rope swing hung from one of the larger limbs high in the tree. There was a small board with a hole in it, the end of the rope passed through the hole with a large knot on the other side of the board. About five feet up the rope was another knot. Lily could visualize a young teen standing on the board, holding on to the knot and jumping from the platform that was nailed to the tree trunk and swinging out over the swimming hole. The teen would either do a straight down drop or perform a dive off the swing board. Across the swimming hole the bank went straight up in a sheer rock formation. At the base of the rock bank a few huge rocks jutted out into the swimming hole. This was the place the swimmers could swim to then lounge on the rock in the sun or do shallow dives.

Lily took off her shoes and waded into the water. She was immediately startled by the extremely cold water. How in the world could anyone swim in this cold water? Sweetie also tested the water but scrambled back to the beach. The kids that swam here just did not feel the cold when they were having fun or trying to impress the opposite sex.

Lily joined Sweetie on the gravel beach and sat down in the sun. She could hear the rippling of the water on her left and marveled at the rock formations that had to have been there for hundreds of years. For centuries, the water was relentless in it's pursuit of a lower level, wearing slowly into the rocks.

Lily became focused on a leaf that was floating slowly on the surface of the water crossing the swimming hole. When it got to the rapids, of course, the leaf was swept away with the increased rate of flow over the rocks. She pondered at the parallel that the leaf made to her life. She felt she had always floated along on the surface of life, moving in the direction that everyone pushed her.

Lily wanted to take control of her life and that is what prompted her to get on a bus bound for anywhere and ending up in a small southern Arkansas town. There were also times she felt like she was racing to fast to be able to see or feel anything. This was the feeling she had after her mother had killed Jake and went to prison. It was a flash in time that she went through in a numb, mindless state. Now she felt it was time to do something in her personal life. Something that she initiated and that she had control over. She felt a very slight stirring in her heart and brain that she would like to have a child. She was not sure where that came from as she had never been around small children.

Lily had just become an instant parent by bringing Jenny and Joshua into her home. Even having two children, there was still an urge in her heart that seemed to swell into a deep ach of desire. She wanted to have a child of her own. However, having been a fatherless child, she did not want this for her child or for Jenny and Joshua. So there was the matter of being open for a partner and husband.

Lily did realize there was no man in her life now but if she was more open and met more people, the chances of finding someone would increase. However, what man would take on a woman with two children already? Well, that's just the way it would have to be, a package deal. That man might never come along, if not, Lily had her children to take care of now.

Lily got up and headed back to her car, Sweetie at her heals. She had gone down to the river for a view of the river but was leaving it with new found determination and vision to change her life. Maybe it wasn't the river that influenced her but having a quiet connection to nature and opening her heart to hear a message. Lily though maybe she had found an answer to why she was spared from being killed by a madman. She had dreams and unfinished business in this life.

Lily did have a small fear that since as a child, she did not have a loving relationship with her mother, she though this could cause her to be detached from her own child. She had to just have faith in that not happening, as she had this desire for a child and from what she had gathered from her mother, Jane did not want her from the start. Lily felt that experiencing the love she had in her heart for Jenny and Joshua, she was sure she would love her own child unconditionally.

CHAPTER 20

RONNIE

By spring time life in this southern Arkansas town, everything was returning to normal. The winter had been filled with tragedy and hope. Everyone was ready for life, as they knew, it to be restored. Lily's business was increasing in her law practice and she was busy learning how to be a mother to two children.

Joshua and Jenny were beginning to blossom. They were catching up in school and learning how to be children free from fear. Lily was also working hard helping the Annie House get started. Maggie and Jane were getting organized and they were receiving some women and children into the home. The death of Annie Hall raised awareness for many people and helped them come out of hiding in the shadows and seek help.

On this normal day in the office, Pam looked up to see Detective Harris walking in the door. She beamed a smile and said, "Lord, I see the most handsome bachelor in town walking in and here I am a married woman! Ronnie, how are you?"

Ronnie had known Pam all his life and he always enjoyed seeing her, "Pam, I'm just fine and I know I missed the boat when I let Hank woo you away from me. Now he is so lucky to have such a beautiful wife."

Pam laughed, "You always were a charmer. What can I do for you today?"

Ronnie said, "I wonder if I could see Ms. Baxter? I know I don't have an appointment but was hoping she could see me."

Pam rose from her chair and took Ronnie by the arm. She pulled him down the hall to Lily's office. "Hey, Lily, look at this handsome man I found in the office. Can you talk with him a little while?"

Lily looked up and was pleasantly surprised to see Ronnie there, "Sure Pam, Ronnie, come on in. How nice to see you when there is not a disaster going on." Lily got up and presented her hand for Ronnie to shake.

"Thank you, Ms. Baxter, for seeing me," Ronnie said as he shook her hand.

"Please, call me Lily and I will call you Ronnie, if you don't mind?" Lily said.

"Oh, sure, thank you. I have been meaning to talk to you as I wanted you to know how much I admire you for all your work on the safe house. The house is great and was really needed. I also thought it was very nice to name it after Annie Hall. That was such a tragedy but it happens a lot. How are the kids? I understand they live with you now."

"Yes, they are fine and they are so precious. I'm the one that is blessed with them. They are both so smart and are just coming out of their shell more and more each day."

As they were talking, Ronnie was looking into Lily's beautiful eyes and he was so mesmerized that he had to force himself to stay focused on the conversation. This was probably the first time since Katy had died that Ronnie had thought of a woman as being sexy and attractive. He was surprised that his heart was beating rather loudly, or it seemed like it was to him. He cleared his throat and tried to continue. "I don't know if you are aware, but I was married until a few years ago when my wife, Katy, passed away." Ronnie had to stop and control his emotions before he could continue, "Katy took her own life."

Lily was very surprise, "Oh, Ronnie, I didn't know that. I'm so very sorry. I know that had to be so devastating for you."

Ronnie continued, "Yes, for me and her wonderful parents. Katy was an only child and her parents were so devoted to her, she was their entire life. I knew Katy all through high school and we were together as a couple the last two years before graduation. When I graduated from the police academy, we were married. I thought everything was good. Katy was sometimes moody or sad, but I had no idea what pain she must have been in.

'Something you said when you were starting the safe house was that women in trouble had no where to turn. I have thought maybe if Katy had a place to turn or someone to talk to, maybe she could have seen a different solution.

'My idea is that maybe we could start a hot line that people can call for help. I don't like to say a suicide hot line but a life line. I have researched for federal grant money that would help if we apply and there is money available for this. I don't know where or how to start. Do you think this is something that would work?"

Lily was really intrigued; she was impressed that Ronnie had felt so strongly about this that he had made a plan to help others. She knew he had felt more pain than she could imagine and wished she could help him relieve some of that pain by helping him with his plan. She said, "Ronnie, again I'm so sorry for your loss, but I think maybe you have a good idea. Maybe we could incorporate it with the safe house. I have the best director, Maggie, who would be great with the organization of the answering service. And my mother, Jane Leslie, is a licensed counselor so she could train the operators.

'We could do some fund raisers but if we had some of the women staying at the house train to answer the phone; we could contribute some of the rehabilitation federal money to the cause.

'Why don't we have some meetings with Maggie and Jane to get this thing off the ground. I think you know Elizabeth from the boarding house? She is very involved with the safe house and is a wonderful source for fund raising and getting attention from all the civic groups."

Ronnie felt better than he had since Katy had died. He felt he was doing something that would honor Katy and keep her memory alive. "Lily, this is so wonderful." Tears filled his eyes, "I'm sorry I'm so emotional but this is the first time I have been able to feel better since Katy died. I would like to talk to her parents, Doug and Ruth, but maybe we could call this the 'Katy Harris Life Line if that would be okay with everyone."

Lily smiled, "Ronnie that would be wonderful. I think you should see if Ruth and Doug would like to be in on our meetings. This might help them feel they are doing something for Katy."

Ronnie was amazed at how sensitive and smart Lily was, "Thank you so much. This is great. Just let me know when we can start. I will talk with Doug and Ruth to see what they think. Lily you are amazing." Ronnie said that with so much feeling that Lily was very touched. She was really taken with this handsome, sensitive, thoughtful man. She assured him she would get started on the project immediately. Lily stood and walked around the desk. She took Ronnie's arm and escorted him out of the officer to the front door. Ronnie waved at Pam, "thanks, Pam, now you be good! I don't want to have to take you "down town" for something."

Pam said, "If I knew you would put the handcuffs on me, it would be worth the trip." They all laughed as Ronnie left. Pam lifted up her eye brows and said, "Well, you two look really good together. Ronnie's a great guy. You better not let him get away."

Lily responded, "Pam, you read to many romance novels and watch too much TV. I do admit Ronnie appears to be a good guy but I am a package deal now with the kids. That will certainly cause men to take a second thought before taking on all that baggage." Even though Lily was talking like she was in denial, she did have to take a few minutes to compose herself and get her mind back on her work and off the handsome man that was just sitting across the desk from her.

Over the next three months, there were many meetings to discuss the new life line program. Grant money was obtained and fund raisers had brought in money. Some of the civic groups in town had committed time and money for the project. Elizabeth had presented the program to all the important people in town. She had amassed statics to show the problem was more far reaching than anyone realized. The fact that the number of teen suicides were increasing brought a lot of interest from parents. Elizabeth and Lily had even been asked by other towns to come and present their program and tell them how they got it stated. Lily encouraged Ronnie to talk at these meetings to give his personnel experience. Ruth and Doug joined in the group and gave their story on how losing Katy had affected their life.

The "Katy Harris Life Line" was set up at the safe house. An office was set up for the operators and the operators were trained by Jane and Maggie. The operators had specific procedures to follow when talking to callers. They were taught to recognize when they needed to call for help and how to refer the callers for professional help. Every call was recorded and documented and a team reviewed all the calls. This helped improve information and see if follow up was needed. The importance of an operator talking to someone that needed help was paramount. Every call had the potential to save a life and the operators and the team also had to realize, there were going to be people that they could not help. It was important that the team did not get emotionally involved to the point that they were depressed. Therefore, the operators were interviewed periodically to assure they were staying focused.

Maggie, Jane, Ronnie, Lily and Elizabeth worked closely together. Ronnie was becoming more interested in Lily. However, he was shy and felt that Lily was so out of his class therefore he did not move forward with his feelings. Ronnie had always been confident in himself. He had been a football star in high school and had advanced in the police force. Ronnie was used to being positive and proactive. He was very articulate and his job was based on communication. However, when it came to Lily, he was a shy boy and could not think of anything to say. He felt Lily was so educated and smart that he could not reach her level. Therefore, he kept their communication on business matters.

Lily was certainly attracted to Ronnie, but he seemed a little nervous and strained around her. She did not want to make any advance and be out of line, so she kept their communication business also. Lily did look forward to any opportunities to be with Ronnie. When she was with him, she felt very calm and comfortable. She did occasionally have thoughts that it would be nice to have a relationship with Ronnie. She did not know how to advance their friendship, so she waited for Ronnie to make a move. She had no idea that the move that Ronnie would make would be sabotaged by a flash from her past.

CHAPTER 21

MAGGIE

As life in a small town went on, everyone continued their routine work but they were all excited about the life line. Doug and Ruth found that talking about the life line and working to achieve something that might prevent the tragedy that they had gone through, had helped them cope a little better. The pain was more of a dull throb now instead of the sharp, debilitating sensation that made them double over and cry. They were also able to learn more about recognizing warning signs of problems that could escalate to a person taking their own life. They became advocates for parents who thought their child had problems or just sitting and listening to grief stricken parents that had lost a child. Reliving their tragedy was always hard, but at the same time it was a life-saving mental therapy.

Maggie was very involved in the life line project. She had come to the realization that John had been on a self-destructive path after he lost Lily. She did not blame Lily in the least. In fact, she was grateful to Lily for giving John the one happy time in his life. She saw a different person in John when he was with Lily. She saw the love in his eyes and a sweetness that he possessed when he was with Lily. These memories were all Maggie had left.

Maggie gained insight to some of the inner problems that John lived with as she dealt with people with problems. Of course, she knew that Jack had been unbelievably cruel to John. She had tried to forgive Jack if only for her own peace of mind. Maggie learned that many times, when a loved one took their life, the surviving loved ones blamed each other. They would channel their pain and grief to blaming others.

Depression is not an emotion that is open to reason. Depressed people cannot just "get over it." The fact that they have a good, easy life or a bad, hard life does not change the occurrence of depression. Maggie thought about all she had learned from Jane, from the women in the shelter and from their work with life line. She acknowledged that even though Jack had a negative effect on John, she could not ignore the fact that she stayed in a marriage that was toxic for both her and her child. She had taken the easy way by staying with Jack.

Maggie also could not ignore that she was financially well off when she was with Jack. When she analyzed all the facts, she realized she was just as much to blame for the environment that John was raised in, as Jack. She was also the example to John that she sacrificed everything for wealth and security. Since John saw that his mother was submissive to her abusive husband, he felt this was the way a relationship was supposed to be. John did not realize that Lily was not going to stand for this type of relationship.

As Maggie went through this realization, she knew she had to forgive not only Jack but also herself for the spiral downward that John went through. Maggie felt that John caused his own death and it was sad that a beautiful horse had to be sacrificed for John's choice of death.

Maggie called Jack one day and when Jack came to the phone she said, "Jack, this is Maggie. I have called to tell you that I have decided that you were not the total blame for John's death."

Jack was stunned into silence then he recovered and stormed at Maggie, "how dare you call me and blame me for John's death. He was killed by the horse that he mistreated."

Maggie was unfazed and continued, "I know John contributed to his own death. However, how you feel is up to you. I do blame you as you were very cruel to John his entire life. You degraded him, criticized him and reduced him to nothing in his own mind."

Jack said a little less aggressively, "You can not blame me for this. He was a grown man. He had no character!"

Maggie continued, "I don't care what your opinion is. I have realized that I was just as much to blame as you were as I allowed you to abuse me and John. I had the option to leave and take John with me. I didn't do that. I failed John as his mother."

Jack started a verbal attack on Maggie like he had done so many times before. But this time it was on deaf ears. He said, "You were spineless, you could not live without my money. You were nothing before you started dating me. You were just a book reading wall flower until I dressed you up and made you presentable."

Maggie remained calm, "yes, the money and position were part of it for a while. But the fact is I forgive you for your part in causing the death of our son. I have to acknowledge that I knew all the time I should have left but I didn't. I am at peace now knowing that no matter what the environment is, some people have a mental illness that causes them to self-destruct. John had some mental problems and we did not help him, in fact, we set the worst example of life."

Jack stormed again, "John was not mentally ill. You are the one that is completely insane. I don't care if you forgive me, I did nothing to forgive. You need to go to hell."

Maggie took a deep breath and said, "Jack, I've already been to hell, which was with you. Now I am okay and I'm whole again. I feel sorry for you. Good bye." Maggie hung up and she felt a wave of relief and peace flood through her for the first time since she was told her son was dead.

CHAPTER 22

JAMES

As winter slid into spring, Lily's business continued to do well. She was very busy with her practice, her children, the safe house and the life line. It was a normal day with clients in and out of the office. Late that afternoon, Pam walked into Lily's office and said, "There is a very good looking man in the office who says he is an old friend."

Lily said, "Did he give you his name?"

"No," Pam replied, "but he sure is handsome."

Lily smiled at Pam's comments about the stranger. She got up and walked into the reception area. She stopped short when she saw the handsome stranger in the waiting room. It was a flash from the past, and something she never thought would happen.

From across the room, James said, "Lily, you are still the most beautiful woman I have ever seen. And those emerald green eyes are still just as startling."

Lily spoke after taking a deep breath, "And, James, you are still the most handsome man I have ever seen. Your sky blue eyes are still very startling."

James told her, "I have looked everywhere for you and suddenly I see you on the news and I had to come see you. I could not believe that you were so far south. I knew you would make something of yourself; I am proud to see you are a lawyer. I hope you can forgive me for letting my father come between us. I have regretted that more than you know."

"James, it's good to see you," Lily walked across the office and put her arms around James. She hugged him and gave him a kiss then backed away. "Where are you living now?"

264

James said, "I'm a partner in a practice in New York. It's pretty intense and stressful work. I'm kind of on the edge right now as to what I want to do. But what about you, other than what I saw in the news. Did you really shoot and kill that intruder?"

Lily smiled, "Yes that was me and it was him or me, as he was attempting to kill me. I got lucky." Lily turned to Pam, "Pam this is James Anderson. James was my high school sweetheart. James, this is Pam, my friend and my receptionist."

Lily led James to her office. As they walked in Sweetie got up for an introduction. "This is Sweetie, my best friend. Sweetie saved my life when I was almost killed. She bit the intruder and caused his first shot to miss me, then the second shot hit my shoulder instead of a more lethal place."

James knelt down and patted Sweetie on the head. "Thank you, Sweetie for saving this wonderful lady. I will be forever grateful to you as I have a second chance to see Lily again."

James and Lily sat down on the couch in her office. They chatted about family and college. James ask, "Would you like to go somewhere for dinner tonight?"

Lily looked at James. She was having a problem spanning the gap in the time since she had seen James. He seemed to want to take up where they left off but things change with time. She said "I have two kids now that I am responsible for, so I need to go home. But if you want, you can come for dinner at my house. You could meet my children."

James smiled, "I'd like that; I just need directions."

As Lily drove home she was very conflicted. She didn't think she was in a place in her life to get into a relationship, especially an old relationship. She was just getting accustomed to having children. The children needed a lot of special attention to help stabilize their life. They were dealing with grief for their mother, shame for their father and a totally new environment. Lily had to admit that her heart skipped a beat when she saw James. She had loved him so much and then had spent years trying to forget him; now here he was out of the blue. She would just have to see how this played out.

When Lily first saw James in her office and they were greeting each other with a hug and a kiss, a hand reached for the office door. When Ronnie looked through the window of the door, he saw Lily move into the arms of a man he had never seen. The stranger was very handsome and was wearing a very expensive looking suit. Ronnie removed his hand from the door and stepped back. Before he turned to leave he saw Lily take the stranger's arm and led him to her officer. They looked very close and familiar with each other. As Ronnie eased away he knew he had expected someone to step in before he had the courage to get closer to Lily. He'd have to keep his eyes open to see if this new man was going to be in a relationship with Lily. He did know one thing, if he saw an opening he was going to step up this time and not miss another opportunity to get to know Lily better.

James came to Lily's house that night and met Jenny and Joshua. James was a natural with kids. After supper, they played games and he told them stories. After the kids went to bed, James and Lily sat on the couch and talked remembering the good times that they had while in high school. Lily explained how she had been allowed to foster Jenny and Joshua and hopefully adopt them. After a while James said he should go back to the motel, Lily walked him to the door. James took Lily in his arms and kissed her. She returned the kiss. It seemed natural; it was good for Lily. She needed someone at this time to shelter her, protect her and give her some attention. She was a little overwhelmed having to do all the protecting, nurturing and being responsible.

James said, "Lily I would like to come down as often as I can so we can have a chance to reconnect. I will always love you."

Lily did not know what to say. She could not truly say she loved him because she was not sure how she felt. She said, "James, I would be happy to see you any time you want to come down. This has been a big shock to me and I have had a lot of shocks lately, so I need time."

James assured her, "You take all the time you need. I have to go back on Sunday but if you let me, I'd like to spend Saturday with you and the kids. Maybe we could have a picnic or go to the park. Whatever you say, we will do."

Lily said, "Sure that would be fun for us all. Good night."

That night Jenny slipped into Lily's bed and cuddled up to her. Jenny and Joshua had asked to call her maw. Lily was not happy with that name, she told them that was what they called Annie and she was not going to replace their maw. So she told them they could call her mom or mother if they wanted to. Jenny said, "Mom, I like Mr. James. Are you going to marry him?"

Lily laughed, "Jenny, Mr. James is an old friend. When we were teenagers we were in love, but it didn't work out. So I don't think we will be getting married any time soon. Don't you like just you, Joshua, me and Sweetie being a family?"

Jenny cried, "Oh yes. I thought if you and Mr. James got married, you might not want us anymore."

Lily hugged Jenny, "I will be here and you will be with me until you grow up and you make a family of your own. Even then, I hope to be a part of your life. We are a family."

Jenny smiled and said, "I love you, Mother." Then they both drifted off to sleep.

CHAPTER 23

LILY

As the summer drifted along, Lily was having a great time with the kids. With Sweetie along with them, they explored everything. She taught them to swim and they were like fish in the water. It was always a surprise to Lily how the smallest thing they did together was a really big deal to them. They never ask for anything and were really shy about taking something new. Every possession they had, they cherished and took good care of it.

Lily found that the biggest help in getting the kids to feel comfortable was Sweetie. Both Jenny and Joshua would spend a lot of time just sitting with Sweetie petting her and talking to her. This gave Lily the idea that pets could be a part of the program at the Safe House. She was going to talk to Dr. Davis about helping her find a suitable dog or cat for the shelter. She also thought Dr. Davis was so good with people she would be interested in talking to the kids at the shelter about animals.

Lily was going to start a search for some pets for the shelter. She went by the Veterinary Clinic one day to talk with Dr. Davis. After she had explained her mission, Dr. Davis was very excited.

Dr. Davis said, "I have taken dogs to the rest home here for several years. I have a great dog that stays at the clinic that was a companion to a lady that had to go in the rest home. She is a Doberman Pincher. I've taken her to schools to let kids see her and play with her. She is always a big hit. Her name is Sky. She would fit right into the environment in the shelter as she had always been a house dog. I think Sky would also be a good watch dog for the shelter. Even though she is gentle with people she is still a good watch dog. I tell you what, let's try her out. I will take her to the shelter for a walk through and then we can go from there.

Another thing I will do is look for a good cat. I always have a "clinic" cat that hangs out in the clinic. Cats really are great with kids. They seem to sense when a child is sad or scared. Also, any pet you take to the shelter; I will volunteer all the medical care for them. I'll see to their vaccinations and any other things that they need such as grooming."

Lily was thrilled and wanted to see Sky. Dr. Davis had one of her assistants bring Sky up to the office. Sky went right to Lily and put a paw on her leg. Lily was so surprised but Dr. Davis said, "I knew she would like you. She knows a "dog person" when she see one."

Lily said, "I guess you heard of my experience with an irate intruder in my practice?"

Dr. Davis responded, "I did hear about that. I am so glad you are okay and sorry that you had to take drastic action."

Lily said, "Thank you. Do you remember that you told me; what you do for a dog, they will do for you? Well, Sweetie saved my life. She attacked the intruder. She bit his leg and distracted him enough that he shot the wall rather than me. I got one shot off but he wasn't dead and he shot me in the arm before I shot him again. Sweetie is the best friend I have ever had. Thank you for helping me learn about being a pet owner. This experience has been wonderful. Another positive thing from having Sweetie is I have adopted two children that have had a traumatizing childhood. Sweetie has been a positive influence on them and has helped them transition to a better life."

Dr. Davis was so touched her eyes welled up with tears. She hugged Lily and said "Thank goodness you are okay. I am excited about partnering with the shelter to help the best way I know how, which is with the animals."

During the summer, James came south several times. After the first couple of times that he came down, Lily invited James to stay with her and the kids. Lily was nervous the first time James stayed with her. They had never had sex when they were going together as teenagers so this was basically their first time. When the kids were in bed, James and Lily went into her room. Lily suddenly was shy, "I am probably the most inexperienced women you have ever been with. You are going to have to be patient with me."

James went to her and put his arms around her. "I'm not a play boy. I have not been with a lot of women so we will move forward together." He slowly kissed her.

Lily and James had some awkward moments but over all, things went well. Lily found that some things just come naturally. Lily felt passion for James, but she thought something was missing but she just did not know what. James was kind and gentle. Lily thought maybe she had to deal with the feelings of abandonment from being left behind by him so many years ago. She had forgiven James but some deep part of her was holding back. She could not trust that James would not bale out again if the going got tough. Right now, everything was easy but there were bumps in the road coming along and she didn't know if James was willing to do what it would take to make this family work. However, for now she would just give it a chance. James seemed very happy with their situation.

Near the end of the summer, James asked, "How about you and the kids come to New York for a vacation before school starts? We could explore lots of interesting things and see what the big apple is like. What do you think?"

Lily thought that this would be a wonderful experience for the kids to see a totally different way of life. So she said she'd work out a schedule and take him up on his offer.

Lily called Joshua and Jenny in the house and ask them, "Do you two want to take a trip to New York?"

At first they were totally quiet and then they started jumping up and down and shouting a loud, "Yes".

At the end of the summer, Lily had scheduled a few days to go to New York to visit James. She got her mother to take care of Sweetie and then they were on their way.

The airplane ride, alone, was a wonderful experience. Lily arranged for Jenny and Joshua to have a window seat on the plane and they could not stop looking out the window until they were so high above the clouds that they could not see the ground.

James met them at the airport with big hugs and kisses. His apartment building was a high rise and his apartment was on the thirty fifth floor. The elevator was all glass on the outside so as they went up they saw a magnificent view of New York City.

James' apartment was beautiful. The living room wall was all glass, so the view from the apartment was wonderful. James showed the kids their room and they got settled. He took them to a Yankee ballgame that night. Then the next day they explored New York. It was a wonderful experience.

The second night they were at James' apartment, Lily went in the kid's room to tell them goodnight. As she sat on the bed, Jenny climbed into her lap and Joshua sat beside her. Lily asked, "Are you two having a good time?"

Joshua said, "Oh, yes. We have never seen anything so big or seen so many people."

Jenny was quiet for a minute before she said, "I miss Sweetie. Do you think she misses us?"

Lily responded, "Of course she misses us. We are her family."

Joshua said, "Sweetie would not like it here. It is too loud and no place for her to hunt and play."

Lily thought a minute then said, "Well, you are right. This would not be a good place for Sweetie. But just think of all the things you and Joshua could do here. This place is a wonderful place to learn so many different ways of life."

Joshua said, "I like our way of life at home. There's woods and space to roam. I love our house, my room and our Sweetie."

Lily said, "Well, let's have all the fun we can here and learn new things. But in the end, we will go home to stay."

The next day James wanted everyone to come to his office and meet some of his co-workers. He asked them to come around noon then he would take them to a nice lunch. The day was windy but nice as Lily and the kids took a cab downtown to the heart of New York. The building that James worked in was a huge high rise with his office on the top floor. When they got off the elevator they were in awe at the beautiful and expensive decor. They were met by a woman that led them to James' massive office.

There was a stunningly beautiful woman talking with James when they walked in. She was dressed in a tight dress with spike heels. James introduced her as Mandy; she was one of the partners in the firm. Mandy nodded politely and started to walk out of the office but first she touched James arm and said, "I'll discuss this more with you later. Will you be staying late tonight?"

James answered her, "No, I have company and I'm taking them out tonight."

Mandy then reminded James in an authoritative tone, "Remember, we just have a week to finish this case."

James nodded, "Yes, I am aware of that." Then James turned and greeted the kids.

Mandy said, "James, may I speak to you outside for just a moment?" She turned to Lily and the kids and said, "Lily it is nice to meet you and your lovely children. I hope your stay is interesting and the trip home is safe."

James sighed and told Jenny, Joshua and Lily, "I'll be right back."

In the hall, Mandy put her hand on James arm and leaned in very close to him as she spook to him. Lily was well aware of the message that Mandy was sending. Lily was way out of her element and Mandy was in control here. Lily did not like how she was feeling. She was getting a closed in feeling and certainly feeling like a second fiddle. It was becoming obvious to Lily that this was not the world she was meant to be a part. Her children would never be happy in this high intensity world. She knew they would all drown in this sea of humanity. James was trying hard to make up for walking away from her so long ago, but what he didn't realize was; Lily had moved on and in an entirely different direction from him. Lily knew it was too late for a long lasting relationship between her and James. It was up to her to make the break this time.

When James returned they went down in the elevator. When they were on the first floor, Lily asked James to sit down with her. She told the kids to go look around in the gift shop. James was puzzled but said, "I'm sorry it took so long up there, but we can go now."

Lily took his hand and said, "James you were my first love. That was years ago and we have moved very far apart. My world compared to your is very small and slow. But it is what works for me. I have two children to raise. They are struggling to get over a tragic episode that would impact even the toughest people. I have to keep life simple and familiar so they will have a chance to grow up into responsible adults. I've decided we are going home now. I know after you think about it this will make sense to you. You can't change the past, you can only move on. So, this is good bye. I wish you all the best in your life." Lily stood up and walked toward the door. She called the kids over and spoke to them, both turned and raced to James and gave him a big hug, "Bye, James," They both chimed, "We love you." Then they ran back to Lily. The three of them walked out the door and out of James' life forever. This time, Lily had made the decision that this relationship was not going to work out for her and her children.

CHAPTER 24

JOSHUA

Lily and the kids had gotten back in the swing of their life after coming back from New York; they still had a little summer left before school started. Lily noticed that Joshua was not as energetic as he had been and he seemed a little depressed. She watched him closely and one day he was sitting on the front porch and she decided to talk to him. Jenny was up stairs, happily playing with her Barbie doll. Lily eased out of the house and sat down next to Joshua on the porch steps. Lily said, "How are you doing, buddy?"

Joshua responded, "I'm fine."

Lily waited a minute then tried again, "Well, you don't look or sound fine. Is something bothering you?"

Joshua was still not opening up but said, "No really, I'll be fine."

Lily sat quietly for a while, then said, "Joshua, you know we are a family now. Families share their problems with each other so they can work together to solve them. A family shares feeling with each other so we can know what caused us pain and try to ease that pain. You have to be willing to open up even the deepest wounds so they can heal."

Joshua said, "Something happened to me a year ago and I tried to hide the memory away but I started thinking about it again and it makes me so sad."

Lily put her arm around him and said, "Joshua, things are never as heavy to carry when you have someone to help carry the load."

Joshua began his story, "Last year, maw was pregnant. I was so worried about her and for good reason. When the baby came a midwife came but it was terrible. Maw screamed for hours but then a baby girl was born. The baby sounded fine as she cried really loud. That night I wanted to see the baby, so I went to maw's room but I saw paw leaning over the crib, so I went back to bed without saying anything. Paw woke me up the next morning to go dig a grave 'cause he said the baby died. I did as I was told and dug a deep grave. Paw brought the baby wrapped in a blanket and left her with me to bury by myself. I was really mad at paw for leaving me alone to bury this sweet baby. I cried and screamed before I could go on. I wanted to see who she looked like so I moved the blanket off her face." Joshua had to stop talking for a minute before he could go on, "Her nose was black and the mark of a large hand was over her mouth. Paw had killed his own baby. He was such a monster. I buried the baby and all I knew to do was say the Lord's Prayer." Joshua began to cry.

Lily was shocked and saddened, "Oh, Joshua, I am so sorry. You should have never been subjected to such a tragedy alone."

Joshua continued, "The grave is under a big cedar tree in the back yard of our old house. It's a quiet and beautiful place but it seems like she was just thrown away without anyone caring. I know my maw cared. She grieved till she died. Maw and I named the baby. We named her Emma Marie."

Lily said, "That's a beautiful name. As long as you remember Emma she will live in your heart forever."

Joshua thought a while then said, "Do you think someday we could get a small stone with her name on it and her birthdate to mark her grave?"

Lily said, "Joshua, that is a great idea and we most certainly can do that. Then you can visit her grave any time you want to and anyone that sees the stone will know who was buried there." Lily hugged Joshua and thought how could such a dear, sweet boy be the son of a monster like Ray Hall?

Jenny, Joshua and Lily went to where monuments for graves were made and sold. They picked a small heart shaped stone. They had Emma Marie Hall printed on it with one date. They also had an angel etched above her name. Under the angel it said 'Child of Annie and Sister to Jenny and Joshua'. Jenny and Joshua made all the decisions on how they wanted it to look.

When the stone was ready, Lily, the kids and Sweetie took a trip out to the Hall house. Lily had not been there before and was surprised at how isolated the house was. Then she was shocked at the shack that they had lived in all their life.

When Lily pulled up in front of the shack she was worried about the effect this would have on the kids. They had been through so much in that house and they had seen their mother dead on the floor of the kitchen. Jenny and Joshua sat still and did not say anything, at first they just stared at the house. Lily told them to take all the time they needed until they felt ready to get out. Eventually they all got out. Sweetie was very nervous about getting near the house. She had her tail down and emitted a low growl as they walked around the house to the back. It took both Joshua and Lily to carry the stone even thought it was small. They had it on a blanket and carried it between them.

They got to the grave and placed the stone at the head of the small indention in the dirt that was shaded by the large cedar tree. Lily asked if they would like to say anything. Jenny had a poem that she read and Joshua recited the Lord's Pray again. Sweetie lay down beside the grave while Lily, Joshua and Jenny held hands and Lily said, "We are here today to place this stone on Emma Marie Hall's resting place. This shows that even though she was only on earth a day, she will be remembered forever by her brother, Joshua and her sister, Jenny. May she rest in peace."

They placed some flowers on the grave and walked together back to the car. For Joshua and Jenny this was the beginning of their new life out of the shadow of abuse and sorrow for the loss of their mother and sister. It would take a life time for these kids to heal from the deep wounds that they had suffered at the hands of an abusive parent. Even when the wounds healed there would still be scars.

CHAPTER 25

STRANGER

The summer was over, Lily and the kids had several adventures during the summer. The events of the summer had brought Lily and the kids very close together as a family and they were happy. But Jenny and Joshua were excited about getting back in school. In the mornings, Lily would drive them to the end of the drive way to meet the bus. After they got on the bus, she would go to work. In the afternoons, Lily would get home before the bus came and if the weather was good, the kids would walk home from the bus stop. Lily would be waiting with a snack and they would start homework. Life was steady and stable. Joshua still watched over Jenny and felt responsible for her. Lily was working toward freeing him of some of that responsibility so he could be a normal growing boy.

When Lily and Sweetie would get home in the afternoons, she would let Sweetie out to get some exercise and Sweetie would go meet the kids when they got off the bus. Fall was everywhere in the south and the weather was beautiful. The leaves were turning all different colors and beginning to fall in preparation for winter. Lily had let Sweetie out and had gone about her business. When Joshua and Jenny came in they were running, "Mom, where is Sweetie? She did not meet us."

Lily looked up and was puzzled but not that worried, "She is probably running a rabbit in the woods. She will show up soon."

After about an hour and Sweetie had not returned home, Lily was getting worried. This was not like her at all. She wanted to be with them all the time. They all decided to go out looking. They roamed the woods, calling for her but it was getting dark so they went back to the house. Lily told the kids to get ready for bed, she was going to take a flash light and look some more. After about an hour and no luck, Lily returned home. Jenny and Joshua were waiting at the door. Lily sadly said, "No, luck. We can't do any more tonight, let's go to bed and I'm sure we will find her tomorrow." Lily was not confident at all that they would find Sweetie, she was very worried.

The next morning, Lily got up early. She opened the back door and there was Sweetie. She had mud all over her and her left back leg was bloody. When Lily reached down to touch Sweetie's leg she got up but she could not put any weigh on that leg. Lily brought Sweetie in the house and called for the kids to come and bring a blanket. They put Sweetie on a blanket then carried her to the car. Lily said, "We are taking her to Dr. Davis to take care of her."

At the Veterinarian clinic, Dr. Davis examined Sweetie. She started IV fluids and gave her some shots. She explained, "I'm treating Sweetie for shock because she has lost some blood. The fluids will help balance her electrolytes. I'm also going to take some x-rays of her leg to see if it is broken. There is a hole in the skin which looks a lot like a gunshot wound. The bullet should still be in the leg if it was a shot because there is no exit wound on her leg. You all will have to sit up front while I take the x-ray so I don't expose you all to the x-rays. My assistants and I wear lead aprons and gloves for protection."

After the x-ray was developed, Dr. Davis had them come back to the treatment room again to review the x-ray on the light box. Dr. Davis was pointing out what they needed to see. "Here is the femur, which is the first bone in the rear leg. You see that it is broken. Also there is the bullet right where the bone is broken. It looks like a 22 caliber bullet."

Lily was shocked, "Who would shoot Sweetie?"

Dr. Davis said, "It might not have been intentional. A bullet will travel a good distance if it misses what the shooter was aiming at. Sweetie could have been in the wrong place. But the good news is, she is doing really well with her clinical signs and I can perform surgery to remove the bullet and put a steel pin in the bone so it will mend. In six weeks, I will remove the pin and she will be good as new."

Lily asked, "What do we do to help her recover?"

Dr. Davis said, "Even with a pin in her leg she has three other legs that she can get around on just fine. She will need to stay as inactive as possible. Just tender loving care will take care of everything. I can tell Sweetie will be well taken care of and will be spoiled also. So for now, you all need to go on to school and work. You can come this afternoon and visit. She will need to stay one night but then can go home. I just want to be sure she builds her blood back that she lost and I will check that in the morning with a blood test."

Lily and the kids loved on Sweetie some more then reluctantly left her in Dr. Davis' hands. The surgery went find. Dr. Davis took another x-ray after the surgery to assure the pin was set right. She also saved the bullet to show the kids. Lily picked Sweetie up the next day and everything got back to normal, or so they all thought.

A week after Sweetie was shot, Jenny and Joshua got off the school bus as usual. When the bus pulled away, a car turned into their driveway. It passed the kids and turned in front of them, blocking their way. It was an old model car with the paint peeling off and rusty spots everywhere. It was very loud as it did not have a muffle. The front door opened and a large man got out. Jenny and Joshua were beyond shocked. It was as if they were looking at a ghost. The man looked exactly like their paw, but they knew he was dead.

The man leaned back on the car, he spit tobacco juice on the ground and laughed, "Guess you think I'm your paw, back from the grave!" he laughed loudly, "Scared you didn't I? Guess you'll thought your paw had come back to beat the hell out of you two for livin with that lawyer bitch. Did you know she's the one that killed your paw? Shot him through the heart, he was dead on the spot."

Joshua had recovered a little from his shock as he remembered his paw had a twin brother named Rafe. It had been a long time since he had seen Rafe because Rafe had been in prison. Jenny would not even remember him as she was a baby the last time they had seen Rafe. Joshua said, "Uncle Rafe when did you get out of prison?"

Rafe said, "never you mind. I'm here now. You and Jenny are my kin. Kin stays together. I've come fer you both."

Joshua said, "We live with Lily now. She's our family."

Jenny began to cry, "Joshua, don't let him take us. Mommy will worry."

Rafe said, "Oh, it's "Mommy" now. You two ungrateful brats, already forgot your maw?"

Joshua said, "No, Lily said she will not replace our maw. She wants to raise us. Lily loves us."

Rafe said sarcastically, "Can't she have her own rug rats? Why she want two scrawny kids like you two? You two ain't worth nothing to her. She'll dump you both in the ditch when she gets tired of you. I see she got you new clothes and shoes. Even in new stuff, you two are still poor white trash underneath."

Jenny cried, "Mommy loves us. She is good to us. We don't want to go with you."

Rafe said, "You don't know nothin! You shut your mouth." Rafe raised his hand to strike Jenny."

Joshua jumped in front of Jenny, "Don't you dare hit her. Lily said no one has the right to hit us ever again!"

Rafe grabbed Joshua by the shirt and pulled him up to his face. "You little piece of shit. I will beat you till you learn to have some respect." He tossed Joshua to the ground. Joshua hit his head on a rock and began to bleed, but he jumped up to protect Jenny.

Rafe laughed, "you look like a gnat coming up against me. Don't try that again." Then Rafe started looking around like he was looking for something and said, "Hey, where's that mutt that always meets you all when the bus comes?"

Jenny said, "Sweetie got hurt. She had to stay at the house."

Rafe responded, "Well, how sad. She should have run faster."

Joshua cried, "You shot Sweetie, didn't you?"

Rafe said, "Maybe."

Jenny said, "You are mean, you could have killed her!"

Rafe laughed, "Missy, if I wanted to kill her, she would be buzzard bait right now. I can shoot the eyes out of a snake a mile away. I jest wanted to let ya'll know I was here and meant business. I had to get that mutt out of the way so I could get to you without being mauled by her. That damn dog is always with you two."

Joshua reached for Jenny and said, "We got to get home. Come on Jenny lets go."

Joshua knew he could run and get away but Jenny would never make it, so he would not leave her. Rafe stepped in front of them, "Whoa, I just need to talk to you some more. You think this lawyer likes you both a lot?"

Jenny said, "Yes, Mommy's going to be mad at you for hurting Joshua!"

Rafe laughed, "Oh, I'm really afraid of her! Joshua, maybe she would be willing to pay me to go away and not take you two with me?"

Joshua saw where this was going, "Yes, maybe. I'll ask her when we get home. Come on Jenny." He started off again, but was stopped by a big hand on his shoulder.

Rafe said, "Well, I bet she will pay but I think I need to have some insurance." For being a big man, Rafe could move fast. He grabbed Jenny by the arm and jerked her to him. He put his arm around her waist and held her to him. Jenny screamed but Rafe put his hand over her mouth, "You run as fast as you can and tell your 'Mommy' I'm taking Jenny with me. If she wants her back, I need ten thousand dollars or she will never see her again. Tell her I'll be in touch, fer her to jest get the money. I'll think of a place fer her to bring the money. Then Jenny can come back. Tell her not to call the police this is between us. She better not mess with me, cause I'm meaner than Ray ever thought to be!" Joshua ran at Rafe and tried to pull Jenny away from him. "Let her go," he screamed.

Rafe backhanded Joshua so hard that he flew back several feet and hit the ground again. Joshua was stunned but raised up to see Rafe throw Jenny into the car, jump in and take off.

Joshua got up, stumbling at first then running as fast as he could toward home.

Lily was working around the house while waiting on the children to get home. She lost track of time until she heard Sweetie whining at the back door. "What's the matter Sweetie? They will be home soon." Then she looked at the clock and was puzzled that they were late. Lily looked out the window and was startled to see Joshua running toward the house without Jenny. Her heart skipped a beat as she instantly felt something was wrong. She raced out the door to meet Joshua.

Joshua stumbled and fell in Lily's arms. He was panting so hard he could not talk at first. Lily was frantic, "Joshua, where is Jenny? What happened to your face and head? You are bleeding. Just calm down and talk to me."

Joshua tried to become calm, "He took her!" He finally said.

"Took her? You mean Jenny? Who took her?"

Again he tried to talk, "Uncle Rafe. He hit me and took Jenny. He's the one that shot Sweetie!"

"Joshua who is Uncle Rafe? Tell me, was Jenny hurt?"

Joshua took a deep breath, "Uncle Rafe is my paw's twin brother. He went to prison a long time ago. We haven't heard from him since he left. He is out of prison now and he wanted to take both of us. At first he said we were kin and needed to be together. When we said we wouldn't go with him, he said he thought you would give him money to get Jenny back and for him to go away. He said he wanted ten thousand dollars by tomorrow or we would never see Jenny or him again!"

Lily could not believe what she was hearing. How was it possible for this to happen? She said, "Joshua, where was he going with Jenny?"

"I don't know; he just took off. He said if we called the police, it would be really bad for Jenny." Joshua began to cry, "I tried to protect her. I would have run, but Jenny was not fast enough so I could not leave her. He hit me hard so I couldn't do anything?"

"Joshua, you could not have kept him from taking Jenny. You did fine. Let's go in the house so I can take care of your wounds. We will figure something out." Lily was trying to act calm when on the inside she was a storm of emotions. She was furious this goon took Jenny; she was scared he would hurt her and she had no idea what to do next.

They went in the house and Lily got a wet rag to wash Joshua's face. While she cleaned his wounds she asked him questions to see if she could get more information. "What was Rafe driving?"

"He was in a old, rusty loud car. It was green with a white top. It did not have a license tag on it."

"That's good, you remembered a lot. Now which way did he go?"

"He went toward town."

Lily assessed the wounds on Joshua's face to only be abrasions and one cut. She put ointment on them then sat down by Joshua. She took his hand and said, "Joshua, you did a good job, but we are going to need help with this. I know he said not to call the police but I'm going to call my friend that is a detective and get his advice. I know he will do everything he can to keep this quiet. Are you okay with this?"

Joshua shook his head yes, "I just want Jenny back. Mom, Uncle Rafe is meaner than my paw. They never got along. My paw said if he saw Rafe again, he was going to shoot him. Uncle Rafe don't care nothing about us! Just give him the money and he will give Jenny back."

Lily looked at Joshua and said, "Honey, people like Rafe never go away. If he gets away with this now, he will come back only he will be worse. We have to take care of this but we need some help." With that Lily went to the phone and called the police station.

When Lily got an answer at the police station, she requested to speak to Ronnie, "May I speak with Detective Ron Harris?" Lily was put on hold. When Ron answered, Lily said, "Ron, this is Lily."

Ronnie was pleasantly surprised, "Hello, Lily. It's nice to hear from you."

Lily continued, "Ron, we are in trouble. I need you to keep this quite, just between us until we get this sorted out."

Ronnie walked to an empty room and closed the door, he was very concerned, "Lily, I'm alone so you can tell me what is wrong."

Lily began, "Joshua and Jenny were attacked when they got off the bus by a man named Rafe Hall. He is the twin brother of Ray Hall. He's been in prison a long time but just got out. He knocked Joshua around and kidnapped Jenny." Lily was near tears and had to stop as she could not talk for sobbing.

Ronnie said, "I will be there as quickly as I can. You stay put and try not to worry." Ronnie hung up and told his partner, Joe, to come with him immediately and they left.

When Ronnie got to Lily's house, he and Joe went in the house. Lily looked at him and he knew she was wondering why he brought someone with him. He said, "Lily, I have to have back up in cases like this or we could get into a real mess. Joe is fine, he is a good detective." He turned to Joshua and said, "Joshua, hey buddy, what happened?"

Joshua recounted every detail he could remember. When he had finished his story, Ronnie thought for a minute then started asking questions, "Can you think of any place that your uncle would go to hide or a place he could stay?"

Joshua thought a moment; then he had an idea, "When my grandpa died, my paw got really mad 'cause grandpa gave Uncle Rafe the old home place. Uncle Rafe got the house grandpa lived in and a big barn. He also gave Uncle Rafe his truck for when he got out of prison. My paw got our house which was on grandpa's land, and the land it was on. Paw didn't think Rafe deserved all that he got."

"Okay, that's good Joshua. Now you need to tell me where your grandpa's place is."

"It's a long way out of town, but I can take you there." Joshua said.

"Okay, we are going there. I do need to tell you when we get there, if Rafe is there, I will have to call for back up. I know you want us to do everything we can for Jenny and I think we need a strong force to flush Rafe out."

"Detective Harris," Joshua said as he put his hand on Ronnie's arm, "Uncle Rafe is a real mean man. He used to beat my Paw up all the time. I'm real afraid that he will hurt Jenny." Joshua began to cry.

Lily hugged him to her and said, "We will do everything we can and so will the detectives. Jenny is going to be fine." Lily wished she was as confident as she sounded. Lily was terrified that Rafe would hurt Jenny but she wanted to keep Joshua as calm as possible since they were reliant on him to direct them to the possible hiding place of Rafe.

Ronnie was also very concerned that Rafe was going to be hard to find and could be dangerous. He looked at Lily and saw fear in her eyes. He felt very sorry for her because she had already been through so much. He wanted to just take her in his arms and tell her everything would be fine. He just hoped everything would be fine.

Ronnie had not seen Lily in a few months because after he saw that she was involved with another man, he decided it was time for him to take some time off. He had been planning to go to an advanced training school for detectives that lasted three months. He had been accepted and had just gotten back from the school. This was the first time he had seen Lily in over three months. His feelings were still very strong for her. He hated that this was such a serious situation. He had to put all his feelings aside and get Jenny back safely. He did notice there was no indication that Lily had a steady partner right now.

Ronnie said, "I need you, Lily, and Joshua to go with us and see if Joshua can show us how to get to his granddad's old farm. It's a long shot but he maybe there with Jenny."

Lily was ready, "Sure let's go. It's better than waiting here."

Joshua also readily agreed. Ronnie had Lily and Joshua get into the back of his car which was an unmarked police car. He and Joe got into the front. As Joshua began to give them directions, they began to drive south on the highway. Soon Joshua indicated they should turn on a small county road. Several miles later, they turned on a gravel road which soon narrowed to a one lane dirt road. The trees on either side of the road grew so tall they leaned over the road and made a tunnel that the road went through. Even though it was night, the moon was full and the moon light made the night almost like day except in the tunnel. It was pitch black in the tunnel and it appeared very spooky with the trees so close to the road.

Joshua said, "I told you we lived a long ways from town. We had to either walk or sometimes get a ride to the bus stop which was about a mile from our house. Even in the day, this part of the road was very scary. Jenny always held my hand on this part of the road. We would run through here." Lily flinched as she thought of the children running through the dark part of the road alone and being so scared. She had been their guardian just a short time but she already felt like their mother. She was very protective of them and it hurt her to think of the life they had before. She was also terrified at how traumatized Jenny must be right now in the hands of this horrible man. Even thought he was Jenny's uncle, Lily knew he did not have any love for her or anyone.

After a mile, Ronnie slowed the car as Joshua told him the old house was just around the next bend in the road. Ronnie turned off the head lights and proceeded by the light of the moon. Soon they saw an old house up a small hill. Behind the house, they could see the tail-end of an old beat-up car. Ronnie stopped the car, "OK, Lily, you and Joshua stay here. Joe and I are going to ease up that hill and see if we can see anyone in the house. I have back-up coming to help if he is in there. Will you two be okay?" He asked.

Lily said, "Sure, but please, be careful."

Ronnie looked back at her and he saw concern and fear in her eyes. He felt like he wanted to say something to comfort her but could not think of anything to say that would be appropriate. So he just smiled a weak smile at her and got out of the car. Ronnie and Joe pulled out their guns and moved up the hill. Soon Lily could not see them for the bushes and trees.

Lily saw Joshua shaking; she said, "Joshua, Jenny will be fine. Ronnie and Joe are really good detectives and they will find her. You have been such a big help. I know you are worried. I'm right with you."

Joshua said, "I know you're right, but I'm sacred!"

Joshua suddenly saw something that excited him. "Lily, look." He pointed down the small road. "There's the big barn down this road. The truck that grandpa gave Uncle Rafe was stored in that barn. Maybe they are in that barn!"

Lily could see the large structure of the barn and thought it might be a good place for Rafe to hide. She said, "Ronnie and Joe are to far away for me to call them. Let's you and I go down there and see if we can see anything."

They got out of the car, being easy with the door so it would not make a noise. They started to move down the road. The moon light was just enough for them to be able to navigate in the night. As they got close to the barn, Lily pointed out to Joshua at what she thought was a flickering light that could be a small camp fire. When they got to the barn, they pushed through brush to get down the side of the barn and peered through a gap between the barn slats. They were able to see the outline of the truck and behind that there was a small camp fire. Rafe was asleep on a blanket beside the fire. Lily was frantic to find Jenny and finally saw her huddled in the corner. Lily whispered to Joshua and he also saw her. "How will we get her attention without waking Rafe up?"

Joshua had an idea, "Jenny and I used to play in the woods and call to each other by making the sound of a dove." He put both his hands together making a hollow center and blew air between his thumbs. The sound was a low, moan-full dove sound. Lily was watching Jenny while Joshua was making the dove sound. Jenny lifted her head and began to look around. She got up and moved toward the sound and when she got close to the wall, Lily whispered to her, "Jenny, it's me and Joshua. Honey, come closer."

Jenny leaned to the wall and peered through the gap. She whispered, "Mommy, please come get me. I'm so scared Uncle Rafe will wake up and hurt me."

Lily said, "Jenny, don't worry, we will think of something. I'm just glad you are okay." She started looking around, "Are there any doors that you can get out?"

Jenny answered, "No, all the doors have big boards holding them closed. I can't lift them."

Lily continued to think while she looked all around the barn by peering through different gaps in the wall. She told the kids to stay where they were, she was going to walk around the barn to see if there was a possible escape hole. In the front of the barn, she saw that at the top of the barn was a big opening. It was the loft where, long ago, the men would hoist bales of hay up to the loft for storage. Lily peered into the barn again and saw a ladder leading to the loft. If she could get Jenny to climb the ladder to the loft, she could get over to the loft opening. Lily was concerned that the loft was one story up and there was no ladder down the outside of the barn.

After thinking some more, Lily decided she would have to get Jenny to jump and trust that she could catch her. It was very risky and Lily didn't know if Jenny would do it but it was worth a try.

Lily returned to where the kids were and whispered to Jenny, "Honey, you will have to be very brave and trust me. Go over to that ladder that goes to the loft. Climb up to the loft and walk over to the opening in the front of the barn. Then I'll be outside and give you more instructions. Okay, can you do this?"

Jenny was very scared but she said, "Yes, I will try. I really want out of here." Jenny slipped over to the ladder and quietly climbed up the rungs. Once in the loft, she was on her way to the opening in the barn when she heard Rafe scream, "Jenny, you get back here. You can't get away up there. I'm coming to get you." Rafe began to climb the ladder. Jenny ran to the opening, looked down and saw Lily and Joshua below. Lily looked up and said, "Jenny, you are going to have to jump! I will catch you. You have to trust me. So jump!"

Jenny screamed, "I can't, I'm scared." Rafe had reached the top of the ladder and looked around for Jenny, "Jenny, you come here. You can't get away."

Jenny looked over her shoulder and saw Rafe. She looked back at Lily, closed her eyes and jumped. She screamed all the way down until she fell into Lily's arms. The impact of Jenny's body caused Lily and Jenny to crash to the ground. For a second, they both had the breath knocked out of them and couldn't speak but they were not hurt.

At that moment, they heard the engine of the truck in the barn roar to life. Joshua grabbed Lily by the arm and said, "get up, Uncle Rafe will run over all of us if he breaks out of the barn!" He pulled until Lily was able to get onto her feet. She still had Jenny in her arms and she and Joshua ran out of the road into the brush and tall grass. They fell together in a heap and stayed very still.

The barn door exploded as the truck rammed through it. Wood and debris flew everywhere and rained down on the three hiding in the ditch. The truck sped out of the barn then slid to a stop. Rafe jumped out of the cab and screamed, "You bitch, you have stolen my kin and I plan to kill you. Come out, I have a gun and I'll start shooting. I may hit the kids and it would be your fault." At that moment, there was the sound of multi sirens from police cars from up the road. Rafe stopped talking and looked in that direction. "What the hell," he said, "Where the hell did they come from?" He jumped back in his truck and floored the accelerator. The back wheels of the truck started spinning, dirt and rocks started flying, then the truck lurched forward and raced up the road.

The lead car with the police was Ronnie driving his unmarked car. When he returned to his car, he saw that Lily and Joshua were gone. His heart jumped and the adrealin started pumping. Then he heard the loud noise of a truck breaking through the barn door. He jumped in his car and started in that direction. He saw the truck roaring up the dirt road toward him. All Ronnie had on his mind was to stop Rafe, he was saying to himself, "If Rafe hurts Lily or the kids, I will kill him with my bare hands." Ronnie's car was speeding straight toward the truck.

When the two vehicles got close to each other, for a split second Ronnie could see Rafe's mean, red eyes through the truck windshield. At the last possible second before the truck and Ronnie's car would collide, Rafe jerked the truck steering wheel and shot out into the field just missing Ronnie's speeding car. Ronnie did not stop, he continued toward the barn. He slid to a stop in front of the barn and jumped out. He started calling, "Lily, where are you? Joshua, Jenny it's me Ronnie."

Ronnie heard Lily call back, "We're here." Struggling out of the weeds, into the headlights of the car, Ronnie saw them. Lily was carrying Jenny and Joshua holding Lily's other hand as they walked toward Ronnie. They were all a dirty mess but a beautiful sight to Ronnie. He ran to them and took Jenny out of Lily's arms and hugged Lily to him. "Thank God, you three are alright. Come on, get in the car. Let's get you all home."

Lily got in the back seat of the car and took Jenny into her lap. Joshua slid in beside her. She put her arm around him and held him tight. When Ronnie began driving them home, he looked into the rear view mirror and the sight of Lily and the kids clinging to each other made tears come to his eyes. His heart filled with love for these three and he planned to do everything his could to protect them.

As Ronnie drove past the other police cars he saw that the policemen had apprehended Rafe. Rafe Hall was handcuffed and being escorted to the police car. Ronnie wanted to get out and hit Rafe in the face for what he had put Lily and the kids through. He could only hope that justice would win and Rafe would be in jail a long, long time. When Ronnie got to Lily's house, he took Jenny from Lily and carried her in the house. Lily and Joshua followed behind. Ronnie carried Jenny up to her room and laid her on her bed. Lily followed closely. She sat on the side of Jenny's bed and said, "Sweet girl, you were the bravest girl in the world. You are safe now and you will never have to worry about Rafe Hall again. Now go to sleep and tomorrow will be a great day. I love you." She kissed her.

Jenny said, "I was so scared, Mommy. Thank you for saving me. I love you." Jenny and Lily looked up as Ronnie came into the room. He was carrying the injured Sweetie. He said, "Sweetie was really upset she could not come up stairs with her hurt leg. She was really worried about you, Jenny."

Jenny smiled for the first time since getting home, "Oh, Sweetie, I missed you so much. Can she sleep with me? She will keep me from being afraid."

Lily said, "Of course, she can sleep with you." Ronnie laid Sweetie on the bed next to Jenny. Sweetie licked Jenny's face then curled up next to her. Jenny put her arm around Sweetie and nestled into her fur, closed her eyes and went to sleep.

Lily went into Joshua's room as he got in bed. "Joshua, you saved your sister and me. You were very brave. I love you so much." She kissed Joshua on the cheek.

Joshua said, "Mom, I love you. Thank you for taking care of me and Jenny. Tell Detective Harris I thank him for listening to me and taking us to get Jenny."

Lily said, "I'll tell him but I'm sure he knows we are glad he was there for us." Lily went back down stairs and there was Ronnie standing in the living room. "I am so grateful to you. Joshua asked that I tell you he is thankful that you listened to him and took us to get Jenny. So you are very much the hero here. At least the kids and I think you are. Thank you so much."

Ronnie smiled, "Lily, I am so glad you all are okay. I have to tell you, if you were not alright, I would be devastated. I want you to know that I have really developed some strong feelings for you. I hope the stranger I saw you hugging in your office a few months ago is gone."

Lily smiled back at him, "You must mean James? And yes, he is not in my life now. He was my first love, but that was years ago and I've changed. But Detective Harris, I had no idea you had seen that hug and kiss. If you would have investigated then, maybe it would not have taken me months to figure out that James was a thing of the past. I thought detectives were supposed to be smart and investigate when they had questions."

Ronnie took a step closer to Lily, "Well, I guess I need to ask you if I might have a chance to get to know you better?"

Lily took a step closer to Ronnie, "Well, you need to know that I have a very colorful past. I was born without a father, was a teenage stripper in a bar, my mother went to jail for manslaughter and, as you know, I shot a man to death."

Ronnie said, "You have a pretty long rap sheet. Are you trying to tell me you are a bad woman?"

Lily took another step, closing the gap between them, "Yes, a bad woman that can be good but I'm also a good woman that can be bad." She said with a low, sexy voice.

Ronnie took the last step between them and they were touching each other. He looked directly into her eyes, "Did anyone ever tell you that you have the most beautiful emerald green eyes?"

Lily looked him in the eyes and said, "Well no more than a dozen handsome men."

Ronnie laughed, "Well, if there's only been a dozen, maybe I have a chance to flatter you. I'd love to see both the good and bad Lily Baxter." Then he kissed her.

When the kiss ended, Lily said, "I'm a package deal, Detective Harris; Jenny and Joshua are mine forever. And Sweetie has been with me longer than anyone. Actually, Sweetie is my best friend. She never argues with me or gets mad at me."

He kissed her again and said, "I know you have a lot of baggage and I would be honored to carry some of it for you. But, unlike Sweetie, I will probably give you some grief and tell you what to do sometimes. As for the family deal, I would not have it any other way. I love both of those kids too."

Lily laughed, "You may try to tell me what to do, but that has not worked with anyone before."

Ronnie kissed her again then said, "Well, maybe I'll try to persuade you, rather than tell you, what to do. For instance, I think you might like to take me into the bedroom and show me your good/bad side."

Lily fluttered her eyelashes and said, "Well, since you put it that way, I guess I will have to do what you ask me to do."

After Ronnie and Lily made love, Lily lay in Ronnie's arms and felt like she had never felt before. She had never felt the passion that generated between them. After the climax of their union, Lily felt like her skin was glowing and she was so stimulated. Lying with her back to Ronnie with his arms tight around her, she wanted to melt into him and be forever one with him. Her heart was overflowing with love for this man and she would be grateful to him for the rest of her life for making her life complete. Lily knew at that moment that she had found the love of her life and soul mate.

At 4 AM the next morning, Ronnie whispered in Lily's ear as he held her to him, "I need to go. I don't want Jenny and Joshua to have to deal with this so soon after their trauma. We can ease them into our relationship."

Lily smiled and rolled over to face Ronnie, "Oh, you think this is a relationship? It may be a one night stand."

Ronnie grabbed her and tickled her as he said, "You may think it's a one night stand, but I will be around for a long, long time. That way you have time to improve!"

It was Lily's turn to tickle Ronnie. As he was trying to get away, she said, "I'll make you think, improve. I'll have you know, you just had the best!"

Ronnie became serious, "You are right and I never want anyone else, ever!" He kissed her one more time before he got out of bed and started getting dressed.

Lily was also serious when she said, "Ronnie, last night was the most wonderful thing that has ever happened to me. I have never felt so absolutely in love with someone in my life. Please, come back to me, I love you." Tears welled up in her eyes as she looked at him.

Ronnie took her in his arms and said, "I am here and will love you forever and ever.

EPILOGUE

As the beautiful summer day was drawing to an end four years later, Lily was sitting in the swing on her porch, gently swinging her eighteen month old baby girl, Emma Rose. Her other children, Jenny and Joshua were playing kick ball in the yard with Sweetie. Across from Lily sat her mother, Jane, and her father, Robert. The screen door opened and Ronnie walked out of the house. He walked to the swing and took a seat by his wife. He reached over and took Emma into his lap. Jenny, Joshua and Sweetie ran up on the porch. The sun was slipping behind the trees leaving the western sky a brilliant orange, blue and purple color. The shadows were returning for another night as the remaining light of the day hid behind objects that blocked the sun rays.

Standing on the porch with their parents and grandparents, Jenny and Joshua would not be hidden in the shadows of childhood abuse by a parent, ever again. They had been rescued from the dark, fear and pain by a loving, caring person. They would grow up to be productive, loving adults but they would always carry the scars from the brutal treatment that we can never imagine that one human can inflict on another. The shadows in their mind would hide as much of these painful memories as possible but these hurtful memories would periodically emerge and the children would relive their trauma in the form of post-traumatic stress disorder. With therapy and possibly medication they would get the help they need to live a good life.

The shadows of alcohol addiction and mental illness would not be as dark on Jane because she had learned how to work every day to stay in the light. She also continued to work hard to show Lily that she had always loved her. Jane was glad she had the chance to help other women who were paralyzed by an abusive relationship or bound in hell by mental illness. Jane still had a shadow that was hiding something that she did not ever intend to share with anyone. She had been instrumental in ending her mother's life. Her mother was in a hell that no one could imagine, she was completely insane and in a lot of pain. She had asked Jane to end her life for her but the question for Jane was if she was committing an act of mercy or a sin, by ending her mother's life. This is one thing that would be between Jane and God. Jane had also taken the life of two men, only one of which she was held accountable for by society. This too would be something for Jane to deal with over the rest of her life. Her mental illness was under control, but the devastation that she caused before she got help would hide in the shadows of her mind forever.

There would be no more shadows of doubt for Robert Leslie. He had overcome his self doubt, with the help of a Viet Nam veteran. He learned to stay focused on the future that he had worked so hard to obtain and was now the professor and director of a university. He had learned that he was human and not above sin. He had to learn to forgive himself and move on with his life. Jane and Robert were proud and active grandparents of Jenny, Joshua and Emma Rose.

Detective Ronnie Harris was able to move out of the shadow of being a survivor of suicide by a loved one. His idea for a hot line managed by trained people to counsel those contemplating suicide had brought him peace of mind and a sense of doing something positive after living through the tragedy of suicide. He was able to move on with his life and he intended to be the best parent and husband he could be.

Attorney Lily Baxter-Harris had escaped the shadows of child abuse, abandonment, abuse at the hand of a lover and being the victim of a viscous attack by a killer. She had pulled herself out of the shadows by being strong and determined. She was realizing her dream of being the mother of three children and the wife of her soul mate. Lily was working to help other women pull themselves out of destructive situations and become independent and productive individuals.

Emma Rose was the baby Lily dreamed she would someday have. The name Rose was in honor of Lily's dear Granny, who gave Lily a chance at life by teaching her how to live. The name Emma was in remembrance of the sister that Joshua and Jenny lost. Emma joined Lily's other two children and all three were equally loved and adored by their mother and father, Ronnie.

We can't forget Sweetie, who was curled up on the porch in the middle of her family. She had been in the shadow of being a homeless, abandoned dog. No one had wanted this strange looking multi-color shaggy female dog, especially since she had the strangest, ice blue eyes with one ear sticking up and one flopped down. But she found Lily who named her Sweetie. Lily had not known anything about dogs but had immediately gone to the veterinarian to get help for her new found friend who was injured. Sweetie had been lucky to find a human that gave her a home, a family, love and devotion. Sweetie would forever give back all her love, devotion and do her best to protect her family against all enemies.

Everyone has shadows in their life. Shadows created by obstacles that obstructs the light and allows weaknesses to be hidden from not just others, but from ourselves. The obstacles must be first identified, then removed in order for life to be lived to the fullest. Everyone in this story moved out of the darkness of their obstacles. They did not do this alone, but had faith in a higher power, used resources available and partnered with the people around them. God helps those who help themselves and forgives those that ask for forgiveness.

Author Biography

Brenda Davis lives with her husband of 24 years, Clifton (Hugh) in Cordova, TN. They live with their five dogs; two Doberman Pinchers, one shitzu and two poodle mixes. Brenda graduated from Oklahoma State University in 1975 with a Veterinary Medicine Degree. She practiced veterinary medicine in a mixed animal practice which she owned and operated for twenty five years in Hope, Arkansas. After selling the veterinary practice in 1997, Brenda was an Associate Veterinarian with Dr. Ricky Hughes in Malvern, Arkansas for 3 years. Brenda joined the USDA Food Safety and Inspection Service as a Supervisory Public Health Veterinarian in 2000. She retired in 2012 at the age of 62. Brenda's husband, Hugh, also retired from USDA FSIS as a Consumer Safety Officer. Hugh is a Viet Nam veteran having served in the Navy assigned to the marines as a corpsman. He received two purple hearts for being wounded during the war. Brenda and Hugh have a blended family with six children; four boys and two girls. They have, as of now, 16 grandchildren. Brenda and Hugh love to go camping and trout fishing on the White River at Bull Shoals, Arkansas. They travel a lot to visit their extended family and have the grandkids spent time with them in the summer. Brenda has to limit her activities due to having fibromyalgia, arthritis and back joint compression but is enjoying retirement with her husband. This is the first fiction novel that Brenda has written. If you would like to contact Brenda with questions her email is brendadvm@yahoo.com